Facing
THE MUSIC

Facing THE MUSIC

A.J. BUCHANAN

4 Horsemen
Publications, Inc.

4 Horsemen
Publications, Inc.

4 Horsemen Publications, Inc.
1497 Main St. Suite 169
Dunedin, FL 34698
4horsemenpublications.com
info@4horsemenpublications.com

Cover & Typesetting by Autumn Skye
Edited by CI Stearns

Library of Congress Control Number: 2024933428

Paperback ISBN-13:
Hardcover ISBN-13:
Audiobook ISBN-13:
Ebook ISBN-13:

"There may be trouble ahead. But while there's moonlight, and music, and love, and romance, let's face the music and dance."

~ Irving Berlin

Table of Contents

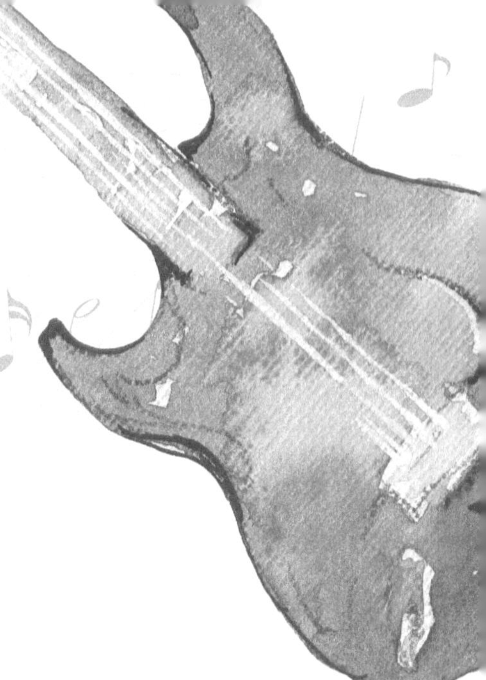

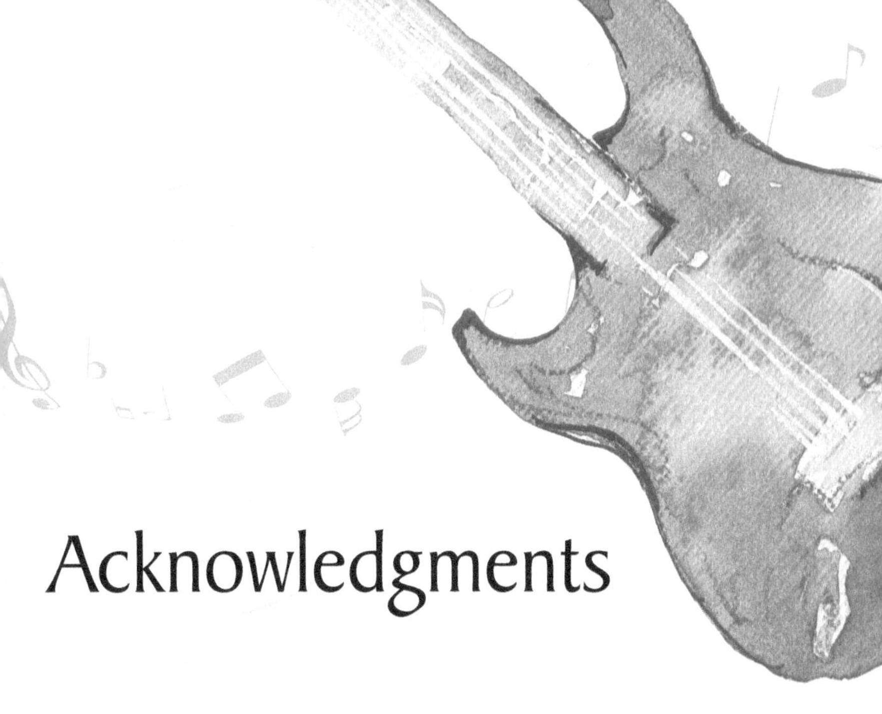

Acknowledgments

I enjoyed everything about writing this novel, but I wouldn't have been able to do it as well without my wonderful helpers. All my gratitude to:

- Linda, my sister from another mister and one of my faithful writing partners.

- Tana, my other helpful writing partner.

- Ron, who isn't the cover artist for this series but chose to be my beta reader.

- Mia from Down Under, for her help with the blurb.

Prologue

Lots of men never found a forever love.

"**W**e are Third Generation!" The leader of the band, looking every bit the rockstar that he was, gestured to his bandmates, who began their ending spiel.

"I'm John."

"I'm William."

"I'm Henry."

"I'm Tristan."

"And I'm Riordan. We love you, New York City! Goodnight!"

The crowd roared as Riordan, aka Rory Stewart, the band's lead singer, bowed, his blond locks falling over his face when he stood tall again. The other members of the band took their bows, the drummer playing a drumroll crescendo to end it. The guys had played three encores and they were exhausted, but they stayed an extra thirty seconds and soaked up the adulation of their fans before exiting the stage.

Rory grinned as the crowd continued to chant, whistle, and shout, clearly demanding and expecting them to return for a fourth encore.

"I'm knackered," Henry Thackery, their rhythm guitarist, wiping his drenched brow with the towel he always kept handy. "Thank God this is the last show. I'm ready to go home."

"You and me both, Henry." Tristan DeVere, bassist, swept his sand-colored hair away from his face. "It's a good thing we did that meet and greet before the show. All I want right now is a shower, some food, and a bed."

The others chimed in their agreement with Tris's comment, all making their way—after the usual debrief—to their dressing rooms to shower and change. Their manager had organized a meal for them back at the hotel where they were spending their last night before flying back to London the next day. Tris dozed all the way to the hotel in the big SUV and barely managed to stay awake in Rory's suite when the food arrived.

Sitting quietly by himself in the overstuffed easy chair by the picture window, he watched as his bandmates and their wives and girlfriends laughed and joked with each other. He was the only member of the band who was still single, and most days it didn't bother him. He was used to being the odd one out, being also the only member of the band who was gay. He loved the men he worked with like brothers, never questioning their support.

But sometimes, like right this moment, watching them together was almost painful. How had he reached the grand old age of thirty-six and still not found a life partner, or even a long-standing boyfriend? What was wrong with him? Why couldn't he land a worthy catch? For a while, he'd shared single status with Rory, until Chrissy, Rory's now-fiancée, had reappeared in his life and pulled him out of the funk he'd fallen into when she'd ghosted him for six months.

Tris sighed, taking another bite of his sandwich. Maybe he was destined to be the lone wolf of the group. Lots of men never found a forever love, never married, and lived perfectly contented lives. And if he were being honest, after that whole ugly business with Devon, he wasn't really looking anymore. Once bitten, twice shy, as the saying goes. And the lessons learned when he was young stayed with him, a caution he would never again ignore.

"Falling asleep over there, Tris?" Rory called out to him, pacing over to where he sat. "Or are you just brooding?"

Tris gave his friend the evil eye. "What do I have to brood about, Ror?" he asked, filling his mouth with more of the melty *croque-monsieur* sandwich that he loved. "We just ended a great tour on a high note, made a lot of money, and are up for some more major music awards again. Nothing sad about any of that."

Rory's knowing smile told him he wasn't fooling his friend. "All true, but you're not celebrating sitting over here by yourself away from the rest of us. If you don't want anyone else asking questions you'd rather not answer, you'd better join in. We won't be up much longer, and you can take your mopey arse to bed to sleep it off."

He turned away, leaving Tris to wonder why he hadn't pushed for a better answer. But then he turned back and added, "Don't think you've escaped this conversation, by the way. I just need you to be awake and less defensive for it."

He grinned and winked, and Tris groaned. Sometimes he hated having nosy friends.

First class on any airline was better than coach, but it didn't help Tris enjoy the flight any more than he enjoyed any time spent in the air. He tried to sleep, but his brain just wouldn't shut down. He'd have a week off before it was back on the treadmill of his life, starting with a fundraiser for Hope House, the organization for abused women where Chrissy worked. He was looking forward to it, because his little brother Teagan and his group, The Barrington Strings, would be the featured artists at the event.

Tris hadn't seen him in a long while because Tag lived in the States and rarely visited his family in the UK. Not that Tris could blame him. With a father like theirs, distance was the best option. Not wanting to pursue another painful thought path, he tried to lose himself in the movie choices offered by the airline but found nothing to hold his attention. Maybe he could play one of the games he'd downloaded on his phone.

By the time the plane landed at Heathrow, Tris was nursing a headache. Knowing his bandmates and their partners knew to leave him alone made deplaning and getting through customs less stressful, and when they all stood outside ready to get into the waiting SUVs, he breathed a sigh of relief into the foggy London air.

"Right, then," he said to the group before getting into the first vehicle. "I'll see you all soon. Call me if you need anything."

"I'll check in with you tomorrow," Rory said, reaching out to squeeze his shoulder. "Eat something before you take those pain pills."

"Yes, Dad," Tris mocked.

"Want me to send over some dinner later, Tris?" That from Gen, Henry's beautiful Japanese wife.

Tris smiled at her. She was a total delight and he loved her as fiercely as he loved her husband, the oldest member of the band. "You don't have to, Gen," he demurred, knowing that that was what she'd want to hear. An outright refusal might hurt her feelings. This way, he left the choice up to her, knowing that at best, he'd have delicious food for at least a couple of days, even though he knew that his housekeeper would have ordered in meals from his favorite meal delivery service to last him a few days, as well.

"I'll send Henry over with it later. Get some rest, love." She stepped up to him to kiss his cheek, patting it in a motherly gesture of affection that was endearing.

"Will do," he promised. No sassing Gen ... that kind of teasing was strictly reserved for Rory and the others.

Now that he was close to home, he let himself relax, let the feelings he'd been avoiding sweep over him, let the melancholy wash him. He breathed a quick prayer that his housekeeper had already gone, even though she normally stayed longer and did more to get the place ready for his return. He wasn't up to chatting with anyone about anything, not even the weather. He'd have a drink or three and fall asleep from utter exhaustion. And who knew, maybe when he woke up, he'd be pain free and positive. A guy could hope, right?

Chapter 1

Priest

How long since he'd last been attracted to a man?

Benedict Priestley drew his dark brows low over his slate grey eyes, frowning at the laptop screen. The contract his solicitor had prepared for the latest project was complex and he wanted to make sure he understood every clause before the meeting where he'd present it to his clients. The Priestley Group was well known for the fairness of its contracts and the high quality of its work in every area, from architectural design through construction to interior design and landscaping. He would always be vigilant about every aspect of each project that his company accepted. Not only his livelihood but his reputation was on the line every time.

The intercom on his desk buzzed. "Yes, Jan?"

"I'm sorry to disturb you, Mr. Priestley, but Dr. James is on the line. She needs a quick word about the fundraiser."

Dr. Anna James was the director of Hope House and his late wife Jane's best friend. They were on the board of directors together, and he was happy to take a few minutes away from work to talk to her. Anna never called during the day unless it was important. He picked up the phone.

"Anna, good morning!"

"Morning, Priest, sorry to disturb you. I know how busy your days can be."

"Not a problem, Anna. I'll always make time for you." She had been one of the pillars of support for him in that first horrible year after Jane died. "What's up?"

"I just need to double check the items that your company is contributing to the silent auction and to find out when they will be delivered to the event site. Also, have they been insured if they need to be, and have you forwarded those documents to us, as well?"

She sighed and Priest could hear the tension in her voice. This was a big event in Hope House's social calendar. And this year in particular, they were also going to launch a second branch in Birmingham. He knew Anna wanted to make sure that nothing happened to set them back, no matter how small.

Before he could reply, she continued, "I'm trying to make sure everything goes smoothly and leave myself with as little to worry about as possible on the night of."

"I understand, Anna, and you're right to be proactive. So let me have Jan put together all the information you need including copies of the insurance documents. I'm sure everything is in order, but if something is missing, Jan and I will sort it for you ASAP. I know it's not PC to tell people to calm down, but you know me. I'm only PC when it suits me. It doesn't suit me now, so calm down, love."

She chuckled, which was what he wanted. He hated when the people he cared about were stressed out, and he always tried to lighten the mood, even if he couldn't do anything else to help. And he knew he could fix this issue for her.

"Better?" he asked when her amusement died down.

"Much. You're very good at diffusing stress, aren't you? And you'd think, after all the years I've been doing this, that I'd be less flustered, but every single time feels like my first time." She sighed heavily.

"That's because you care, Anna, and you want the best outcomes each time you ask people to dig into their pockets for that extra pound. That is one of your most admirable qualities. Don't ever change." He meant every word of his statement.

"Thank you, Priest. It'll be good to see you again in a week. We haven't spent much time together recently."

Priest nodded, even though she couldn't see him. Life had been particularly busy for him these last few months, and he hadn't had much time for socializing. When he wasn't working, he was doing dad stuff with his two children.

"I'm looking forward to seeing you and Rod, as well."

Anna's detective husband was as busy as his wife and Priest were, so it would be a wonderful reunion at the fundraiser. After Anna rang off, he got back to the contract, and spent the rest of the morning making notes for his lunchtime meeting with his solicitor. By the end of the day, he hoped to have a contract he could review and hopefully sign with his clients so the next project could begin.

It was Friday. Tonight, he and the kids would make takeaway food at home and binge watch a television show or movie they all decided on—as they did every Friday night when he was home—but so far, they hadn't sent him a list of their shopping needs. He'd have to call if they didn't by the time he was ready to leave, because once he got home, he wasn't going out again for the evening. When his cell phone chimed as he was packing his briefcase, he grinned, recognizing the tone he attached to his children. It was like they had a direct line to his thoughts. He read the message aloud, nodding as he did.

"We want hamburgers and American-style French fries, Dad," Shannon, his twelve-year-old daughter had written. "But we don't have any potatoes and the ground meat isn't enough. Also, can you bring home ketchup and brown sauce, please, and onions?"

Sounded like he needed to make a proper supermarket run, but that would have to wait until the next day. He sent a thumbs up in reply, running the list over in his head as he locked his briefcase, shrugged on his overcoat, and closed his office door behind him. The cleaner had already arrived, and he waved a cheery goodnight to the woman who had been doing his offices for the last seven years.

"Try to get home before the rain, Mavis," he told her, smiling as he walked by the closet where she was getting organized for the work ahead. "And have a good weekend."

"And to you, Mr. Priestley," she returned in her East London accent.

Outside, the sky was gray ... no surprise there, given the way the weather had been these last few weeks. It was springtime, which meant rain was inevitable. And by the looks of it, Mavis was in for a soaking, unless she had a ride home. Pulling the collar of his coat up to block some of the raw evening breeze, he hurried to his car and drove to Sainsbury's. By the time he parked, there was already a fine drizzle misting the air. Priest cursed under his breath as he rushed in and picked up the items he needed for family night.

The rain was pelting down when he exited the brightly-lit store, and by the time he got into his car, he was drenched. Sighing heavily, he made his way through the now snarled traffic of a London evening to his home. The outside lights popped on as he drove under the motion sensors, and he used the remote control to open the garage doors. As the doors slid shut, more light spilled into the garage from the open door that led into the house and an elegant dog barreled out to greet him.

"Onesie!" He let the whippet get in a few hello kisses, rewarding him with affectionate scritches behind his ears and under his chin. Then he called his son Mason to help him with the bags. Once inside, he dumped his briefcase in his office, changed, and returned to the kitchen to help with the food prep. Shannon was already seasoning the meat for the burgers, and Mason was making the salad they'd have with their meal.

He paused for a moment to watch them. They worked silently, though his daughter was shaking her hips to whatever she was listening to on her phone, the cordless earbuds just visible under the wisps of hair escaping her ponytail. She had her mother's coloring ... curly strawberry-blonde locks, blue-gray eyes, and honey-gold complexion. Seeing her made him think of Jane, but thankfully, these days the piercing pain of her loss was muted, and only bittersweet—more sweet than bitter—memories remained. He had learned, over these last three years, to let the memories take him to a place of love and warmth and not down the road of despair and rage.

Shaking off the thoughts that might yet make him melancholy, and wondering why tonight he seemed to need to practice the thinking that would hold those feelings at bay, he fell into the meal prep with his children. He grilled the meat patties, Shannon toasted the buns, and she and her brother built the burgers. He fed the dog and Lilbit, their crossbreed, one-eared cat who had outgrown her name in the year since she'd arrived, a bedraggled mess, on their front steps.

"D'you want a beer, Dad?" Shannon asked, opening the refrigerator and pulling out two bottles of fizzy pop, as she liked to call the drinks she and Mason preferred on Friday nights.

"Thanks, love. How many are left?"

She turned to look back inside and said over her shoulder, "Just two. Sorry, Dad. I didn't look earlier."

Priest smiled. "It's alright, Shan. I'll need to do a Sainsbury's run tomorrow anyway. So you'll need to let me have your list by then."

It had become his habit, after Jane died, to include his children in the food shopping and in helping keep the house picked up until the housekeeper came in once a week to do the real cleaning. He had needed to give them something to focus on, other than their grief, something to help him build a closer relationship with them, and his plan had been working well.

"So, how was your day?"

"I had three tests today," Shannon began, wiping mustard off her bottom lip. "I don't think I did so well on the science one, though."

Priest studied her face, searching for any sign that she was upset. Shannon was a perfectionist; failure was not an option for her.

"Are you worried that you failed the test?"

She frowned in thought, then shook her head. "No, but I know I didn't get a high mark."

"Do you know where you messed up?"

"Yes. Lizzie and I are going to go over it together to check each other and figure out the right answers. Miss likes it when we go back to class already prepared to explain where we think we went wrong. We get credit for reviewing on our own first."

Satisfied that his daughter was okay, he turned his attention to Mason. The boy was ten and favored him with his straight dark hair, longer on top and falling into dark gray eyes. He was nowhere near as chatty as his older sister, being more inclined to keep his thoughts about school to himself and needing to be coaxed to share.

"And how about you, Mase? Had a good Friday?"

The one thing Priest knew with absolute certainty was that Mason wouldn't lie to him if anything bad had happened because he knew that his father would find out anyway. Priest loved that the boy faced things head on, that he didn't avoid his problems, even if he did have to be prodded to share them.

"It was okay," Mason replied, sipping his drink. "Remember, I have football practice tomorrow, Dad."

"I remember, son. We'll get you there on time. Anything else? Any tests?"

"Only some practice questions for the math SAT." He took a bite of his burger, chewed and swallowed before adding, "I did okay."

Priest nodded. Mason was the exact opposite of his sister when it came to his studies. As brilliant as she was, he did what was expected of him and was responsible about his work, but he didn't push himself. Only in one area was Mason as driven as Shannon was to succeed and it was in football. Truth be told, he was an avid sports fan and had been asking his dad when he could try out for the rugby team.

Priest had managed to put off answering him so far, hoping the boy would move on. He knew from his own years as a rugby player how brutal and dangerous a game it could be, and the last thing he wanted was for his son to be hurt. He couldn't bear it if anything happened to either of his children. Football was risky enough, but he and Jane had agreed to let Mason join the mini-soccer team when he had expressed an interest and he'd graduated now to the 9 v 9 team, where he'd stay until he turned thirteen.

Bringing his focus back to the table, he waited for his turn to share. The children always wanted to know what he'd done at work, what big plans he had, and whether he had signed any celebrity contracts.

"So, Dad, did anything new and exciting happen for *you* today?"

Something about the way Shannon worded the question made Priest look at her sharply. "Why do you ask that? What have you heard, love?"

"Aren't you on the board of directors of Hope House?" she asked, ignoring his question.

Priest tilted his head to the side, watching her face for any clues as to where this line of questioning was going and coming up empty. "I am. Why?"

"On the bus coming home, I heard that there's going to be a big event with celebrities, including Third Generation."

Priest smiled. Shannon was obsessed with the rock band, and from things she'd said before, he suspected she had a bit of a crush on the bass guitarist.

"Well, I don't know about Third Generation, love, but the featured performers for the evening will be The Barrington Strings. Have you ever heard of them?"

She shook her head. "No. What do they play?"

He spent the next ten minutes explaining chamber music to his children while they finished eating. Shannon was unimpressed. Mason seemed to perk up at the idea of playing a big instrument like the cello. Would *this* be the instrument he'd decide he wanted to play? He had shown no interest in the piano, which Shannon was learning to play. Priest didn't push the boy. He only wanted his kids to do what interested them, not what he would like for them. Their lives were theirs to live as they chose.

After dinner, they decided against a movie in favor of one of Third Generation's concerts. He managed to get them to keep the decibel level acceptable and smiled indulgently as Shannon immediately got into the swing of the music, singing along with the songs she knew, which appeared to be all of them. Meanwhile, Mason cycled between tapping his foot to the catchier tunes and scrolling on his phone. If Priest had to guess, his son was probably researching the cello.

Turning his attention to the television, he focused on the musicians, on the songs, on the artistry. They were brilliant, no doubt about that, and the bassist was handsome and electric in his performance. After a while, Priest couldn't take his eyes off the man. He was tall, rangy but clearly fit, sandy blonde hair falling into his eyes as he played. His facial hair gave him a sleek, sophisticated look, and truth be told, he rocked a sexy vibe that Priest found exceptionally appealing.

How long had it been since he'd last been attracted to a man? He mulled that over as he watched the guitarist move and followed his fingers as they made his instrument speak in arousing tongues of passion. The man's expression as he let himself be carried away by the music was intense, fierce, sometimes hungry. What would a man like that bring to a relationship? *Was* he in a relationship? Did he bring that same intense passion to his bed that he brought to his music?

What the hell? Priest blinked. Where were these highly inappropriate thoughts coming from? He didn't know the man, had never even met him once, and the likelihood of his ever meeting him was slim to none. Why was he suddenly reacting to an illusion, a fantasy, a ghost?

Shaking his head, he looked at the screen again, choosing to focus on the lead singer, another blond god with rich vocal tones that caressed and made love to the notes and words he belted out for the audience. Better … this man was as beautiful, if not more so than the bassist but Priest's reaction to the lead singer was nothing like the compulsive one to the man his eyes strayed back to as they did their ending spiel.

"We are Third Generation!" The blond leader of the band gestured to his bandmates.

"I'm John."

"I'm William."

"I'm Henry."

"I'm Tristan."

"And I'm Riordan. We love you, Amsterdam! Goodnight!"

Tristan … his name is Tristan. Damn! Tristan's voice was whole worlds of suggestion and heat, smoky, fiery … dangerous. He'd have to find out if the man and his band were really going to be at the fundraiser. Something told him that meeting the hot guitarist would be revealing.

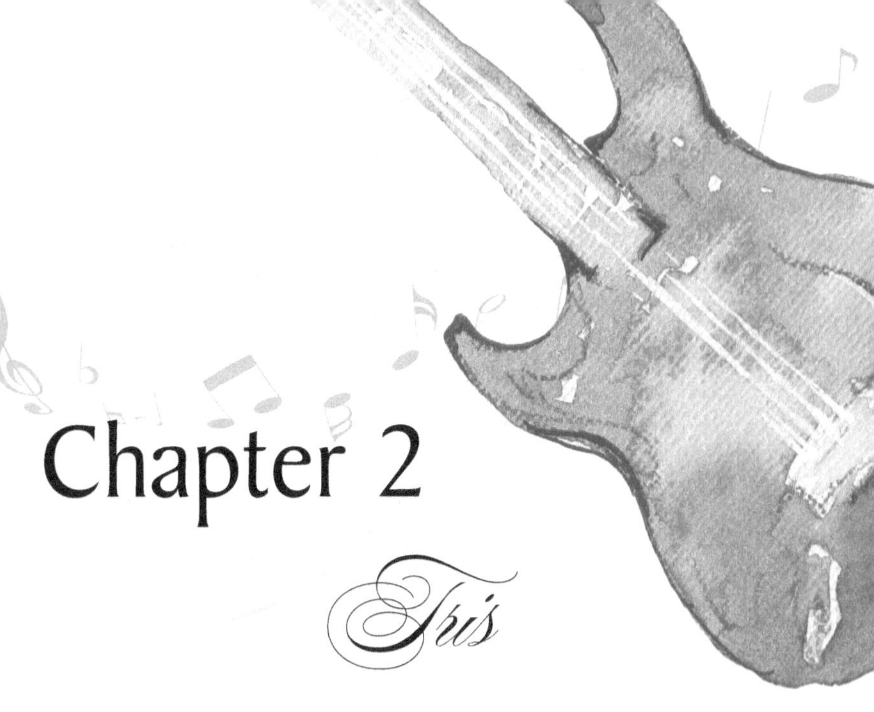

Chapter 2

Tris

Benedict Priestley's image was imprinted on his brain.

Tris breathed a heavy sigh of relief as he closed up the boat. If he weren't so wiped out, he'd take the drink he'd been looking forward to and sit on the houseboat equivalent of a patio and soak in the night sounds, bathing his face in bright moonlight and sparkling starlight. But he desperately needed sleep, as much as he could get before the world closed in again. He'd remembered to call Gen and ask her not to send Henry over until tomorrow, because he knew he would pass out once his head hit the pillow in his opulent master suite.

The houseboat had been his dream home since he'd been able to make enough money to move out of the charming but cramped cottage he'd shared with his housemate-turned-friend once he'd finished uni and needed to play the part of a grown-up for real. It was an elegant space, colored in neutral tones of cream and beige and sand, with pops of warm reds, golds, and other jewel-toned hues to add flavor and excitement to the spaces. There were three bedrooms, two with ensuite bathrooms, and a third small one that he'd had kitted out as his soundproof studio when he needed to play out his frustrations without getting ticketed for breaking the noise ordinance law.

Stripping to his skivvies, he washed his face, brushed his teeth, and drew a weary hand over his haggard face. He had a call scheduled with his realtor in a couple of days. He needed to find an architect and builder to bring his vision for the fixer upper to light and make it into his permanent home. Despite his mother's opinion of his decisions, he knew he couldn't keep living on the boat, no matter how luxurious it was. *Adults who can afford it buy a proper home.* He could almost hear her acid tones as she berated him yet again for living on a boat like a vagabond.

He sighed heavily, moving away to his king-sized bed. None of that, he admonished himself. Thoughts of his parents filled him with a mixture of rage and longing, and he had no emotional bandwidth to handle that kind of stress at the moment. Everything could wait until he woke up.

Tris's boat was moored at Old Windsor on the Thames and when he finally woke up after a solid twelve hours of sleep, the view still made him smile. Sunlight sparkled on the river and on the beautiful homes that lined it on both sides. The mooring his houseboat occupied was attached to the property that he had bought. His realtor had done all the hard work for him, obtaining the necessary licenses so that he could go ahead and hire a company to get the job done.

Making his way out to the deck with his tea, he settled into the over-large chair, loving the warmth of the soft leather at his back. River traffic would increase as the day wore on, and since it was the weekend, a fair amount of foot traffic would also pass by on the wide, grass-verged foot-path that separated his mooring from the low iron fence and lawn that led up a gentle slope to the house on the property. Maybe he'd take a walk himself, venture into town for lunch and a walkabout to re-orient himself to the spaces that filled him with a sense of home.

His cell phone chimed, and he put the cup down and hurried in to fetch it from the bedside table where he'd left it.

"DeVere," he said brusquely, belatedly wishing he'd added a polite "Good morning."

"Good morning to you too, Tris." Henry's tone was ripe with amusement. "D'you still need more sleep, Grumpy?"

"Fuck off, Henry," he replied, chuckling. His bandmates all knew he didn't function well on too little sleep, that his ideal sleep time was at least eight hours. They teased him mercilessly when he came to rehearsals looking like death warmed over because he'd been up late and hadn't had enough sleep.

"Done. The boys come back tomorrow, so we're taking advantage before then."

Tris could almost see his friend waggling his brows salaciously. Despite the vast differences in their circumstances and experiences, Tris still felt a close affinity to Henry that he had given up trying to understand. Henry was just the big brother he didn't have.

"I don't need the dirty details of your sex life, bro," he sassed him. "So if that's why you've called…" He let his words trail off and listened as Henry laughed in his ear.

"Shut it, you cheeky bugger! Gen's gone food shopping, and I'm to bring your dinner and be back for afternoon delight, so I'm heading there now."

"I'll be here. Bring beer."

Henry would arrive within the hour, so Tris took a shower and changed into dark blue sweatpants and a white t-shirt, pulling out his favorite old anorak to wear when he went into town. Freshening the pot, in case Henry wanted a cuppa before he left, Tris went back out to the deck to watch the world go by until his friend arrived.

"Permission to come aboard!"

Tris grinned as he turned at the sight of Henry carrying a picnic basket. "Come through," he answered and walked back in to welcome his guest. He was an inch or so taller than Henry, but the man was as wide and solid as a rugby player, making Tris feel almost delicate by comparison.

Henry put the basket on the counter in the kitchen and reached for Tris in a one-armed hug. Then he stepped back to look him over. Tris bore his scrutiny; it was their ritual. Henry was the mother hen of the band, and he'd taken Tris under his wing from the beginning, as though he'd sensed, even before Tris had shared his story, that underneath the cool, reserved exterior was a wounded and cautious man.

"Good. You look rested."

Tris smiled. "I feel rested, though I'm sure if I sat for too long, I'd nod off again." He turned to the teapot he had on the warmer. "Tea?"

"Just a quick cuppa," Henry said. "What are you plans for the day?"

"Just going into town for lunch and a bit of a walkabout. I'll have to start reviewing the files the realtor sent me. I need to choose an architect and builder to get the house remodel going."

Through the window, both men looked at the house, its faded yellow walls taking on the warmth of the sun. Tris had no plans to change the exterior colors, merely to deepen them, though he would listen to any ideas the architect might put forward. He was ready to set down roots. He didn't see his single status changing, and he was no longer prepared to wait for the one who would make his heart sing.

"It's got good lines," Henry said. "And you can't beat it for location, can you?"

"No, you can't. That was one of its selling points. That and the low asking price. Made me wonder what secrets it held … you know, dead bodies in the cellar, rotting floorboards, things that go bump in the night, that sort of thing."

Henry's laughter filled the cabin. "And did you find answers when you did the tour?"

"Nothing other than dingy, dark rooms and dank cupboards. And some structural damage. But I can see it being something fresh and bright, somewhere I'll love to come home to even more than I do this boat."

Henry looked at him quizzically, sipping his tea for a moment before asking, "Have you decided what you'll do with this once the house is built?"

"I've been thinking about turning it into an investment property. You know, like one of those holiday homes for rent. This is a pretty part of England, and the riverfront adds to the appeal, and thus to the overall pricing. Win, win, yes?"

Henry nodded. "Indeed." He drained his cup, rising to rinse it out in the sink before turning back to add, "I'm really proud of you, Tris. We all are. And I hope you know that everything you've accomplished and all the things you plan to do are signs of someone who is worthy. I hope they have eradicated any feeling you may still be harboring that you are somehow less because you're you."

Tris knew what his friend wanted him to hear, and the gratitude and affection he felt bloomed in his chest. Henry wasn't old enough to be his father, but he was the best example of what a father should be that Tris knew. He wasn't interested in flying the rainbow flag over his head in some misguided attempt to prove his pride in himself. The people who needed to know he was gay had no issue with who he romanced, but they were really only the other members of the band, his siblings, and his friend from his uni days.

Needing not to get lost in his head and all the questions that plagued him, he smiled at Henry. "Thanks, mate." Then he rinsed out his own cup and followed his friend back out to the door.

"When are you coming back to London?" Henry asked. "Will we see you before the fundraiser?"

"I don't know yet. I'll call you."

"Right then. Take care, Tris."

Once Henry left, Tris locked up the boat and followed the footpath into the little town, finding a hidden cafe to order himself a thick cheese sandwich and a beer for lunch, sitting in the sun to watch the tourists and locals milling about. One of the reasons he'd decided that Old Windsor would be his permanent residence had been the fact that no one recognized him, or if they did, they chose not to approach him.

His cell phone buzzed as he was heading back to the boat. Checking to see who was calling, because he still really wasn't up to socializing, he huffed when he saw his realtor's name.

"Ms. Danvers, good afternoon."

"Mr. DeVere, welcome home!"

"Thank you. How may I help you?" He wasn't up to extended pleasantries, even though he was sure that what she was calling about would be something he would want to hear.

"I wonder, have you reviewed the files I sent you regarding possible architects and builders?"

"I haven't had the chance yet," he said, feeling annoyed and embarrassed at the same time. "Why?"

"Well, I have a new candidate that will most likely make all the rest seem poor by comparison. The Priestley Group is renowned for the highest quality work, and the company includes all the components that you will need for your house remodel. I've just sent their information to you, and suggest you give them a look immediately. They've recently announced that they're open for new contracts, which is a rare thing indeed, so you'd be advised to act fast if you don't want to miss them. They get snapped up rather quickly."

"How are they price wise?" he asked, not really understanding her urgency, and not willing to throw away money on a high-priced company that might be more show than substance.

"They're pricier than half the options I've sent you, but well within your budget."

She paused as if choosing her words, and Tris wondered what else she could have to say. He was just about to speak when she continued. "Will you be reviewing the files soon, Mr. DeVere?"

He rolled his eyes. The woman was clearly trying push him without appearing to do so, and he supposed since she knew what she was about, he should probably take her advice and get a move on with the looking.

"I'll get on it as soon as I get back to the boat, Ms. Danvers. Thanks for the heads up."

"You're very welcome, Mr. DeVere. I look forward to hearing your decision."

Once he decided which company he would go with, Tris had no further need of her services, but he appreciated everything she had done in searching for, identifying, and finally helping him procure his property, so he would happily tell her what he decided when he made a decision.

"You'll be the first to know," he promised her. Well, the first after his mates, but she didn't need to know that.

He resisted the urge to take a nap before checking his emails because he knew that would disrupt the sleep schedule he needed to reset in order to minimize jetlag. So he sat in his living room, his laptop on his knees, and went through all the files that she'd sent him. However he left the one she'd just sent that morning for last, feeling somehow that if that was his best option, he wanted it to be the crowning moment in his decision-making.

Three of the companies he immediately crossed off the list as being much too expensive for the kind of work their website showed. That left one other and The Priestley Group. Both companies were exceptional. Their websites were creative and professional, the work they put on display was stellar, and the cost, while not inexpensive, was also not prohibitive. He needed to see them laid out side by side so he could decide.

Once he printed the pages he needed, he set them out on the dining table and studied them. Lawrie & Associates had been around for more than seventy-five years, and their experience and attention to detail showed in every photograph of the work they did. But after another hour of looking back and forth between the two groups, Tris knew he would go with The Priestley Group. The vibe he got from their work felt right for what he wanted.

Knowing he would revisit his decision before announcing it—he preferred to be meticulous rather than impetuous— he left the papers on the table and prepped his dinner. Gen had sent over roasted leg of lamb, with mint sauce, roasted potatoes, and steamed carrots and peas. The flavors scenting his kitchen as he reheated the food in the oven—"You're the only bachelor I know with a microwave who never uses it," Rory liked to tease him—made his mouth water.

Dinner was delicious, but Tris couldn't shake the hint of loneliness that pushed into his thoughts as he ate. He had never been bothered about eating alone or spending time in his own company before. What was suddenly making him miss the sound of voices, the feel of a warm hand at his back, the sight of a bright smile? He tried to cycle back through the last few weeks to see if he could find an explanation for this new and disturbing trend in his emotions, but could think of nothing that might have triggered him.

Maybe it was because he was following through on his plans for home ownership. The idea that he was going to own a big, family-style house when he had no family he cared to be with who didn't already have their own houses was a quelling one, to be sure, but that had always been the case. He'd been house hunting for months before the realtor had found the perfect place to suit his needs. Why was it only now settling over him like a wet blanket?

He hated the feeling. Looking down at his half-eaten dinner, the flavors turning to ash in his mouth, he dropped his fork onto the plate and stood up. He needed to blow the funk away. Sliding the plate into the unused microwave, he locked the boat and walked into his studio, shutting off the rest of the world. He'd play until his spirits settled.

By Tuesday morning, Tris was finally ready to be around others. Driving was one of his greatest non-music joys, and the Range Rover Evoque he'd bought only a year ago was stylish and comfortable, the kind of vehicle his parents would highly approve of, if they knew he owned one. Thankfully, their approval had been the furthest thing from his mind when he'd had to decide between it and the Volvo SUV.

He grinned now as he switched to the fast lane on his way to meet his bandmates for lunch at a popular hangout spot in Belgravia. The food was good, the prices were reasonable for the neighborhood, and any fans they met were respectful of their privacy. He pushed the volume of Third Generation's latest studio album up a notch and hummed along as he drove. The motorway was happily flowing smoothly, and he got to Henry's house with time to spare.

"Tris! How lovely to see you. Come in?"

Gen's warmly affectionate greeting was just what he needed after his self-administered isolation. He had needed the reset and he felt easier now that he was back with his found family.

"Thanks, Gen. It's great to be here. Where are the boys? I brought them something."

Henry and Gen had twin boys, age ten, and they loved car racing. He'd ordered two Formula One models for them, and they had arrived the day before.

"They're in the den. Go through. I'll let Henry know you're here."

Nicholas and Lucas were playing a racing game when he walked in, but they abandoned their controls to jump on him when he appeared.

"Uncle Tris!" Twin cries of greeting were followed almost immediately by an identical question: "What did you bring us?"

Because why would the gift bags in his hands be for anyone but them, eh? He chuckled and handed them off, watching as they fought with the packaging until they got to the cars inside. Their shouts of joy pierced the otherwise quiet house, much to Tris's amusement.

"Boys! You're too loud! What do you say to Uncle Tris?" Gen's stern question belied the twinkle in her eyes.

"Thanks, Uncle Tris," they said belatedly.

"Now, clear up this mess and then you can get back to your game." As they tidied up, Gen smiled at him. "You're looking much better."

"I'm feeling much better, thanks. How's Henry doing?"

"Top of the world, as you can imagine."

Gen was the quietest of the wives, but she had hidden depths that she only shared with a few. He was chuffed to be included in that inner circle who got to see more of her than she showed to the world at large. He grinned at her implication just as Henry walked in.

"Morning, Tris. Ready to go?"

"More than. I have news to share."

"About the house?" Gen asked as the boys settled back into their game.

"Yes." Tris followed Henry back out to the front. "I have a meeting tomorrow with the company I chose to get started on the planning."

"Great! I'm sure you won't be disappointed. You can stay over tonight," Henry offered. "You know your room is always ready."

Tris chuckled. "I do, and thanks. I think I will."

He was sure he wouldn't be disappointed either, especially if he got to meet the man himself, the co-founder of the company. He had spent most of the night before studying The Priestley Group's website, learning everything he could about them in their almost meteoric rise in the industry. He was impressed by the highly professional presentation of the website, by every image chosen to demonstrate all aspects of the work they did, by the text describing what they offered, and by the warm introductions of the major partners.

The man after whom the company was named was a burly man with a winning smile and a handsome face. Benedict Priestley was a father of two, a Cambridge graduate, and a former rugby player, whose hobbies included playing the piano and gardening. They had music in common, and if the examples of houses he'd worked on were any indication, he was a master in architectural design.

Something about the man drew Tris to him. He'd read all the other bios, but Benedict Priestley's image was imprinted on his brain from the number of times he'd gone back to ogle his picture. His gray hair was cut short on the sides, longer on top with a side part, and his low, dark brows presided over equally dark eyes. His wide smile revealed deep dimples, which Tris envisioned licking into before he could squash the thought. A mustache and thin goatee, the same silver-gray as the hair on his head, framed wide lips that Tris skated his glance over. He couldn't keep perving on the man without ever having met him.

Ten o'clock the following day found Tris standing at the receptionist's desk in a bright foyer, lit by the sun from three large windows. Bright paintings decorated the fourth wall and the one separating the reception area from the offices beyond it. A cheerful periwinkle blue contrasted quite elegantly with the gem-bright abstract art.

"Good morning, sir," a cheerful young woman said, her smile as bright as the rest of the room. "Welcome to The Priestley Group. How may I direct you?"

Tris looked at her name badge before responding. "Good morning, Maxine. I'm Tristan DeVere. I have an appointment."

Maxine looked down at the screen before her, touched it, and then nodded. "Ah, yes. You're meeting with Mr. Priestley regarding a house remodel?"

"I am," he said, ignoring the way his heart rate kicked up at having his wish come true. He hoped like hell that he'd be able to disguise his unprofessional interest in the man. He didn't need an inconvenient attraction to mess with his plans for his home.

"Please have a seat, sir. I'll let him know you're here."

Tris stepped away to stand by one of the wide windows overlooking the busy street below. London traffic was as snarly as ever, but he wasn't really seeing it. His thoughts ran to the friendly smile of the man he was about to meet and how their meeting would go. Would he recognize Tris? Would that make things even more awkward than his own unexpected attraction? What if he didn't like rock music or had some preconceived negative ideas about rock musicians? Would that make their working relationship difficult?

He couldn't imagine any businessman, no matter his prejudices, refusing to work with someone who had the means to pay them for their work. This man wouldn't have become as successful as he clearly was—if the understated elegance of the front office was any indication—if he had been overly sensitive about who he chose to work for. And somehow, Tris doubted the man in the picture was the sort of man who let his personal biases determine how he ran his business.

"Mr. DeVere?"

A hesitant voice dragged him back into the room from his ridiculous reverie and he turned sharply to see a tall, willowy young woman looking at him questioningly. How long had she been there trying to get his attention? Feeling foolish, he extended a hand.

"Yes. Sorry. I was ... lost in thought."

She shook his hand with a smile. "I'm Erin, Mr. Priestley's admin assistant. Please come this way."

Tris followed her to the end of the hallway, then to the left where a corner office door stood open. He walked in behind her and waited for her to announce him to the man who was standing at a drafting table studying something on the laptop before him.

"Mr. DeVere is here, Mr. Priestley."

She waited until her boss turned to look at them before excusing herself and closing the door behind her. Tris froze for a second at the sight before him. Benedict Priestley wore a pin-stiped gray suit, crisp white shirt, and black tie loosened at the collar. Tris did his best not to do more of a stare-down than he'd already done. The last thing he needed was for this man to notice he was ogling him.

He wondered, after a pause, if he was still wearing the bit of his breakfast sandwich that had spilled on his shirt. He thought he'd managed to clean up pretty well, but the way his host was staring, he might have missed a spot. Then he seemed to gather himself, blinked, and found a strained smile.

"Ah, good morning, Mr. DeVere. Please, have a seat."

His voice somehow matched his ruggedly handsome features ... it was sharp-edged, with a husky undertone as though he'd once been a smoker. The sound sent a shiver up Tris's spine, which he tightened against the back of the chair, holding himself erect to help his body handle the sensation. He watched as the man straightened his tie, and something about the way his hands tightened the Windsor knot was the hottest thing Tris had seen all day.

"Thank you." Tris wished he knew how to start the conversation, because the man who had taken the seat across from him behind a massive desk appeared once again to be lost in thought. Had he been wrong in his choice after all? Nothing on the company's website had suggested that their CEO was scatterbrained, but he had to admit these first few minutes with him were not showing him in his best light.

Unless ... Tris shut down the fanciful idea. There was no way in hell the man looking at him was attracted to him too. He knew he was easy on the eyes, but the air of experience that the architect exuded meant he'd lived a fuller life and had probably enjoyed every bit of it far more than Tris ever had his own. Besides, with two kids, he was most likely straight, right? Ignoring the faint shot of disappointment at that thought, he looked up when Benedict Priestley spoke at last.

That's right, Tris, back to business.

Chapter 3

Priest

*He wasn't ready for any more stimulation than
he'd already had with this man.*

What were the odds that the man Priest had spent almost a week thinking about would be his newest client? If he were a betting man, he'd have lost a ton of money on that bet because as far as he was concerned it had definitely *not* been a sure thing. And yet, here they were, sitting across from each other while his client was probably wondering if he could escape from the lunatic staring him down. *Get your shit together, Priest.*

"Ah, sorry. Thank you for coming in." *Really, Priest? Of course he would come in, because you invited him here. He's looking to hire you, fool!*

An upward quirk of his lips was Priest's only indication that the man found his awkwardness amusing. He was not a fan of being laughed at, even if *he* was the reason it was happening. He really had to get this briefing onto a professional footing pronto.

"Before we begin, I'd like to review the questionnaire you completed online for today's meeting. This way, I can be sure I understand what you need from us, and we can discuss how best to provide it and how much it will cost you. Sound good?"

Tristan nodded, then swallowed and answered, "Yes." Was he nervous? *Why in the hell would a famous rockstar be nervous with me?* Ignoring the silly notion, Priest passed a tablet across the desk to him, already open to the questionnaire, and opened his own on his laptop.

"So, I see you're in the music industry. May I ask specifically which part of it?" Better to pretend he didn't know exactly who Tristan was, even though he hadn't known his surname until just now.

"I'm a member of Third Generation. You may have heard of us?"

Priest noted to the tone of Tristan's reply. The humility was stunning. He had always believed that famous people had an arrogance about them that was almost part of their persona, but this man was nothing like he imagined a rockstar would be. It was very appealing to him.

"Yes, I have. My daughter is a rabid fan of your band." And she would lose her mind when he told her who his latest client was. The thought made him grin.

"I'm guessing, by your expression, that that's not a bad thing," Tristan commented, bringing him back to the moment.

"Not at all. We listen to all kinds of music in my house." He ventured a smile in the star's direction before moving on purposefully. "So, you're looking to put down roots. I see you currently live on a houseboat. Why the change of plans?"

He refused to entertain the thought trying to slip into his head that the man was in a relationship and making things permanent. Fate, God, the universe, whoever or whatever was in charge, wouldn't be so cruel as to reawaken his absent libido with a man who was unavailable, would they? Dammit, he hadn't felt even a moment of interest in anyone for three years. No one, male or female, had made him want to look twice, let alone all the things he wondered about with this man. It would be dreadful to have to deal with a man belonging to someone else.

Focus, Priest! He listened as Tristan explained his need to settle down, his belief that he'd be a bachelor—*thank you, God!*—for the duration, and his desire to have a home large enough to accommodate his band mates and their families. It sounded to Priest as though these men were filling a gap left by his blood relatives, and he wondered what the story was there. But it would be inappropriate to ask that question. They were barely acquaintances, not friends.

"How much time do you spend on tour?" he asked next.

"It depends. Most of our tours are planned at least two years out, but we do spend a lot of time in England. So, maybe half and half, though that varies depending on where we're booked and for how long."

They continued through the questions, Priest making notes on his laptop. Tristan wasn't sure exactly how large he wanted the house to be, just that he didn't want a McMansion.

"Just because I have money doesn't mean I should waste it, you know? A single guy doesn't need a huge house."

That opinion so accurately matched his own views on the matter that Priest added another tick to the growing check boxes of things to admire about his client. Tristan didn't know what style of house he wanted, just that he wanted a master suite on the first floor, a cellar or daylight basement—Tristan wasn't sure what it was called—where he could set up a soundproof studio to practice.

"I want there to be a lot of windows. I need as much direct sunlight as possible. But I also need remote-controlled retractable blinds in the master suite, so I don't have to get out of bed to open or close them."

Priest smiled. "Total darkness for sleeping, eh?"

Tristan looked abashed. "Something like that."

Again, there seemed to be more to the story than that clipped answer, but he wouldn't pry. Instead, he asked the next logical question. "Do you have any ideas for the facade of your house?"

"Well, I don't want it to look too different from its neighbors, but I would like it to be water and airtight at the same time. And I'd like to keep the color, if possible. Deeper, but the same tone." He pulled out his cell phone and scrolled through until he found what he was looking for. "Here, have a look."

Priest took the phone from him, careful not to touch him. He wasn't ready for any more stimulation than he'd already had with this man. He studied the pictures Tristan had taken of the house he wanted remodeled, and ideas immediately began to filter into his brain. Returning it, he said, "Can you send me those pictures, please? And I'd like to schedule a time to see the place in person."

Tristan did as he asked, using the cell phone number on Priest's business card. His phone buzzed with the new message but he ignored it, intent on completing the briefing. "How much are you willing to spend on this remodel?" he asked.

Not that he expected Tristan to have any sort of an accurate estimate, given that he didn't know what he wanted in vital areas, but it always paid to know what a client was prepared to spend to make their dream come true. He didn't think Tristan was a skinflint, but it was a standard question and it needed to be asked.

"I'd rather answer that after you've had a look and done some initial drawings, if you don't mind. I'm willing to pay for what I want. Will that do for now?"

Tristan held his gaze as though he understood what Priest was doing. Another tick in a box. Any man who held his gaze unwaveringly when money was the subject was worthy of his respect. And Tristan's answer was the perfect one for the situation. Why so many other clients couldn't muster the same level of common sense had always baffled him.

"That's fine. Do you have any questions for me before we continue?"

"No questions, really. I started looking at houses to see what I liked and it's a mishmash of styles, I'm sure. I started making a file. Perhaps I can send it to you when I'm satisfied I have everything I want in it? Just don't expect there to be any kind of common sense. It's all just things that please my eye. I'm a musician, not an artist."

Priest bit the inside of his cheek to stop himself from saying "But what a musician you are!" That would just give away that he knew more about Tristan than he'd let on at the beginning of this meeting. His clients needed to trust him, so he had to keep that bit of knowledge to himself for now. Maybe the next time they met he could let that tidbit free. It would seem more plausible that he'd gone and listened after finding out who Tristan was.

"Send it as soon as you're ready," he replied instead. Turning to his calendar, he added, "I'm not available for the rest of this week, and I'm not in town for the following week and half. What's your availability in a fortnight?"

"The band is working on a studio album, so we're here for a while."

"I'll have Erin send you a date and time." He tapped something out on his laptop before standing and walking around his desk, his hand outstretched. "I'm sorry, but I have another meeting in a few minutes. It's been great meeting you, Mr. DeVere." He truly wished he could prolong the time he spent in this man's company.

"Tristan, please," the musician said. "No one calls me Mr. DeVere. That's my father's title, and he's welcome to it."

Tris's dry tone and pinched lips told their own story, yet another one Priest would love to find out more about. He knew that accepting that their children were adults could be difficult for some parents, but thankfully, his relationship with his own was warm and affectionate. Part of that might have to do with the fact that they lived in Spain these days and had for years. "Absence makes the heart grow fonder," as they say, added to the fact that once he hit his 40th birthday, he had given them the boot from his life in a much firmer way than he'd been able to manage before.

Would he ever find himself in a situation where Tristan would share what made his voice so tight when he talked about his dad? The idea didn't seem feasible. Reining in his vagrant thoughts, he went to open the door for his guest.

"Hope to see you soon, Tristan," he said. "Take care."

Priest watched as the hot rockstar walked briskly down the hall and turned to head to the elevator, disappearing from sight when he did so. Erin appeared before him, her tablet in her hands.

"Mr. Banks is waiting for you, sir," she told him. "Shall I bring him round?"

"Thanks, Erin. And don't forget the coffee."

She nodded and turned down the hall while he walked back over to his desk to get ready for his next meeting. After that meeting, he had planning sessions with his builders, and then he left early to take Shannon to ballet. Wednesdays were busy days for him, between working a full day and doing the parent shuttling thing for the kids. Mason had football practice as well, and they'd all be exhausted by the time he drove them home.

By Friday night, when they were making pizza for dinner, Priest was more than ready to be alone with his kids and his piano. It was raining again, but he didn't mind that because at least this time he hadn't been caught out in it. Now, as he put out food for the pets, he acknowledged that his life was good. His children and his pets were happy, and he was … content.

Well, he was resolved to be content, at least. Nothing had changed in his life except that he'd finally met someone who made him begin to think about how much more than merely content he could be. And now that wasn't enough. When had he become that person, dissatisfied with the life he had been living without an issue for so long? He had nothing to feel this melancholy about. His children were growing into even-tempered, well-rounded human beings, he loved his job and was succeeding in it, and many others would envy the general serenity of his existence. Was he being ungrateful, entitled, to suddenly want more?

"Dad, the pizza's ready."

Shannon's voice pulled him back into the moment, away from the curious emptiness that he fought to keep from spreading in his chest. He wouldn't let one man disturb the calm he had found after the devastation of Jane's death. No one else was worth the upheaval of emotions that loving brought with it, and certainly not someone he didn't really know.

"Right then, let's eat. I'm starving."

He forced himself to stay present with his children as they enjoyed the homemade pizza, pop, and the trifle that was Shannon's favorite dessert to make. The usual hums and slurps and random other sounds of people enjoying their food were somehow just the notes he needed to hear. The usual questions about the week ensued, and when Shannon asked about his week, he debated for half a second as to whether or not he should tell them about Tristan.

He'd managed to calm the swelling emotions from before, but now, having to bring the man back into his mind was doing a number on him.

Heaving as quiet a sigh as he could, he said, "Well, I met your heartthrob on Wednesday. I'll be doing a total remodel of an old house he's bought."

"Who's my heartthrob?" Shannon asked, looking genuinely puzzled. Had she already moved on from the Third Generation bass guitarist? Oh, the fickleness of youth!

"I believe he's the bass guitarist of Third Generation," he said as nonchalantly as he could.

Shannon squealed a high-pitched sound almost painful to the ears. Clearly Onesie agreed with his master's assessment, because the dog looked up, eyed his mistress disdainfully, and put his head back down with his paws over his ears.

"Mind you don't deafen the dog, love," Priest teased her.

"What's he like, though, Dad?" she asked, ignoring him, her food forgotten.

"He's just like he was on television last week Friday," he answered, trying for a neutral expression. "And he's very ... polite and well-spoken." *Well done, Priest! Now you sound like your mum describing the neighbor's boy.*

"When are you going to see him again?" she wanted to know next.

"In a fortnight." Best to keep his answers short.

"Will you get him to sign something for me, Dad?"

"Shannon, I'm doing a job for him. I'm not his fan." *No, you're just silently perving on him.*

"You *should* be, Dad. You've listened to his music. I have a t-shirt I can give you."

"I can't make you any promises, love. We'll see."

Relieved when she accepted that answer, Priest helped them clean up from dinner and they all went into the den with dessert. He settled in his chair in front of the television and lost himself in the action of the first of two The Transformers movies that they wanted to watch, listening with amusement as they argued about which Transformer was the best.

"Dad, isn't Optimus Prime the best?" Mason demanded.

"Of course he's not, stupid!" Shannon retorted.

"Shannon, no name calling. You know the rule..."

She cut him off. "Sorry, Mason, but come on! How can you think a truck is better than a fighter jet?"

"But the Decepticons are the enemy, Shan! They're evil!"

It always amazed him how innocent his children were, especially living in the world that they were growing up in, and yet even movies with no semblance of reality got them to talk about deep issues like good and evil and who should be admired.

"Daaad!"

Shannon's frustration as she called him to be the final judge made his heart swell with pride. How long would it be before she wouldn't value his opinions, would probably actively oppose him if he tried to suggest a way to look at things that didn't coincide with her own? At least for now she understood that whatever he said could go against her own ideas and she was okay with that.

"Well, there's a lot to that question. For example, what exactly do you mean by 'best'? Are we talking best in terms of abilities and performance, or best in outward appearance, or best in character?"

He let them talk, only chiming in when they asked. He liked helping them to form and understand their opinions by stimulating their thinking with questions. In another life, he would have been a teacher. But he knew it was one thing to have patience for the children you helped bring into the world, and it was entirely another to do the same for other people's children in the artificial atmosphere of most schools.

"Alright, you lot, time for bed. I have an event tomorrow night and a lot to do before then. And you're going to be getting your rooms into shape before Mrs. Marks gets here." He was grateful for their grandmotherly babysitter. She was the right mix of indulgent and stern, which was just what his preteens needed at this point in their lives.

Priest knew that Mason usually felt his absence more keenly than Shannon did, so he wasn't at all surprised when the boy said, "I wish I could go with you, Dad."

He reached over to offer him a comforting hug for a moment as they cleared up the dessert bowls from the living room. Shannon rinsed the bowls, Mason took the dog out to do his business and clean up after him, and once everything had been set to rights, Priest kissed his children's foreheads and bid them goodnight.

"Lights out at midnight," he called after them as they made their way up the stairs.

"Yes, Dad!" echoed back down to him and he chuckled. He knew he'd find Shannon's light on when he went up to his own room after midnight, but he could never be angry with her, because she'd have fallen asleep with her earbuds in her ear, listening to whatever was on her phone.

Sleep took its own sweet time coming as it had done since Wednesday. His thoughts kept cycling back round to Tristan DeVere and the effect the star had had on him. He rolled in bed, facing the window, and instructed his Nest Hub to play soothing music for sleep. The sounds of ocean waves, waterfalls, and streams, interspersed with birdsong and the sweet strains of pianos wafted into the room.

He wondered what Tristan did to fall asleep when he couldn't shut off his brain. If he had a partner, maybe he never had that issue. They'd make love and wear each other out, and the stress and anxiety and worry would leach out in their orgasms. His unaccustomed dick perked up inconveniently at that idea and he rolled over again, closing his eyes against the images trying to invade his brain. Aside from being an entirely inappropriate train of thought, it wouldn't help him to fall asleep any faster, which had been his goal when he'd changed for bed.

What would Optimus Prime do in a case like this? The ridiculous question popped into his head, making him chuckle, and the tension in his limbs and his wayward dick eased at the new images invading his brain. Transformers making love ... impossible. He didn't know when he fell asleep.

Chapter 4

*Tris needed to let go of this yearning that
had taken up residence in his chest.*

"You look a million dollars, little brother," Tris remarked when his brother walked over to greet him. They were standing in the large space that the board of directors of Hope House had hired out for their fundraiser. "Where are your mates?"

"Joel and Blair are already at our table with Noah and his fiancé," Tag replied. "You're with us. Where's the rest of the band? They have the table next to us since they've brought their plus ones."

"They're just behind me. The ladies needed a touch up. You know how that is."

Tag chuckled. "No security tonight?"

"No. We figure the people who would misbehave and act like idiots won't be at this event. Any fans we might meet here will be the cool kind who won't expect or demand autographs. Unless the odd one has a kid who is a fan, and then it's a parent asking for a child, not a fan wanting attention. Besides, the venue hired out for professional security so we're good to go."

Tag nodded. "Well, come on then. Everyone's been asking for you."

Tris followed Tag to the table closest to the musician stand and smiled a greeting at everyone seated there. The women at the table he knew from having met them when the band was on tour in the States.

"May, Jessa, how lovely to see you both again." He accepted the hands they extended but instead of shaking them, he turned them so he could kiss the backs of them, making the women giggle.

"Go on, you charmer," May, the older one, said.

Blair, the violinist, shook his hand vigorously and clapped him on the shoulder. "My sister is a married woman, buddy."

Tris laughed. "Sue me for being a gentleman," he retorted with a grin. They all laughed as he moved on to shaking Joel's hand. The violist gave him a side hug.

"It's good to see you again, Tristan." It amused Tris that the man never shortened his name, but Joel had always been the most formal of the bunch, even after they'd become friendly. He didn't mind ... what would be the point? The man was showing respect in the way that was comfortable to him, and Tris was all about having people who were comfortable around him.

Finally, he moved to Noah. "How's life, Noah?" he asked, smiling at the violinist who had had to give up his career because he'd been involved in an accident that made playing for long impossible. He looked good, healthy and happy, and if the silver fox sitting next to him was the reason for that glow in his eyes, Tris could well understand.

"Tris. I'm glad I could come this time. This is my fiancé, Jax."

The older man shook hands and smiled. "Pleasure to meet you. It's kinda cool meeting the members of a rock band in person. Forgive me if I get a little starstruck."

Tris laughed. Clearly the guy was a charmer and anything but shy, but he appreciated the humor. He had a commanding presence that Tris assumed was one of the things that Noah loved about the man. "We'll be gentle, I promise."

More laughter followed his answer, and then the band members and their wives arrived and more introductions followed. The Barrington Strings had already been set up in their corner, and the room glittered with elegantly appointed round tables, as well as long rectangular ones laden with items for the silent auction. As he understood, having never before participated in a silent auction, each table would be opened individually, and once those items were sold a new table would be opened.

All the items for sale were listed on separate bid sheets by table, and the only thing that was of any interest to Tris was an unusual painting by a well-known but reclusive artist named Averille Shand. The painting, "Hope's Promise," showed a treble clef artfully presented in the shape of a voluptuous, naked woman. The vibrant colors suggested a myriad of emotions, and the note said it had been specially painted for Hope House to commemorate the work that the organization did with abused women.

Tris looked around as the director for Hope House, Dr. Anna James, finally stood at the podium to open the night's proceedings.

"Good evening, everyone, and thank you so much for being a part of this evening's gathering. As you know, we're here to raise funds for Hope House, which has served the

Greater London area for the past ten years. We are blessed to be able to work with the women who pass through our doors, to help them find a successful way forward for themselves and their children. But we couldn't do this work without all of you. So, thank you very much."

She raised her hands to clap, and everyone clapped with her. Then she continued. "This evening, in addition to the tickets you purchased for dinner and the finest chamber music, we have set up a silent auction. You should each have received the bid sheets for each table, and if you are participating, we invite you to place your bids on the app you should have downloaded at the time you purchased your tickets."

Tris wondered how many other people were interested in the rare Shand artwork and hoped he wouldn't have to spend too much more than he'd planned to in the event he had competition for the piece. He listened as the people at his table talked about what they liked. Among the things for sale, the four other musicians all liked the painting, but only Blair seemed interested in bidding on it. Well, at least he knew one person who he would be bidding against.

Dinner was a thorough delight, and Tris was grateful that despite the elegance of the presentation for each course, the food was filling. He usually avoided black-tie affairs like these because the food always bordered on pretentious, with a lot of smoke and mirrors and very little real substance. Thankfully, Hope House knew who to hire to please a crowd's eye and fill their bellies at the same time.

Since they'd opened the bidding on the last table, where the painting he wanted was displayed, he'd been placing his bets and watching as the bidding raged on. He didn't know when the bidding would be closed, but he noticed that after a while, when the bids began to grow, only he and one other person were still battling to the finish. He cast his eye over the crowd, wondering who his competition was. He'd already figured out that it wasn't Blair, who had long since pocketed his phone and was preparing to perform with his mates. The dessert course was almost over, the chatter of the other diners a low rumble echoing in the room.

He surreptitiously studied the people at each table, trying to see who was still on the phone, but Dr. James interrupted his scrutiny when she returned to the podium, calling the guests to order.

"Ladies and gentlemen, I hope you have enjoyed your meal. Thank you for your enthusiastic participation in this evening's silent auction. Bidding is now closed on all items, and those of you who have won out against your rivals will be able to collect your purchases at the end of the evening in the checkout area which is clearly marked at the back of the hall." She paused and looked over to the musicians, who were seated and ready to begin. "And now, to introduce tonight's performers, please help me welcome our chairman of the board, Mr. Benedict Priestley!"

Tris's heart skipped a beat, then another, then another, while his skin prickled with heat and his limbs froze. The man standing to his feet, the clearly bespoke tuxedo fitting him like a second skin, literally took his breath away. As he smiled at the crowd, looking over the sea of faces before him, making eye contact with individuals, Tris tried to catch air in his lungs, since living depended on breathing.

Still, he must not have done too good a job of it, because Jessa, Joel's girlfriend, touched his arm lightly and asked, "Are you alright, Tris?"

Pulling himself together, he nodded. "I'm fine, thanks Jessa." He really didn't understand the kind of visceral response he was having to a man he'd barely spent a couple of hours with two days before, a man he'd only met then and barely knew. The sexy, smoky voice was speaking, and Tris had missed the first minute of his speech. He tuned in.

"Hope House was one of my late wife's most beloved projects and because of her influence, I became a member of the family there. I am proud to be part of the leadership of an organization dedicated to the safety and well-being of all women and their children, and proud to serve alongside the other members of the board. What we have achieved in these last ten years is due in great part to your continued generosity and philanthropy. As we move into the next decade, our plans to expand the program will no doubt continue to benefit from your active participation in events such as these."

He raised his hands, clapping enthusiastically, and once the applause died down, he continued. "As a token of our deep appreciation and gratitude, we chose a vibrant and talented group of young men to perform for us tonight. The Barrington Strings was formed while these young men were still in college in the US, and today, eleven years on, they have carved out a niche for themselves in the world of music, distinguishing themselves in classical music as well as in more modern and experimental pieces."

He turned to look at them, his dimples deepening as his smile widened. "We are proud to have them perform for us this evening. Please help me welcome Blair Adamson, violinist, Joel Butler, violist, and Teagan DeVere..." He paused and looked up as if the last name had suddenly struck him. The pause was barely a second long, but it seemed to drag on forever before he ended, "...cellist."

Applause broke out in the room, and despite the formality of the occasion, a wolf whistle or two rang out. Tris understood, and he needed that reality check to bring him back to the moment, away from the surreal feeling threatening to overwhelm him. Forcing himself not to follow the architect with his eyes, he focused on the music.

Classical favorites were followed by trendy modern pieces including an unusual adaptation of one of Third Generation's best loved songs. The band had given the group permission to use the song, and Tris couldn't wait to hear what they'd done with the work they'd chosen. No doubt his band mates were just as eager. Tag stood to his feet to introduce the piece.

"Good evening, everyone. I'm Tag, aka Teagan DeVere, and as only few of you know..." he paused to look pointedly at the band's table and then at Tris, "my big brother is the bass guitarist in Third Generation."

An audible hum built in the crowd but Tag pressed on, ignoring the audience's shock. "When we were younger, growing up in England, we loved both classical and rock music, and we played both the cello and the bass guitar. I guess we love the lower registers of music best. They have a kind of sensual power that we find impossible to ignore, right Tris?"

He looked over at Tris, who managed a smile even though his mouth was a dry desert, before continuing. "Still, as we matured, and I migrated to the States, we chose paths that would take us in the direction of our dreams. I enjoy the almost cerebral quality of the cello, while Tris loves the earthier, meatier textures of the bass guitar."

He sipped from a glass of water next to his stand before continuing. "What, you may wonder, does any of this family history have to do with our performance this evening? The group and I, along with our colleague Noah Santiago, who did the lion's share of the work, have chosen one of Third Generation's most popular songs and have arranged it as a classical piece, in honor of my brother's and my love of both classical and rock music. And so, I give you, 'Revelation'."

Resuming his seat, he began the signature piece with the cello introduction, and Tris played his guitar in his mind as his brother poured his soul into the song. He knew the lyrics as well as Rory, who sang them with deep feeling each time they performed it. He could hear the classical inspiration—Saint-Saëns's "The Swan"—that Noah had somehow married to the music of the original rock song. How had they never thought to do this adaptation? It was a perfect marriage, and tears welled in his eyes as he followed along.

> *Time was*
> *I knew my heart —*
> *or thought I knew —*
> *how I would feel*
> *when kith and kin find places of their own,*
> *how I would act*
> *when I was left alone to my own soul.*

Rory's words always made his heart full, and now, with the possibility—or the hope of such—with a man he had not expected even to meet, that fullness overflowed. He wiped at his eyes surreptitiously. He was being an idiot. Benedict Priestley was an unknown quantity. They moved in different worlds, and the man was straight. He'd confirmed as much earlier with talk of his wife. Tris needed to let go of this yearning that had taken up residence in his chest since Wednesday morning.

Maybe he should try one of those dating apps again. Maybe his luck would change this time, and he'd find someone worthy of his attention, his affection, his commitment. Maybe ... the sound of chairs scraping as people stood and the musicians rose to thunderous applause. Tris stood belatedly and cheered his brother and his mates. After a few minutes of non-stop applause, Dr. James called for order one last time.

"What a wonderful performance, ladies and gentlemen! Our deepest gratitude goes to The Barrington Strings." She turned to look them in the eye. "Gentlemen, you have outdone yourselves and should be justifiably proud of your amazing achievement here this evening. I hope you will be as blessed as you have blessed us tonight."

Turning back to the audience, she ended, "And so, ladies and gentlemen, we've come to the end of our time together. Many thanks to you all for your unwavering support of Hope House. Our mission remains unchanged ... to work with women who need assistance to move on from abusive and harmful situations to safety and security for themselves and their children. Many thanks to our sponsors, donors, staff, and volunteers for their hard work in planning and preparing for this event."

She looked towards the back of the room and nodded faintly. "Those persons who have won their bids should have received the notification on their phones. The checkout area is now open for you to redeem your purchases. Thank you all, and goodnight."

Applause greeted her final words, and the buzz of voices rose again as people made their way to the checkout area or said goodbye to each other and left. Tris checked his app and saw that he had won. Elation rose in his chest. Whoever had been bidding against him had done his best to get the painting, and Tris couldn't help but wonder why the man or woman had just dropped out. It was clear that he or she could afford it. He shrugged; it didn't matter why he'd won, just that he had.

"I'm off to get my painting," he announced to the others at the table. "Are you all joining us for drinks?"

"Most definitely," May said with a grin. "Who would be crazy enough to refuse to hang out with a bunch of hot rockstars?"

Tris laughed. "And their women. Don't forget their women."

"Even so," she persisted. "Just because I can't have them doesn't mean I can't enjoy hanging out with them. Bragging rights, you know? Pictures or it didn't happen."

Still laughing, he stepped away to join the queue for the table where his artwork was displayed. When only one person remained ahead of him, he pulled his wallet from his inside breast pocket and prepared to pay for his purchase. Then a familiar voice said, quite close to his ear, "So you're the lucky Shand winner, eh, Tristan?"

Tris turned, feeling his heart swell in his chest. Needing to calm his nerves, he tried for a joke. "Are you the unlucky loser, Mr. Priestley?"

He smiled. "Call me Priest," he said. "Let's just say, I fought a good fight, shall we? Congratulations! It's a beautiful piece."

By now it was Tris's turn and he paid and signed off on the receipt, accepting the brown-paper-wrapped painting. Turning back to Priest, he said, "I'm not sorry I won the bidding, obviously, but I do feel your pain at losing this gorgeous work."

Before the man could reply, Rory came up. "We're heading out now, Tris." Then he saw Priest and smiled. "Oh, hello, Mr. Priestley. I'm Rory Stewart. This was a really great evening." They shook hands before he added, "We're going out for drinks. If you've nothing else planned, would you care to join us?"

Tris's heart skipped three—or three hundred—beats, he had no idea. Part of him wanted the architect to say yes with an almost rabid desperation. He wouldn't refuse any extra time that he could spend with this man. But the other part of him wanted to keep his attraction a secret, and he knew he'd never pull off a nonchalant act with Henry and Rory there to see.

"I'd love to. Tell me where we're meeting, and I'll be there as soon as I can."

"We'll be at Alford's. Tris can ride with you and show you where."

Rory avoided looking at him, making Tris wonder what he was up to, but he had no time to consider it more closely because the man at his side agreed enthusiastically, as though he didn't have a satnav in his vehicle. Could this mean he was interested after all? And if he was, what did that make him ... a closet gay man with kids? A bisexual man? Pan? Did it matter?

"...okay?"

Tris blinked. Rory had disappeared and apparently, he'd checked out while Priest had been talking to him. "Sorry, what?"

Priest's smile radiated amusement. "I just asked you to wait for me here. I'll be with you in a few."

"Sure." Tris managed to keep his embarrassment hidden. He wouldn't be winning any cool points if he kept wool-gathering in Priest's company. The man wasn't likely to remain interested—assuming he was—if Tris couldn't get his act together. Moving away to stand by the window, he watched as the hall emptied, trying to avoid staring at Priest as he made his final rounds. The man stood tall and ele-gant, gliding from one person to the next, his warm smile a beacon drawing Tris's eyes to his full lips and deep dimples.

He barely managed to pull his gaze away before Priest looked up, heading towards him. Picking up the painting he had rested by his foot, he moved towards the door.

"Let's go. The car will be out front in a minute."

Chapter 5

Priest

*His eyes met Tristan's, and something
sparked to life between them.*

Priest's SUV was all sleek luxury and style, the interior a rich midnight blue. He settled his spine against the plush leather seat, his strong hands gripping the steering wheel as he pulled out into traffic. He could barely see Tristan's profile as he drove, and he bit back a grin at the way they'd ended up together alone in his car. Not that he objected; in fact, he'd been thrilled when Rory had suggested that Tristan give him directions to their club. The spicy scent of Tristan's cologne made him want to pull him closer, to inhale him deeply.

Worried that his companion might feel awkward about their current situation, Priest said, "I appreciate you keeping me company, Tristan. D'you mind putting the address in the satnav?"

"Not at all."

He did as requested as Priest asked, "How did you discover Averille Shand's work?"

"I was gallery hopping a few years ago and found her in a little shop off the High Street in Oxford. It was a print of one of her most famous pieces, The Pianist. I ended up buying that as well as one of a harp."

"I think I know the two you have. I have a few other pieces that my wife bought. She was the one who introduced me to Averille. They were friends, if you can believe it."

He caught the hint of a smile when he glanced over at Tristan, but the man didn't reply, and before long Priest was handing off his keys to a parking valet once again. Then they were ushered in by the liveried doorman, and he followed Tristan, who headed over to where his bandmates were waiting for them. He noticed that Rory caught Tristan's eye first and winked at him. Hmm ... what was that about? He observed Tristan's response. He inclined his head slightly, smiled, and spoke.

"Guys, let me introduce Benedict Priestley. Priest, my bandmates and their significant others."

Going round the room, he named each member of the group and Priest shook hands and smiled, thanking Rory, when he got to him, for the invitation to hang out. Then he smiled widely when Rory said, "This is my fiancée, Chrissy."

"It's lovely to see you again, Chrissy. Dr. James did mention your engagement. Congratulations to you both!"

"Thank you." Chrissy's smile was radiant.

The others made room for them, and Priest wondered if Tristan could feel the heat emanating from his body. He had to force himself not to react to the need coursing through him to sit shoulder to shoulder, thigh to thigh with the younger man so he could share that heat with him. Henry ordered champagne for the tables and toasts rang out for the men of the hour, breaking the spell he was caught up in.

"That was a truly masterful adaptation," he said, grateful for the distraction. "'The Swan' is one of my most favorite pieces of music, and my daughter Shannon also loves it. Speaking of which..." He paused, trying to decide if he should say what he had been thinking.

"Yes?" Tristan prompted him to continue. Priest had a feeling Tristan knew what he was going to ask and why he was hesitating.

"Let me apologize first. I'm not that guy who bothers celebrities..."

Henry stopped him immediately. "No, you're the guy we invited to hang with us. So just say what you need, and we'll be happy to oblige if we can."

Priest smiled a little awkwardly, then plunged on. "I had no idea that I would be meeting Shannon's favorite rock band tonight, so I don't have a t-shirt or any merch of yours for you to sign for her, but if you could all sign the program, I'll make sure she gets it." Turning to Tristan, he added, "Yours will need to be extra special, as she's mad about you, in particular."

Tristan chuckled. "No problem. I'll go last."

The drinks flowed, and everyone shared stories back and forth, including Priest effortlessly in the conversation. He, Henry, and Gen bonded over raising preteen children, and he and Noah's man, Jax, spent time reminiscing about their experiences in Vienna. He kept his eyes on Tristan as often as he dared, watching as he let the talk flow around him. He seemed happy just to soak in the sense of family that permeated the space. He rarely spoke but didn't appear to feel excluded and no one, not even Priest, tried to force more from him than he gave.

Finally, however, Priest rose to leave. "This has been a truly wonderful evening, everyone. I really enjoyed every aspect of it and hope we can stay in touch. As you probably know, I'll be doing the remodel of Tristan's home, so I imagine we will meet again." He lifted the program he held and added, "Oh, and thank you for this. Shannon will be over the moon."

"What about your son?" Chrissy asked. "Won't he be jealous of her?"

Before he could reply, Will said, "Why don't we send them both some merch, signed, so they'll each have something to brag about?"

"That's a great idea. We already know Shannon loves Tris." Will grinned and winked at Tristan. "What does your *son* enjoy?" he asked.

"Mason loves football more than anything else in the world."

"We're on it," Henry said. "We'll get your details from Tris."

Priest turned to him. "Walk me out? I have a question about the house."

Tristan rose and followed him, clearly ignoring his friends who were all grinning like loons as Priest turned away. He was doing his best to hide his own grin, though he hoped Tristan didn't mind if his mates knew why Priest had called him aside. He needed to be alone with the sexy guitarist, and he hoped Tristan could handle the ribbing he'd likely get when he got back to the table.

At the door, Priest turned to him. "This was an unexpected but delightful surprise," he began. "I hadn't thought I'd see you again for two weeks."

"You mean, at the house you wanted to talk to me about?" Tristan teased. Oh, so he was feeling brave, was he? Priest could live with that.

He smiled. "I do want to talk to you about it." At Tristan's disbelieving stare, he chuckled. "You saw through that, huh?" He held Tristan's gaze.

"I'm sure *everyone* saw through that," Tristan replied, his gaze sparking as Priest pinned him with his dark eyes. "So, what can I do for you?"

Can I ask you out? Would you say yes if I did? That's what I want you to do for me. Keeping a lid on his less than professional thoughts, because he *had* said he wanted to talk to him about his house, Priest said instead, "Since I have you here, I can take one thing off Erin's To Do list. I need more than the few images of the house that you've already shared with me. I've been brainstorming a few ideas, but I need more detailed images. I'll email you to set up a time for my colleague to come by to take the images I especially need to see."

"Of course. I'll get back to you as soon as I get it." Was that disappointment in Tristan's eyes? Surely not! The guitarist was so buttoned up, Priest found it hard to read his expression.

A tense pause followed before Priest replied. "Well, I'm off. See you soon. Have a great weekend, Tristan."

His eyes met Tristan's, and something sparked to life between them. Priest watched his eyes go dark as they trailed down to his own parted lips and then he turned away and walked out to the street. What had that look been about? Could it have been the same outrageous desire to press his lips against Tristan's that had gripped the other man? The thought shook the calm he was fighting to maintain.

Back on the road, he reviewed the evening. It had been wonderful, entertaining, and arousing. Between the good food, excellent performance, and the time spent with the musicians afterwards, Priest was ... happy? When was the last time he'd felt this deep contentment? He couldn't recall. It must have been before Jane died. And the thoughts of the man he was apparently crushing on like a randy teenager added a whole other dimension to the feelings into which he let himself sink.

Tristan was clearly the quietest, perhaps most reserved member of the band. Even his younger brother was more talkative than he was. Priest liked that about him. He was secure in his own skin, unafraid to be himself and unapologetic. His vibe said take him or leave him, and Priest found he wanted to take him more every time they met. He couldn't wait for their next encounter.

For now, he'd send the email requesting access for pictures, as he'd said he would. Even this small task was another connection between them. He wished he could call, but the things he wanted done needed more words than he'd be able to push past the ones he dared not say. Writing them was best.

At home, he undressed, pulling on sleep pants, and settled on his big bed with his laptop across his knees. He tapped out a brief message, erasing and rewriting, changing words, reworking it like he was writing his capstone essay for graduation. Then, finally satisfied, he read it aloud to make sure it was perfect.

"Hi, this is Priest. Will it be okay for my colleague to come by on Monday or Tuesday to take some pictures? I need specific images that he'll have the details for, both inside and outside. Let me know which day and what time will be best for you. Regards."

The feeling that he hadn't struck the right note sat heavy in his gut. Should he say something about the evening? Wouldn't that muddy the professional veneer he was trying to project? But was it professional to begin with "This is

Priest?" His nickname had no place in business correspondence. It didn't help to remind himself of that because he wanted to get personal with this man, not be bloody professional.

Sighing heavily, he hit send before he could add a PS with some totally inappropriate message. This job was going to be a challenge of an order he had never experienced before. Only with Jane and his first boyfriend in college had he felt the levels of attraction he was feeling for Tristan. With 50 staring him in the face, he had thought that kind of intense emotion lost to him, and he really wasn't sure how he was supposed to feel about what was an inconvenient, if thrilling, attraction.

Would Tristan still find him attractive if he knew that Priest was almost ten years older than he was? Would he be turned off by the fact that Priest was bisexual? Would he want a man with two children approaching their teen years? And speaking of children, how was he to explain his own desire for a man to them when they had no idea that he was equally drawn to men and women? And how would he explain to his 12-year-old daughter that he thought about Tristan in the same way that she did?

He shuddered. He'd never thought he'd have to have *that* talk with his kids ... the one where he told them he was an equal opportunity lover. It was bad enough he'd eventually have to talk to them about sexuality and the place of intimacy in their own personal relationships. That was a conversation he was dreading, but as it had never come up until now, his own preferences had been securely veiled behind the curtain of marriage to a woman he had loved to distraction. And as he'd not been attracted to any man for a while before he and Jane got together, he'd forgotten that part of himself. Until now.

Pushing the laptop to the side, he lay back, pulling the sheet over his body, and clasped his hands behind his head. He missed having a warm body to cuddle with in bed. He missed having a lover to shower with affection, to ravish with desire and lust. He missed Jane, and the spurt of guilt that lanced through him at the thought that he might be moving on from her wounded him.

Logically, he knew he was being ridiculous. His therapist had helped him figure out that feelings of guilt were a part of the grieving process, that in fact, if he ever fell in love again, it would not be a betrayal of his wife. He really knew that, but now the idea of finally having someone to share with again, after all this time, brought those feelings surging back. And with the guilt came fear, because there were no guarantees when it came to matters of the heart. Shutting his eyes and breathing deeply, he tried to force thoughts of Tristan from his mind. He had a late morning flight and there were things he needed to do before he headed to the airport.

When he woke a few hours later, his head throbbed faintly from lack of sleep, but he did his best to wash it away with a hot shower and drown the rest of it in hot tea. Biting into the buttered toast he'd made, he checked his watch and saw that he had a few minutes to spare to say goodbye to his kids before he left for ten days. Just as he swallowed the last of the toast with the rest of his tea, they both tumbled down the stairs, rushing into the kitchen.

"Morning, sprogs."

They came over to him, ignoring his greeting in favor of tight hugs. Wrapped around his children, Priest let their sleepy morning scents wash over him, soaking in their love and missing them although he hadn't yet walked out the door. They were the reason he'd finally pulled his head out of his arse and got back to the business of living when grief over his loss threatened to drown him in permanent waves of depression.

"I'll call you every night, and if I can't, I'll send you a text message. Be good while I'm gone. Don't give Mrs. Marks any grief." He knew they wouldn't, but he liked to make them promise anyway. "And if you're very good, I'll have something special for you both when I get back."

Two pairs of eyes studied his face for a moment before Shannon pulled away to ask, "Is it something we're going to like, Dad?" Her eyes were filled with suspicion.

Priest laughed. "Name one gift I've given you that you haven't wanted."

She paused, thinking hard, and when she was still speechless after fifteen seconds, he said, "I rest my case."

"Well, remember that wooden doll? The Japanese one," she clarified before he could ask her which one. "I didn't know what to do with it."

"Ah, but that wasn't a gift that I bought you, love, if you'll recall. And once your mum explained what it meant, you found a place for it in your collection, didn't you?"

He knew he had her when she pursed her lips. "Okay, okay. You got me."

"Don't worry. I'm sure you'll be wild about the surprise I'll have for you. Trust me."

He'd decided to keep the signed program from the fundraiser to present to her along with whatever merch the band members chose to send. That would satisfy her soul for a while. Pulling up the handle of his suitcase, he rolled it to the front door, turning back to kiss each child on the forehead.

"I love you both with all my heart. Be good until I get back. I'll miss you. Don't miss me too much."

Mason clung a little more tightly before finally letting go when his sister pulled him away with a frustrated, "Mason! Stop being so clingy."

The cab he'd called was waiting for him at the curb. On his way to the airport, he reviewed his itinerary. First, he was going to close out the job he'd done the designs for in Edinburgh. Then he'd travel to Madrid to investigate the possibility of bidding on another project before heading back home, only making a short stop on the Isle of Wight to see the progress on the house his friend was renovating as a holiday home. It would be a busy ten days.

Had Tristan answered his email as yet? Was he even up as yet? It had just gone eight in the morning and on a Sunday, with nothing to do and nowhere to go, why would he be awake, especially after the night he'd just spent with family and friends? He probably hadn't even seen the message as yet. There was no reason for him to check his inbox after midnight on a weekend. Anything could wait until he woke up, right? That was certainly how Priest lived his life—when he wasn't failing to fall asleep and checking his emails instead—so why would Tristan be any different?

He sighed heavily, wishing his thoughts didn't always seem to cycle back to Tristan. Hopefully he'd be too busy to moon over the sexy rockstar, and by the time he saw Tristan again he'd have regained his common sense and his equilibrium. He crossed his fingers as he watched the traffic outside the cab's windows.

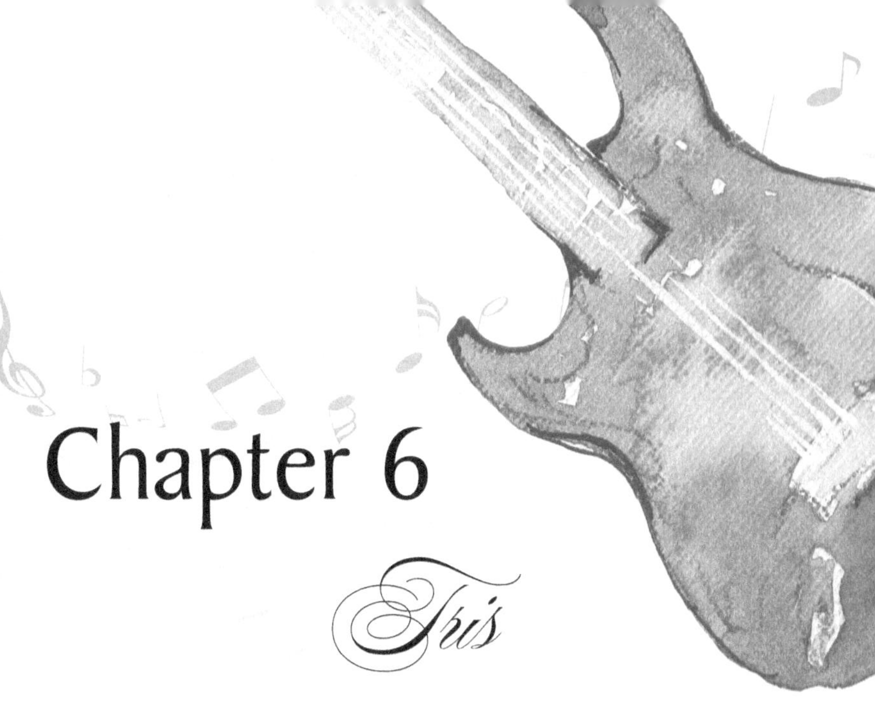

Chapter 6

Tris

There's just something about him.

Tris woke slowly, the sun slanting a bright stripe across his eyes between the slightly open blinds. He stretched, glancing over at the phone he'd set on the upright charger. Reaching over, he woke it with a touch and saw that it was almost ten in the morning. His body felt like it could use another couple of hours in horizontal bliss, but his brain had snapped to attention almost as soon as he'd opened his eyes and images from the night before returned with unexpected clarity.

After Priest had walked away, Tris had taken another moment to gather his control around him. The urge to press his lips to Priest's had been almost overwhelming. Had the man noticed the way his eyes trailed down to their plush softness? Shaking his head at himself, he put on his poker face before returning to his friends, prepared for the ribbing that he was sure would follow. So he was shocked when he got back, and no one said anything about Priest's request. Maybe he'd get away with it.

Except, on his way back to Henry's place, Gen had turned to look at him in the dark car and asked innocently, "So, Priest, huh?"

Tris had heaved a heavy sigh. He hadn't been sure exactly what she was asking, but whatever it was, it was the first shot over the bow of his pretense at disinterest, and he knew from past experience that he'd lose not just this first skirmish but the whole damned war with her and Henry.

"That's what he told me to call him." It was the truth, and he hadn't felt inclined to offer anything else. No need to interpret it as meaning anything more than the man being friendly, as *he'd* been when he'd told Priest to use his first name.

"Hmm." He could barely see her smile as she'd added, "And what did he want to ask you about the house?"

"He wanted to know which day I'd be home as he needs to send someone to take more detailed pictures before our next meeting. He has some ideas, and he needs the details so he can present them to me."

Happy to be able to give her the truth, he watched her turn to face forward again and hoped he'd managed to squash any further interest in his dealings with his architect. He wasn't sure what was happening between them, or what it meant that he was so insanely attracted to a man he'd only met briefly twice now, but he'd rather not engage in speculation with anyone on the subject. Thankfully, Gen dropped the interrogation.

"Are you sleeping over?" Henry asked when they got back to his house. He hadn't contributed to the conversation, but Tris knew that didn't mean anything. His friend would grill him when he was ready. In the meantime, Tris would take any reprieve he could get.

He returned his attention to Henry's question. Although he dearly wanted to be on his own, Tris knew it would probably not be smart to drive with the alcohol still sloshing around in his system. Crisps and nuts weren't enough to soak up all the booze he'd had all evening. He could bite the bullet this once. Gen had long since invited him to leave a change of clothing in the room she called his, so there really was no reason to refuse.

"Yes, if it's alright with you."

After a hot shower, he'd lain sprawled in bed, naked except for a clean pair of boxers, his mind going on an endless loop over the evening, particularly the parts with Priest in it. Those last few moments by the door of the club, when Priest's eyes had lingered on his lips, were set to keep him awake long past the time when he needed to be asleep. What would it be like to be kissed by the big man?

Despite the extra two inches that Tris had over him, Priest's body made him appear larger than life, a giant among men. The tuxedo had done nothing to hide the powerful body it covered. Anyone could see the man was ripped. How would it feel to be wrapped in those powerful arms, to be cradled, held impossibly close? What would their bodies feel like pressed together?

Tris remembered how restless he'd been as he tried to slow his wide-awake brain. He'd rolled onto his belly, hugging the pillows, trying desperately to stop the round of his thoughts. He needed sleep. It had been a long evening and he had things to do before rehearsals began again on Monday. The thought of Priest's body tight against his own slid back into his mind when his dick pressed into the mattress.

"Bloody hell!"

He'd rolled onto his back. He did *not* need to be thinking about a man he was in business with in any sexual way whatsoever, but he also knew that something had been set off at the club. He had felt the live-wire connection sparking between them, unseen but full of unexposed energy and power. He couldn't say how he knew, but he knew that Priest was attuned to that same energy arcing between them. How could that be? The man barely knew him but was obviously attuned to what he was feeling. It was a bit unnerving, if he were honest.

The charisma that had ensnared Tris was clearly not lost on his bandmates either. Tris had felt such pride when Henry had interrupted Priest's apology earlier. He understood the other man's reluctance to ask for something most people demanded as their right. That was one of the reasons Tris loved Henry like a big brother. He had no airs about him, and showed respect to people who deserved it. People like Priest.

Tris sighed. He needed to keep Priest squarely in the friend zone. He was probably in his forties, which wasn't a bad thing, just not his thing. Not anymore. He'd been disappointed by older men all his life, starting with his own father. And the one man he had given his heart to had turned out to be a two-timing toad with a mistress and a secret kink for gay boys. Never again! No matter what was happening between him and Priest, he couldn't, *wouldn't* entertain it.

Sleep hadn't been any closer than it had been an hour earlier, so he'd picked up his phone and signed into his Grindr app. Maybe he could find a hookup. He'd swiped half-heartedly through a few profiles, but nothing held his attention. After a few minutes of unfairly comparing the bodies—and in one case an enormous dick screened by white boxer briefs—to Priest's, he'd shut down the app, sighing heavily.

That last profile had his brain going to places it didn't need to be. What Priest looked like under his trousers was *not* Tris's concern, and he had no business even contemplating it for a second. Flinging himself back onto the pillows, he'd pulled up a Third Generation soundtrack on his phone and lost himself in the music. He didn't know when he fell asleep.

His restless night was probably why now, almost halfway through the morning, he still felt like he could sleep for a while longer. But he wasn't on his boat, and no matter how much he loved spending time with Henry and his family, he needed to be alone with his thoughts. He got out of bed and went into the bathroom, relieving his overfull bladder before washing up and brushing his teeth.

Back in the bedroom, he dressed quickly and took the tux with him down to breakfast. He could hear movement in the kitchen, so he headed there, setting the clothes on a chair as he greeted his hostess.

"Morning, Gen. Sorry I got up so late."

Gen smiled at him. "No need to apologize. Henry just woke up as well. He'll be down in a few. I had to get up to feed the brats because you know, growing boys and all." Tris chuckled. "I hope you slept well," she continued. "Help yourself to what you want, love. I have a load of laundry to put in."

"Thanks, Gen."

He could hear the twins in the den playing a video game. He'd make sure to say hi before he left. He checked under the food covers and chose eggs, beans, sausages, and bacon, and dropped two thick slices of bread into the toaster. While he waited, he poured himself a cup of tea from the pot on the warmer and set his breakfast next to the spot where his clothes sat. The toaster popped, and he slathered butter on the hot slices, then sat and devoured his meal.

He hadn't realized how hungry he was until he'd taken a sip of the delicious Earl Grey tea. When he was almost done, Henry walked in, his loose-fitting sweats hovering at his hips beneath a ragged-looking band t-shirt.

"Morning," his friend grumbled, heading straight for the teapot and pouring himself a huge mug. Adding in sugar and a squeeze of lemon, he sat across from Tris, sipping it with his eyes closed.

"Not ready to be up, are you?" Tris asked, smiling.

"Gen insisted I get up. Something about it being almost halfway through the day or some such nonsense." Although his lips were cupping the mug, Tris could hear the pout in his friend's voice.

"Well, think of it this way. At least you don't have an hour and a half drive ahead of you before you can go back to bed."

Henry harrumphed. "We'll be back at it tomorrow," he said, not responding to Tris's comment.

"I know. I'm kinda looking forward to getting back to work. I'm finally feeling like my old self again."

"The advantage of youth," Henry muttered into his mug.

Tris laughed. "Says the guy who is only three years older than me."

"Shut it!" Henry glared at him, then put the tea down and looked him in the eye. "So, what's going on between you and the chairman of the board?"

Tris blinked. The question blindsided him, though he didn't know why it should. He had known Henry was just biding his time hours earlier. He hurried to answer.

"Nothing, absolutely *nothing*, is going on," he put air quotes around the last two words, "between me and the chairman of the board."

"So giving you permission to call him by a nickname and having you walk him out to talk about something he could have sent you an email about is nothing?" Henry used his fingers to emphasize the last word of his question.

"None of that means anything. He's a friendly bloke who likes to give that personal touch in his business dealings whenever he can, that's all." He needed to believe that as much as he wanted Henry to believe it, because it would make letting go of his attraction easier ... he hoped.

"Hm ... except for the part where he took every chance he could while assuming he wasn't being watched himself to observe you. I've seen that look in people's eyes before, when they see something they want but don't think they can have it."

Tris opened his mouth but couldn't find a ready response, so he closed it again, completely stumped. Was that how *he* looked at Priest? Had anyone noticed his own furtive glances at the man? He'd done his best to keep his attention elsewhere, but the magnetism of Priest's personality kept him returning for another glimpse, another chance to see him interacting with his bandmates and friends.

"And let's not talk about the times *you* snuck in your own admiring glances," Henry continued, picking up his mug and taking a deep swallow of tea. "So tell me again how there's nothing going on." When Tris still didn't answer—because what could he say to that?—Henry continued. "You know I'm not just being an interfering friend, don't you, Tris? I'd never presume to tell you who you should and shouldn't be attracted to. I'm just worried."

Tris sighed. He should have known that Henry would be the first one to worry about him. He held their friendship close to his heart and took his big brother responsibilities very seriously. Tris smiled, suddenly glad he had a solid man in his corner. No matter what did or didn't happen between him and Priest, he knew he'd have Henry's full support.

"Thanks, mate. You know I appreciate you looking out for me. I promise I won't let things get out of control."

"But you *are* interested, yes?"

"Yeah." He wished he weren't. "I know it's highly inappropriate showing any interest in someone who basically works for me, just because things could get awkward if the interest fizzles or he breaks my trust. And I know we've only met twice. But there's just something about him..."

His voice trailed off and he finished his breakfast in silence. Henry said nothing further until he stood up to clear away his dishes.

"Leave them, Tris. I'll deal with them. I'd better eat now before my ever-hungry twins return to clean up whatever's left with space left over to inhale lunch."

Tris laughed as he set the dishes in the sink. "Thanks. I'll call you when I get home."

Henry stood up, taking his tea with him, and accompanied him on his way to the front door. He stopped to greet the twins, who rushed him for a hug.

"Take care, mate," Henry told Tris, and waited to wave him off.

Traffic on the motorway was the expected mix of easy and snarled all to hell because of an accident that was cleared away by the time he got to it, but he managed to make it back to his boat just after lunchtime. He'd drop his tux off at the cleaners on his way in to work, but for now it could live on the chair closest to the door so he wouldn't forget it on his way out. The deck was calling to him, so he changed into shorts and a t-shirt, poured himself a drink, and went to sit in the unusually warm sunshine, loving the calm flow of the afternoon.

His phone buzzed with a reminder from Rory about the next day's rehearsal, which was going to start an hour later than normal at his home in Kensington. They had some planning to do before heading into the studio in London. After responding, he decided to check his emails, suddenly recalling that he was expecting one from Priest. His belly fluttered when he saw that the architect had sent the message in the early hours of the morning. Had he also been having a hard time falling asleep? The thought pleased Tris.

The message was simple but he read and re-read it as if he hoped to find some other meaning in it than what was actually there. Then he answered with a quick note. "Tomorrow morning is best, as rehearsals won't start until 11:00. If your colleague can get here by 8:30 or so, that would be fine. Will it take longer than an hour? Please let me know ASAP."

He hovered over the send button. Could he add a personal note without sounding like a romantic idiot? *Should* he add anything personal to a business message? He worried his bottom lip trying to decide, then muttered, "Blast it!" and added, "I hope you had a safe journey. Regards, Tris." Then he hit send and exhaled hard. He was a grown man, not a teenage girl crushing on her idol. He needed to stop acting that part and be himself ... an adult interested in another adult. Let the chips fall where they would.

Sun-drunk after a couple of hours soaking up the rays, he went in, drank a whole glass of cold water, and fell into bed for an afternoon nap that turned into three hours of deep, revitalizing sleep. He must have been more tired than he'd known. Evening was closing in when he woke again, his belly snarling at him. Hangry ... was that the word for the kind of feeling he was experiencing in his gut? As if his belly was berating him for making it go so long without sustenance? He chuckled as he checked his freezer. There was still one frozen dinner left over from his shopping trip a week ago. Pulling it out, he preheated the oven and prepped it, making himself an iced mocha drink before putting it to cook.

He checked his phone while he waited, his pulse kicking up when he saw a reply to his message from Priest. Leaving his drink in the fridge to keep cold while dinner cooked, he sat at the table and read it aloud.

"John can be there by 8:30 in the morning and it shouldn't be longer than an hour. And thanks, I got here safely. Have a great rehearsal. Priest." His belly fluttered again ... was he having an upset stomach?

Dinner was palatable, and the iced coffee was a fitting dessert drink to elevate it above the merely ordinary. He spent the next few hours going over the songs they had planned for the new album, working on the one in particular that gave him the most grief because the blocks were complicated. Finally feeling like he'd gotten the rhythm right for a change, he showered and went to bed, making sure to set the alarm to give himself enough time to shower and get dressed before the photographer arrived.

By the time John showed up the next morning, the fog on the river had loosened its grip and only a light mist remained, accompanied by the expected drizzle of an early Spring day. He greeted the man with a cheerful good morning and an offer of tea.

"I'll have that when I'm done, if you don't mind," John said with a grin. "This is chilly weather."

Tris led him up to the house and watched as he took measurements and pictures before heading out to do the same for the exterior.

"This is a sweet spot," John remarked when he was finally done, looking admiringly from the house down to the boat and the river. "It must be grand having a houseboat here."

Tris smiled as he led him back onto the boat, offering him a seat at the table. He'd left the tea to steep and keep warm, and it was ready for pouring.

"Help yourself to whatever you like," he invited the man, indicating the biscuits he'd arranged on a plate along with milk, sugar, and lemons before adding his own fixings to his cup and sipping. The morning still held the deep chill of a Spring night, so the tea was a welcome shot of warmth in his bloodstream.

"Will I get a set of the images you'll send to P... Mr. Priestley?" He caught himself on the nickname, not sure what Priest's coworkers knew about him and not willing to open any avenues for gossip. It was bad enough *his* mates may have some idea from his side of things. Tris didn't need to open up another can of worms on Priest's side.

"Most definitely, sir," the man said. "You'll be copied in the email."

Thankfully, he was so fascinated by their location that he spent the rest of the time talking about what it was like living on "this gorgeous houseboat," about living in Old Windsor, about the commute to London for rehearsals.

"People think rockstars have an easy life, but it doesn't sound like it's all that different from my life, aside from the whole living on a bus thing," he commented with a grin as he finished his tea. "I don't envy you, really. Not even the money. I like my own little place to go home to every day after I do my nine to five."

Tris understood. Sometimes he wished he lived that simpler life too. Wasn't that why he had bought the house, why he was having it renovated? So, he could have a greater feeling of normalcy than he did at the moment? He smiled his agreement, and as the photographer stepped off the boat, he said, "Take care and thank you."

With a wave, John disappeared along the pier to his car, and Tris cleaned up before heading out. If all went well, he'd get to Rory's just on time.

Chapter 7

Priest

Why was his stupid heart beating harder?

"**D**ad!"

Every time Priest came home after a work trip, his greatest joy was the welcome his children gave him. A small part of him dreaded the day when they would no longer want the hugs he loved to share with them. He held them tight to his body, loving the warmth radiating from them.

Shannon released him first and stepped back to say, "We've got mail."

Priest grinned at her. "We?" He was sure there was more to her announcement.

"It's two packages from someone named Henry Thackery, addressed to Mase and me, in care of you." She quirked a brow at him.

Priest shook his head. "Don't know who that is, love. Do you?" He could guess, but he wouldn't let her know that.

"No." Her shoulders slumped. "Mrs. Marks said we had to wait until you got home to open them. I felt sure you would know, and that was the surprise you had for us."

"Well, maybe it is." He decided to throw her a bone. "We'll know after I've had a shower and changed, okay?" He knew they couldn't hold out until after he'd had some supper. He kept moving through the house, pulling his suitcase with him until he got to the stairs. "I'll be back down soon."

"Mrs. Marks left you something for supper. Shall I get it ready for you?"

"That would be lovely, Shan. Thank you."

He was exhausted, but he could sleep after he spent time with the children. They were his whole world. He spent a few minutes letting Onesie remind himself that Priest was his human and carried Lilbit upstairs with him so she and the dog could stay close to him while he showered and changed. He had long since figured out that it was best for all concerned if he let the animals mount a guard by his bed—well, Lilbit's spot was in the *middle* of his bed—to ensure he didn't leave again before he was allowed.

Back in the kitchen, the signed program from the fund-raiser in his hand, he immediately noticed the two packages on the opposite side of the table from where his supper was laid out. The children stood by them, almost vibrating with impatience.

Smiling, he said, "Before you open those packages, here's something I think you'll be happy with, Shannon."

She rushed to take the program from his hands, and he watched her eyes widen in disbelief, swiftly followed by unrestrained excitement. Then tears filled her eyes, and he swallowed his own emotional response to her happiness.

"Dad! The band was there? You met all of them? Oh my God!" She reached for him, burying her face in his chest and squeezing him tight before pulling away. "Thanks, Dad."

Priest couldn't have asked for a more heartfelt expression of gratitude. This was why he never made promises to his children that he couldn't keep. Their honest appreciation gave him wings. He smiled at her.

"You're welcome, love." As he sat down to enjoy his bacon butty and bread and butter pudding he added, "Now you can go ahead and open the parcels." He bit into his sandwich while they tore into the packages and grinned as they each squealed with delight at the bounty they'd received.

"Dad, look what I got," Mason cried, coming over to show off his haul. "Did you know the drummer used to play football? His name is A. John Walker but they call him Beats. He signed a poster for me."

Mason held up the poster which showed John kicking a football and wearing the jersey of a local club. Priest smiled at his son, knowing that now he'd find the drummer fascinating, not because of the music but because of the football. Next, Mason pulled a black t-shirt with an image of John in mid-beat at his drums and slapped a cap on his head with the band's logo and images of the members round it.

"Thanks, Dad," he said, grinning broadly.

"You're welcome, son." He turned to look at Shannon, chuckling at the awed look on her face. "So, what did *you* get?"

Instead of answering, she walked over and laid her treasures on the table for him to see. Besides a tote bag with signed images of the band on the front, a signed lyric book, and a colorful throw with the band logo and signatures, she had also received a signed t-shirt. Hers, however, had an image of Tristan with his head thrown back, the guitar held aloft in a final note of triumph. It was a riveting shot and every thought he'd been shunting to the back of his mind for the last ten days came rushing back, forcing him to swallow some of the tea he'd poured himself to ease the sudden tightness in his throat. Still needing to clear it, he spoke after a moment.

"That's a great shot, love."

"It's a pity he's a grown-up," she said, her voice small and a little sad.

Priest could guess why she was feeling forlorn, but apparently, he needed to punish himself for his own thoughts about the guitarist. "Why is that?" he heard himself ask.

"He's... I... He's so hot, Dad!" Her face flushed crimson at the admission, but before Priest could respond, she rushed on. "I know he's too old for me, but..."

Why did his daughter's first crush have to be on a man three times her age, and more importantly, a man he himself was doing his best to keep in the friend zone? And how was he going to handle it if Tristan and Shannon ever met in the flesh? He'd always done his best to keep his personal and professional lives separate, and so far, he'd been very successful. But what would happen if he and Tristan...?

Shutting down the thought and the panic that was simmering, he beckoned her closer so he could wrap an arm around her shoulders. "Come here." When she settled against his side, he said in his most comforting voice, "There's nothing wrong with finding people attractive, love. I want you to know that first. But I'm glad you're smart enough to realize that nothing can come of this. It won't be easy, but you'll get past it, I promise."

Maybe it was better that she was crushing on someone she knew she couldn't have. It would pass quickly—he hoped—and give him time to prepare for when her heart got broken by a boy her own age. He'd take the comfort where he could. When she pulled away from him, her eyes were red-rimmed but dry. Trying to give her something else to focus on than her incipient heartache, he added, "I told him that you're a big fan of his, and he said he'd leave you a special message. What did he say?"

Her eyes welled up again and Priest wished he'd kept silent. But she smiled through her tears and reached for the program, turning it to the back.

"Hi Shannon," she read. "Your dad tells me you're a big fan. Thank you. I'm very flattered and appreciate you so much for keeping our music alive. Stay as cool as you are, for the next generation. Cheers, Tristan."

The message sounded just the right note from a star to a young fan, and Priest appreciated that it didn't either gush and sound insincere or like the standard meaningless tag-line he'd use to sign an autograph for every other fan.

"The others just signed their names with a heart-shaped smiley face," she said, wiping her eyes.

"Then it's really kind of him to send you a special message, love."

"Can I write him a thank you note? Would you give it to him for me?"

Priest didn't need to think twice before agreeing. Tristan had gone out of his way to do something special for her, so it was appropriate for her to respond to him specifically. He would send a note to the whole group thanking them for making his kids happy. That would be enough.

"I'll be seeing him again tomorrow, so if you want him to get it soon, you'll need to have it ready for me in the morning. Do you need a note card? I have an open box of Thank You cards in my office."

"No, Dad, I'll make my own."

Mason piped up then. "Can I send one to John too, Dad? I want to ask him about his team and what position he played."

"Sounds like you plan to write him a letter, son. Want me to help you with it?" The boy hesitated long enough that Priest added quickly, "Or you can have your big sister look it over for you if you prefer. I know, I know. I'm an old fogey." He got the laugh he wanted. "Now, I have a bit more work to do before I can rest, and it's almost time for bed for you two. Clear up your treasures. Did you finish your homework?"

"Yes, Dad," they answered in chorus. "You need to sign mine," Mason added.

"Bring it down when you're ready. Thanks for supper, Shan."

The rest of the evening was spent finalizing the notes for his conversation with Tristan the next day, and preparing the email that he'd send to him before he went up to bed. He would admit, in the privacy of his thoughts, that he was more than a little excited at the prospect of seeing the guitarist again.

Would the energy be as high this time, or would time and distance have muted it? Should he be harboring any hope that it would have at least remained the same? And how on earth was he going to respond if it had increased? He had every intention of being entirely professional when they met, but after so long without a spark between him and anyone else, he wasn't sure how successful he would be.

Losing himself in the work was easy enough and making sure the children's thank you notes were acceptable took up the rest of his evening. Once they were in bed, he chose the suit he'd be wearing the next day, refusing to think about why he wanted to look extra special. His client was a famous person, and he wanted to represent his company in the best style he could. When he was down to two dress shirts, he chose the dark blue to go with the light gray suit he'd wear and the patterned, silver-gray tie to match.

Thankfully, his travels had left him so exhausted that he fell asleep as soon as he slid beneath the covers, and when he woke it was the first time he'd stirred all night. Eight hours of solid, uninterrupted sleep felt good in his bones. A quick shave and shower and as he dressed, he thought back to the images he'd been sent of Tristan's house. It would be a dream to remodel and part of his excitement for the new project was directly related to the plans he had for the space that he hoped Tristan would like.

Downstairs, the children were waiting for him. He'd drop them at school on the way to Tristan's. They handed him their handwritten messages for the stars, and Priest couldn't suppress a grin at the faint scent of lavender on Shannon's envelope. He may be too old for her, but Shannon would not pass up any chance to make Tristan remember her.

"What did you make for breakfast?" He didn't see any dishes on the table or in the sink when he went over to look.

"Mrs. Marks made extra bacon butties, Dad. We'll have those and the last two chocolate milks."

"And have you fed the pets?" He assumed they had since neither animal was currently wrapping itself around his ankles in a bid for attention.

"Yes, Dad," Shannon replied. It was her job to feed the animals and Mason's to walk the dog and clean up after him.

Satisfied, he poured himself his usual car mug of coffee, and they all trooped out to the big car. At eight o'clock, traffic was as expected, but he managed to make it to their school with half an hour before their first class, so they'd have time to eat.

"Have a good day, you two. I'll see you later."

He was scheduled to be in Old Windsor by ten, so he had time to sip his cooling coffee, which he preferred to tea when he had visits more than an hour away. It also gave him time to settle his thoughts, bring the professional to the foreground of his brain, so that by the time he was knocking on the front door of his newest project, he was mostly in the zone.

He had asked Tristan to meet him at the house, hoping that that would help him remain professional, but when he opened the door, all Priest's cool fled like crooks ahead of the coppers. *Bloody hell!* Priest closed his eyes for a moment, gathering every vestige of his control back around him and opened them to find Tristan watching him curiously. He cleared his throat to speak, but Tristan beat him to it.

"Are you alright?" When Priest nodded wordlessly, Tristan added, "Good morning. Come in, please."

Priest stepped inside, fisting both his hands in an effort to halt the faint trembling in them. What he really wanted to do— reach out to brush his thumbs across Tristan's cheeks— was not part of the script for a business meeting. Keeping himself firmly under control, he took in the sunny warmth of the house after the chill of the air outdoors, and as Tristan led him into the bright kitchen, he cast his eye over the view again. Down the rise, across from the hiking path was Tristan's houseboat, the Thames beyond it reaching to the other side where beautiful homes resided. A narrowboat slid slowly up the river, a woman lounging on the deck with a dog beside her.

"This is absolutely the best view," he murmured. "In each of the three plans I've made for you to choose from, this will be the focal point of the first floor, and of the master suite on the second floor."

"Sounds amazing," Tristan replied with a smile. "I can't wait to see what you've got for me."

Priest watched him move away from the scarred wooden table that he had brought in for them to work on to the kitchen counter where he had set up a tray with two thermos flasks and a plate of digestive biscuits. He brought them over and placed the two flasks before Priest.

"I wasn't sure whether you'd want tea or coffee, so I made one of each. Help yourself to the biscuits."

"I'll have the tea, please. I've already had my coffee fix for the day."

Tristan poured him some tea, and he helped himself to the fixings in little packets on the tray and dunked a biscuit into the hot liquid. The snack warmed him up, and he appreciated Tristan for thinking of it. Maybe they could have lunch together in town. He'd ask, even if his brain was screaming at him not to do it. He had another biscuit, finished his tea, and stood up to rinse the top of the thermos that had served as his teacup.

"Ready?" he asked, once Tristan had moved the tray back to the counter.

"Yes, please."

Priest loved how, in that moment, the rockstar sounded like a child waiting to pull the Christmas cracker. He smiled and pulled his chair around next to Tristan's, retrieving his laptop and placing it on the table so Tristan could see while he reviewed all the notes he'd taken from their pre-design meeting, and walked Tristan through his preliminary sketches. He took his time, explaining the different options, answering every question that came up, making note of things Tristan liked and things he wasn't particularly keen on.

Of the three options they finally settled on, he knew which one he would like best, and though it wasn't the most expensive, it felt like the one closest to who Tristan appeared to be, both as a man and as a professional musician. He hoped he hadn't gotten it wrong, that Tristan would choose that one. It had fewer bedrooms but a larger space for entertaining, and an open loft space in the attic that could be converted into office space or extra living space.

"So, which are you leaning towards?" he asked when Tristan seemed to have run out of questions.

"I really like the one that gives me more studio room in the basement, and that adds height to the attic." Tristan looked over the models that Priest had also printed so he'd have his own hard copies of the drawings, in case he wanted more time to decide.

It had been his experience that most clients preferred both a paper and a 3-D digital copy of potential designs. He waited patiently, not sure what the younger man was thinking and not wanting to influence him unduly with his own preferences. He was there to provide sustainable design options and once they were agreed upon, to provide accurate detailed drawings of the final plan, so that his builders could get moving on the job.

"I think I like this one best." Tristan spoke at last, indicating the set of sketches that Priest liked best. "But can you change the basement plan to this one?" He indicated a different design.

"Absolutely. Whatever you need, as long as the building systems will support it, is fair game."

Carefully tagging the sketches Tristan had approved, he packed up and checked his watch. Time had gone by so quickly as they'd both been engrossed in the work. And Priest was pleased that he hadn't become distracted by the other man's nearness. Not that thinking about that was helping him now, as he watched Tristan pack up the rest of their snacks and put everything into a picnic basket. His tight arse was a tempting sight. Priest dragged his eyes away.

He stood up, suddenly questioning whether or not he should ask Tristan out to lunch, after all. They wouldn't be working together directly anymore unless Tristan wanted more changes, and he couldn't guarantee that he would be able to keep the professional distance he wanted to maintain. Tristan walked over as he was debating with himself and took the decision out of his hands.

"How about lunch before you head out? Rehearsals won't start for another hour, and they can begin without me."

So much for keeping his distance. He could no more say no to the casual invitation than he could refuse to breathe. How had that happened so fast? He had really believed that out of sight would be out of mind, but clearly he'd been deluding himself and instead he was living the "absence makes the heart grow fonder" version of reality. He sighed inwardly and replied, "Sure." Then he moved away to the front door, to put some distance between them, because the man smelled like sex on a stick, which was not what Priest needed at that moment.

He followed Tristan back down to the boat, going aboard when Tristan invited him. The craft was all masculine design and understated elegance like its owner was, and he could see this becoming a favorite holiday rental for anyone who wanted time away on a boat.

"Before you take a seat," Tristan began, "how about the penny tour? Lunch will be ready in five."

Why was his stupid heart beating harder? Priest passed a hand absently over the misbehaving organ, then quickly slid his thumbs into his belt loops and nodded. The layout was perfect for a single man: two bedrooms, two bathrooms, a studio for one—"For those nights when I'm too restless to sleep, or when I need to get something right for rehearsals"—the spacious eat-in kitchen and the elegant living room. There was even outdoor seating. This was the perfect place for romantic trysts and hookups.

"Do you entertain here often?" he asked before he could censor himself. Had he really just asked Tristan about his love life? Lord help him, he had, and he wanted to feel guilty about it, but he didn't. Hopefully his runaway mouth hadn't offended his new client.

"The lads come here once in a while," Tristan replied, either deliberately ignoring the gaffe or unmoved by it.

Either way, Priest heaved a quiet sigh of relief. "How is it in winter?" Asking acceptable questions about living conditions in bad weather was entirely preferable to intrusive ones.

"When I'm away on tour, it's mostly locked up except when my housekeeper comes to clean. But I usually send her notice in enough time so that by the time I get back it's warm enough that I'm not freezing."

Tristan turned to the slow cooker plugged in on the kitchen counter. The scent of cooked meat flavored the air in the cabin, and Priest's belly rumbled. Tristan laughed and pulled two plates from the cupboard above the stove.

"I hope you like beef stew," he said, dishing up two heaping servings of mouthwatering brown stew. Between their plates, he set a third with thick slices of bread and butter on the side. "What would you like to drink?" he asked.

"What do you usually have with this?"

"I like a Guinness stout every now and again. My housekeeper made this, and she always leaves me Guinness to have with it."

"Guinness is fine with me." Priest wasn't a fan of the stout by itself, but he had enjoyed it with stew before, so he knew it would please his palate.

Tristan finally sat down, sliding a fork over to Priest, who found he loved Tristan's informality. It meant he was relaxed around Priest, that he was being his authentic self with a man he was only now getting to know. And something told him this might also be Tristan's way of saying "take me or leave me." Was he up for the challenge? His brain and his dick were not necessarily in agreement.

Spearing some of the stew, he took a huge bite and moaned, the sound reminding him of those over-the-top porn stars pretending to be enjoying the fake lovemaking on late night television. Except *his* emotion was genuine. The stew was delicious ... well-seasoned, cooked to melt-in-your-mouth perfection. He was glad Tristan wasn't a talk-and-eat kind of person, because he had no brain cells left over for speech when he was soaking in the scent and taste of the meal. The Guinness went down almost unconsciously, and when he was done, Priest patted his belly.

"That good, eh?" Tristan teased, swallowing more of his drink.

"You said it," he replied. "Compliments to the chef. She can make stew for me any time."

"The lads love it too, so when we're having potluck and I don't take drinks, I take beef stew. It's always a winner."

He stood up to clear the plates away, but Priest stopped him. "Let me," he said. "You provided lunch. The least I can do is clean up."

He was proud of how he managed to offer without touching Tristan. He didn't think he was ready for the electricity that would inevitably follow from any physical contact between them, no matter how innocent. Thankfully, Tristan didn't object, offering him dessert instead.

"If I can take it with me, thank you."

He had to go before the desire rising inside him again got out of control.

Chapter 8

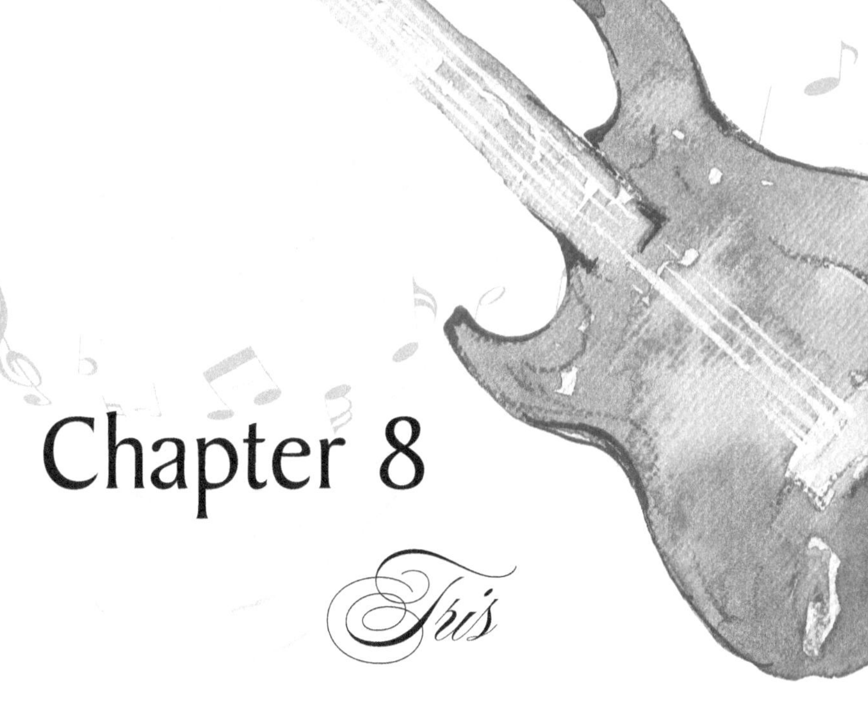

Tris

"Did you sleep well?" Tris asked Tag the following Saturday.

The Barrington Strings had played at two more events since the fundraiser, and they were returning to the States the next day. This would be the brothers' last time together for who knew how long, and Tris was glad that his little brother had made time for him. Despite the age difference, they were close, for reasons that went beyond their blood bond.

"I did," Tag replied, grinning at him. "You know I always do when I spend time on this boat."

Tris chuckled. "Yeah. Because usually when you're on this boat you make free with my beer and whiskey, and then you have to sleep it off. How's your head this morning?"

"I'm fine. I didn't drink all that much last night, and it was only beers. But I can eat, if you're offering breakfast."

Tris shook his head. "Typical. I'm only here to satisfy the needs of your bottomless belly."

"What else are big brothers for, eh?" Tag was unashamedly unrepentant.

Tris served up the full English breakfast he'd made while his brother still slept and they sat down to their meal, eating in silence broken only by the strains of classical music pouring from Tag's phone. Once the meal was over, they cleaned up and went to sit on the deck, taking a second cup of tea with them.

Tris loved the early days of Spring, when the weather couldn't seem to decide if it was coming or going. Would there be a wintry chill today, or would it be comfortable enough for shorts and a tee? He'd taken the middle road, slipping into an old worn-thin pair of sweats and a long-sleeved Henley shirt. He cast his gaze over his younger brother. Tag was an inch shy of six feet, but where Tris was built like a swimmer, Tag looked like a boxer. That was the only thing he got from their father.

Thoughts of their sire made his stomach curdle with anger and sorrow. Tris hadn't seen or spoken to his father in more than a decade, even on the odd occasions when he went home to visit his mother. He always made sure his father would be away from home, or he'd arrange to meet her in the quaint village cafe where she loved to stop for a cuppa and a scone.

"So, two questions." Tag's voice interrupted his thoughts.

He cocked an eye at his brother. The look on his face said neither question would be one Tris wanted to answer, but his brother was like a police dog. He wouldn't let go once he found his target. He sighed, sipped his tea, and waited.

"Have you been to the estate recently?"

Neither of them considered the rather grand mansion that their parents still lived in their home. It hadn't been home for Tris since he was twenty years old, when he'd been more-or-less driven out by his father. The words and the implacably harsh tone of his father's voice that had driven him away from home were forever imprinted in his brain.

"I do not approve of your ... sexual proclivities, Tristan. You are free to remain in our family home as long as you do not expect your mother and me to welcome any friend of yours that we deem to be unsuitable. Is that clear?"

Had it been clear? Crystal. Tristan shook the thoughts away and did his best not to show how deeply wounded he still was by the rift that had become a chasm between him and the man whose DNA he bore, whether he wanted it or not.

"I haven't seen Mum in more than a year. Why?"

"I got a call yesterday. She's worried about you and angry that you're 'not making an effort.'" He put air quotes around the last four words so Tris would know he was quoting their mother directly.

"Making an effort at what?" He tried not to feel guilty for not speaking to his mother more, and resentment swelled like ocean waves as he continued. "I'm often on tour but I try to call her at least once a month. What more does she expect when I've not been welcome where she is for sixteen years? How much of an effort has she made for me? Does she expect the same effort from Tara?"

He swallowed back the anger and immediately apologized to Tag for raising his voice. He wasn't upset with his brother, or with his sister Tara. He was angry with his father and disappointed in his mother. None of that had anything to do with either of his siblings. They had gone their own way as well, and even Tara, who had married and moved to the north of England, had been out of touch. Like him and Tag, she had a job that had her traveling frequently, and making it back to the estate to be with her parents was low on her list of priorities, what with her demanding job and two small children.

"Sorry, Tag," he said again, sipping more tea. "I'll call her soon. What's your other question?"

His brother wasn't the one who needed the promise, but that was the best he could offer in answer to that question. He knew Tag would follow his lead and move on. That was one of the best things about his youngest sibling. He knew when to push and when to back off.

"Let me know how that goes, okay?" When he nodded, Tag continued. "So, what's up with you and the board chairman? He's a hot silver fox, by the way. You could do a whole lot worse."

Tris chuckled. Apparently, he hadn't been subtle at all, any more than Priest had been, if yet another person was asking him about the architect. He'd had to weather a bit of ribbing after the first rehearsal at Rory's when all the boys had teased him mercilessly about his crush on the sexy older man. The memory of their probing questions and ribald jokes still made his cheeks heat. And of course, his brother noticed the warmth growing in his face and latched on, not waiting for his answer before continuing.

"That," he made a circle with his index finger, "is the face of a man with a secret. Come on, big brother, own up!"

"There's nothing to tell." That had been his answer at rehearsal, and he was sticking to it. "We've met three times and twice it was for business."

"But the second time, at the fundraiser, you were both making eyes at each other. Don't think you were hiding your interest any more than he was. And I know you, so talk to me."

When Tris stayed silent, Tag leaned forward, resting his now empty teacup on the table between them, leaned back, and crossed his arms over his chest and his legs at the ankles. It wasn't even noon, and Tris knew his brother wouldn't return to the hotel where the group was staying until it was closer to the dinner hour. He readied himself for a lecture.

"Look, Tris, we both know our father has been a huge disappointment to the two of us. When you needed him most, he rejected you. So you didn't have any good role models going into that shit show with Dickhead Devon, but that doesn't mean you should spend the rest of your life afraid to commit. And just because the dishy chairman is older doesn't mean he's contemptible like the men you thought you could trust."

"Really, Tag, nothing's happening between us..."

Tag interrupted. "Yet. Nothing's happening yet. But I know your usual MO is to scent something possible and run like the wind in the opposite direction. You tried the hookup thing and that didn't work for you, because we both know you're not that guy. So why not stop running and see where this might go? What can it hurt to get to know this man who has caught your attention? Especially since it's clear he's as caught in your web as you are in his?"

Trust his brother to hit the nail on the head. Tag had always been the one to drag him back to practicalities whenever his overthinking brain tried to shove him over the edge of what ifs. And Tag was right too. If he wanted more from life than a solitary houseboat and third wheel status in his friends' lives, he had to stop running. There was nothing wrong with being attracted to older men, and not every older man would disappoint him. If Priest showed any interest, he wouldn't run.

He nodded, swallowing the last of his tea. "He asked me to call him Priest." Well, bollocks! That had not been what he'd wanted to say at all, but the words rolled off his tongue, a hope in them that he dreaded.

"Ah, nicknames already, eh?" Tag teased. "And did you return the favor, brother dear?"

"I told him to call me Tristan." Before Tag could answer, he added quickly, "That probably means nothing, so don't go getting excited. We'll be seeing more of each other regarding the house, so it just makes sense to be less formal."

Tag shook his head slowly, amusement brimming in his eyes. "If that makes it easier for you, I won't judge. Just promise me you'll tell me when things change."

"When? You're an optimist!" Tris chuckled.

"And proud," Tag said. "So promise me."

"What are we? Twelve?" Tris tried to laugh it off.

"We're brothers." Tag kept a straight face, not giving an inch. "At least promise I won't hear about it from anyone else before you tell me. And by anyone else, I mean the gutter press and Internet stalkers."

This time Tris nodded. They'd always shared the big moments in their lives, and that would never change. But he was also ready to move on, to find a way to explore his connection to Priest.

"Since you've spent the whole morning grilling me about my non-existent love life," he laughed when Tag rolled his eyes at him, "it's my turn to be nosy. What's up? Last I heard, you were thinking about some woman I'd not heard about before. Who is she and what have you been doing with her?"

"She's in the past, as Rafiki said to Simba." When Tris grinned, Tag chuckled, adding, "It would never have worked, to be honest. She was barely out of college and didn't understand what being with a working musician would require on her end. And her older brother was a complete arse. So, I'm back on the market but not really looking. You of all people should know what that feels like."

"Yeah. There's not a lot of time for searching, is there? And if you do find someone, you've got to get through all the crap of getting to know them and finding out who they are under the facade they used to get close to you in the first place."

His mind went immediately to Priest, who had done nothing to ingratiate himself with Tris. The energy between them was obviously intensely sexual, even if neither of them had acted on it as yet. He appreciated Priest's restraint. At least he was acting like a grown man not a fan-girling adolescent. How much better would it be when they got close enough for Priest to surrender his control? If he ever did? Was he really going the optimistic route like Tag now too? The thought stirred a deep ache in his gut for just that kind of response. He wanted to make someone wild for him ... someone like Priest, someone ... Priest.

"Just remember, not every guy is a closet cheater. Not every guy will break your heart. You've lived long enough and guarded your heart hard enough now to recognize the good guys. You know more about your board chairman than I do. Trust your gut, big brother."

Later that evening, as he sat with his band mates at Rory's house after dinner, he listened as the others talked about their plans for holidaying with their partners once the new studio album was complete. What would he do? He had no idea. Maybe he'd visit Tag in his home in New York or go up and spend some time with Tara and her clan. He could do with some bonding time with that branch of his family.

But his heart wasn't in those private plans because he wanted what his mates had ... someone to hold onto who was his, who had his back in a different and more intimate way than his friends and his siblings did. Tag's words came back to him as he smiled his thanks when Chrissy brought him dessert. He refocused so he could add words to his smile.

"Thanks, Chrissy. This looks delicious! Apple crumble and ice cream are one of my favorite treats."

She moved on with a warm smile. Tris watched her stop next to each man, sharing a smile and a soft word with them, and leaving her fiancé for last. When Rory pulled her down onto his lap, she settled against him, her posture at once relaxed and alert, as though she were trying to keep herself from falling into the well of his love with company present. Someone to hold him close ... the idea resonated inside him like a song waiting to be written.

"So, what are your plans, Tris?" Rory's voice startled him.

"I'll probably visit the siblings and their families." He was pleased that he could give an honest answer, even if it wasn't the one he most wanted to give.

"Doesn't your sister live up north, close to Scotland?" Will asked. "Or is it in the Lake District?"

"It's in the Lake District," Tris said. "Beautiful country thereabouts. I haven't seen the babies in a while, so it'll be a nice change of pace for me."

The conversation meandered on with Tris paying scant attention until Rory came to sit next to him. Immediately, he knew he was in for more interference. He managed to hold back an amused grin when Rory wrapped an arm around his shoulder and asked,

"So, why are you planning tame family times when you could have something far more..." he paused, clearly choosing his next word with care, "... invigorating with a friend?"

Tris couldn't hold in the chuckle. "I could, could I? And who might this friend be?" As if he didn't know.

"Come on, mate, don't act all coy with me. We both know you'd like to jump that dishy silver fox's bones." Rory held up a hand when Tris opened his mouth to protest. "I know, I know, you're not interested in hooking up anymore. I get it. You know I was exactly where you are a year ago. But if you're going to compare yourself to me, then you should at least stick to the script."

Tris looked at his friend, curious to see where he was going with his argument. "The script?"

"I wanted Chrissy, and even though she'd ghosted me for six months, when fate or whomever sent her back into my orbit, I pursued her until I got her. She was the one I wanted, and I had to let go of a lot of my own insecurities, as did she, before we got together. And I wouldn't change even one second of what we've got going now. She's my whole world."

He cast his eye over to where his love sat listening to Henry hold court. She was a sweet, beautiful woman, and the envy Tris had been fighting against all evening slammed back into him when she looked up, as though she felt Rory's eyes on her, and smiled at him. There was so much in that look, in that smile ... affection, passion, love.

"All I'm saying is, if Benedict Priestley makes you want things you haven't wanted in forever, maybe you should find out if he could be the one to pull you out of your shell, to give you what you want and fear you'll never have. Maybe he'll be the one to make it so you lose that wistful look you have every time you sit back observing the rest of us. But it won't happen if you don't make a move, Tris. That's all I'm saying."

"Make a move? You mean like invite him out? I'd have to call him to do that. And really, what reason would I give? We've only met regarding work, aside from the fundraiser."

"What more reason do you need than that you want to see him again in a non-business kind of way? And anyway, why do you need an excuse to call him? Have you been off the scene so long that you've forgotten how dating works?"

Rory sat back to observe him, and Tris felt his stare stripping away the layers he wore between himself and others all the time, until he was laid bare. Could Rory see the trepidation he carried at the idea of an invitation from him being rejected?

"You'll never know how he'll respond unless you ask. And if he's not interested, at least you won't spend any more time on him, and you can move on to someone who deserves you."

Tris inhaled a harsh breath. This was the push he needed. "Have you and Tag been talking behind my back?" Rory laughed but didn't answer, so he went on. "You're right, of course. Both of you. I should follow my gut and ask him out. Something tells me he won't say no. I'm just worried that things might not work out and I'm not sure I'm ready to face that."

"There are no guarantees, Tris, but it's time to stop riding the fence and get a move on with your life."

Another heavy sigh escaped before he nodded. "Okay. I'll call him now. Just give me a few to figure out how to start that conversation."

"Or maybe send him a text message if you're worried about talking the first time around."

Tris wasn't sure what he was more worried about ... making a fool of himself by starting a conversation with a man he wasn't sure of or being rejected by said man. But he'd already stepped into the kitchen so he could speak privately, and so that, if he were honest, he could cringe without an audience if he got shot down. He tossed around Rory's suggestion to send Priest a text message. It might delay his response, but so would having to leave a message if he didn't answer when Tris called. Either way, he'd be a knot of anxiety until he got an answer.

He pulled up Priest's number and held his breath when the phone rang. Priest's voice filled his ear a second later.

"Priestley."

Tris said the first thing that came into his head, because this wasn't the time for hesitating. He didn't want Priest to hang up on him if he remained silent too long.

"Hullo, Priest, it's Tris." Wait, he hadn't told Priest to call him Tris.

"Ah, Tristan. Good evening. How are you?"

"I'm fine, thank you. Sorry to bother you so late." It was barely eight, but Tris didn't know what Priest's preferences were relating to calls after hours.

"You're not bothering me. How can I help you?"

Those rumbly tones were going to be the death of him. They certainly weren't helping him to get his invitation out. Swallowing a sigh with his nerves, he replied, "I just wanted to ask if we might have a drink together some time..." His voice trailed off. That had to be the driest, most unenthusiastic thing he could possibly have said. Nothing about that would tell Priest that he was being invited out on a date. Tris hurried on, trying to salvage the situation before it got any worse. *In for a penny, in for a pound.* "I'm asking you out, in case that wasn't clear."

Bollocks! That isn't any better, Tris! He tried to quiet his brain while he listened to Priest's reply.

"Thanks for the clarification. It helps to know you're not inviting me out for a drink as my client."

Was that amusement in his voice? Tris waited, hoping that that wasn't all Priest had to say. He hadn't agreed, which was really all Tris wanted to hear. Would he say yes, after that bloody awful beginning? Tris's mouth dropped open in silent shock at Priest's next words, which were nothing like he'd been expecting. Not even close, but very welcome, for all that.

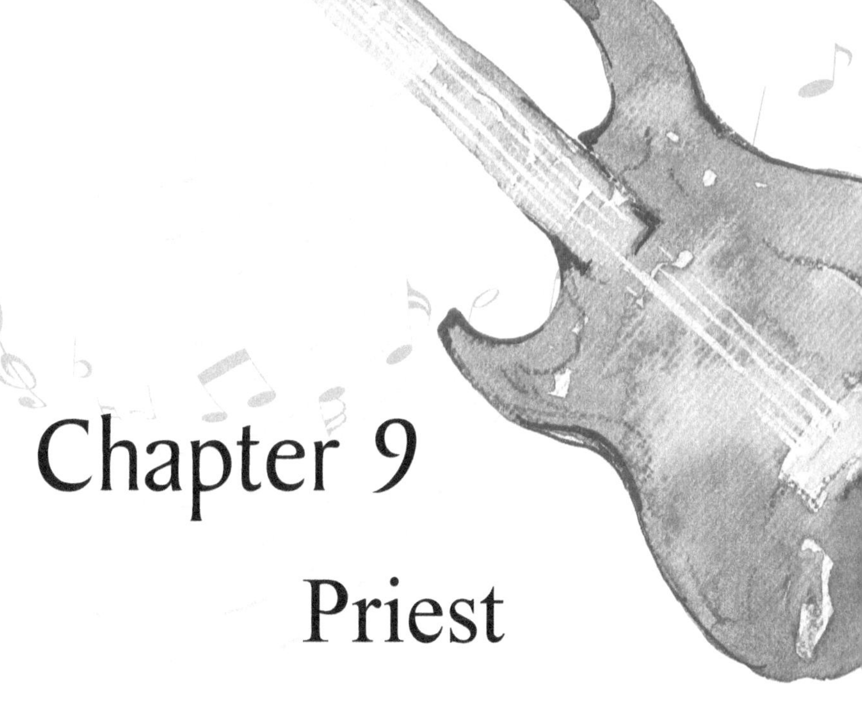

Chapter 9

Priest

*He couldn't have found a better man to
recapture his dating rhythm with.*

Nothing had prepared Priest to hear the voice of the man he'd been thinking so hard about since their last meeting at Tristan's house. After he'd run off as if the hounds of hell were chasing him and he thought he could escape them, he had reviewed the time they'd spent together, including that last fraught moment when he had wished desperately to kiss Tristan goodbye. The very thought of it still had the power to make his insides tingle with heat. Like they were doing now, at the sound of his voice.

"You beat me to it," he said, surprising himself. That was probably not what Tristan wanted to hear, but he continued. "I'm going to take it that you recognize the pull between us and want to see where it goes just like I do." He paused, waiting for the answer he needed before he would continue.

"Yes," Tristan answered. Priest could almost feel him searching for the right thing to say after that stilted opening. "I wasn't sure if I was reading you right, but my brother and my mates all seem to think I should give it a try."

"So, this invitation is to please them?" Priest's tone was sharp. If this wasn't what he had been hoping it would be, he wouldn't entertain any further conversation. He was too old for obligatory dates to appease anyone. Best to make that clear at once. He spoke again. "Because if there's no real interest beyond that on your part, we should call a halt before we begin. We can continue as architect and client."

"No, no!" Tristan hurried to deny the assumption. "No! I really would like to get to know you better outside of the job. It's been … on my mind since I read your profile on your company page."

That was a good sign, right? He must have realized that he had to give Priest something as proof of the truth of his words. That admission would do nicely. It made the tingling turn to flame inside him, and he had to clear his throat before replying.

"It's nice to know I'm not the only one in that situation."

His voice was huskier than usual, but with an added layer that he hoped Tristan would read as indicative of how very pleased he was. He wished in that moment that he could show the other man exactly how much he liked the idea of being the object of his thoughts and that was playing havoc with his attention.

Tristan's question—"How so?"—reminded him that he had been withholding a secret as well that he probably ought to share. He had been shocked to see the rocker turn up in his office that first time, so he could well understand Tristan's confusion.

Time for his own confession. A small, wry chuckle preceded his reply. "Your name came up in conversation in my house before the fundraiser. Shannon said she'd heard that your band would be there, and then she'd gone off in rhapsodies about the music and about you. I wanted to see what you all looked like, and when I saw you, I was hooked. You are a riveting man, Mr. DeVere." He could relax enough to tease.

"No more than you are, Mr. Priestley." They shared another warm chuckle that settled around him like a comforting hug, and then Tristan asked a question that Priest had come to expect from anyone whom he'd invited to use the nickname. "Why do they call you Priest and not Ben?"

Ben ... no one had ever called him that. His parents never shortened his name, and his siblings called him every derogative version of Dick that they could think of when they were upset with him, or else they called him Benny. Maybe Ben could be Tristan's private nickname for him?

"Priest?"

Tristan's voice brought him out of his musing yet again. "Oh, it's mostly because in school we called each other by our last names, and the short form of mine was easier to say. But also, among our group, I was the most ... shall we say, law-abiding, the one who followed all the rules, the one who kept everyone else's secrets and did my best to bail them out of trouble when I could. Sort of like their priest, you know?"

"So what you're telling me is that you were Mr. Goodie Two Shoes? Mr. Butter Wouldn't Melt In Your Mouth?"

The amusement in Tristan's voice sent fire licking up Priest's spine and into his limbs. "Something like that, though to be honest, I wasn't drawn to rebellion and experimenting. I was much too keen on getting the highest marks and winning the most in everything I took part in to have time to be a tearaway."

They'd moved seamlessly from awkward beginnings to a conversation that was exactly what two people getting to know each other should be having. This was the perfect moment for Tristan to share something of his own childhood. Would he talk about his parents? Priest could only hope he'd share some of his own childhood trivia, even if he was reluctant to open up about his past completely.

"I'm the oldest of my siblings," Tristan began, "and named after my father—hence, The Third—and I was never allowed to get away with anything, even as a small boy. I learned fairly early that if I did everything that was expected of me, I'd be fine."

"Why does your youth sound so much more boring than mine?" Priest kept his tone light, making a joke of the question, in case the answer was too heavy for Tristan to share.

"Probably because it was." And because it was not just boring, but perhaps also untenable? Priest kept *that* question to himself as Tristan continued, "Anyway, you still haven't answered my question. Will you go out for drinks with me?"

"Yes, I will." Did he even have a choice? "When do you want to do this?" If his hesitation was anything to go by, Tristan hadn't thought that far ahead, leaving the choice up to Priest, who found it oddly endearing.

"Most of our rehearsals go until about five. So whenever is good for you…"

"Tomorrow evening too soon?" Had Tristan heard the eagerness in Priest's tone? He was losing his cool spectacularly, but he didn't much care right now. Once they hung up, he'd cringe and berate himself for acting like his twelve-year-old daughter.

"Not at all. Where should I pick you up?"

"That depends, but you don't have to…"

Tristan interrupted him. "I'm aware, but I'm old-fashioned like that. I've asked you out, so I'll provide the transportation." The steel in his tone meant Priest was better served letting that go.

"Alright then. What time should I be ready? I don't know where you're coming from."

"Kensington. Where will you be?"

"I'll be at the office until six." A crash and Mason yelling angrily put paid to any notion Priest had that they could continue the conversation.

"Sibling bonding?" Tristan asked with a chuckle.

Priest's next words answered his question. "Something like that. I'm sorry, Tristan, but I have to go play referee now. I'll see you tomorrow, and thanks for calling."

"Tomorrow," Tristan agreed and hung up.

Where would Tristan take him on a first date? Priest didn't know much about the guitarist, but *he* didn't care for the kind of nightclub that the twenty and thirty-somethings frequented. Which meant he hoped that Tristan would choose a more grown-up space. Maybe they should have waited until each knew more about the other before trying to date. Going on just their obvious attraction to each other wouldn't be enough to sustain a conversation, especially since he was not in the market for a hookup any more than he thought Tristan was.

Still, despite his reservations, his anxiety a few minutes before six the next evening had little to do with anything other than how his first date in three years would go with someone he was more wildly attracted to than he'd ever been to anyone other than Jane. His last first date had been well over a decade ago, for God's sake, and as he waited for Tristan, he tried to prepare himself to be somewhat more than the currently insecure mess that he could probably win prizes for.

"Calm down, Priestley! He's just a man, not the Almighty. This isn't a big deal. It's just drinks."

He waited for a full thirty seconds, counting them off in his mind as he headed for the elevator, in hopes that the verbalized pep talk in his father's severest tone would do the trick. He breathed deeply when it seemed to work. His mind was not whirling around worst-case scenarios, and he actually felt calmer. Imagine that! Maybe he needed to do impressions of his sire in no-nonsense mode to get him through.

Then his cell phone rang as he stepped out of the car on the ground floor and his confidence dipped and swayed, like a bird ready to fly away.

"Priestley." At least he didn't sound as nervous as he suddenly was again.

"I'm across the street." Tristan's deep voice rumbled through him, spiking and settling his nerves at the same time.

He looked up and saw the tall musician standing beside a BMW sports car. He hung up, crossing to where his date stood looking like a dream in skin-tight black jeans and a skin-tight plain white tee under a midnight blue blazer. His hair was slightly tousled, as though he'd just run his hand through it, making Priest want to do the same. Only, in his version, he'd hold on and pull Tristan in for a kiss hello.

Instead, he smiled and extended his hand. "Hi! Nice car."

Tristan's smile lit up his face. "Hi yourself, and thanks. I'm into fast cars and motorbikes."

The thought of riding behind Tristan made his limbs twitch, but Priest held it together. Tristan was a man's man, it seemed, and yet Priest knew that on some level, he was as vulnerable as everyone else in the world.

Once they were in the car, he turned to the fascinating man and asked, "So, where are we off to? I hope I'm not overdressed." He'd worn a light gray suit and dark blue shirt and had put the tie in his briefcase as he was getting ready for the date. He caught Tristan's eyes as he glanced over at Priest in the passenger seat.

"You look great. We're going to a piano bar. I thought you'd appreciate that."

Priest's heart went all fluttery butterfly wings in his chest, warming him with gratitude. Apparently, Tristan had paid attention to the bio on the website and was doing his best to make Priest feel comfortable in his company. They could probably spend hours just talking about their shared love of music, and his earlier almost-meltdown over whether or not things would get awkward suddenly seemed like a foolish waste of emotional energy.

"That's very thoughtful of you."

He wanted to do more to acknowledge Tristan's effort on his behalf and the simple "Thank you" that he added didn't seem nearly enough. If this was a true measure of the man driving them patiently through the early evening London traffic, then he couldn't have found a better man with whom to recapture his dating rhythm.

Eventually, they pulled up before a trendy-looking club called Oasis. Tristan pulled into a convenient spot and led him into the establishment that was much larger on the inside than it appeared on the outside. There was a long bar, a few booths and tables for two set around a stage where an imposing baby grand and a drum kit were set up. There was enough space on the stage for three or four musicians, plus the pianist.

"We're early," Tristan said as he weaved his way through the other guests to the table closest to the piano. "The real fun doesn't begin for at least another hour, but I wanted to make sure you ate something before the music starts."

"You've been here before, then?" Priest asked, not sure he wanted to hear the answer.

"A time or two with a friend."

Priest noted that Tristan didn't look at him as he spoke but had picked up the menu and was studying it as though he would be tested on the contents at the end of the date. So ... he'd either been taken here on a date or had brought someone else. The thought left a weird feeling behind Priest's breastbone, almost like heartburn, and his tongue dried up in his mouth.

"I need a drink," he announced more loudly than he'd intended. "What would you like?" he added, modifying his volume.

"I'll just have a beer for now. I don't want to drink too much as I'm driving tonight."

Right ... I should have thought of that. Priest nodded and went to order their first round. If he was going to react poorly to every new revelation about his date, he'd need a lot of alcohol to get through the evening. Better to resolve now to be the adult he was and remember that Tristan was a few years shy of forty and had clearly lived a full life. He was a rockstar, for heaven's sake! He would definitely not have lived like a monk, even if he *wasn't* a player.

"Good evening, sir. What can I get you?" The barman was a wiry fellow with tightly muscled tattooed arms and a full head of riotously curly strawberry-blond hair. His smile was as glorious as his hair, spreading his full, glossy lips around slightly crooked teeth.

"Two of your most popular IPAs, please." Priest returned the cute barman's flirty smile.

"Coming right up, stud!" the barman replied, making Priest chuckle.

Had he been out of the scene for so long that being flirted with felt new and a little forbidden? Not that he would encourage the man's obvious interest, because he wasn't that clueless that he'd do anything to upset Tristan, but it was a boost to his ego nonetheless.

"Here you go! When you're ready to order, a server will be over to see to your needs."

Another chuckle escaped Priest at the blatant double entendre, but he only nodded and took the bottles and glasses back to their table. Tristan's eyes were on the bartender and as soon as Priest sat down, he said, pouring his beer into the glass, "Friendly guy, isn't he?"

Priest grinned. "You noticed that, did you?"

"Hard not to," Tristan replied, sipping his beer. "This is good."

Feeling possessive, are you, Tristan? Priest let the thought percolate while he sipped his own drink and let his eyes wander round the space. Other guests were enjoying their food, chatting, laughing, and one or two couples were making moon eyes at each other. The vibe was cheerful and warm, not especially romantic, but he could see, when the lights were lowered for the performers, how it could morph into something much more intimate and conducive to thoughts of a sensual nature.

He decided he would like it very much if Tristan was feeling a little proprietorial of him. He hadn't had that in three years, and really, after a while Jane had been so certain of his complete devotion to her that long before her death, she had let go of that knee-jerk reaction. Still, it did his ego good to know that a hot guy like Tristan could feel even a moment of envy because of him.

If anything came of this connection between them, it would be his absolute pleasure to dismantle every bit of the younger man's uncertainty where he was concerned and replace it with bone-deep trust. In the meantime, he followed where Tristan led, adding his own words of praise about the brew.

"Ready to order?" Tristan asked next.

"What's the best thing you've had here?" Priest didn't really care what he ate.

"I like sharing a charcuterie board, or we could do a mini tasting menu. Those are great too."

"Whatever you decide is fine with me." Once Tristan placed their order, Priest continued, "So, tell me a bit about yourself. What made you decide that being a bass guitarist in a rock band was your life's work?"

Tristan looked over at him sharply, suspicion bright in his gaze. "I know it's not what most people think of as a serious profession, but music has always been my life, for as far back as I can remember."

He did his best not to sound defensive, but Priest still heard the strain in his voice and hastened to reassure him. "I'm not most people, Tristan. I'm genuinely interested."

Something told him that that reaction was at least in part due to some parental disapproval, more than likely from his father, based on his past responses to any mention of the man. Priest watched as his shoulders relaxed.

"There were always instruments available in our house when we were young, because my parents were raised that way. Art, music, dance, sports, gymkhanas ... you name it, we did it. I loved the cello and the bass guitar the best, and from that I discovered a love for music theory and composition."

He harrumphed, taking another swig of his drink before continuing. "I've played the piano my whole life and was supposed to have gone on to a master's degree in composition. But things didn't go the way I planned."

He took another swallow of the ale and closed his eyes briefly. Priest waited, hoping he would continue, but whatever came after was clearly not something Tristan wanted to dwell on and certainly not to share. Not sure where to go next, he was saved by the arrival of their food. Tristan had chosen the tasting menu, and his eyes sparkled as he saw the first courses placed on the table.

"We begin with amuse-bouches to tease your palette," the server began, pointing out the food as she continued speaking. "And appetizers to prepare you for the main course bites. Here we have toasted tomato-basil bruschetta and crispy bacon-wrapped dates, and here we have ceviche spoons and smoked salmon with cream cheese. Finally, we have shrimp on seasoned crackers with pepper jelly and cream cheese and cranberry brie bites."

Once the server left, Priest lost himself for a long moment in how Tristan enjoyed everything he placed in his mouth, and only came to his senses when he looked up, the ceviche spoon poised at his lips, to ask, "Priest? This isn't all for me, you know."

Priest's face felt warm under Tristan's amused stare, and he hurriedly popped something from the platter into his mouth without noticing what he'd taken. The cranberry and brie flavors from the bite burst on his tongue. It was good, even though he suspected he should have left it for after the pepper bite. Still, he ate everything and hummed in satisfaction as he sipped the wine they had paired with these first courses.

"Delicious!" he said at last, pleased he had regained his composure. "I'm glad I let you choose what we ate."

Tristan's smile was a little bit shy. "I'm glad you like it. I'm sure you'll love everything else they bring out tonight."

And he was right, from the surprisingly lightly-dressed salad to the gazpacho shots and prosecco that served as palate cleansers, everything was tasty. And the dessert, fruit poached in wine, was surprisingly delightful. By the time they'd had their fill of seafood, meat, and cheese, Priest was pleasantly full, and almost as soon as the busboy cleared the table, movement on the stage grabbed his attention.

"This pianist is part of the house band," Tristan told him. "But they often have visitors up to play, as well. In case you're interested in doing the piano version of karaoke." His eyes gleamed with curiosity, as though he wondered if Priest would take him up on his offer.

Priest chuckled. "Nice try, but I only play for my enjoyment at home. No public displays for me, thanks. I'm happy to listen and enjoy."

"Pity. I was looking forward to hearing you play."

The next words out of Priest's mouth were a complete surprise to them both. "Maybe we can set up a playdate sometime."

Blimey, Priest, what have you done? He looked away from Tristan as he asked himself the question. He hadn't intended to do anything of the sort. Inviting him to his home hadn't even been on his radar at this point, and now he'd look like a fool if he tried to retract the invitation. What the hell was he to do?

Chapter 10

Priest

It's not permission. It's consent.

T hankfully, the pianist greeted the audience, interrupting their conversation. "Good evening, ladies and gents. I'm Josh. Welcome to Oasis! I hope you've been enjoying your meals, but now it's time to add a different flavor to your evening. Sit back, relax, and savor these delicious musical numbers!"

He began a lively jazz set that completely quieted the audience, giving Priest a much-needed and welcome reprieve. Tristan hadn't responded to his ill-timed invitation, even if the intended play on words was clever. The pianist stopped to switch his music sheets and wait for the rest of the band to take their places. As they prepared to play a second set, Tristan spoke.

"I don't expect that that will happen any time soon." Priest frowned, wondering what he meant. "I mean, the playdate idea," he explained. "You've got kids and I know at-home routines are important for children. I wouldn't want to mess with those."

Priest closed his eyes. He couldn't allow himself to show his relief at Tristan's words. Neither of his children knew his true sexual orientation and as he hadn't brought anyone home in three years, there was no way for them to know anything other than that he liked women. Introducing Tristan to his kids would completely upend their idea of him, and he didn't know how to handle any fallout that might occur as a result.

Still, the time for such unsettling thoughts wasn't when he was out with the man in question. He'd take the excuse that Tristan offered and run with it.

"You're right, of course," he replied eventually, hoping Tristan took his delayed response for a thoughtful one. "Perhaps someday." He didn't want to appear to be shutting down the idea. Giving that open-ended response made him feel a little better, even if it *was* rather lukewarm.

The second set with the band was as thrilling as the first had been. They played some tunes that were new to Priest, though Tristan seemed to recognize them, some oldies that took him back to his youth, and what sounded like some sexy Latin rhythms.

When they returned after a ten-minute water break, the pianist said, "We have a treat for you this evening, folks. We've got rock royalty in the house, and in his honor, we're going to play a set from his band's recent hits. You'll notice that cards have been placed at each table. In order to win the prize we've got for you this evening, you'll need to be the first up here with the title of each song we play and the name of the band."

The man paused, grinning at the crowd and laughing at something one of the guests at the back yelled out to him.

The drummer began a quick beat and the pianist called out loudly, "Are you ready?"

The room filled with screams of "Yes!" and "Ready!" and the music began. Priest looked down and noted that while two cards had been placed at their table, Tristan hadn't picked up his but was smiling at the band and tapping his fingers and bobbing his head to the beat. He had no clue what the first or second songs were and only picked up the stubby pencil when the third song started. Only three weeks ago, he'd heard that song, artfully arranged by The Barrington Strings at the Hope House fundraiser.

Glancing over at Tristan, he found the man staring at him and when their eyes met, Tristan winked. Bloody hell! He wrote the name of the band on the card, and the name of the song, which popped into his mind without thought. Well, he knew he wouldn't win whatever the prize was, because he didn't know the last two songs, either, but he didn't care. The rock royalty that the pianist had mentioned was his date for the evening, so he'd already won the prize.

Once the band played the last note with a flourish, a tiny woman dashed up to the stage to hand her card to the pianist. He looked over her answers and nodded, speaking to her for a moment and then waiting until the applause had ended before saying, "Well, ladies and gents, we have a winner. Please give a round of applause to Linda." After a few moments, he continued, "Congratulations, Linda. Before we award you your prize, let's see a show of hands. How many of you chose the band Third Generation?"

Priest raised his hand and looked around to see who else had got it right. More than half the audience members had their hands raised. He watched as two servers spread through the crowd to leave something on the tables. A CD was placed on the table he shared with Tristan. He glanced down at it—the title was "Greatest Hits"—and then up at Tristan who smiled quietly at him.

"How...did you...?" He was interrupted as he tried to figure out what to ask when the pianist began to speak again.

"So, Linda, we're happy to present you with some Third Generation swag. And when you leave the stage, someone will direct you to the band member's table so he can autograph whichever item you'd like him to. How does that sound?"

"Brilliant!" Linda replied, her voice as tiny as her person. "Thank you so much!"

A quick congratulatory hug from Josh and then Linda was being led over to their table. A second spotlight was added to the one over the stage, this one directed at Tristan who stood to hug Linda and smile at the crowd, whose applause swelled as they recognized him. Priest watched as Linda blushed at whatever Tristan whispered in her ear, and then he signed the t-shirt and swag bag that she presented for his autograph. Phone cameras flashed for the few minutes that Linda stood at their table, and when she leaned in to kiss his cheek shyly, more camera flashes went off.

The spotlight dimmed, and Tristan seemed to relax. Priest wondered about that. How could a man who made his living performing in front of hundreds and sometimes thousands of people, be ill at ease in such a small space with so few people? He didn't like the way the last few minutes had changed the dynamic between them. Tristan was clearly happy not to be in the spotlight any longer. His expression had become tight and guarded.

"Are you alright?" Priest gave in to the need to check on him.

Tristan's eyes met his in the once-again darkened room. "It's fine," he said. "Just wondering if you're ready to leave?"

The blatant hope in his tone, in contrast to the studiedly neutral expression on his face, meant Priest needed to get them out of there with as little fanfare as possible. Channeling his knight-in-shining-armor persona, he answered, "Ready when you are." He added a smile for good measure, needing Tristan to know he wasn't disappointed that they were leaving.

They headed out, Priest waiting patiently while Tristan signed a few more autographs on his path to the door. Once they made it outside, Tristan offered him a tight smile.

"Thanks for being patient. I always try to sign at least a few autographs if I'm spotted and anyone asks. It's good for business, you know."

Priest nodded, unwilling to add anything to the conversation until they were in the privacy of Tristan's car. He really wanted to understand the puzzling reaction of a man who should be accustomed to the limelight. When Tristan pulled into traffic, he asked, "Back to the office?" He glanced at Priest.

It took him a second to figure out the reason for the question. "No, home. I took a cab in today because I knew you were picking me up."

"Go ahead and put in your address, then."

Priest did as requested, adding his address to the satnav and then he turned slightly in his seat so he could look at Tristan and asked, "So, is it okay to ask why you seemed so tense once Josh identified you? You don't seem to enjoy the spotlight, for someone who makes his livelihood in it. What's that about?"

Tristan spared him a quick glance and then sighed. "I don't know if you've watched any of our concerts or interviews, but I'm the most reserved member of the band. I say the least. I'm not one for too much talking, unless it's about the music, and even then only if it directly relates to what we're playing or to my part in it."

"I *have* noticed that you aren't exactly Mr. Communication. I'm just curious as to why. You don't strike me as the shy type."

Tristan's answering chuckle startled him. That wasn't the response he'd been expecting. "Oh, I'm not at all shy," he replied. "As my invitation proves, I think. I may be a bit rusty in the dating arena, but in general, I go after what I want. It's just how I've always been. Growing up believing one thing to be true and finding out it was all a lie delivered quite a shock to my already quiet tendencies."

"How does that *not* interfere with your performance? Do you really just imagine naked people when you play?"

He was only half joking. The idea that Tristan was juggling two personas whenever he was out in public was almost unfathomable to Priest. There was definitely more to the man than the things he kept revealing of himself, and Priest was ready to peel back every layer that he exposed.

Tristan's soft laughter warmed him, set his pulse racing, and made him have to struggle to recall what they were talking about. In the greatly reduced confines of the vehicle, his scent was overwhelming, leaving Priest hungry for more than conversation about a topic he'd lost interest in as soon as Tristan had laughed.

"It's really hard to see people when you're on stage," Tristan replied. "Because the lights are so bright up there, they're kind of blinding. And anyway, once we break the ice with the first song, there's nothing but the music after that."

The depth of his love for his work sent a bolt of electricity straight to Priest's suddenly alert cock. He'd never been aroused by anyone's love for their job before, and he didn't understand what made this man any different.

Straightening in his seat—because he didn't need Tristan catching even a glimpse of the trouble he was in— he said, "So it's not stage fright, either. You just aren't a rock-star when you're off stage. I mean, you leave that persona up there, you don't carry it around with you like a crab carries its house."

Another sexy laugh filled the car, and Priest's cock hardened a little more. "That's a good way to think of it, yeah. Just call me Tristan the Shell-tered." He glanced at Priest with a wicked grin. "See what I did there?"

Priest echoed his amusement. "I did. Very good. Sort of like my word play earlier."

Not that he wanted to remind Tristan of the invitation he hadn't meant to give, though he *had* meant to make a pun.

"So, you like to play on words as well as on your piano, do you?"

There was an edge to Tristan's tone, as though he had more in mind than the simple question. Priest didn't want to think too hard on what it might mean, especially not with a stiff dick in his pants. It was bad enough that his body seemed to have a mind of its own where Tristan was concerned. He didn't need to deepen his predicament by imagining himself playing with the man. He replied as coolly as he could.

"I do indeed. It's required for being the father of two pre-teens in my house. I have to be able to keep up with them."

Tristan's chuckle did nothing to ease the strain in his trousers. What was it about this man's voice, about his laugh, that made Priest hard? He'd never had such a reaction to anyone else in his whole life. Maybe that's what grieving did to a man ... it made him hyper aware of every stimulus, made his body hypersensitive to all of them, left him open and pulsing with buried needs.

"They sound like they'd be fun to hang out with."

Tristan's comment, spoken nonchalantly, sent tension twisting into Priest's shoulders. Was Tristan asking to meet his kids? That was not going to happen any time soon. All this awareness might be just a physical thing between them, and Priest had no intention of inviting anyone into their lives who would just turn out to be a non-starter. That would be as irresponsible as leaving an unexploded grenade in a playground.

He settled for a non-committal reply. "They're a treat to spend time with."

It wasn't a lie, but he deliberately didn't answer any question that Tristan might be subtly asking. He'd provide a better answer if he were asked a direct question. They might not have anything more than chemistry between them at the moment, but he didn't want to ruin whatever chance they had at finding more by being too blunt too soon.

Silence reigned in the car for some time after that, leaving Priest to wonder if Tristan sensed he was unwilling to bring his kids into any further discussion. He wondered how the young man felt about that door being slammed in the face of his possible curiosity. Tristan had some soft ballads playing on the car radio, and Priest chose that to start a new thread.

"Do you enjoy all types of music?" He was pleased at how normal he sounded despite the uneasiness trying to disturb his peace.

"Yes and no," was Tristan's puzzling response. Priest waited for him to elaborate. "I will listen to anything once, but I do have some favorites."

"Such as?"

"Obviously, rock music," he replied with another cock-hardening chuckle. "But I also love classical music, folk songs, classic reggae by the classic bands like Bob Marley and the Wailers and Third World. And I love Christmas music, especially those grand old hymns."

Priest smiled. "Something else you share with Shannon. She wanted to be a cathedral organist once, and still says she wants to learn to play the pipe organ."

"That's pretty cool. I'm sure she'll do well with it. Does she play the piano like you do?"

"She does and is really good at it too. In fact, she has an end of term recital coming up where she'll play a solo piece as well as be the pianist for two of the orchestral selections."

"That's fabulous! Maybe the boys and I can come and see her ... you know, incognito and all. If that's okay with you, shoot me the details and if we're available, I know we'd love to come. You can keep it a surprise until afterwards, if that will help. I wouldn't want her concentration to be shot to bits because she's excited about seeing us."

Priest could already imagine the squeals and tears of delight if that were ever to happen, and he supposed there'd be no harm in inviting them without letting her know. But how would they, and the school, manage the high probability of the band being recognized and mobbed by a bunch of teenage girls with no impulse control? He didn't think that would go over well with the headmistress, who was as staid as the best maiden aunt around.

"I don't think it'll be possible for you all to be incognito in her school," he said ruefully. "You and your mates are too well-known in her circles, and I don't think the head of her school would appreciate pandemonium breaking out in the auditorium once you're all discovered."

"You're probably right, of course."

Was that disappointment in his voice? Why would he care that he couldn't see a school concert, even if the kids were really good, which they were? He traveled the world on tour and played for bigwigs all over. A school concert was nothing. Still, Priest felt a twinge at having to dash Tristan's hopes, but it also served to keep him away from his children, so he wouldn't regret the decision.

The silence felt awkward after that, though Priest assumed it was more on his part than Tristan's, since *he* was humming tunefully along to a Luther Vandross song. Priest couldn't remember if he was one of the backup singers in the band, but there was no time to ask that now as they had pulled up at his gate and were turning onto the driveway.

Tristan parked and sat quietly, turning to him in the dimly-lit car to say, "I had a really great evening, Priest. Thanks for coming out with me."

Priest turned to look him in the eye. "I had a good time, as well."

They held each other's gazes for a long moment, as though each man was trying to decide what to do or say next, and when it threatened to become awkward, Tristan leaned forward. The scent of his cologne was rekindling the arousal that had been simmering in Priest's body all evening. He echoed Tristan's movement, wanting more of the sensual flavor before he had to go into his house, and gasped when Tristan's warm breath brushed over his lips as he said, "I've been wanting to do this for almost a month. I hope you won't mind. I'll ask forgiveness after, if you do."

Before Priest could fully decipher his meaning or prepare himself in any way, Tristan's lips were on his, a gentle press, as though he just wanted to feel them, to know their weight, to sample their flavor. Priest wanted to devour him in the moment when Tristan's tongue teased the seam of his lips, but he stiffened his shoulders and held himself rigid, just letting the younger man have what he needed.

When he pulled away, Priest felt regret that he had remained passive. Would Tristan take that as disapproval? Distaste? He didn't want to give the wrong impression, but he needed to rein in the enthusiastic mental gymnastics that had him doing back flips of sheer exuberance. Then Tristan spoke again and stole his breath and his common sense.

"Do I need to ask for forgiveness?" He paused, breathing through his mouth so that his breath caressed the damp lips he'd just tasted. "Or are you giving me permission to do it again?"

For some inexplicable reason, the mischievous promise in that question was more than Priest could bear. He reached up, placing a finger on the lips teasing him and said, "It's not permission. It's consent." Because as far as he was concerned, permission didn't require his participation, but consent did, and he was all in.

Tristan groaned as Priest pulled him close again and took his lips, controlling the kiss and giving him what they both wanted. Their tongues touched, danced lightly around each other, the kiss not deep but no less sensual for all that. It was as though they had agreed beforehand not to go where they shouldn't until they knew each other better but needed to ensure that the other understood how much he wanted more.

Finally dragging his mouth away, Priest sat back in his seat, his cock making his trousers impossibly uncomfortable. He was glad that his children would not be home until later, because he didn't want to have to explain why it had taken him so long to get inside. Snogging his date like a teenager in the front seat of his car was not something he felt ready to discuss with anyone.

"I'd better go in. The kids will be home soon." There was nothing he could do about the way his voice sounded like his throat had been scraped raw.

Even in the dim confines of the car, Priest could see where Tristan's eyes were trained, and the weight of his gaze did nothing to relieve his aching erection. A small, secret smile curved his lips when he looked back into Priest's eyes.

"That was a tasty way to end a tasty evening, Priest. I hope we can do it again some time."

Did he mean the date or the kisses? Or both? Heaving a quiet sigh, Priest opened the door. Either way, he was totally on board with the plan. He smiled.

"I hope so too, Tristan."

Then he stepped out, returned Tristan's wave and watched him turn and head back onto the road.

Chapter 11

Tris

Priest was already proving to be a huge distraction.

"**B**last it!"

Tris's frustrated exclamation burst from him as he missed the timing yet again. Granted, it was the most complicated part in the song they were rehearsing, but it wasn't as though he couldn't play it. He'd done some intense practice on the boat before today's rehearsal precisely because he knew this was a challenge he had to overcome.

He also knew *why* he was flubbing the set.

"Okay, guys, let's take a break. We've been at it all morning. How about lunch? Chrissy made us a feast. Everything's been laid out. Help yourselves to whatever you like and be back in an hour."

Tris stood to head up with his bandmates, but Rory stopped him. "Not you, Tris. We need to talk."

Tris sighed heavily and hung back, taking a seat on the futon that Rory kept down there for when he was too tired to make his way up to bed. Tris suspected he knew what Rory wanted to talk about. He wasn't ready to discuss the reason for his distraction with anyone, but Rory was more than just his friend. He was also the leader of the band and managing rehearsals was part of his job description.

He settled his back against the seat and waited, dreading what Rory was going to ask or say. Rory settled next to him, angling his body toward Tris before speaking.

"What's going on, Tris? I know you can play this. It's not the hardest thing we've ever done, but you're screwing it up royally, mate. So talk to me. Why are you so distracted?" When Tris didn't answer at once, Rory went on. "Is this about the silver fox CEO?"

Trust him to hit the nail on the head right out of the gate! Tris sighed again, wishing he knew a way to avoid this conversation. How did he explain that he'd initiated lip locks with his sexy date? That they'd been the best first kisses of his life and that he'd left Priest with a raging boner that had only been relieved when he'd taken himself in hand as soon as he got on his boat?

How did he explain his near-constant state of arousal at the memory of the way he had left Priest in a similar condition, his cock straining against his fly? That knowing that wasn't helping him concentrate because all he wanted was to explore that hard body before attending to what looked, even in the dim light filtering into the car, like a pretty impressive package? Above all, how did he explain that for some totally unknown reason, the bass line of this song reminded him of Priest's voice, which meant he was fighting without weapons against something he had no idea was even possible?

He opened his mouth, hoping words would come, but all he managed was, "Yes."

He hated the amused chuckle that was Rory's first response before he sobered and asked, "What happened?" And, after another tiny pause, an even more concerned, "What did he do?"

The conflicting feelings of affection and annoyance that swept over Tris at the last question confused him, just like everything else about his reactions to anything Priest-related did. He loved that Rory was so protective of him, but it irritated him that his friend would think Priest had done anything to upset him, as though he thought that Tris was somehow incapable of looking after himself without needing an intervention.

"Nothing happened." Rory raised an eyebrow in obvious disbelief, so he clarified. "Nothing *bad* happened."

"Okay. So what good happened that has you all in a tizzy?" He studied Tris's face as if he thought he'd figure out the truth just by looking at him. "Did you sleep with him? Already? Thought you weren't looking for another hookup? I mean, I can see why that would be a concern, why you'd be a little distracted, especially if the sex was that good."

Tris could feel the blood heating in his veins, no doubt staining his skin a warm red. It was as much embarrassment as it was anger. What he did in his private life was nobody's business but his own, and he wouldn't be judged for how he lived it by anyone, thank you very much! He got ready to tell his friend as much when Rory held up his hands, palms out in surrender.

"Sorry. That was uncalled for. I know you wouldn't go against the very thing you've been holding onto for so long without a good reason, and even if you did, it's none of my business. I'm just concerned that whatever's happening between the two of you is messing with your performance, and we have a deadline for the album that I'd like us to meet, so we can get Sam off our backs, yeah?"

Tris huffed, still feeling the energy of righteous indignation simmering in his veins. He nodded, unable to speak just yet. But when Rory still waited expectantly for his response, he said, "Thanks. I appreciate the apology."

"Is there anything I can do to help you focus better after lunch?" Rory was back in leader mode, and Tris was grateful for it. Figuring out how to get past the emotions that were stymying his efforts to be productive was really the way to go, or else his whole day, not to mention his band mates' own, would be a colossal waste of time.

"I don't know." But that wasn't strictly true. He knew one thing that would definitely help in the short term. "I mean, maybe if we rehearse something else this afternoon, it would give me some space to figure things out."

Why had he thought he'd get away with that odd request? Their rehearsal schedule was planned beforehand and very few changes were ever made. And when those changes occurred, it wasn't for a sea change in the middle of a number.

"What's wrong with the song?" Rory's brow was furrowed in puzzlement.

Tris heaved a third sigh, then shrugged and answered as coolly as he could. "It's not the song. It's me. I…"

Thankfully, Rory's amusement didn't make it past his lips this time, and his tone was neutral as he said, "Something about the song messing with you? Reminding you of him?"

"Something like that." The embarrassment he thought he'd feel at making that admission was curiously absent, but Tris wasn't going to question it. He was just grateful he wasn't reddening up again like ripening strawberries.

"You do know there's research into that, right? It's not unusual for music to have an effect on us that we're mostly unaware of. I can't say I know how to help with that, but I figure that at the very least you can stop trying to control it. Maybe that's why you're distracted, because your brain is trying to do two things at once. So, for this afternoon, how about you focus on one thing—getting the play right—and whatever else happens, just ignore it, instead of trying to control it?"

It wasn't the worst idea, even if Tris hoped he wouldn't become a distraction himself if he popped a boner as he played. The thought made him cringe, and he started trying to think of ways to avoid that when Rory's voice interrupted his close-to-panicked musing.

"Stop fretting. No one will pay you any mind if you get it right later, trust me. They'll be too relieved that we can finish this number today instead of having to go back to it at the next rehearsal. You'll be doing us all a favor if you let go."

There was no denying the teasing note in his voice by the end, and Tris shot him a two-fingered salute in response, but they were both laughing as they headed up for lunch. When he followed his leader's suggestion and lost himself in the music, pushing his almost physical reaction to it into the background, he played seamlessly, and when they finally recorded it for a final listen, he could hear how flawless his performance was.

Afterward, as they were leaving, he leaned in and hugged his friend. "Thanks, Ror. I guess that's why you're the boss, eh?"

Rory shoved his shoulder playfully. "Shut it, you!" Then he returned the hug. "Any time, Tris. Even if I have to pretend I can't see the effect it's having on you."

When Tris pulled away from him, shock written on his face, Rory winked and laughed. "Go on, then. Chrissy will be home soon, and I don't need anyone else here to interrupt *my* concentration, you get me?"

"Sod off!" He tried for a pout as he voiced the insult, but the grin he couldn't hold in was all Rory needed to know that he wasn't really angry. "Say hi to Chrissy for me."

"Will do."

All the way back to his houseboat, Tris ran over the notes from the song, trying to figure out why they made his dick hard. Nothing came to mind, except perhaps that the mid-range bass notes reminded him of Priest's voice for some reason. And adding in that smoky quality on top just made him shiver even now as he thought about it. Tag hadn't been wrong when he'd said that Tris preferred the earthier sounds of the bass guitar. And now he'd apparently discovered why he did.

Between his voice and those lips that Tris now knew were pillowy soft, Priest was already proving to be a huge distraction. Should he keep pushing, or should he let Priest make the next move? How long should he wait before giving up or trying again? Tris sighed as he reheated leftovers for dinner and took a swig of the beer he'd opened. He couldn't remember a time when he'd been so captivated by another person.

Even Devon, whom he had thought he loved completely, had never made him feel this off-kilter. There had been lust and passion with him, for sure, but now, in the sober light of hindsight, Tris had to wonder if there'd been anything more. Devon's twelve-year age difference had been an irresistible attraction, but it hadn't seemed to mean much in the maturity department. Not that he'd have noticed, because the man had been very good at distracting him with gifts and sex.

Thoughts of Devon left a sour taste on his tongue. He swallowed more beer to wash it away. The man who had been cheating on him with the woman he'd eventually divorced after a two-year marriage, had gutted him with the words he snarled as Tris walked out with the last of his things.

"Oh, grow up, Tristan! We were headed nowhere fast, and you know it."

There had been no remorse, no shame, nothing to suggest he was even bothered for a second at having been caught balls deep in someone who wasn't the man he'd been living with. How could Tris have been so foolish, so blind, so utterly clueless? The shame that had burned in him, right alongside bitter anger and resentment, still reverberated in his memory even now, well more than a decade later.

Once bitten, twice shy. He would never allow that to happen to him again. It was now firmly imprinted on his brain that he didn't need anyone to be complete, that when his good right hand wasn't enough, he'd find someone to scratch his itch without allowing a deeper attachment. And he would certainly never again let himself fall for anyone, especially not the older men he'd favored all his life, because they clearly could not be trusted to watch out for him in any way that was beneficial to him.

The timer beeped and he shut off the oven, removing the hot plate to a charger on the table and settling down to eat. The casserole was delicious; the pork, ginger, turnips, and potatoes all spiced with some mouth-watering Asian sauce, went down smoothly and he cleaned his plate with relish. After opening a second beer, he did the dishes and sprawled on the couch in the living room, drowsy and replete.

Through the picture window across from him, he could see the lights of the houses beginning to sparkle on the darkening river, and the odd boat making its way up or down its length. The scene was tranquil, the growing darkness hiding the mean and cruel world from view for just a little while. Would Priest like it here? Was he a boat kind of man? Probably not a houseboat. More like a yacht kinda guy.

Tris snorted quietly. There didn't seem to be anything he could do about Priest invading his every thought. Not that he minded, since it gave him the chance to plan his next steps. He'd wait a week, and if Priest hadn't called by then, *he'd* call. Now all he had to do was figure out what he wanted and how he asked for it. He had three more days to wait.

By Friday afternoon, he and the boys were all ready for a pint after the grueling pace they'd set for recording the new album. They could use some down time and really wanted to blow off some steam, so they'd all jumped at the chance to hang out at Sam's country place. He'd invited a few people for a weekend house party, which Tris knew meant there'd be a mix of business and pleasure. He didn't plan to stay past the night, if he got too pissed to drive himself home, but as the others were all bringing their plus ones, it meant he could bring a date as well.

Would Priest be available, he wondered? After all, it was Friday, and he had kids. And would he even be interested? Sam's parties could get pretty wild, depending on the tastes of his guests, but there was nothing to say anyone had to do anything they didn't choose to do. And it would be the perfect opportunity for Tris to see how Priest would behave in a situation outside his norm. Maybe he'd ask him to go with him.

There had been no communication between them since their date the week before, but he would stick to his plan. The most Priest could say was no, and Tris was prepared to let it go if the man refused. He would just ignore the part of him that dreaded that outcome. Before he could talk himself out of it, he pulled his phone from his pocket, but it buzzed before he got further. Glancing down, he saw Priest's name pop up. He took a deep breath before answering.

"DeVere." He worked hard to keep his tone cool, to pretend he didn't know who was calling.

"Tristan, it's Priest. How are you?"

The man's voice was doing a number on him again. "I'm doing fine, thanks. It's nice to hear from you." He didn't like the way the words sounded accusatory. Priest owed him nothing, but his next words indicated that he'd read something in Tris's voice.

"I'm sorry I haven't reached out until now. It's been a bit crazy here this week. I've had a couple of pretty big obstacles come up that I had to help my clients handle. Between that and managing my kids' schedules, I've been knackered by the time I got home every night."

"You don't need to apologize." Tris hastened to reassure him. "I understand how it can be sometimes, even without kids of my own. I hope you're feeling less exhausted now, though." This was the perfect time to extend the invitation. Before he could voice it, though, Priest continued.

"I am, thank you. I was wondering if you're busy tomorrow night. Friday nights are family take-away-homestyle nights in the Priestley household, so they're pretty sacred, and I don't like to spend them away from the children too often."

Tris's heart skipped a beat. This was more than he had hoped for. That Priest was about to invite him out at the same time that he was getting ready to do the same thing meant that the interest had not waned, that the pull was still there. It was also immensely touching that he prioritized his children over anyone else. That sounded like the actions of a great dad, something he wished he had. He wondered what "take-away-homestyle night" meant.

"Tristan?"

Priest's voice broke into his distracted thoughts. "Sorry. The answer is yes and no. The guys and I have been invited to a weekend house party, and I was just about to call to invite you to go with me. But if you have a better plan, I'm in." He didn't mind ditching his bandmates to spend another evening with the fascinating architect.

"Your idea sounds like way more fun than mine. I was just going to ask you out for a meal."

Tris grinned. "Well, there'll definitely be food at the party, as well as dancing and gaming, if you're into those sorts of things. Or you can just mingle and meet some new people." He chuckled as he added the next bit. "Fair warning, though. There may be a lot of, shall we say, high octane people at this party."

"By high octane do you mean over-the-top famous types?" Priest didn't seem especially bothered by the possibility. Amusement rang through his question.

"Something like that," Tris agreed. "You may get to see how the other side parties and why the gutter press always has a field day with some of them."

"Well, if you don't mind introducing a staid architect into that fabulous crowd, I'm fine with going. What time shall I come get you? And before you protest, please remember *you* got *me* last time. It's my turn."

Tris laughed softly. "Okay, if you say so. We can get there any time, so just let me know when you're leaving. By the way, what on earth is 'take-away-homestyle night?'"

Priest's amused chuckle spread heat through Tris's chest. "It's movie night with take-away-style food made at home. The kids tell me what take-away food they want for dinner, and I get the ingredients. We make it together, then watch a movie or two before they go to bed."

Something sharp twisted in Tris's chest. There had been a time, before the breakup with his parents, when *their* family had had traditions that kept them together and fostered love between them. Well, he had thought it was love, but he'd clearly been wrong. Or something. Still, now wasn't the time to get mired in the ugliness of a past he would never outrun.

"That sounds quite sweet," he said instead. "What's for dinner tonight?"

"Fish and chips."

"And the movies?" Tris wondered what his kids' taste was in movies and whether or not Priest also enjoyed them.

"They usually decide over dinner," Priest answered. "I just go along with whatever they choose, because they know better than to choose anything I'd veto. Oh, the unbridled power of parenthood!"

They laughed together at that, and then Tris said, "I'd better let you get on, then. Enjoy dinner with your family." He was sorely tempted to ask Priest to say hello for him, but that didn't seem like a smart idea when he really didn't know the children and didn't want their father to think he was trying to push his way in.

"Have a good evening. See you tomorrow."

Chapter 12

Tris

*Why does everything this man says
have to sound so damned sexual?*

Priest rang off and Tris felt curiously empty, as though his cup had been drained by the conversation's end, and only a repeat would fill it up again. And suddenly, he didn't want to be alone on his fancy houseboat feeling sorry for himself. A pub dinner sounded like an excellent idea. Maybe he'd meet an acquaintance from town, and they would keep each other company until closing time.

Of course, he'd have to spend the next morning alone, as well, but he'd cross that bridge when he got to it. Decision made, he showered, changed, and went down to his favorite riverfront pub. Almost as soon as he walked in the door, he spotted the publican's son, John, a schoolteacher who gave karate classes on weekends. He was the closest that Tris had to a friend in the town. John grinned when he spotted Tris and beckoned him over.

"Well, it's been a month of Sundays since I last saw you in here, mate. How in the world are you?"

Tris let himself be bro-hugged and back-slapped and returned the grin and the warm greeting.

"I'm even better now you're here," he said. "How are the wife and kids?"

"They're thriving. They've gone up to visit her mum for the weekend, and I'm on my own, reliving my glory days as a wild bachelor."

Tris laughed. "I doubt *he'd* let you get away with that in here." He gestured over his shoulder at John's dad who was chatting with a customer at one of the tables. "Everyone knows he loves his daughter-in-law more than you," he teased.

John laughed. "You're probably right, at that. Care to join me and my mates? It's pub quiz night and we need a fourth."

"Don't mind if I do." This was turning out to be even better than Tris had hoped for as a distraction.

"Ralph, Joe, this is Tristan."

Tris noticed that the men shook hands and smiled politely but with absolutely no recognition, and he relaxed. It always helped when he could hide in plain sight.

"How much to play?" he asked as he sat down. "And does it come with food?"

"Five quid and yes."

Tris handed over the money and John went to add him to their team and place the additional food order. By the time the evening ended, Tris had a bit of extra cash in his wallet and a belly full of beer, sandwiches, and crisps. He was pleasantly buzzed, glad he hadn't ridden his bike, and grateful that John was the designated driver for the evening.

"Thanks for the lift, John," he said when the car stopped at his gate. "I had a good time tonight. Thanks for inviting me."

"Good to see you as always, Tristan. Don't be a stranger, yeah? When are you off again?"

Tris liked John not being more specific, especially with two other men in the car who obviously had no clue who he was. That was something he appreciated about the man … he was discreet and respectful of Tris's privacy.

"Not for a few months yet," he told him.

"Then you've no excuse for not showing up to the pub more often," John replied in a no-nonsense voice. "Looking forward to the next time."

Tris laughed and waved as he drove off. He didn't do nearly enough of that, spending far too much time alone and with just his bandmates. He could be sociable when he made the effort. He needed to get out more, find friends who weren't also his workmates, do ordinary things that relieved the pressures of being a star. Maybe he'd feel less lonely if he did. Definitely something to think about going forward. What could he do in the hours before Priest came to get him? He needed to figure that out.

Lying in bed, his hair still damp from the shower, he considered his options. It would really be great if he could spend the whole day at Sam's family estate. The man was part owner of his family's stables where they boarded horses, gave riding lessons, and hosted horse shows, polo games, and gymkhanas. He also owned a couple of quad bikes in case anyone wanted to do a little off-roading, and there was a pool, a game room, and a tennis court. Maybe he could go up in the morning?

Before he could rethink it, he sent Priest a text message, only thinking after he'd hit Send that it might be a bit late for messaging anyone. Glancing at the clock, he saw that it was almost midnight. *Blast it!* Groaning at his thoughtlessness, he put the phone down, then almost jumped out of his skin when it vibrated on his side table. It was Priest. Were he and his kids still watching a movie? He hadn't meant to disturb them, either.

"Read the message, Tris!" he told himself. Waking his phone, he found it.

[Priest: I'd love to spend the day with you, Tristan. What time shall I come to pick you up?]

[Tris: How long will it take you to arrange childcare?]

A longish pause followed, but Tris could see the bubbles so he knew Priest was answering him. He was glad he'd thought of it first, because he needed Priest to understand that he would never come between him and his kids.

[Priest: I had already lined up the sitter for the afternoon. I'm sure she won't mind spending an extra two hours with them. She adores them like they're her own flesh and blood. I'll call her in the morning and then call to let you know when I'll be starting off, okay?]

[Tris: Sounds like a plan. Sorry for getting in touch so late. Goodnight.]

[Priest: No need for apologies. I was still up. See you tomorrow. Sleep well.]

Tris was up with the birds the next morning. He didn't need to be up so early, but after tossing and turning and growing more awake instead of sleepier, he slid out of bed, relieving himself and washing his hands before grabbing his phone and heading out to the living room. Maybe a movie would help him relax. Scrolling Netflix was as dissatisfying as tossing and turning had been, but he eventually settled on a romcom and pulled the blanket he kept on the couch over himself.

He didn't know when he fell asleep, but he was painfully aware of what woke him a few hours later. His cock was leaking precum, a steel rod in his boxers, and his heart was galloping faster than a prize pony at the races. He'd been dreaming about Priest, and specifically about no-holds-barred foreplay that had been about to get downright dirty when he woke with a shout. He could still almost feel Priest's fingers inside him, making him see stars.

Gasping, he sat up on the couch, a hand to his chest. Bloody hell! That had never happened to him before. He had dreamed about men before, but there had only ever been make-out sessions in those dreams. This sex dream was on a whole other level. It had been fevered, too real to be merely a figment of his imagination. Maybe a wish fulfillment? That seemed to be closer to the truth of things.

He'd slept for three and a half hours, had missed two calls, and had text messages waiting. Rubbing a hand over his face, he listened to the only voice message. It was from Henry.

"Morning, Tris. Are you coming up or not? Don't forget to bring swimwear. I know you love Sam's heated pool." He'd call back in a few minutes. First, he needed to see what Priest's messages said.

[Priest: Morning, Tristan. How do you feel about leaving at eleven?]

The second message, tacked on as an afterthought, wanted to know where they were going. Wishing he was ready for the sucker punch that was Priest's voice but knowing it would be unwise to call him when his body was still humming from the sexiest dream he'd ever had, bar none, he answered the message.

[Tris: We're headed down to Guildford. The band's manager lives there on an estate with a lot of fun things to do. And eleven will be fine. It's about an hour's drive when the motorway is clear.]

His phone rang immediately, and he looked to see it was Priest calling. Gathering his control around him, he answered as coolly as he could.

"DeVere, good morning."

"Good morning, Tristan. I hope I didn't wake you?"

He shivered as Priest's voice trickled down his spine, through his arms and legs to the tips of his fingers and toes, and wrapped around his balls, renewing his finally waning arousal.

"Morning. No, you didn't." Strictly speaking, it had been a dream about Priest that had woken him up. "I just answered your messages."

"I know." Something in his voice made Tris sit up and pay attention. "Should I bring a change of clothes?"

Whatever the darker note in his voice had been, it was gone as quickly as it had appeared. Tris felt curiously bereft, as though he'd missed something vital, and that empty feeling from the day before returned.

Shaking off the odd sensation, he replied, "Yes. There's a huge, heated pool as well as horseback riding and polo or tennis."

"Okay. I'll see you at eleven then."

Of course, Tris spent the time between Priest's call and his arrival—after he called Henry to confirm his attendance and sighing in relief when his friend didn't ask if he was bringing anyone—fretting like a teenager about what to wear. Should he take the black board shorts or the Hawaiian print one? What should he wear down? Finally getting a hold of himself, he settled on a pair of dark olive chinos and a black button-down shirt for dinner. He'd go horseback riding in the faded jeans and long-sleeved Henley that he would change into now that he'd made up his mind.

Making himself tea and toast with marmalade, once he'd showered and changed, he wondered how the rest of his day would go. After that erotic dream, his mind was a whirl of mixed thoughts. How was he going to manage this clearly out-of-control lust that was manifesting itself in his dreams? If that wasn't a sign that even his subconscious was sold on Priest, he didn't know what was.

His phone chimed an alarm, for which he was grateful, distracted as he was by his thoughts. He wanted to be up at the house when Priest arrived, and not force the man to have to come fetch him from the boat. He headed across the footpath and up the slope and had just rounded the corner of the house when Priest's SUV pulled up to the curb. His heart rate sped up and as he returned Priest's wave, he reminded himself to be cool.

"Good morning, again," Priest said as Tris approached the vehicle. His smile was warm and welcoming, and he took in Tris's appearance with a heated gaze as he got into the passenger seat. His eyes sparked with heat that Tris could almost feel on his cheeks.

"Morning. Thanks for the lift." Tris glanced at him as he returned his smile, aiming for a casual air. "How was the ride down?" He closed the door and strapped himself in. "Was there a lot of traffic? I know the motorway can be a misery sometimes."

Why the hell was he running off at the mouth? *Shut up, Tris, for God's sake!*

"It was an easy ride, thanks." Priest's voice had that same quality he'd heard for a moment in their phone call earlier.

Tris glanced over at him again and found Priest's eyes on him, but he said nothing as he looked away and drove off. Then he spoke, clearing his throat to make himself heard.

"It'll be about an hour's drive. Sling your bag in the back seat and be comfortable. Music?"

Reaching between his legs for his rucksack, Tris turned to drop it on the back seat. "Whatever you want to listen to is fine with me," he answered. He was pleased when Priest chose a classical music station.

They listened to popular favorites from Brahms, Beethoven, Chopin, while Priest hummed along, clearly very familiar with the music. Apart from the music, the silence wasn't unbearable, but Tris needed to hear his companion speak. He loved the cadences of Priest's tones, the smokiness, the way the lower his voice went, the more turned-on Tris became. He loved the music, but he had to break the silence between them.

"Do you ride?" he asked without thinking, then looked up sharply when Priest made a choking sound. "What?" he asked when he saw the almost feral look that Priest slanted his way. Immediately he understood and the heat crawled up his neck to his cheeks.

What a bloody awkward time for a Freudian slip! "I mean ... horses. Do you ride horses?" he hastened to explain, closing his eyes against the embarrassment of the moment.

"Yes, I do." Priest sounded amused. "Apart from rugby, which was my passion, I was a fair polo player. And I'm sure you know that requires you to have a good seat and strong thighs, among other things."

Why does everything this man says have to sound so damned sexual? It's polo, for heaven's sake, not sex!

"Do you ride?"

Tris would have to have been deaf not to have heard the teasing note in Priest's voice as he echoed his question. For some unknown reason, being teased by the man he was panting for eased his embarrassment and he managed a believable chuckle.

"Yes, I do. Before the fallout, I enjoyed riding."

"The fallout?"

Tris rolled his eyes at himself. Not only was he losing his battle against Priest's attractiveness, but he was losing control of his words, as well. The last thing he wanted to do was talk about his father. But he'd opened the door for the question so he had no choice but to answer it, and hope Priest would accept his brief response and move on.

"My father and I don't see eye to eye. Haven't since I was twenty-one." Would he be forced to talk about a subject he still found very painful, or would Priest take the hint and let it go? Based on the little he knew of the man, he thought—he hoped—it would be the latter.

Priest's next words confirmed it. "I'm sorry to hear that. When was the last time you were on horseback?"

Tris wished he could kiss him just then, so great was his relief at the obvious change of subject. He could so easily fall for this man he still barely knew, because so far, Priest was doing everything right. He smiled instead.

"That would be the last time we went to Sam's for the weekend. He does these house parties at least two or three times a year, and *we* go at least once."

"Is that a normal relationship between a manager and his clients?"

Tris shrugged. "I don't know, really. It's just what we've forged together over the years. He's been our manager from the beginning, when he was also new to the game, so we've sort of grown up together. We're like a rowdy bunch of brothers."

Priest's chuckle settled him, and he let the music take over once again, finally content to just enjoy the intimacy of their budding friendship or whatever it was that was growing between them. Priest's humming aroused and soothed him at the same time, and he let himself enjoy the tension between the two feelings. It kept a pleasant buzz simmering in his chest, and by the time Priest was parking where the other cars already were, he felt energized. Anticipation thrummed in his veins at the thought of what might happen between them.

"This is pretty." Priest's tone was appreciative as he looked around him.

"It is, isn't it? We love coming here, and when Henry and Gen bring the kids, they never want to leave."

Priest turned to smile at him. "I can understand that. I imagine my kids might feel the same way."

Tris tried not to attach any meaning other than the obvious one to Priest's words. If he started thinking that Priest might want to introduce him to his kids and about what that might mean about his interest, he'd be a ball of nerves for the rest of the day. He'd rather enjoy the time they would spend together.

"Let's go in. I didn't tell anyone I was bringing a guest, so the boys will be glad to see you. Hope you don't mind if they tease you a bit. It'll really be me they're ribbing, just so you know."

Priest laughed. "I'm a big boy. I can hold my own."

Tris bit back the flirtatious question on the tip of his tongue. Wondering aloud about how big Priest was in answer to his statement was *not* the way to avoid hardening his cock and making an embarrassing display of himself before a group of people who liked to push his buttons. Instead, he led the way to the door which opened as they made it up the last step.

"Took you long enough," Sam groused in greeting, reaching to hug Tris anyway. "I thought you were ditching me." Turning his eyes to Priest, he added, "Though, to be honest, I wouldn't fault you if *this* guy was the reason."

Tris groaned, noting that Priest just grinned. Well, at least he wasn't offended by Sam's forwardness. "Sam Keswick, meet Benedict Priestley. Priest, Sam."

He hoped neither man would mind that he had left out explanations of their roles in his life. He needed to keep things as simple as he could manage. Thankfully, Sam seemed to understand his desire and extended his hand with a warm smile.

"Welcome to my home, Mr. Priestley. It's a pleasure to meet you. Please, come in. The others are in the back. You can drop the bags here for now."

Cheers rose up when they walked out to the covered back porch where the others were gathered. They had arrived just in time for lunch. Cheers, hugs, and back slaps greeted them as they settled down in two empty seats next to each other. Tris tried to ignore the suspicion that they had been deliberately set up to sit together, because Sam was leaning against the door leading outside, his legs crossed and a half-full glass of beer in his hand.

"Good of you to join us, Tris," Henry said above the chatter, smirking at him. Then he turned to Priest and added, "Thanks for prodding his lazy arse to come today, Priestley. How would you like the job of pulling him out of his shell? It's a volunteer position only, you understand. Your only reward would be his agreement to be less of a recluse."

Priest laughed right along with everyone else. Tris visibly cringed at Henry's blatant attempt to mind his business for him and set him up with the sexy silver fox. He should be more used to being harassed about his tendency to hide, but this teasing in front of someone they were still getting to know was a first. Did it mean that his friends had already accepted Priest? That would be monumental, if it were true, because all of them were protective of him. He acknowledged a hidden desire to be more open about himself in relation to the man and it eased his embarrassment.

That actually wasn't such a bad idea, after all.

Chapter 13

Priest

Priest couldn't keep his eyes off his prize ... Tristan DeVere.

The Keswick estate was medium-sized, in comparison to some that Priest had visited before, but it was lovely country bordered on one side by the river. The stables were on that side, and the setup for the gymkhanas and other riding-related activities, as well as any horse sales, were in a field adjacent to them. After an enjoyable lunch, in which Tristan and his friends regaled him with stories of their adventures on the estate, seasoned with plentiful laughter and endless teasing, a few of them went for a meandering ride to work off the food.

His mount was a strong, feisty black stallion but he didn't mind the spirited animal between his thighs because he was much too distracted by the man astride the black and white mare riding ahead of him. Tristan sat tall and straight in the saddle, chatting away with Rory and Henry who rode on either side of him. He himself was between John and

William, who asked about his work and about the progress on Tristan's home.

"Work hasn't actually begun as yet. We're finishing up the design phase. But it will begin soon. He'll have a really great home when it's all done."

"I'm more of a condo kind of guy myself," John said. "I'm just too lazy to be a true homeowner."

They all laughed at that, though Priest could well understand the sentiment. Home ownership was like parenting teenagers, except that there was even less communication between the owner and his house than between him and his kids. They all chuckled when he voiced the thought as they were finishing the tour, passing by the guest house where Henry and Gen were staying—"because it has two bedrooms for them and the kids"—on their way back to the stables. The ride had taken the chill out of the Spring air, and Priest was pleasantly warm by the time they dismounted.

"I think I'm ready for a swim to cool down," he remarked as the others gathered round.

"Your things have been sent up to your room," Sam informed him. "I hope you don't mind sharing with Tris. He didn't say he was bringing a plus one."

"If he doesn't mind," Priest looked over at his unintended roommate. "I don't."

At Tris's grin, Sam continued, turning to him. "Top of the stairs, far left corner. You know where the pool is. We'll see you in a bit."

Priest nodded, glad that they had put him and Tris in the same room. Not that he had expected it ... well, maybe he had, just a little bit. But knowing that they weren't staying over had prompted his wish for some alone time with his crush. He scoffed at his thought as he headed up the stairs.

What was he ... twelve? Only preteens and teenagers had crushes. He was a grown man, already middle-aged.

This thing, whatever it was, would either blow over or strengthen into something real. He knew which he'd prefer, but if Tristan was as reserved as his mates said he was, Priest would need to call on all his patience to win him over if he remained aloof. To be fair, though, he'd also need to make his own adjustments, like telling his children he was seeing a man, thus revealing his bisexuality.

Someone bumped into his back, and he came to himself in time to notice that he'd stopped on the landing and was just staring into space. Lord help him, he was distracting himself at a time when he needed his wits about him. He wasn't exceptionally good with strangers outside of his work, but he wasn't completely inept in social situations, either.

He turned, an apology on his lips, and found himself face to face with Tristan. His breath stuttered in his lungs for a second before he spoke. "Sorry. I got sidetracked."

Tristan's smile was knowing, though what he thought he knew was a mystery. "No problem. Our guest room is this way."

Priest's pulse ticked up as he followed Tristan. Inside, the space was large and airy, the walls a cool teal, the bed linens complementary shades of sky blue, pale peach, and gray. The flooring was hardwood with an ocean blue rug under a queen-sized bed. Their bags were on either side of the bed. Through a door to their left was a walk-through closet that led to a small bathroom with a shower.

"I'll go first," he offered, noticing Tristan standing uncertainly by his bag. They both needed some more time away from each other, it seemed, even though all he wanted was to wrap the other man up in his arms.

Grabbing his bag without making any further eye contact with Tristan, he hustled into the bathroom, closing the door leading to the closet and dumping the bag on the closed toilet lid. Two sets of towels filled the space on the towel rack and upon closer inspection, he found shower gel, shampoo and conditioner, and even body lotion—presumably for when the room was used by female guests—in a stylish built-in shower caddy.

Shedding his sweaty clothes, he pulled a t-shirt and his board shorts from the bag and stepped from the cool white tiles onto the mat by the shower. Reaching around the half glass wall to start it, he waited while the water came to a reasonable temperature and then stepped under headfirst, letting the warmth rush over his heated skin.

Thoughts of the man in the adjoining bedroom assailed him as he washed his hair and soaped his body. Damn if he wasn't as aroused now as he'd been since Tristan had gotten into his car. He gripped his thickening dick and wavered between tugging himself to a quick release or ignoring the desire pulsing in his veins and getting the hell out of the shower before he did something he'd regret, like wank to thoughts of a man he'd only kissed a couple of times.

Hurriedly drying off and donning his swim shorts and t-shirt, he exited the bathroom to find the bedroom empty. Where had Tristan gone? Pulling the clothes he would change into after his swim out of the bag, he was just hanging them in the closet when the bedroom door opened, and Tristan walked in. Priest barely glanced at him, noticing nothing amiss.

"Bathroom's yours," he said, focusing on getting the shirt just so on the hanger as though his life depended on it.

"Already showered."

Tristan's comment made him spin around so fast he could have given himself whiplash. What the hell? Something uncomfortable rose inside him ... dismay. Why had he gone somewhere else to shower? What was so bad about waiting until Priest was done? Or had he been in there so long that Tristan had gotten tired of waiting? And above all, why the hell was he upset? He felt his forehead furrow, the wrinkled skin tight with his confusing reaction.

"Is something wrong?" Tristan asked, clearly equally puzzled by his frown.

Priest closed his eyes, turning away to bring himself and his expression back under control before responding. "No. Everything's fine. I forgot to bring a towel for the pool. I'll just go get the one I used..."

His voice trailed off. He was talking too much and getting needlessly agitated again. He turned instead to head back to the bathroom but found Tristan in his path. Before Priest could step around him, Tristan grasped his biceps in his strong hands.

"Hey, I'm sorry I didn't wait. I needed some time to calm down."

Priest's eyes widened. "Calm down? Why? What's happened?"

Tristan chuckled. "You. *You* happened." Leaning in, he bussed Priest's lips. "We'd better get back downstairs before rumors start flying about what we're up to in here."

Priest held Tristan's wrists as he tried to pull away, keeping him where he was. "You don't think maybe we should give them something real to talk about? You know, like that Bonnie Raitt song says?"

It was Tristan's turn for wide-eyed surprise. "You've got hidden depths, haven't you?"

"What?" Priest slid a hand up to his face, passing his thumb gently over Tristan's lips as he cupped his jaw. "You think I only listen to Third Generation's rock music?"

Tristan laughed. "I didn't say that," he protested.

"But your surprise implied it." Priest pulled his face into a frown again, this time trying to affect disapproval. "Now, take your punishment like a man so we can go for a swim."

And then he kissed him, teasing Tristan's lips with his tongue before seeking entrance into the warmth of his mouth. When Tristan opened for him, Priest wrapped his arms around him, pulling him closer and deepening the kiss. Relief settled in next to the arousal rising in him when Tristan looped his arms around his neck and returned the kiss.

He could feel Tristan's plumping dick rising against his own, and he pulled away reluctantly. Clearing his throat, he said in a low voice against the lips he wanted to keep savoring, "We're definitely going to give them something to talk about if we show up hard." A final light peck on Tristan's lips was all he allowed himself before he moved away.

"I'll meet you down there."

Tristan's voice was hoarse with unfulfilled lust. The sound made Priest's cock twitch with renewed interest, while his chest warmed with foolish pride at the thought that he had been the reason for that.

"Okay. See you in a few. Thanks for taking the heat for me."

Tristan laughed. "Don't worry, you'll get what's coming to you," he promised. "You know the drill. Stiff upper lip and all that."

Priest grinned as Tristan walked out, dropped his dirty clothes in the bag and made his way down after him. He supposed he had it coming for riling them both up earlier, however briefly, but he remained pretty confident that he'd be able to manage any ribbing that came his way. At least his cock had lost interest once Tristan had left the bedroom, so by the time he made his appearance on the terrace, he was back in control. That had to be his focus until they left at the end of the evening.

Tristan and Rory were doing slow laps in the pool, which looked to be at least half the size of an Olympic pool, when he got down, and as he stripped off his t-shirt, he watched them begin to race each other to loud cheers from their mates. The vibe was all fun and frolic, and he imagined they needed it when they worked so hard at all other times. Blowing off steam like kids was highly underrated, as far as he was concerned.

"I've been waiting for you," Henry informed Priest when he sat next to him. "We're a team. The others have already paired up."

"A team? You sure you want to win?" Priest found himself liking the guy who seemed to be the unofficial band dad. "I haven't been in a pool in a while."

Henry shrugged. "It doesn't matter. Neither have I. But we need to keep these whippersnappers on their toes, show 'em how it's done."

"So it's not about winning?"

"Nope. It's about endurance. How fast can you do ten laps without stopping?"

Priest inclined his head dubiously. "I'll be lucky if I last five laps in that pool."

"Then it'll be good exercise for you." Henry was unmoved by his protests.

Priest liked that none of them had felt it necessary to corner him for the "don't hurt our friend" talk. Maybe they still would, but he was certain that even if they did, it wouldn't be hostile. He watched the men as they swam, leaving the pool with heaving chests and runny noses. The sight of Tristan's tall frame, dripping water as he emerged from the pool like a golden god, was almost too much for his poor tortured dick to bear. He dragged his eyes away, reaching for the bottle of water he had snagged on the way to the lounge chair.

A sprinkling of water droplets chilled his skin, and he looked up to find Tristan grinning down at him, goosebumps pebbling his arms as he passed a towel over his broad chest.

"You're on," he informed Priest. "Show us what you've got."

By the time Priest got out of the pool, he was exhausted, but his ego hadn't let him stop when he'd grown tired. Ten laps should have been nothing for someone who tried to keep his heart rate up with jogging and time in the gym, but Priest would be the first to admit that he wasn't in as great shape as he used to be before Jane died. His exercise routine had become sketchy at best. If he planned to try for something with Tristan, he'd need to get back on track.

"Wow! You're a beast," Henry remarked admiringly, coming up then. "Thought you said you hadn't been in a pool for a while?"

"I hadn't, but I have a big ego, and it needed to prove itself," he heard himself admitting, an uncharacteristically diffident smile lifting the corners of his lips halfway.

"You old guys both still have game," Tristan remarked, as if sensing Priest's discomfort. "I'm with King Louie. I wanna be like you."

"Who's King Louie?" Both Henry and Priest looked at him inquiringly.

"From *The Jungle Book* Disney movie," Tristan clarified.

"Oh yes. I remember that." Priest chuckled. "My son loved that movie, though with typical Mason logic, he wondered why Mowgli couldn't have been raised by tigers, because then he and Shere Khan would have been besties."

General laughter followed his statement before the younger men began trading friendly insults as they rested. Priest finished a bottle of water and munched on a few grapes from the snack tray that had been placed on the table for them. An hour passed in desultory conversation, and he did his best to participate when he was called on to do so.

Footsteps approached where they all sat around the pool, and a tiny but elegant woman led four Black men out to where they were sitting. Priest noted how she silently glided over to Sam and leaned in to kiss his lips before moving on to greeting the band members and blowing them air kisses.

"Mona!" they called out in unison.

"Where are the ladies, boys?" she asked, looking around while the newcomers settled on other chairs.

"Coming up later. They had something planned to do before," Henry answered for them.

"And yes, the twins will be here."

"Excellent! My lot will be back by then, so they'll have company." Mona clapped her hands in glee, then turned her sharp eyes to Priest. "Hello there, Mr. Priestley," she greeted him. "Welcome to our home."

Priest apparently hadn't managed to hide his shock at her addressing him by his name, because she chuckled and continued, before he could reply, "I was at the Hope House fundraiser with Sam," she told him. "And one of my closest friends lives in a Priestley Group house. She can't stop singing the praises of you and your team."

Priest was not a shy man, but the unaccustomed attention made his skin heat up. "Thank you," he answered, feeling like a fool.

"Introduce Mr. Priestley to the others while I go get more drinks, love," Sam said to the woman Priest assumed was his wife, rising and walking back into the house.

Mona smiled obligingly. "Benedict Priestley, meet Brandon Marsh, Elijah Hawkins, Levar Hunter, and Oliver Washington." She indicated each man as she said his name. "Together, they are Blackbeat, an up-and-coming American vocal band. Boys, Mr. Priestley is the CEO and chief architect of The Priestley Group based in London."

As they shook hands, Priest marveled at the combined good looks on display before him and the size of the men in question. They all looked like they'd played some tough sport like football when they were younger. None was shorter than he was, one of them more than a couple of inches taller than him. Was he the bass singer? Immediately his mind went to Tristan, sitting across from him chatting with one of the Blackbeat band members.

Would anything more happen between them than the few stolen kisses they'd already shared? *Should* anything more happen? There were so many things that neither knew about the other, and on his side, so much that could hinder any relationship they might try to start, beginning with his children not knowing that he liked men as well as women. Why was he even putting off the discussion? He couldn't keep Tristan away from his kids for much longer without making it appear that Priest was treating him like a dirty secret, like he was ashamed of who he was and who he loved.

Before he could wander any further down that troubling thought pathway, the subject of it said above his right ear, a hand cupping his shoulder, "Are you alright?"

Priest looked up, noticing the concern on his companion's face. "Yes, I'm fine. Why?" His skin burned where Tristan's hand still touched him.

"You were a million miles away. The new guys are going to change so we can play a game of water polo. You in?"

Priest chuckled, ignoring the way his pulse rate had kicked up at the continued contact. "Thanks, but no thanks. I've had more than enough exercise for the day. I'll be satisfied just watching you lot."

Tristan smirked. "Well, at least you know your limits. That's so mature of you."

Priest shoved at him with his elbow, dislodging his hand. "Bollocks! Maturity has nothing to do with it. I'm just lazy and not afraid to admit it. Besides, it's my day off and I have no interest in doing anything more strenuous for the rest of the day than eat and maybe watch a movie before I drive you back."

They shared a laugh before Tristan went back to his friends. The game was full of shouting and insults that resulted in laughter which made things even more hilarious. It was clear that only two or three of them knew the rules, that the rest just needed to let off steam, and that all the men in the pool were fit and strong and unfairly sexy. Even given all that, Priest couldn't keep his eyes off *his* prize ... Tristan DeVere.

A gong sounded, startling them all. Mona stood in the doorway and banged it again, and this time they all laughed.

"Dinner will be in a couple of hours, boys, and we'll be having a few more guests. So if you know you need a bit of rest, now would be a good time to get on it, yeah?" She paused to look over at Henry and her husband and added, "I can think of at least two people who shouldn't refuse my thoughtful suggestion."

Priest laughed out loud at that pointed remark and she turned her amused eyes to him and added, "Oh, you think *you're* excluded from that comment?"

Now *he* was the butt of the joke, but he didn't mind. Somehow, it relaxed him to know that his being a newcomer to their inner circle and a person of note didn't earn him the kid glove treatment. He could be himself, which might mean he could relax with Tristan as well, especially since he was sure the guitarist's mates already suspected that they had something going on between them.

He wasn't sure how much rest he would get if he went up to their shared room with Tristan, but he'd figure something out. He'd take a shower to wash off the chlorine and then he'd see what happened after.

"Coming up?" Tristan asked, dripping water on him again as he stood over him. Something in the question made him look up and Priest caught the banked fires in his gaze.

"Yeah." He picked up two more bottles of water on the way and handed one to Tristan.

"Thanks."

The air crackled between them as they walked up the stairs together behind a couple of the guys from the other band. *They* were talking in low tones and chuckling between themselves while an electrified silence reigned between him and Tristan. In their room, Tristan grabbed his Dopp kit and headed into the bathroom immediately with a murmured, "Won't be long."

The evening was growing chilly after a warmish afternoon, so he didn't begrudge Tristan first use of the shower. He'd been frolicking in the pool most of the afternoon and needed to warm up. While he waited, he checked his phone. No messages meant all was well at home. If he got his wish, he'd have to call the children later to tell them goodnight, but that was a big if. Tristan might not invite him to stay over at his place and he'd be making the lonely drive back. Best not to think about the disappointment that that would be.

"Shower's yours," Tristan said, bringing Priest's head up from the email he'd been reading.

He swallowed roughly at the sight as Tristan walked back into the room, a towel wrapped around his waist, a second towel drying the excess water from his hair. His chest was lightly furred, the hair growing subtly darker as it arrowed down his middle to his groin and whatever was hidden under the towel. A drop of water rolled down his chest as Priest watched helplessly, raising his eyes only when it was soaked up by the towel.

"Like what you see?"

Again, Tristan's voice, as well as the question he'd asked, brought Priest back to the moment. Remembering the sight of the tall, defined body in the pool and the way he'd had to force his mind away from all the dirty thoughts that had been threatening his cock all afternoon, he chose to answer honestly. He didn't have the energy for subterfuge.

"Very much." His throat was dry even though he'd finished the water he'd brought up.

He stood up and took his own kit into the bathroom, brushing by Tristan on his way. Conscious that he was running away from the challenge he could see in Tristan's eyes and unable to say more, he held tightly to his control, ignoring the soft gasp from Tristan when Priest's arm brushed his naked chest.

"Where's the fire?" Tristan murmured as he walked by.

In my balls! Priest glanced up. "Don't start anything you won't finish, Tris."

He'd shortened his name unintentionally, completely unnerved by the lust that was riding him. He didn't want to hook up with this man in a stranger's guest bedroom, especially when that stranger was also Tristan's manager and friend. There was just something distasteful about that idea ... or maybe it was just his hypersensitivity to the entire situation making him find reasons to deny what it was clear they both wanted.

"Who says I won't?" The challenge was clear.

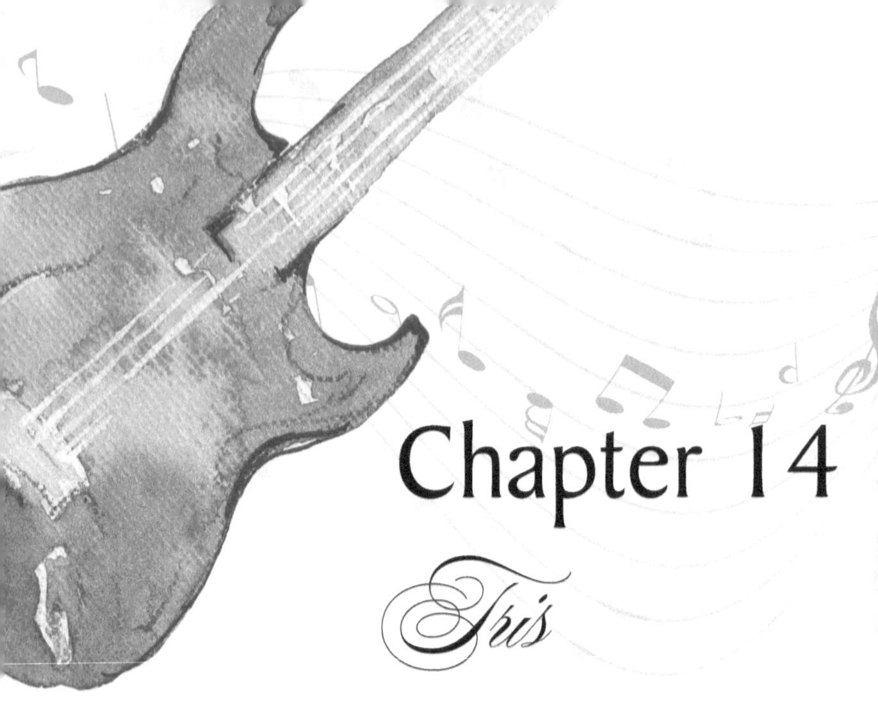

Chapter 14

Tris

I want exclusivity, as well. What's mine is mine.

What the bloody hell are you doing, Tristan Alan DeVere? Reprimanding himself in his father's voice helped bring Tris back from the edge he'd been about to throw himself over. He'd been a second away from pulling a clearly reluctant Priest into his arms and taking the kiss he'd been wanting all afternoon. After all the time they'd spent together, from the passive moments on the ride to the more active frolicking in the pool, he'd been distracted and aroused by Priest's body. His muscular limbs, broad shoulders, and toned abs with the dark treasure trail of hair bisecting it down to his carefully camouflaged package had stirred fresh need in Tris.

But whatever demons of desire were tormenting him, he couldn't allow them to win this battle for control. Something was holding Priest back, and Tris wouldn't go where he wasn't invited. That flirty question had been unnecessary at best, unwise at worst. He moved away, letting Priest pass him, and squelched his disappointment when the only response he got to his teasing comment was a raised brow and a half-smile. Sighing as he listened to the shower go on, he acknowledged that it was a good thing that at least one of them was thinking like an adult and not a hormonal teenager.

Maybe he would be better off resting somewhere other than this bedroom with its one bed. The sitting room on this floor had some comfortable couches and a lovely view. He could hang out there, maybe catch up on some reading. Dismissing that idea almost at once—because hanging out in a public sitting area in his skivvies and a bathrobe seemed a bit too informal in mixed company—he sighed and grabbed the robe, settling against the headboard on the side of the bed furthest from the bathroom. He'd listen to an audiobook.

The shower was still going when he found the one he hadn't finished and put his air pods in. Closing his eyes, because he needed every defense against lust that he could muster, he forced himself to concentrate and prayed that the story would distract him. But his simmering disappointment continued to fester, bubbling inside him, and the words being piped into his ears mixed with his increasingly unsettled thoughts became a cacophony of mounting irritation.

Opening his eyes again, he found Priest just tying his own robe at the waist. Tris had to address the issue, or he'd be a right mess for the rest of the day. This wasn't who he was. He didn't let people get to him, but Priest's effect on him was unexpected and he didn't know how else to handle the confusing emotions than to air his complaints and let things go where they would. Stiffening his resolve, he spoke, injecting a coolness he wasn't feeling.

"We need to talk," he began. "I need to clear up some things."

Priest eyed him speculatively, and Tris could almost see the wheels turning in his head. He waited none too patiently for the older man to respond. Would Priest be okay with whatever he said? What if he wasn't willing to go further than a light flirtation and making out? That wasn't what Tris wanted. Nor did he want to be a secret, and he suspected that Priest hadn't shared his bisexuality with a lot of people, which made him essentially a closeted man.

"What do you want to clear up?"

Priest's question was reasonable, but it still annoyed Tris. Was he going to pretend he didn't know what Tris wanted to talk about? He didn't feel like playing those kinds of games. Not now. Not ever, in fact.

"Are you going to stand there and pretend you don't know what we need to talk about?"

Priest's eyes narrowed, but he didn't show any other reaction. "I think it's a reasonable question. I'm not a mind reader. I find it's always better to ask if you're not privy to what someone else is thinking. It would be like starting a road trip without directions."

Why he felt like throwing a terrible-twos tantrum, Tris couldn't say, but he managed to control the urge to pout at Priest's entirely too logical response. But before he could reply, Priest added, "By the way, Mona came by to remind us that dinner will be at seven."

Tris could feel Priest's gaze on him as a fraught silence settled between them. How could he say all that was bubbling in his brain without making things more awkward? He opened his mouth and spoke whatever came first to his lips.

"What are we doing? Are you just messing around? What did you mean by not starting anything I won't finish? Do *you* want to start something?"

He ran out of steam and let his voice trail off. That was more than enough to get a conversation going, and Priest had better not come off all aloof and superior like he'd been a minute ago, or Tris would lose his shit. This was the closest he'd been to anger in a while, and it dismayed him that he was having such contradictory feelings towards Priest. These last few weeks had been the most unsettling and emotionally unstable of his life, aside from the feelings about his father that sometimes swamped him.

Priest sat on the edge of the bed, turning to face him before he answered. "I have those same questions, Tristan. I feel the attraction as deeply as you do, and I want to follow it to its logical conclusion."

"I sense a 'but' coming."

"But there's a lot to consider, as I'm sure you know." Priest paused as if searching for words.

Tris helped him. "Things like my touring schedule and your work schedule, like your kids and our other family and close friends knowing about us, like what we want out of this. So far so good? Anything you want to add?"

"Will this be exclusive? I'm very much a proponent of monogamy, so if we chose to pursue this, I'd want your word that I'd be the only one you're seeing while we're together. I don't share well. Or at all, really."

Those last words flooded Tris's whole being with warmth. He needed commitment and the promise of Priest's single-minded focus. He didn't share, either. He wasn't wired for that kind of freedom.

"I want exclusivity, as well. What's mine is mine."

"What happens if things don't work out between us? Should we take that risk? Will it affect our working relationship?"

Tris hated those questions, but he knew they were important. Priest was right, after all. It was a risk they would be taking if they chose to become lovers. There were no guarantees when it came to romance. He knew that better than most.

"I'd like to think that we're adult enough to work together without ripping each other's throats out if things fall apart."

He pushed a confidence into his voice that he wasn't feeling. Because he also knew that that was what he would want to happen, even if it would be the hardest thing he'd ever do.

"I'm sure we are."

Priest's smile was tentative, as though he was also doing his best to believe the words he'd uttered. What a pair they were! How would a relationship work between them if they couldn't talk without this awkwardness, without tiptoeing around each other? That was a discussion for another day. He had wanted to say his piece about the things that were currently weighing him down. Now he'd just have to wait and see how things progressed. He would do everything he could to make their journey together fulfilling and if Priest's heated gaze was any indication, he was equally committed.

"So, are we good now?"

Priest's question pulled him out of his head. "For now, yes. Thank you."

He hoped his smile would help the man sitting on the edge of the bed to relax. The last thing he needed was any awkwardness between them that would be noticed by his sharp-eyed friends.

"Good." This time his smile was unfettered. "I need to check in with my kids."

Tris nodded and put his air pods back in, closing his eyes this time and going back to where he'd been before to let the story really sink in. He must have fallen asleep because when he opened his eyes, Priest was tucking his shirt into his trousers. Tris eyed him slowly, glad his back was turned so he wouldn't notice Tris's greedy perusal. The man's body never failed to send his pulse into hyperdrive.

"You really ought to get going, Tristan."

Priest's amused voice made him blink. What? "How did you know I was awake?" he demanded. "I didn't make a sound."

"The hairs on the back of my neck stood up when you started eye-fucking me," Priest replied, letting his amusement free with a chuckle. "Dinner is in half an hour, and we don't want to be late."

"Eye-fucking you?" Tris pretended to be affronted. "I was doing no such thing!"

"The rocker doth protest too much, methinks!" Priest teased him.

"Shut up!" Tris replied, pouting. "It's not very gentlemanly of you to tease me."

Priest had come over to where he still sat up in bed and when he smiled down at him, Tris melted, butter in a hot skillet. He looked up into the stormy gray eyes staring down at him intently and breathed a sigh of relief when Priest leaned in and kissed him. It was sultry and hungry, reclaiming the lost ground between them. Tris could still feel the restraint in the way Priest held his body, not touching Tris anywhere except his lips.

"Get dressed, hot stuff. I'll meet you downstairs." Priest picked up his bag and walked out, whistling softly.

Tris could still feel the warmth of Priest's words on his lips as he dressed. Had there been something more than teasing in his voice just now? Now that they'd both said what they wanted with each other, it wasn't unreasonable to imagine that Priest might want to recommence intimacies and perhaps take them further. Tris was ready for anything, really. If wishes were horses!

Downstairs, the numbers had swollen with a few additional guests, including his mates' women and Henry's and Gen's twins. Cocktails preceded a buffet dinner filled with laughter. Once Gen took the twins off to bed, Tris watched as the guests separated into smaller groups and drinks once again flowed freely. Priest was in deep discussion with a couple of the singers from Blackbeat, and Tris didn't bother to hide his appraisal of the man from where he sat by a window.

Priest's whole body was broad and buff, and his height made him seem larger than life. Tris swallowed at the mouthwatering sight of Priest's wide chest and muscled arms straining his dress shirt, and the thick thighs encased in snug-fitting trousers. What would it be like to have that powerful body above him, holding him in place while they kissed and humped each other? Or better yet, when Priest was taking him to paradise in his strong arms?

"Earth to Tris. Come in, Tris."

Fingers snapping in front of his eyes and a highly amused voice calling him back to attention brought heat into Tris's cheeks. Rory was quietly laughing in his face when he blinked and focused on his friend. And then he noticed the others who had all been watching him for God knows how long, all sporting the biggest grins. John was waggling his brows at him, and Henry's gaze was knowing. Will made a point of looking over to where Priest still sat talking before turning back and wagging a finger at Tris.

"So," Rory dragged out the word, "are you staying the night? I know you hitched a lift here, but one of us can take you home tomorrow night."

Tris bit back the sharp denial that wanted to burst from his lips. Although his friends all knew his attraction to Priest, he wasn't about to give them any more opportunities to tease him than he could avoid.

Squaring his shoulders, he said, "I'm leaving with Priest. I never planned to stay over, and you all know that."

"Pity," John chimed back in. "It would have been nice to see your faces the morning after."

Guffaws loud enough to bring other guests' eyes over to where they were seated made Tris cringe.

"Shut it, Beats," Tris replied, a warning in his voice. "Not that there would have been anything to see, but even if there were, it's none of your business, is it?"

He was only a little bit irritated, but he played it up, hoping they'd drop the subject. John was about to answer him when he saw Priest approaching and closed his mouth. Tris watched as Priest came close enough to speak.

"I'm sorry to break up the fun, but it's late and we need to get going." He turned to Sam, who had followed him over. "Thanks for a great evening. I had a good time."

Sam smiled. "Glad you did, Mr. P..."

"Call me Priest," he said, shaking hands all round.

"We'll see you Tuesday, Tris," Henry said. "Enjoy the rest of your weekend, you two."

Refusing to rise to the bait, Tris made the rounds with Priest, ending with Mona. Tris reached over to hug her and when he went to pull away, she held on and whispered in his ear, "Your friend seems like a nice gentleman. Try not to chase him off, darling!"

Tris disentangled himself with a quiet chuckle. "I don't know what you're talking about," he demurred, and laughed out loud when she just pursed her lips and winked at him.

"Mr. Priestley…" she began, turning to Priest.

"Priest, please," he said again. "Thanks for a lovely day."

"I'm glad you enjoyed yourself, Priest. I do hope you'll come again." She smiled warmly at him. "And bring your children next time. Henry and Gen's and my lot would love some more company."

Priest smiled but didn't answer. What did that non-response mean? And why was everyone assuming that there'd *be* a next time? Just because he and Priest had come to an agreement—which no one else knew about—didn't mean anything if it didn't last. And Tris had learned not to take permanency for granted. He grabbed his bag and followed Priest out to the car.

"Sorry about my friends," he said as he slung it into the back seat beside Priest's. "They can be a bit much sometimes."

Priest's chuckle reached him over the top of the car as they got in, but he didn't answer until they were strapped in and waiting for the engine to warm up a bit. The night had gone quite chilly, and Tris was grateful for the seat heater while they waited.

"Your friends are lovely," Priest said, breaking the silence.

"Don't tell them that though. It'll just go to their heads, and they're already too big," Tris joked in response.

"They care about you, and that's the best thing you can ask for in a friend."

Tris had no argument against that. "They've been with me for well over a decade. It's like I told you … we're like brothers."

"Will you tell them about us?"

A reasonable but tricky question and one they hadn't discussed. "I probably don't need to, since they've all assumed, anyway," he hedged.

He hated this uncertainty that had him confused about how to act, what to do. It really was no one's business but his own and if things didn't go the way he wanted them to, the fewer people who knew, the better. He breathed a sigh of relief when Priest didn't pursue it.

"So, what did Mona whisper in your ear?"

Dammit! Another trick question and the last thing Tris expected to come out of Priest's mouth. He thought back to Mona's gentle admonition. Was that really how everyone saw him, as the guy who chased good men away? He stumbled over his answer.

"She said you seem like a nice gentleman."

There was no way he was sharing the rest of her comment with Priest. He wasn't ready for that conversation just yet. They had barely begun to find their way to each other, and oversharing could be the death of anything more between them.

"Was that all she said?" Priest glanced over at him as they headed down the driveway.

"Yes," he lied.

"So, she disagrees with you, it seems."

Tris's brow furrowed in confusion. "What are you on about?"

"Earlier this evening, you said I was ungentlemanly, remember?" The teasing note was back in his voice.

"Belt up, Priestley," Tris groused, then burst out laughing when Priest did. "See? You're proving me right, no matter *what* Mona thinks."

"You're too easy to rile up," Priest answered. "And I really like riling you up."

And just like that, he was back in the guest bedroom at Sam's, kissing Priest and watching him walk out, his fine body outlined in the well-fitting clothes he wore. The sight of the man—the very memory of the way he looked—never failed to distract Tris. But he could flirt as well as the next guy if he tried.

"Is that what you're trying to do now?" That was a good effort if he said so himself.

"Trying? Are you *trying* to impugn my ability?" Priest was clearly having a hard time keeping his laughter under control. "Two can play, you know."

"Ooh, you wanna play, do you?" It was almost like they were riffing off each other, a harmony born of attraction, affection, and desire.

"Don't you? I mean, it should be second nature to you, Mr. Bass Player. Maybe I'm trying to appeal to your baser nature."

Tris laughed at the pun. "Good one, Mr. CEO, good one!"

This verbal sparring was more fun than he had ever had with a date. He wanted more. He wasn't ready for the evening to end, but he didn't know what arrangements Priest had made for his children's care, and he didn't want to push his luck by suggesting anything that would disrupt Priest's plans. He had sensed that there were issues surrounding the children, but he wanted to wait for Priest to bring them up. Still, he could ask.

"Will the babysitter go home when you get back?" That was a fair question, right?

"I asked her to stay the night, in case I didn't make it home."

Tris's heart skipped a beat. He ignored it and asked another question. "You're going somewhere else when you drop me off, then?"

"That depends." Now Priest was deliberately teasing him.

"On?" Tris squashed his impatience.

"On whether or not you have a better offer than home to bed."

Slowing his racing heart rate took a few breaths. *Calm down, Tris!* "Would you like to stay the night at mine, then?"

Priest exhaled sharply, Tris's first indication that he was not as cool as he'd been projecting. The knowledge shot through his system like a drug to the vein.

"There's nothing I want more, Tristan." This time, there was no teasing, no humor, just a quiet, intense seriousness that demolished the last of Tris's control.

How much longer would this drive be? "Can you go any faster?" he asked.

Priest laughed.

Chapter 15

Priest

The emotion spiraling through him was unlike anything
he had experienced since he lost his first love.

P riest had never made love on a boat before, and he would
marvel at that later, after he got off the boat and back
to life as he knew it. Tristan's houseboat was a world apart,
Priest's own little bubble of dreams and wishes and desires,
an alien space where he could be whoever he wanted to be
without considering who else would know or care, or how
it would affect anyone else. And as he pushed Tristan up
against the door they'd just closed with his hips, it was the
last thing on his mind.

Wait a second! Made love? Where the blazes had that
come from?

"Whatever you're thinking so hard about, it clearly isn't
me." Tristan's amused tone belied the displeased words,
but Priest felt no less embarrassed than if he had been
truly annoyed.

"Sorry. Was just thinking it's my first time on a boat. Is it any different on here?"

Tristan laughed and grabbed his hips, pulling him tight against his groin. "Are you asking me if I've brought other lovers to my boat, Mr. Priestley?"

Priest knew he was teasing, but a fresh wave of embarrassment washed over his cheeks. "No. Not at all. It's none of my business, is it?"

"You're running off at the mouth, mate. Shut up and kiss me."

Priest had no trouble obeying the order, pulling Tristan's face to his and opening his mouth over those tempting lips. He teased the divot in Tristan's upper lip with his tongue, then traced the path down to the corresponding space beneath his lower lip, before plunging into Tristan's open mouth and demanding his tongue. He shivered at the hunger in the kiss, the raw need for more that had them both shaking a little where they stood against his door.

"Let's take this into the bedroom," Tristan whispered when he dragged his mouth away.

Priest was too undone to answer with more than a grunt as Tristan led the way back to his room. They were too far gone to indulge in the niceties of extended foreplay. Priest needed to do more than feel the outline of Tristan's cock against his own. He needed the heft of it on his palm, in his fist. He needed the groans that would issue from Tristan's throat when he stroked him, the cries of need when he teased the head, the nonsense words that would fall from his lips when Priest made him come.

"Lost you again, have I?" Tristan murmured as he reached for Priest's shirt and began to unbutton it. "What am I going to have to do to stop you from being distracted?"

"Work faster," Priest said, finally finding his voice.

They fumbled around, laughing as they got into each other's way until they were both naked except for their underwear. Priest walked Tristan backward to his bed and fell on top of him, reveling in how good his skin felt, how toned his body was, how erratic Tristan's heartbeat was against his own, how they fell into the same rhythm of need and lust. He gladly gave Tristan the kiss he demanded as he pulled Priest's head down to his and sucked on his lower lip. Priest let him in, and they lost themselves to the flavor of each other.

As Tristan writhed beneath him, their clothed cocks riding each other, Priest could feel the lust raging in him settling into a burning need to come. It was probably too soon for everything his body was demanding, but he was determined to bring Tristan to completion at least once before he broke.

Turning them onto their sides, Priest pushed Tristan's briefs down his thighs and pulled his heavy cock free. It fit in his fist like it belonged there, and the precum already sliding down Tristan's length from its weeping tip eased his way as he drove Tristan closer to the edge, if his increasingly wild responses were anything to go by.

"You're not planning to cheat me, are you?" Tristan's breathless question came between hot kisses and hard tugs of the steel between Priest's fingers.

"Cheat you? How?"

Priest held his gaze, a teasing grin on his face. The twitching flesh encircled by his fist, the steel he found himself unable to release, told him he was a pump or two away from Tristan's first orgasm with him. Was that how he wanted their first time together to end? Probably not, but he needed to get the edge off his need to touch and taste. He didn't plan to stop at one orgasm for either of them.

"You know how," Tristan gritted out between clenched teeth. "I want more."

Priest's chest swelled with feral lust, his body tightening with need, his blood so heated that beads of sweat popped up on his skin.

"You'll get more," he reassured him. "As soon as I take the edge off."

Leaning in, he sealed his promise with a fierce kiss, curling his tongue around Tristan's and groaning when Tristan reached for his own steely erection and gave him a taste of his own medicine. Priest covered Tristan's hand and both their cocks and moved with him, pumping into their joined fists, loving the slide of skin on skin. He was on fire, a savage heat racing up his spine. He wanted to let his lover know how much he was enjoying their first foray into intimacy, but his brain stuttered on words and only grunts and groans made an appearance.

Their combined precum meant they were soon sliding along each other's length with increasing speed, their hips and hands pulling them ever closer to the inevitable edge. Priest had had enough lovers in his life to know that what he was doing with Tristan was more than humping. It was more than animal lust. The emotion spiraling through him was unlike anything he had experienced since he lost his first love.

Which should give him pause, because he wasn't interested in rebound sex, any more than he thought Tristan was. But as he leaned in to kiss the man swearing and crying out his name as he came, Priest knew it was more. What, he couldn't say, but he'd think about all that tomorrow, when he was back in his own home, in his own bed. For now, he let himself fall over the edge with Tristan, growling out his release in his ear, nipping the lobe and savoring the satisfaction of Tristan's sharp hiss.

Breathing was their prime concern as they came down together from Priest's first orgasm with another person in more than three years. The most that Jane had been able to enjoy in her last few weeks of life had been the butterfly kisses he'd been happy to shower her with, and truth be told, he hadn't even been able to get himself off. His heart had already begun to break in anticipation of her passing, and his whole focus had been keeping that sorrow away from her, only filling her days with as much joy as he could.

Holding his new lover in his arms, he let the warmth of unexpected gratitude wash over him. He hadn't known what to expect when he had sex for the first time with someone else after Jane's death, but he assumed that guilt would be high on the list. Instead, a swell of sweet relief rolled through his belly, settling in his chest, leaving him almost as spent as the orgasm.

Thank God he didn't have any regrets. That would have been an insult to the man whose gaze was piercing him even as they lay still breathing in each other's air.

"What?" he asked, letting his own eyes hold Tristan's. "Is something wrong?"

A slow, heated smile was his first answer, followed by a murmur. "Shouldn't that be my question? You got kinda quiet."

Priest didn't look away from him. Whatever was going to happen between them, they had to be honest with each other. So, even though he had no idea how Tristan would react, he refused to keep his thoughts to himself.

"I was just thinking how relieved I am not to feel guilty about this."

Tristan raised a brow at him. "Were you expecting to?" He cupped Priest's cheek in a surprisingly reassuring motion.

"I was. I suppose I'm still learning that grief and loss play out in various ways, with guilt being one of them. I was just enjoying the relief at *not* feeling guilty for making love with someone who isn't Jane." A mountain lifted completely from Priest's shoulders when he stopped speaking.

"Making love?" Tristan's stunned question, accompanied by a caressing thumb along his jawline, was a reminder that they were still facing each other with cooling semen between their sweaty bodies.

"I think so."

He might as well get that out there. It hadn't felt like anything other than lovemaking, though he would be the first to argue that neither of them could possibly be in love with the other. They hadn't known each other long enough for that. But the mutual hand jobs hadn't just been about sex. At least, not on his side of the question. Still, he wasn't ready for any deep discussion of what it had meant to Tristan.

Eventually, they'd talk about it, but for now, he just wanted to do it again, to do more, to bask in the satisfaction sparking like fireworks through his body, even eclipsing the relief. Giving another gentle tug to Tristan's now limp dick, he pulled off him and said, "Shower time?"

Tristan sighed and nodded. "I suppose we'd better, yes. Come on. Let's see if two can play there."

The shower stall in the ensuite bathroom was barely large enough for two, but Priest didn't care. He pulled Tristan under the warm water and slid his hands up and down his arms. Tristan's body was a dream when he was clothed and dry. Wet, he was a revelation. Priest reached for the shampoo, needing to play out one of his secret fantasies. Tristan's honey-colored locks darkened when wet, and they felt like heavy silk when he passed them through his fingers. The action stirred his blood more than he understood.

Rubbing his palms together to spread the shampoo evenly, he applied his hands to the lush hair on Tristan's bowed head. His lover's groans as Priest massaged his scalp sent his desire spiraling upward, and the feel of Tristan's silky locks between his fingers as he rinsed the suds away hardened his dick even more.

What did they say about older men and rebound time? Apparently, that law of nature didn't apply to him, because he was raring to go again, and it hadn't even been half an hour. He chuckled, unaware that he'd done so aloud until Tristan looked up, his face streaming with water, and asked, "What's so funny?"

Priest didn't reply immediately, just took Tristan's hand and placed it on his growing erection. Tristan's eyes widened but he grinned when Priest finally spoke.

"*Your* hair is one of *my* erogenous zones or an aphrodisiac or something like that."

A faint wash of color crept into Tristan's cheeks. "You like my hair, huh?" he replied, his voice low and rough with arousal.

"I like a lot of things about you." Priest tried to deflect.

"And washing my hair makes you hard. Shouldn't that be the reverse ... you washing my hair making *me* hard?" he teased.

Priest's eyes traveled down Tristan's belly to his own upstanding cock, thrusting out from the dark bush at its root, a pistol ready to shoot.

"You're a one to talk," he growled, then pulled him in for a deep, hungry kiss, the water washing over them.

Eventually, they parted and washed each other, getting distracted by holes, balls, and once again rock-hard cocks, teasing and edging each other until Priest broke away from Tristan's hands and knelt at his feet.

"What...?"

Tristan couldn't finish the question because Priest sucked him in, laving the head of his dick, and teasing the underside with his tongue. Before much longer, impatient hunger made him take Tristan all the way to the back of his throat. Tristan's long cock fit perfectly in his mouth with just a bit of stretch to make him remember what he'd been feasting on when they were forced to part. He licked the head when he finally pulled off, tickling the underside of it with his flicking tongue and holding Tristan steady so he could rock into his open mouth.

"Fuck my face, lover," he urged Tristan, his voice rough with lust and unpracticed deep throating.

They reveled in the intimacy for a minute before Tristan pulled on his short hair, forcing him to release him and look up.

"I'd rather..." he gasped, "do this," another heavy pant, "in bed." He stopped to catch his breath, then added, still panting, "So we can enjoy each other together."

His eyes were dark with need as they pleaded with Priest to agree. And who was he kidding? Sixty-nine with Tristan would likely kill him, but he was ready to sacrifice himself on the altar of desire to give this man everything he wanted and to take some joy for himself, as well. His every nerve ending was on fire for more. Rising to his feet, he planted another deep kiss on Tristan's waiting mouth, and they hurriedly got out of the shower, barely drying the excess water off their bodies before racing back to bed.

For one fleeting moment, as he positioned himself below Tristan and reached for his weeping cock, his thoughts went to the few other times he'd given a blowjob. The first experience had been grossly disappointing, emphasis on the gross part, and none of the others had been any more appealing. That was just one reason that he'd stopped doing what was not mutually enjoyable in the bedroom.

So why was it different this time? Why was his mouth watering for another taste of the man currently setting his heart hammering again? Maybe he'd finally found that irresistible someone who aroused all his senses. That epiphany faded when Tristan assaulted his steely erection with long swipes of his tongue, driving every other thought from Priest's mind except the need to give back in equal measure.

Tristan's dick was weeping when Priest pulled it down to his lips, stroking him as he sipped at the precum and savored the tangy-sweet evidence of his passion. A groan escaped his throat as the scent and taste of the man above him invaded his senses, adding to the jumble of sensations rioting inside him. Not knowing how else to respond to them, he swallowed Tristan to the back of his throat again, needing it to ground him in the moment, or else he would surely float away on a euphoric wave of feelings.

"Fuck, Priest," Tristan growled above him, releasing his dick to protest. "You're going to make me blow before it's time."

Sliding his tongue slowly back to the blushing cock head, Priest kissed it and said, "Any time you want to, I'm ready for you."

He wasn't even sure what he meant by that because he'd never swallowed another man's release before. What if Tristan wanted him to? If he could manage his gag reflex enough to take him to the back of his throat, swallowing shouldn't be a problem, right? All he knew for sure was that he wanted Tristan to be blissed out when he came, and he wanted to be the reason that that happened. So if swallowing would be the way to go, he was all in.

Tristan sucked him harder, taking his leaking flesh all the way to *his* throat as well, and Priest could no more stop himself from moaning than he could stop breathing. He couldn't concentrate for a moment, letting his lover's cock fall from his lips so he could suck in air to stop himself from spurting too soon. He didn't want this to end any more than Tristan did, it seemed.

"Together?"

Tristan's question pulled him back from the edge enough to agree before they were at each other again. Priest savored the weight of Tristan's heavy flesh on his tongue, loving how it jerked every time he licked the tip, and how, when he swirled his tongue around the glans, more precum leaked out. He pulled one of Tristan's balls into his mouth, mimicking his lover's action, and they ratcheted up the lust another notch as they played with each other.

A finger repeatedly caressing his pucker was the last straw for Priest. He broke, his balls tightening and spilling his seed into Tristan's waiting mouth. He had to catch the breath that had whooshed out when he came by releasing his hold on Tristan's dick, but he didn't let him out of his mouth this time. He just breathed around the invading muscle, feeling it spasm repeatedly on his tongue when he finally sucked him down again. A moment later, hot semen flooded his mouth, spurt after spurt of liquid satisfaction.

"Wow!"

Tristan broke the silence first, gasping as he left light kisses down the length of Priest's dick, licking him clean. His warm breaths caressed Priest's sated length lovingly. Priest agreed wholeheartedly, though he still didn't have enough oxygen to voice it quite yet. His lungs still heaved like a bellows as he replenished his air supply.

Leaving his own heated kisses of gratitude on Tristan's cock gave him the time to recover enough to say eventually, "You taste so good, love."

Tristan rolled off him, settling himself to the side without responding, leaving Priest to wonder if he had overstepped with the endearment. Just because they'd slept together twice now didn't mean Tristan was ready for pet names. That spelled a level of intimacy bordering on a relationship, and Priest still wasn't sure that what they had agreed to was the start of such a thing. He didn't want to appear to be rushing Tristan, but the word felt right on his tongue.

"You're very good," Tristan finally said after a long moment. "Between the words that come from it and the actions it does so well, your mouth is without a doubt a thing of wonder."

Priest wasn't sure how to read the tone behind the teasing yet complimentary words, and he wasn't ready for any distance between them just yet. If that was going to happen, he'd rather it happened in the morning when he was driving home again. Rolling to his side, he looked Tristan in the eye. Seeing no sign of amusement, Priest tried to read the expression on his face, but only a serious gaze greeted him.

"What are you thinking so hard about?" Tristan asked, reaching a hand out to stroke his cheek.

"I'm not sure if you're ready for endearments yet. Perhaps it was too soon?"

A smile lit Tristan's eyes before it touched his lips. "If I confess that you became 'babe' when you were sucking my brains out through my dick just now, will that make you feel better?"

This time, the teasing note was hard to miss, and Priest's heart rate slowed in relieved pleasure.

"Babe is probably better than 'baby,' since I'm older than you, wouldn't you say?" he replied, letting his own playfulness loose. "And it is definitely to be preferred to 'snookums' or 'boo.' Those and others of their ilk would completely emasculate me."

Priest hoped the rich irony in his voice wasn't lost on Tristan and clasped a hand over his chest in mock dismay. He was rewarded for his effort when Tristan laughed out loud, slapping his own hand over his belly as he did.

"God, you're such a drama llama," Tristan finally managed between chuckles.

Some imp of mischief seemed to have a hold of him, because before he even registered the urge to do so, Priest was tackling Tristan, rolling over him and growling, "A llama? You're comparing me to the South American cousin of a dromedary? As Shannon would say, how rude! At the very least, I am the camel himself." At Tristan's renewed shout of laughter, he added with a flourish, "Available for rides at your convenience."

Immediately the words left his lips, his pulse quickened with a mixture of dismay and hope. Though it wasn't his intention to do more, the thought of being buried inside Tristan's body or having Tristan inside his own was enough to make his spent cock twitch with renewed interest. Avoiding Tristan's gaze—because he wasn't ready to face disappointment—he rolled onto his back, keeping that thought to himself.

Yet he did nothing to halt the hope that took wing inside him.

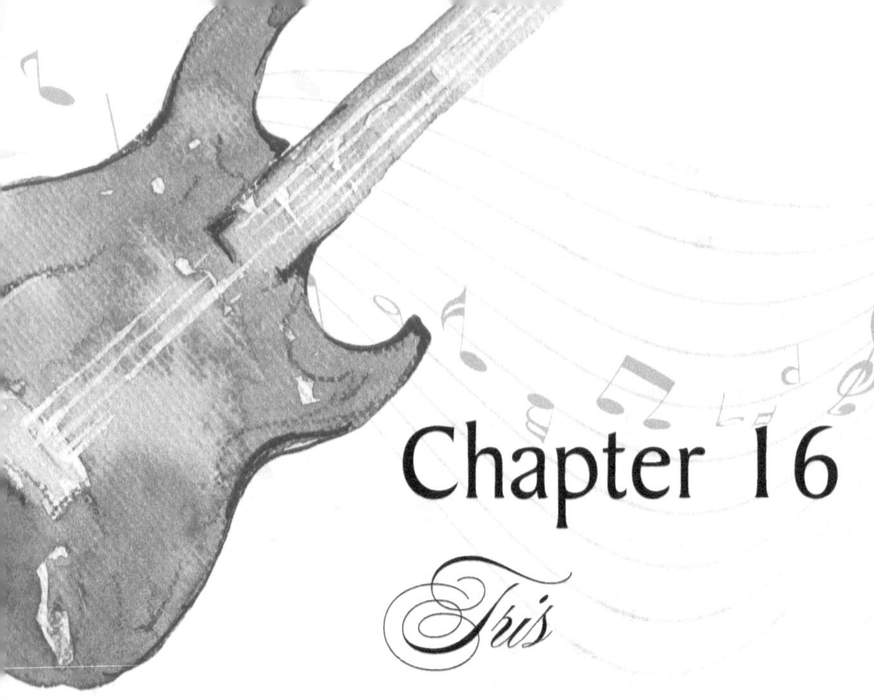

Chapter 16

Tris

*Contentment stole into those deep places in his heart
that he'd barricaded behind anger and cynicism.*

The morning sun slipped between the spaces in the half-open blinds, sending stripes of shadow across Priest's cheek. Tris traced the path of those lines with his eyes, noting how they highlighted his lover's high cheekbones and full lips. He was loath to wake the man who had so completely satisfied him before they'd fallen asleep spooned together. He never stayed with his hookups or allowed them to stay with him. There had never been a reason to … until now. Benedict Priestley had completely overwhelmed his senses and changed his mind about trying again.

As if he knew he was being observed, Priest began to stir. Tris felt the arm over his belly tighten before he slid his dark eyes open, looking directly into Tris's own.

"Morning," he said, his voice rough with sleep. "Been awake long?"

Tris smiled. "Long enough."

"Were you watching me sleep, Tristan? Was my snoring that bad? Or did I drool?"

Tris laughed. He had never laughed with a partner before, neither before or after sex. That must be significant, right? The sex had been intense, and still Priest could make him laugh the morning after. He basked in the complete freedom he felt to be himself and not put up barriers to guard his heart. It was exhilarating.

"We had a dog when I was little that snored loud enough to wake the dead," he began, watching Priest's eyes widen. "You were a great improvement," he added before his lover could protest, tugging him into his arms.

"Cheeky sod!" Priest squirmed in his hold, trying to escape when Tris refused to let him go. "I shall exact a fitting punishment as soon as I relieve my bladder. Unless..." He paused, eyeing Tris up and down before a mischievous smile tugged at his lips. "Unless you're into golden showers?"

Tris let him go and shoved him away. "Get away from me!" He crossed his fingers in front of Priest's face as if to ward off evil.

Priest's laughter trailed him into the bathroom and Tris hurried to do his own business in the other bathroom, coming back in to find Priest rifling through his bag and pulling out his bath kit. Apparently, Priest was ready to leave.

"Are you planning to shower without me?" Tris asked, refusing to let his disappointment show.

"Not quite yet. Just need to brush my teeth."

Tris released the breath he'd been holding. He'd have to see about breakfast in a bit, but first, he'd put on some tea, then come and do his own morning wash. Priest walked out in dark sweats and a t-shirt and pulled him into his arms.

"Do I get a good morning kiss now?"

"Not until I'm as minty fresh as you," Tris demurred, slipping out of his embrace. "Tea will be ready soon."

He hurried to wash his face and brush his teeth, changing into comfortable sweats and an old t-shirt before heading back into the kitchen. Priest was gathering ingredients for something, but Tris couldn't be sure what it would be. His heart swelled at the sight. Priest was willing to cook for him, instead of waiting to be treated like the guest he was. It charmed the place inside Tris that still believed older men thought they were entitled to courtesies that were not their due.

"You don't have to do that," he protested, moving closer to where Priest stood whipping up eggs.

"I don't *have* to do anything. But I *want* to." Priest turned to pin Tris with his gaze. "Now, stop protesting and get the toast going. I like lots of butter and honey with mine, thank you."

He went back to his egg mixture while Tris cut thick slices of bread from a crusty loaf and placed them in the toaster. Thankful that he'd done a bit of shopping earlier, he set butter and spreadable honey on the table, and laid out knives, forks, and two mugs.

"Would you like some fruit with breakfast?" he asked.

Priest nodded as he headed to the table carrying what turned out to be omelets done the French way, with slices of cheddar on the side. Tris put the container of pineapple slices that he hadn't yet opened on the table, adding cream, sugar, and lemon slices.

"As morning-after meals go, this is delightful," Priest said, winking at him. Tris chuckled, but before he could reply, Priest was at his side, pulling him around to face him.

"No more stalling," he declared. "Your breakfast for a kiss."

Tris's laugh was swallowed by hungry lips eating at his own and a silencing tongue demanding his submission. Tris opened for him, taking as much pleasure from their curling tongues as Priest gave him, returning it with a passion that had been simmering just below the surface of his skin since the moment he'd opened his eyes earlier to find himself tucked against Priest's chest.

When Priest pulled away with a groan, Tris grunted in disapproval. He wasn't ready to stop the taste testing of kisses.

"Omelets aren't good cold," Priest said against his lips. "Let's save the best for last, okay?"

Hauling in a harsh breath, Tris nodded and loosened his hold on Priest so they could sit and eat. The food hit the spot for taste and the pleasure of the company he was keeping. Contentment stole into those deep places in his heart that he'd barricaded behind anger and cynicism. How Priest had managed to poke holes in his reserve, to weaken his defenses to the point where he allowed himself to feel almost happy was something Tris didn't understand.

For now, he'd wait to try until he was alone again. Figuring out why he was floating on a cloud of bliss because he was sharing a simple homemade meal with a hot guy after an equally hot night of sex was something for the inevitable lonely hours.

"Do you cook often at home?" he asked, unwilling to let Priest know where his emotions had taken him.

"Yes. I always loved cooking with Jane, and after she passed, it was imperative that I keep doing it, not just because I needed to keep myself and my kids fed, but also because it made me feel closer to her." Priest's smile was warm as he continued. "It was bittersweet for a long time, but now it's a quiet joy, a sweet memorial."

Tris could understand that, and it added to the things he admired about this man he was so infatuated with. Could he really have a fulfilling relationship with him? It was still really early, and anything could happen before they got to where they'd talk about commitment. Just because Priest wanted to be exclusive didn't mean he'd be around for the long haul, even if he believed he would be. Tris had to be careful, even with his heart in overdrive at how much this man was proving to be everything he knew he wanted in a partner.

"It's your turn to zone out on me, is it?"

Priest's question startled Tris back into the moment. He didn't want to have to answer any questions he wasn't ready for, so he hurried to speak.

"I wasn't, honestly. I was just thinking how much I enjoyed breakfast with you."

It wasn't a lie, which was good since he didn't want to hide behind lies with Priest. But he was aware that not admitting to his doubts *was* prevaricating, which wasn't the honesty he wanted to nurture. He'd give it time. It took a lot to trust someone completely, and he'd been mistrustful for over a decade.

Priest didn't reply. He drained his mug and stood, beginning to clear away the breakfast things.

"No, let me," Tris said, feeling awkward and ashamed. He had messed with the vibe by getting lost in his head, doing what he always did and overthinking things. "You cooked. I'll clean up."

Priest watched him for a few seconds as if he were trying to decide how to respond. Tris hoped whatever he said next wouldn't bring their tryst to an abrupt end. But if it did, he had no one to blame but himself.

"Are we still on for a shower together?"

Relief rendered him speechless, so he nodded and smiled, stilling his hands so Priest wouldn't see the tumultuous effect that his question had had on him. He watched him walk away, then set the dishes down for a moment to calm himself before tidying up and wiping down the counters and table and heading back into the bedroom. The shower was going, and he could hear Priest whistling. Time to salvage the rest of their morning together and make another happy memory before his lover had to leave.

Shucking his clothes, he walked into the bathroom to find Priest already in the shower washing his hair.

"Couldn't wait to start?" he complained as he stepped in behind him.

Priest turned to him, suds sliding over his closed eyes before he swiped at his face and opened them, their gray dark and thunderous, like the silence growing between them. His words, when he finally spoke, did little to ease Tris's tension.

"I'll wait as long as I need to, Tristan, as long as I know you'll be there at the end with me."

That was a gauntlet thrown down if he'd ever heard one, and Tris was at a loss for how to respond. He wanted to assure Priest that he was willing to play the long game, but it was so much more than a game, this thing growing between them. And assurances should be two-sided, right? Was Priest going to promise him that he wouldn't keep Tris a secret from the people he cared about? Would he ever be invited into Priest's life, as he was already in Tris's? Could he ask those questions now?

Just because they'd been intimate a couple of times didn't mean they were at the place for him to make demands, even if he felt that they were reasonable, and Tris was anxious enough as it was without adding to it by introducing anything that might cause further awkwardness. Lost in his thoughts, he barely heard the heavy sigh before Priest was speaking again.

"Don't you think this conversation will go much better if you just tell me what you're thinking so hard about?"

Embarrassed at being called out for pussyfooting around the issue, even though Priest didn't know what it was, Tris looked him in the eye and said, "I was just thinking about when I'd get to meet the people you care about. You know, I show you mine, you show me yours?"

He hoped the line came out as amusing, even though he could barely crack a smile to go with the weak attempt at humor.

"Are you asking to meet my kids?"

Nope ... Priest was definitely not into beating around the bush. That was probably a good thing, since it forced Tris to speak up or shut up. He spoke up.

"Yes." Well, at least he'd been honest, even if he couldn't say more than the one word of affirmation.

"I'll let you know." Not the agreement Tris was hoping for, but it didn't sound like a refusal, either. "Now, enough chitchat. You need to wash away all those heavy thoughts and just be with me."

He reached for Tris, pulling him into his broad chest and leaned in, his eyes hooded, the air between them filling with expectation. Tris met him halfway, their kiss starting slow as the water pelted them, gradually getting deeper and hungrier. Pulling away with a gasp, he stopped Priest as he went for the shampoo to wash Tris's hair.

"Can we hurry up in here and take this back to bed?" He loved that Priest enjoyed playing in his hair, but he could wait to have his hands in it another time.

He was sure he'd never taken a faster shower with a lover before ... well, not after Devon. Priest washed his back, he washed Priest's. They lingered on each other's cocks only long enough to drag needy moans from their throats and rock into their fists. Priest claimed his mouth with breath-stealing thoroughness, leaving him shaking with lust.

Words piled up in his mind as he watched his lover exit the bathroom, his erection standing proud as he approached. The longing to touch, to taste, to feel, overwhelmed him, and he dragged Priest down on top of him, seeking his mouth while their bodies lined up and their cocks synced together.

"Mmm. This feels very good."

There was nothing to disagree with in Priest's sexy words. Tris's moan in reply was more than enough to seal his approval of what they were doing.

"Mhm!"

That wordless agreement would have to do. His mouth and hands were too busy, and Priest's own had flipped the off switch in his brain. Instead of words, more groans and sighs accompanied the skillful way that Priest loved on him. He played Tris's body like Tris played his guitar, eliciting the depths of soul from his instrument, making him speak in tongues of how much pleasure he was taking in what Priest was doing to him.

He must have been doing the same to his lover, whose answering calls swelled in tandem with his own cries until they broke free of the restraints they had been trying to keep on themselves and whatever was happening with them that was more than lust. A thick coating of their combined seed spread between them as the evidence of their passion shot from their cocks almost simultaneously.

Tris was glad that Priest held him down with the weight of his body or he would have floated away on the wings of ecstasy. Gasping for breath as they came down from their shared orgasm, he felt Priest's belly tremble against his own, their deliciously half-hard cocks still pressed together.

"What's so funny?" he asked, recognizing the movement as laughter.

Priest raised himself up on his elbows from where he'd lain, his arms wrapped around Tris as they'd frotted each other to release, and grinned.

"I was just marveling at the effect you have on me," he confessed. "Seems like I'm regaining some of my youthful stamina around you. Thank you." He leaned down then and swallowed Tris's answering smile in his kiss.

Much too soon for Tris, Priest had to leave. Although Tris understood that Priest had children who needed him and a life outside his bed, he was finding it difficult to hide his disappointment as Priest dressed and repacked his overnight bag. He felt like a useless lump on a log unable to do anything to keep the man to himself for more than a day. And the feelings Priest had set off in him were flooding his system, spreading warmth and desire and a curious ache as Tris followed him out to the front door.

He bit back the words that were building behind his lips, because there was no way he wanted to sound like a sappy, lovesick fool. So Priest's next words were a shock to his system. They hadn't known each other long enough, despite the deep and fiery sexual chemistry they shared, so how was it that Priest seemed to know exactly what he'd been thinking?

"I'll call you as soon as I get home. And I'll talk to my kids, I promise. I don't want you to be a surprise."

Tris closed his eyes and gulped to control the rush of emotion welling behind his lids. He nodded, then managed a strangled, "Okay, thanks." When he was certain that the foolish tears gathering in his eyes would not spill over, he opened them to find Priest standing right in front of him.

"There's so much I want to know about you," he said, cupping Tris's chin in his hand and stroking his cheek with a trembling thumb. "And there's a lot you need to learn about me. But I can't shake the feeling that this thing between us is bigger than either of us anticipated, and I don't know about you, but I'm having to do a lot of self-evaluation. I've never lacked for confidence before, but this is new ground for me. So I'm asking you to be patient with me, okay?"

He ghosted soft pecks over Tris's lips, dropped his hand from his face, and stepped away, his bag over his shoulder. He stood by the door, his hand on the latch, gazing down at it as though searching for the answer to his problems in the curved handle.

Then he looked up again and added, "I know it's a lot to ask, but I need you to know that I'm doing my best. You will meet my children as soon as I can figure out how to tell them who I am, who I've always been." He smiled wryly. "Take care, Tristan."

Tris followed him, watching from the doorway as he walked up the slope at the back of his house to his car. When he disappeared around the side to the front of the house, Tris closed the door and went immediately to his studio. He needed to work out his desire and his confusion. The band had a number of songs in various stages of completion. He chose one that was almost done and worked tirelessly on it, pushing all the feelings warring inside him into his fingers and the strings of his guitar.

Was this what falling in love was like? He'd thought he'd been in love with Devon, but this feeling, as though the whole world were settling in his chest, as though the sun was filling him with burning light and heat, was new to him. New and so very overwhelming. And he had no idea what to do with the sadness that still lingered, even as he set the guitar back on its stand and walked back into the living room.

What did he have to be sad about, after all? Sure, he and Priest had had phenomenal sex. Sure, they had touched something vital in each other, if Priest's parting words were to be believed. Sure, they seemed to get along outside the bedroom. But they had only agreed to be committed daters, nothing more. He agreed with Priest that they still had a lot to learn about each other. So missing him after only one night together was a bit over the top, wasn't it?

Who could he talk to about this? Tag was on tour, and he didn't want to burden him with his little crisis. Besides, he was the older brother ... *he* should be the one helping *Tag* through his emotional entanglements, not the other way around. He just knew he needed an ear, and soon, before he lost himself to doubts and recriminations, and the ever-present urge to rush back behind his walls and keep the world, and the threat to his peace of mind that Priest represented, far away from him.

What a brave one you are, Tris! He sighed ... he didn't disagree with his inner voice because the sarcasm was well-deserved. He was a coward and he'd lose any chance for what he wanted most—a happy life with a beloved partner—if he kept running away. Priest wasn't the only one with things to do to be ready for more. He had his own homework to do as well, it seemed. Facing his fear like an adult was absolutely imperative if he wanted to keep Priest in his life.

Chapter 17

Priest

Could he honestly give up his chance at a new love?

"908 Fenton, yes," Priest confirmed. "It'd be good to see whatever pictures they've taken too, so we can gauge what's important to them."

Priest hung up from the call with his photographer and settled back in his chair. Immediately his mind went to Tristan, whom he'd neither seen nor spoken to since the sleepover on his boat. It had been more than a fortnight, and though they'd texted almost every day, Priest had been glad to avoid the subject of his children. They were both busy. The band was producing another studio album, and *he'd* been kept very occupied wrapping up one project and overseeing the start of another in Ireland.

His crew was ready to start on Tristan's project. They were just waiting on the final approvals from the city, but had already begun to gather the materials they'd need for the renovation to begin once demolition was complete. Priest had just agreed to be there on the first day with Tristan to watch the work begin.

Truth be told, he was missing Tristan and feeling guilty about his procrastinating. He could never seem to find the right time to broach the subject of his sexuality with his kids. What would be a good time? On Sundays, when they all lounged around doing a whole lot of nothing? Or maybe tonight, after their family movie session?

Come to think of it, that was a really brilliant idea. If he could find a movie that would allow him to raise the subject naturally, that might make it easier for him to speak his truth. He couldn't think of any offhand, but he imagined he could search online and find some options. He'd have to make sure they were age appropriate.

And how the hell was he supposed to raise the subject without making his kids feel his own awkward embarrassment? Because if he were honest, he was embarrassed to have to have this conversation with two children not yet thirteen, only one of whom had finally reached puberty and needed her aunt to talk her through it. At times like these, he missed Jane more than he could say.

Which raised another issue ... was he ready for what seemed like it could happen with Tristan, with what it appeared was already happening in fits and starts? It was one thing to want a monogamous sexual relationship, but wasn't that much less than he really wanted with the rocker? If he was willing to out himself to his kids, this wasn't just about sex.

The phone on his desk buzzed again, forcing him back to work and by the time he got home that evening he had a plan in place for having the conversation he was dreading. It would probably be only slightly less painful than the one when his sister had called him to inform him that Shannon had begun her journey to adulthood and would he please remind her to wash her bedding in cold water.

He sighed as he recalled how uncomfortable he'd felt approaching Shannon to talk about supplies, which her aunt had insisted that he should shop for with her, so he'd know what she preferred if he ever had to go shopping for her. And yes, she could shop for her own supplies online, but why was he a coward? He was a single dad, and he should know what was happening in his daughter's life so he could protect her when he needed to. What would he need to protect his twelve-year-old from related to purchasing feminine products?

Shaking his head at his randomly embarrassed recollections, he parked and got out of the car, taking the sausages and sweet peas he'd bought for the bangers and mash they wanted for dinner. Something smelled delicious when he walked into the kitchen.

"I'm home!" he called out, not seeing either of his children.

There was no response. Popping the items into the refrigerator, he passed through to the hall and heard the television going. Mason walked out of the hall bathroom just then and grinned when he saw Priest.

"Dad! Did you just get home?"

"I did. What's cooking? Something smells good in the kitchen."

"Shannon wanted to surprise you, so she found Mum's book of handwritten recipes and followed the one for bread-and-butter pudding. We couldn't find anything to add to it apart from sultanas, so she says we'll have cream to put on top."

Priest's heart swelled with pride and affection at his son's words. He had always suspected that Shannon would be a mini version of her mother, and this take-charge attitude was evidence that he was right. Was he a terrible father for not being alarmed that his twelve-year-old had been in the kitchen on her own without an adult present to supervise her? And where had she even found Jane's recipes?

He walked into the lounge to find Shannon scrolling through the channels, no doubt trying to find something for them to watch after dinner.

"Good evening, Shan. What are we going to watch today?"

"I can't find anything I like, Dad. Mason says he doesn't care," she added, reaching up to accept the kiss Priest planted on her cheek. "Do you have any ideas?"

She cringed when she asked and Priest barely concealed his grin, remembering how much they had complained about the few movie choices he'd made in the past three years. Still, he wouldn't look a gift horse in the mouth. This was the perfect opportunity to introduce the movie he'd decided to watch for his big revelation.

"Have you ever heard of *The Half Of It*? It's a Netflix coming of age story," he added, glad he'd asked Erin, his admin assistant, what she thought of it. Turned out she'd gone to see it with her youngest sister and her friends for her sister's sixteenth birthday. "My assistant says it's a great movie. She's watched it with her teenage sister."

"Why were you even asking about it, Dad?" Shannon asked, turning to eye him curiously.

Priest chuckled, unsurprised by the astute question and thankful he had an answer prepared, because he knew his child.

"I was talking about movie nights at the office and sharing some of the ones we've watched. Erin asked if I'd seen it and when I said no, she told me what it was about. I thought *you* might be interested, even if Mason isn't."

That was more or less the truth. He'd searched it online and liked the synopsis, but wanted the opinion of someone younger before deciding. Now, he waited for his daughter's verdict, hoping she'd agree. It would definitely make things easier once the movie was done and they talked about it.

Shannon lifted her index finger to her chin and thought for a moment, then nodded. "Okay." Then she stood, abandoning the remote control and hurrying into the kitchen just as the timer dinged. "The pudding's ready," she announced. "I'll leave it in the warmer so it'll make the ice cream melt when we have it. Did you know we hadn't finished the French vanilla ice cream, Dad?"

"I did not. I'm assuming that's a good thing?" Priest asked as he pulled the ingredients out to cook the sausages.

"It's the best. French vanilla is the only vanilla flavor worth having, and I bet it'll be epic on warm bread and butter pudding," she declared emphatically.

Priest loved her enthusiasm for the simple things. That was another of her mother's traits that he admired. Wait ... that was twice now he'd thought about Jane in the last half hour without feeling like his innards were being shredded to bits by a world-sized, sharp-edged boulder. Healing ... who knew it could happen?

"Let me just go get changed and wash up and then we'll get to work."

The children had the potatoes that they had already peeled boiling by the time he got back downstairs, and once the bangers were fried to their liking, they heated the peas and Mason set the table. Dinner was delicious, and school concerns were the main topic of conversation as they ate. Shannon had a concert coming up, Mason needed a bit more tutoring in maths, and they'd both done well in their quarterly assessments.

"By the way, Dad," Shannon said as she and Mason served up three portions of her pudding with ice cream, "Sara's older brother is at uni in Birmingham, and he told her that Third Generation will be there for a charity concert at the beginning of July. Can we go, please? It'll be summer hols by then."

Priest's heart skipped a beat. He knew about the concert. It was to raise funds for the second Hope House being opened there that weekend. And really, there was no reason that they couldn't all go to show their support. That he'd get to see Tristan perform live was a perk he wouldn't refuse, and it *would* be nice if he could be with him openly with his children there.

"Mason, would you like that?" he asked his son. No matter how much he—and Shannon —wanted to see Tristan perform, he wouldn't allow Mason to feel left out.

"Sure, Dad. Can we meet the drummer? I can ask him about football."

"If he gets to meet John, I get to meet Tristan." Shannon's tone brooked no argument, as firm as his own was on occasion.

"I don't know about that..." he began, but Shannon interrupted him.

"Dad, you're friends with Tristan, aren't you? Why can't you just ask him?" Shannon's impatience with him was emphasized by the eye roll she didn't disguise before she put the rest of the pudding and ice cream away.

Friends? More like lovers. And now he also had to contend with his daughter's crush on the man he'd taken to bed. How was that going to turn out? He already knew there'd be drama if Shannon wasn't over the rocker by the time of the Birmingham concert, but he'd have to cross that bridge when he got to it. Right now, it was enough of a challenge to use the movie—about a girl helping a boy articulate his feelings for another girl while discovering that she herself has feelings for that same girl—to begin the conversation about sexuality in general. And it felt like the best way to tell his kids he was bisexual.

Realizing his daughter was still waiting for his answer, Priest hurriedly replied. "As long as you don't get your hopes up, that's fine. Just because I know them doesn't mean they'll be available. There may not be a meet and greet after the show, in which case you won't get to meet them, anyway." Picking up the tray with dessert, he walked ahead of them into the lounge.

He was proud of how he managed to skirt around her "friend" comment. Time enough to address what his relationship with Tristan was *after* the big reveal. Happy that she let the subject drop, he passed out the dishes with their treats, and they settled down to watch the show. He'd been a little worried when the show started really slowly that he wouldn't like it. Thankfully, the pace increased, and he was pleasantly surprised to find that he rather enjoyed it.

There was humor, pathos, affection, love, and heartbreak. Mason didn't seem bored, for which Priest was grateful, and he could tell that Shannon was full of questions and opinions. Before she could voice any of them, though, Mason surprised him by asking,

"Dad, what if you don't have someone to defend you against bullies?"

That had not been a question he expected to answer, and it made Priest wonder if his son was being bullied. Surely he'd have said something if he were? No time like the present to find out, even if it delayed his big announcement.

"If someone is being bullied, he or she should tell an adult if nothing else works. It's not tattling if you're protecting yourself from harm." He paused, looking between his children to see if they were telegraphing anything he might need to know about, but nothing was out of the ordinary, so he added, "Are you being bullied, Mase? Because if you are, I need to know so I can protect you, son."

"No, Dad, I'm fine, I promise. Shannon won't let anyone mess with me," he said confidently.

Priest could well believe it. He loved that his children got along and prayed that things wouldn't change as they got older.

"You have to speak up for yourself, don't you, Dad?' Shannon asked. "In the movie, Ellie was good with words, but she never said anything."

"You can't always defend yourself with words, can you, love? And given everything she had going on, it's not surprising that she needed a little help, is it?" What better way to start the conversation about difference ... all kinds of difference?

"I guess so. She was almost like an outcast, right, Dad? Because she was Chinese and she didn't have a mum..." Shannon began, before Mason interrupted.

"Just like us, Shan. But she had her dad, so that's okay." Mason had always been easier in his grieving of his mother, though he had loved her as only a child can ... simply and completely.

"And she played the organ in church. Does that really happen? Do the priests really not care who you like?" Shannon frowned. "Because I have a friend who has two mothers now, and she says they've stopped going to church because they're not comfortable there anymore."

Shannon totally ignored Mason's comment, and Priest wasn't sure whether it was because she had other things that she wanted to talk about or because she was avoiding the painful subject. He'd let it slide. He didn't want to get side-tracked from the main reason he'd chosen the movie. And her question was the perfect bridge.

"I suppose it depends on the church, Shan. Remember, this is fiction, and the writer may have wanted to keep the issues as simple as he could."

How much more should he say on the subject? Because it wasn't just the church that disapproved of same sex relationships. There were a whole lot of homophobic people in the world, many of them completely unconnected to any religious organization.

"What do you think about your friend having two mums?"

Shannon thought about it, and he gave her the space to formulate her response. "I guess it's a little odd," she finally said. "Because everybody knows you can't have a baby unless there's a man and a woman, right? But what about a boy in my class who has two dads? Neither of them can have babies, can they? His mum had him for them. She comes to get him from school every day." She paused, then added, "I think he's bullied sometimes, like Ellie in the movie. He gets into fights."

Priest's heart hurt to hear that. It didn't seem that Shannon knew too much about the boy, but enough to know he was like Ellie in the movie.

"It's very hard to be different at your age, isn't it?" Priest took a deep breath and plunged on. "In fact, it's very difficult to be different at any age. Grown-ups are as diverse as kids, and sometimes owning up to their differences can be just as painful for them as it is for kids."

"Why's that, Dad?" Mason asked, curling his legs under him on the sofa. "Aren't grown-ups stronger than kids? They can fight, can't they?"

Oh, the sweet innocence of youth! "You can't always deal with pain by fighting, son. Sometimes, you have to be more strategic. Ellie likes girls just like Paul likes girls. But some people like both girls *and* boys. How do you think *they'd* feel if anyone found out before they did or were ready to deal with it?"

"We had lessons in health class about how people are different. The teacher said it wasn't wrong to like who we like, especially since we're still learning who we are. I like boys and that's okay, but I guess it would be harder for me if I liked girls, or both of them." Shannon's voice was contemplative. "I don't know any girls who like girls or boys who like boys."

"Or maybe you just don't realize you know them because they haven't said," Priest pointed out. He needed his children to know that outward appearance never told the whole story about a person.

"So what does that make Aster, Dad?" Mason's question broke into his discussion with Shannon.

Priest was a little bit shocked that Mason had watched the movie so intently and was interested enough to ask such a mature question. It really was great, these Friday night movie sessions, because there were teachable moments aplenty, even with what might seem like fluff. And what better way to finally come to what he wanted to tell them than to answer Mason's question? He smiled to hide the sudden hit of nerves that had his palms feeling damp and his pulse speeding up.

"Well, if she likes both Paul and Ellie, we'd call her bisexual. I mean, it's not entirely clear in the story, but it is suggested at least, so maybe that's what she is."

"You like girls, right Dad?"

Mason was hitting all the best notes tonight, but Priest was still unprepared for the question. He inhaled slowly, forcing himself to keep his voice steady as he answered.

"I do. And I also like boys."

There ... he'd said it, come out to his kids. Now for the aftershocks. Keeping his eyes on Mason—he wasn't quite ready to look Shannon in the eye just yet—he waited for his son's response.

"So you loved Mum more than a boy and that's why you got married?"

"Very much, son. More than anyone else."

The truth was easy, especially now that the weight of his secret was finally off his shoulders. How had he not realized all this time that he was carrying it around like a boulder? Probably because until Jane's death, he hadn't had to think about it, and afterward, he'd been too bound by grief to care. Until Tristan.

"Do you still love her, Dad?" This from Shannon, whose eyes, now filled with shadows, watched him anxiously.

Priest reached out and pulled her to him. Mason sidled closer without being asked and Priest slipped an arm around him, as well.

"I will always love your mum. Always." It was no more than the truth, even if his feelings for Tristan were evolving into more than lust. "Is that all you want to ask me, Shan?"

He suspected that his too-mature-for-her-years daughter was concerned about who he might love next, about who he might bring into their little family to replace their mother. And it occurred to him as he held them quietly that he would do anything to preserve this unit, even if it meant giving up any hope of a relationship with anyone, man or woman, if his kids felt threatened by them.

Could he honestly give up his chance at a new love, though? He hadn't thought it could happen again, so he hadn't been looking, but if this thing with Tristan was to go anywhere, he had to believe it was more than possible now. And in his deepest heart, he wanted it. He wanted to feel whole again, something he'd only ever felt with Jane. But what if his children couldn't handle it?

Priest sighed. When had his life become so complicated? And what on earth was he going to do about it? He squared his shoulders, waiting for Shannon to lob her real question his way.

"Are you going to get married again?"

Priest smiled. He knew what she really wanted to know. "I don't know, Shan. Are you asking me if there's someone I want to take your mum's place?" he asked gently, giving her a squeeze. When she nodded against his chest but said nothing, he continued, needing to reassure them both. "I promise that even if I find someone else, no one can ever replace your mum." He couldn't count Tristan as that someone until they had cemented something more than just monogamous dating between them.

"But how, Dad? If you marry someone else, they'll be here with us, with you. Mum's not here. How can you be sure they won't...?"

"No one can replace your mum, I promise you. Love doesn't work like that. If I ever find someone else to share our lives with, they won't take her place because they will have their own." He paused, then added, because he needed to set their minds at ease, "And they will never take your place, either."

Shannon sagged against him, and he kissed the tops of their heads, then pulled back to ask, "Anything else you want to talk about, either of you?"

So far, neither of them had asked about his revelation. Was he going to escape with no comment or question? He'd take that lucky escape if it presented itself, thank you very much. He wasn't above avoiding hard questions until he had the answers he would feel comfortable sharing. Assuming they had nothing to add, he said, trying to be fair since it had been a particularly serious evening, "Opportunity going once," he looked at Shannon. "Going twice," he looked at Mason. "G…"

"Did you ever have a boyfriend, Dad?"

Priest sighed inwardly. No escape.

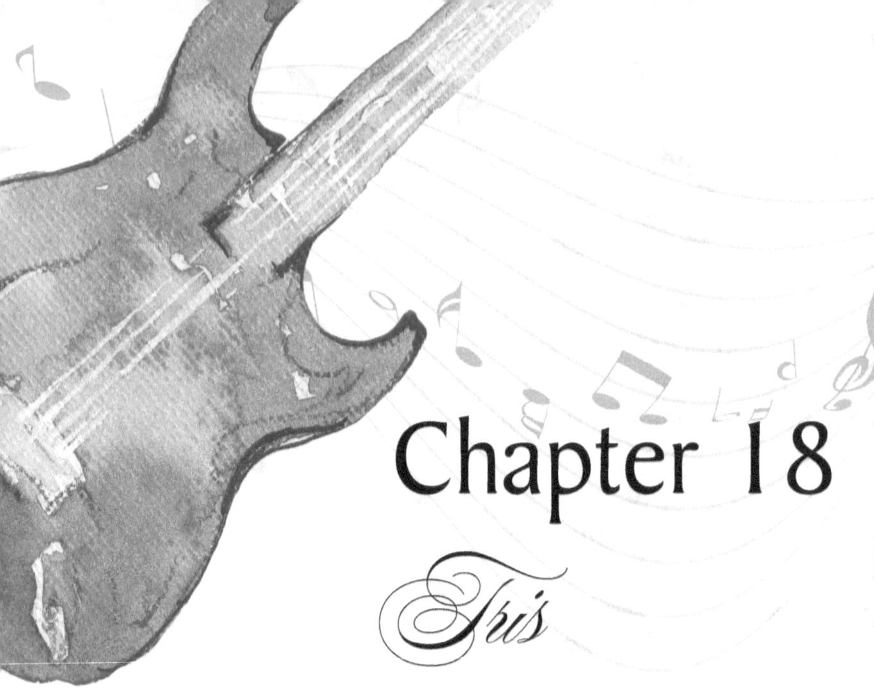

Chapter 18

Tris

Would sundaes be the only dessert on offer?

"So, apart from the Hope House benefit concert that first weekend in July, we've got a host of interviews and appearances and two other benefit gigs taking us out to the end of October."

Sam was reviewing the band's work schedule with them as he usually did after a major event was completed. The studio album was almost done, and they had a series of television and radio appearances planned to fill in the time before the July concert. They were playing the entire weekend with Blackbeat, the vocal band they'd met at Sam's the other weekend, who would be their opening act each night.

Thoughts of that weekend sent Tris's pulse skittering faster. It had been more than a fortnight since he'd last seen Priest, and he'd never had a harder time being an adult than in the past two weeks. Should he call? He nixed that idea at once. Priest was a busy man, as was he. The timing might be off, and he didn't feel like leaving a message. They'd texted, though nothing too salacious.

Although he'd been delighted to receive a message again this morning, it wasn't enough to scratch the itch that burned beneath his skin. He yearned for a bit of the bawdy with this man who had completely captured his attention. So much so that he was completely distracted during this meeting and found all eyes on him when he zoned back in after a hard squeeze on his shoulder.

"Tristan, we need your full attention, unless you need to excuse yourself to handle whatever's stopping you from focusing on business."

Sam's admonishment was delivered in a sharp, impatient tone. Tristan counted himself lucky that his words weren't accompanied by ripe swear words and outlandish threats of physical harm to the oddest places on his body. He fought the blush trying to cover his skin in deep shades of pink and apologized to the assembled group without offering any explanations for his inattention.

"Right. Do we have any other business?"

"Have we decided what we're doing about Canada?" Henry asked.

"We're still in negotiations with the promoters. We'll soon have full details of how many cities, dates, you know, the usual. Plans will be completely sorted in another week or two." Sam drained the beer in his bottle and looked around the room again. "Anything else for now?"

Tris spoke up before he forgot again. "Are we doing a meet and greet in Birmingham? Priest's kids want to meet us." They didn't need to know that the children had asked specifically to meet him and John.

"What do you want to do?" Sam asked. "Whatever it is, I'll arrange it."

"I think it would probably be a good thing to do at least one after the Sunday afternoon show. Make it special … you know the thing. VIP tickets cost a bit more, but we can give Priest and his kids three passes for free. I'm sure he and all the other parents of underage fans will appreciate not having to spend their entire Sunday out with their offspring. We don't have to do any more than that one unless you lads want to." Henry looked at the others who all nodded their agreement.

"I know my woman will appreciate me getting back to the hotel before the wee hours every morning," John joked.

"I'll get those passes to you ASAP, Tris."

Sam's exaggerated wink reminded Tris of Lucy trying to get one over on Ricky with her friend Ethel. He chuckled, giving Sam a playful two-fingered salute. "Or you can just include them in the VIP package like everyone will get sent, yeah?"

"You are such a spoilsport, mate," Will chimed in before Sam could reply. "Where's the fun in that?"

"Fun for whom, exactly?" Tris lobbed back. "You're such a bunch of gossipy old biddies."

General laughter followed the good-natured insult before Sam said, "Okay, that's settled. I'll have them gift-wrapped so you can make a big deal of it when you deliver them."

Tris shook his head. Trust Sam to completely ignore his objection. It was annoying and yet endearing how all his mates were rooting for him and Priest even without knowing much of what was happening between them. They all thought that Priest was a good man, and they just wanted Tris to find his someone. That they thought it was Priest was comforting to his mistrustful heart.

He could never let them know that secretly he was as excited as they were to be able to hand deliver the passes. It seemed he would get to meet the kids after all, though Priest hadn't given any indication of when that would be. Aside from asking if he was available on Friday night, Priest had said nothing else about the kids. Was he going to have another sleepover on the boat or was Tris to be invited to his home for their Friday night family time? That might be too much to ask for on such a short acquaintance, but a guy could hope.

He hadn't wanted to ask what he needed to be available for, just said he had no plans. He hadn't heard back yet, which was part of the reason he'd been so distracted in the meeting. Would they be eating out or doing something else this time? He'd do anything or go anywhere with Priest.

That thought brought him up short. Was that really how far gone he was with Priest already? They'd known each other what, six weeks, seven? How could he already be thinking about the total and absolute surrender of his mind and heart to a man he was still getting to know? A man whose family he hadn't met, even once? A hit of fear flashed through him. He wasn't ready for such heavy emotions, was he? He sure as hell didn't *feel* ready.

"Tristan!"

His name, spoken sharply again alongside a cuff to the shoulder roused him from the panic he'd been about to sink into. He blinked and looked over at Rory, who was eyeing him with concern.

"Are you alright, mate?" Tris managed a quiet yes, but Rory looked unconvinced. He continued, his gaze never leaving Tris's face, "We're heading out for dinner. You joining us?"

What did he have to gain by moping about on his own? "Yes, of course," he answered, forcing outrage into his tone. "Were you lot planning to abandon me to my own devices?"

"You haven't exactly been fully present today, Tris. The others are already on their way. I volunteered to wrangle you." His chuckle helped to settle Tris's shaking heart.

"What am I, a wild horse on the American prairie?"

"And an ornery one, as they would say." Rory dodged the punch Tris aimed his way as they headed out together.

He did his best to focus on his friends for the next couple of hours, even managing not to check his cell phone when it vibrated in his pocket. He'd been distracted around them enough, and he didn't feel like fielding nosy questions about his preoccupation. Still, by the time he got back to the houseboat, the phone was a burning weight against his leg.

Locking up as soon as he got on board, he headed to his bedroom and lay across the big bed, silently hoping that the messages that he'd been receiving all evening—each vibration a torturous reminder of his need to connect with his crush—were from Priest. There were four, though they had felt like dozens at the time, his anxiety no doubt giving their arrival added weight. His hand shook slightly as he unlocked the phone, seeing that they *were* all from Priest.

He read each one slowly, savoring the words as though he were sipping the finest wine.

[Priest: Good evening. It's been a while. How are things?]

The time stamp was minutes after they'd all gotten to the restaurant. The second message arrived ten minutes later, and the last two almost together half an hour later.

[Priest: I've talked to my children. They had questions, only one of which had anything to do with the subject. You would have been proud of how I handled it.]

Why would Priest care what Tris thought of how he'd handled coming out to his kids? Maybe the insta-love bug had bitten him too? The word jolted him, like a strong electric shock to the system as he re-read that second message. Love? Surely not! The third and fourth messages were apparently sent together.

[Priest: I was thinking about ripping the plaster all the way off by having you over for dinner on Sunday evening. I'll cook, and you can get to know each other.]

[Priest: Oh, and did you remember to ask about the meet and greet? If you come over, they're sure to ask.]

He answered everything in one long reply.

[Tris: Good evening. I'm okay. Went out with the lads for dinner. Congrats on coming out. I'm glad it wasn't awful. What question did the kids have? I'd love to come over for dinner. What shall I bring with me? And yes, I mentioned the meet and greet in today's meeting. We'll be doing it after the Sunday afternoon show. I'll let you know everything when I see you next.]

He'd have a whole day to fret about how he'd be around Priest's kids. In the meantime, he'd need to think of something cool to take with him as a hello gift. What kind of gifts do preteens enjoy? And as their dad was a wealthy man, what could Tris give them that they'd appreciate? Remembering his own youth, he knew the gift of cash had usually been the way his father's cronies and old family friends dispensed with that duty. Tris didn't think that that would be appropriate since he didn't know the kids, and anyway, it was his first time meeting them. It wasn't as though it was their birthday or anything else that would require it.

His cell phone vibrated on the bed next to him, and his face heated when he saw that Priest was calling him.

"DeVere," he said, forgetting to adjust his usual greeting to indicate that he knew who was calling. He was suddenly inexplicably nervous, which had opened the door to let every thought fly free.

"Priestley," Priest replied, clearly mocking him. Before Tris could respond, he added, chuckling, "Do you always answer your phone like that?"

"You answer your phone like that," Tristan shot back at him almost defensively.

"Yes, when I'm working. Sometimes I even give my full name." Priest grinned. "Not usually when I know who's calling me."

"It helps people know if they've called a wrong number," Tris hedged, not really sure why his default was to answer the phone like that.

"Maybe it's to make you seem more aloof than you are? You know, to put distance between you and whoever is calling? Is that how your mum taught you to answer the phone?" When he didn't immediately reply, Priest ended, "Anyway, it doesn't matter. I got your text message and wanted to talk a bit, if that's okay."

Tris cleared his throat before speaking this time. "It's okay. I like talking to you too. And no, my mum made us say 'This is the DeVere residence. How may I help you?' Very proper she was. And still is."

"Is that how she answers the phone when you call?" Priest was clearly amused.

When was the last time he'd called his parents? Shaking his head, because he didn't need to go there at the moment, he said, "Yes. it is."

A memory fell into his head just then ... his father answering the phone in his office. Tris could see him as clear as day, his body ramrod straight, his mustache hovering like wings above his top lip, the little dot of hair in the middle under his bottom lip trembling as he said "DeVere." He spoke again without thinking.

"My dad answers the phone like that. Very brusque and business-like. He hates talking on the phone. He claims that you really can't read the people you're speaking to if you can't see their faces."

Tris had always admired that brisk way his father had about him, and now he realized he'd copied it so he could be like his old man. He shook his head again, wishing this little epiphany hadn't come in the middle of his conversation with the man he was interested in. The older, bisexual single dad.

Hurrying to change the subject, he began to speak at the same time that Priest did.

"So, what...?" he began, then stopped because Priest was saying,

"Every little boy wants to be like his dad in one way or another." As if he knew Tris's secret desire and the hurt it had caused when they fell out.

"Thankfully, I'm not a little boy anymore. Thanks for helping me realize I have to upgrade my telephone etiquette."

His voice was sharper than he'd have liked it to be, but what was done was done. He couldn't take back either the words or the tone, and he was done apologizing for being who he was.

"I didn't mean to be critical, Tris."

Priest had shortened his name again, and the sound of the diminutive short-circuited his brain a second time, so that Tris had to focus hard to hear what he'd said. And then he felt like an idiot for making the man think he was angry.

"No apologies necessary," he reassured Priest. "I've just never noticed it before. I like that you listen to me well enough to notice that."

And even if the conversation was unexpected, it wasn't uncomfortable, aside from his embarrassing overreaction to Priest's observation. Time to move ahead, away from the faux pas to something else. Like what to take to dinner at the Priestley house.

"What should I bring with me for dinner?"

"You don't need to bring anything. The children love to show off their cooking skills when I have guests over."

"I'd still prefer not to come empty-handed," Tris insisted. "What about a dessert? What do your kids like?"

Priest chuckled. "An easier answer would be what they *don't* like," he replied.

"You said they like to show off their cooking skills. What if I bring the fixings for a sundae and make it with them?"

"That sounds like something they'd both enjoy." A pause, then, "I'm looking forward to seeing you again."

Priest's voice had gone low and sultry, and something flared to life in Tris's belly. "Just seeing me?" he asked, meeting seduction with seduction.

"To begin with, yes."

Priest's words were a low growl of sound this time, sending the flare higher, as much because of the sexy sound as because of the suggestive comment. Would sundaes be the only dessert on offer? How would they even get a taste of the adult kind without Priest's children being any the wiser? Just because he'd come out to them didn't mean they were ready for him to be in a relationship of any kind with another man, did it?

That reminded him. "By the way, what question did your kids have?"

Priest sighed gently. "Mason wanted to know if I'd ever had a boyfriend, and Shannon asked if I had one now."

"I imagine the first one was easier to answer than the second." Tris kept his tone as light as he could. Priest didn't need to know how his heart leapt in his chest. What had been his answers? Should Tris ask or wait to be told? Would he seem too eager if he asked? Dating was so much harder than hooking up. One had to know so much about pacing and expectations and appropriate reactions. It was exhausting!

"Don't you want to know what I told them?"

I guess I should have asked. "I do, but I wasn't sure I should ask," he confessed. He didn't want to lie to Priest by pretending that he was certain of anything between them.

"You can ask me anything, Tristan. I'll answer whatever questions you have. I don't want to hide from you any more than I do from my kids."

The flare in Tris's belly spread heat through his body at the promise in those words.

"Thank you," he managed after clearing his emotion-clogged throat. "So, what did you say?" Because truth be told, he wanted to know the answers to those questions as much as Priest's kids did.

"I had a few hookups in college, but they weren't looking for more, so no serious relationship until I met Jane." He chuckled. "I gave the children the cleaned-up version of that answer. Of course, Mason wanted to know if I had loved any of them as much as I loved his mum. That was an easy no. I hadn't loved *any* of them." Priest paused, inhaling slowly before continuing. "In fact, at least two of them turned out to be total arseholes whom I couldn't even remain friends with after our hookup."

"So, you're still friends with the others?" Why that mattered to Tris he couldn't say, but he wanted to know.

"Let's say I'm friendly with the few I'm still in touch with," Priest said. "We don't see each other often enough for the fledgling friendships to grow beyond buddies who meet for a drink if they happen to be in the same city at the same time. Two of them are married with children. Another is still single and apparently not interested in ever tying the knot."

Now it was Tris's turn to inhale deeply. "And what about Shannon's question?" He knew what he wanted to hear, but he didn't dare let even a ray of hope in. He needed to know if he and Priest were in agreement about what was truly happening between them.

"I told them I'd made a friend recently. I said I wouldn't give them a name until we were both sure that we wanted to be more than friends. Mason wanted to know if it was Uncle Lanny. Lachlan is my business partner and best friend. My kids love him like family."

"So he's like a brother to you." *Thank God for that!* "How did they take that news? That it wasn't your friend?"

"They were curious, of course, but they didn't seem surprised. I promised them that no one could take their place, and that I'd always love their mum. That was Shannon's worry."

How was Tris supposed to respond to that? Realistically, he knew no one could replace Priest's first love, but what did that mean for him, if he decided to brave the waters of romance a second time? He didn't know how to feel about being second best, if that's what he would be. *Getting ahead of yourself, Tris. You don't know how this will play out.*

Pulling himself together, he said, "I can understand that." Because he really could.

A pause followed his words before Priest said, "Well, I'd better get going. We're going out tomorrow for a fun day. I promised them we'd go to the circus a month ago."

"Sounds like a good time. Enjoy yourselves. I'll see you on Sunday."

After he rang off, Tris lay mulling over the conversation. Priest didn't seem unduly worried about his kids' curiosity, and he hadn't hidden anything from Tris, as far as he could tell. He wanted more between himself and Priest, and he was fairly certain now that Priest had the same idea. Thoughts of his ex filled his head then, and he bolted up, not willing to lose himself to the hurt that still lingered even after all these years. He wouldn't go there.

Playing in his studio for almost two hours wore him out enough that when he finally fell into bed after a hot shower, he fell asleep almost at once. Morning rolled around far too quickly, but Tris didn't linger in bed. He had promised to take Henry's and Gen's twins for a day out, and he'd agreed to take them wherever they decided they wanted to go by the time he got there.

Driving along the motorway gave him more time to think about Priest and what it would be like to have dinner with him and his children. Aside from his sister's and Henry's own, he hadn't been around children much and didn't know how to meet ones he'd never met who were already in double digits. He'd been around the ones he knew when they were still in the womb, so they'd always known and accepted him as Uncle Tris. Priest's kids knew him only as the bass guitarist for a rock band. They'd probably expect him to act a certain way, and he hoped he wouldn't disappoint them, though he doubted he had the rockstar panache they were looking for.

"Uncle Tris!"

His ears rang with the twins' greetings when he stepped into the Thackery home half an hour later. High fives and fist bumps were exchanged before they ran off at their father's bellow.

"Get back in here and finish your breakfast or you're going nowhere," Henry threatened them.

It was an empty threat, but the boys disappeared into the kitchen. When Tris got there, Gen was placing a full English breakfast before her husband.

"Tris! Good to see you. Thanks for taking the monsters off our hands today." She walked around the kitchen island to plant a soft kiss on his cheek.

"It's not a problem at all. I'm glad to help." And it gave him some extra time with the boys, time away from his thoughts, time to enjoy being a part of a family that cared about him. He didn't want to get emotional in front of the boys, so he asked for a glass of water and gulped it down, pretending he didn't see Henry watching him with knowing eyes.

"So aside from babysitting today, what else have you got going on this weekend?" His friend lifted a brow as though warning Tris not to try anything, like lying.

Tris chuckled. "You act like you've got your eye on me," he deflected, though he knew it wouldn't be for more than a moment or two.

"And you act like I can't read you like a book," Henry retorted with a snort. "Now stop trying to distract me and answer the question."

Tris shrugged. "I'm going out for dinner." That was the truth.

"With?" Gen asked, taking over the grilling from her husband. She slanted a knowing grin his way and winked.

Tris groaned. "I'm sure you know who," he groused. "You two are as bad as all the others."

"Where are you going?"

"His house."

Their approval swelled around him. "Ah, meeting the kids at last, then? That's a good sign." Gen's voice was hopeful. Tris wished he could wholeheartedly agree.

"We're still in the early stages," he said. "It seemed fair that I meet them since he's met you all twice already."

"You're either delusional or a fool if you think there's nothing more to it," Henry said, sipping from his mug. "I hope you're not stalling, Tristan!" His friend never full-named him unless he was dead serious. "He seems like a great guy. You should give him a proper chance and not let anything get in the way of something real here." He paused to point his fork at Tris. "Don't forget, I know you."

Which was nothing more than the truth. His bandmates had all known how he avoided anything more than one-night stands, refusing to let his hookups even sleep over. Not getting close to anyone meant not risking getting his heart handed to him again. But he'd already admitted that he was ready to go there with Priest. Now all he had to do was trust him.

Easier said than done.

Chapter 19

Priest

Even quick kisses with this man could undo him.

The children had enjoyed the circus immensely, as had Priest, who hadn't had a fun day out in a very long time. Well, not a child-friendly one, anyway. His thoughts went back to his day out with Tristan that had ended with a sleepover and the morning after. *That* kind of fun had also been in severely short supply until now, and he wanted more. He wanted it back and he wanted it with Tristan.

"Dad, we can't decide," Shannon groused. "Mason wants to get ice cream, but I want merch."

Priest braced himself for the request he knew was coming. He knew what his daughter was doing, but he liked to pretend he wasn't aware that she was being as subtle as a sledgehammer to get him to buy them both a treat and some circus merchandise. She wanted ice cream as much as her brother did, but she also had her eye on t-shirts showcasing some of her favorite acts.

"Can you please decide?" she asked in a huff. As if she thought he would choose one of their requests above the other. She knew better.

He chuckled. "You may have one t-shirt and a scoop of your favorite ice cream. Mase, you can get two scoops of yours or whatever other treat you'd like."

He turned to head toward the shop where all the circus swag was for sale and froze when he saw who was heading toward them with two boys in tow. That was Tristan, wasn't it? He felt hot and flustered, but Shannon's hand squeezing his bicep pulled his gaze down to her.

"Dad!" she stage-whispered. "Isn't that Tristan DeVere? The bass guitarist from Third Generation?"

Priest pretended to notice him for the first time. "It looks like him, yes."

He hoped his daughter wouldn't feel the way his pulse had kicked up at the sight of the rocker. She didn't need to know how the man affected him.

"Can we go say hello, please, Dad? Please!" she implored him, not even trying to hide her efforts to secure his agreement. "I'll give up my treat if you say yes. Please, Dad!"

Priest chuckled. His girl was something else. "You don't have to give up your treat, Shan, but maybe he doesn't wish to be disturbed. He's with other people."

"But if we just kind of walk over as if we're just wandering around..."

She pulled on his arm a little harder to emphasize her point, looking up at him hopefully, and Priest couldn't help the laugh that escaped him. If this were a cartoon, she'd be the cute kitten trying to get her master to give her a snack with large blinking eyes and an innocent smile.

"Besides, the ice cream stall is closer to them. Come *on*, Dad!" She was full on begging now.

By this point, Tristan had also noticed them stopped in the middle of the busy pathway. A tentative smile creased his cheek, and Priest's body warmed.

"Dad, come on! He's seen us!"

Shannon's impatient whisper-shout of excitement could not be contained. As they approached him, it was clear that other bystanders had also recognized him. Would he be mobbed or was Priest just being ridiculous? Tristan didn't seem overly concerned about his privacy right now, so Priest wouldn't spend any more time fretting about it.

"Tristan! What a pleasant surprise!" Priest extended his hand and squeezed Tristan's own when he responded to the handshake. Shocks of electric awareness shot up his arm, and Tristan's eyes popped for a second with that same reaction before they released each other.

"Likewise," Tristan said. "I'm guessing these are your children?" he asked, his face expressionless.

"Yes. I'm Shannon," Priest's daughter introduced herself. "And this is my little brother Mason." She stuck her hand out and Tristan took it, shaking it gently before doing the same to Mason.

"It's nice to meet you both, Shannon and Mason. These are my bandmate's sons, Nicholas and Lucas."

Before he could continue the introductions, one of the boys chimed in. "You can call us Nick and Luke," he said. "I'm Nick and he's Luke." He pointed to his brother, who was clearly his twin. "Uncle Tris isn't our real uncle, but he's our family."

Aww! Priest barely managed to suppress the sound at the boy's words. It was sweet how they claimed him as their own, despite him not being a blood relation. That right there was true family love. Not quite sure how to respond to that, Priest was relieved when Shannon took over the conversation, as only she could do.

"We were going to get ice cream for my little brother," she informed them, and ignored Mason's disapproving "Hey!" to add, "Would you guys like some too?"

"That's where we were going too," Nick replied. "Uncle Tris promised us two scoops each and some fairy cakes." He was apparently the spokesperson for the brothers, as Shannon was for his two. "What's your favorite flavor?"

Priest caught Tristan's gaze, holding it a moment while the children discussed best ice cream flavors. Tristan's smile lit up his eyes for a moment, the banked heat in them mirroring the way Priest was feeling just then, before he looked down at his charges.

"Well, lads, what's it to be?"

Priest tuned out the boys' replies as Mason said, pulling on his arm, "You know what we want, Dad. But can we have them over for dinner? They're in football too."

Mason rarely used his puppy dog eyes on Priest, in part because his sister did a good enough job for the two of them, but also because by nature, he was much more laid back than Shannon was. This was unusual for him, so Priest gave his full attention to his son as he replied.

"I don't know, son. Tristan will have to ask their parents' permission." He turned to Tristan to find them all watching and listening. "Are we ready?"

Once the children had their treats and were sitting together discussing what it was like to have a rockstar for a dad and how much time they got to spend with all the band members and who else had kids, Priest turned to Tristan.

"Mason asked to have the boys over for dinner. I told him that their parents would have to agree. Can you just ask and let me know later? Then you can bring them tomorrow."

It wasn't ideal. In fact, he hated having to make the invitation, but his children would always come first, and this was a small thing to ask. It wasn't as though he and Tristan would be able to manage any adult time together the next day, anyway, so two more children wouldn't make a difference.

"I'll ask."

Tristan's rather curt reply sent Priest's eyes to his, but he was studiously looking elsewhere. "Is everything okay?" He didn't like it any more than Tristan did, but he had to at least make the effort. There was no guarantee that the Thackerys would accept the invitation.

"Everything's fine." Whatever had happened a moment earlier had apparently blown over, or else Tristan was doing a great job of pretending that it had. "What time do you want me over tomorrow?" he asked next.

Smooth change of topic. Priest went with it. There was no point in belaboring a subject that Tristan was clearly not willing to discuss.

"How much time do you want to spend? The children's bedtime for school is nine, so we'd have a bit of time together after."

"I can come later, like five, if I'm on my own. If the boys come with me, I'll have to get them back home by eight, and I know they'll want to spend time with your lot, so maybe three?"

"Sounds like a plan."

"Your kids are very well-behaved," Tristan said next.

Priest had the impression that he was making conversation to cover the silence that was settling between them. He didn't like this strange new awkwardness, but he wasn't sure how to fix it aside from following whatever path Tristan led him down.

"That's mostly down to their mum," he answered. "She was the disciplinarian."

"And you were the pushover?" Tristan's sardonic tone relieved the tension in Priest's shoulders.

"I was not!" he protested. "I was just more easygoing. We all did what we were told."

"Uh huh ... so now you're saying she was bossy?" Tristan teased.

"She was ... decisive," Priest amended with a smile.

How was he managing to talk about Jane without falling apart? Tristan must really have some kind of magical power. Or maybe it was just time for Priest to move on with someone else who could make him laugh and lift his spirits without seeming to try. Whatever it was, he would take it.

"Seriously, though, I can't imagine that you don't have *something* to do with them being such good kids," Tristan added.

Priest wondered what he was thinking to make him say that. "Most lessons about good behavior are learned really early," he said.

"You've been their only parent for a while now, so I'm sure you've reinforced what they already knew and added to their store of lessons, yeah? Don't sell yourself short. I don't imagine being a single parent is easy."

It wasn't, so Priest smiled but didn't comment. The children finished their treats and Tristan called to the boys. "Time to go, lads. I promised your mum I'd have you home for dinner. Say goodbye to your new friends."

Priest watched Shannon's face fall for a second before she schooled her features to show complete disinterest. That was impressive! How had he not noticed that his daughter was growing up so fast? When had he gone from being able to read every expression on her face to this? If he hadn't been looking at her, he would have missed the shift completely. And he had a good idea why too.

Tristan waited patiently while his charges said their goodbyes, oblivious to how he had crushed Shannon's hopes of spending more time with him. Priest heaved a quiet sigh. Her crush had only been enhanced by the few minutes they'd spent together. She'd been remarkably cool about meeting him in the flesh, though Priest knew she was less likely to act like a rabid fan than other girls her age.

She might be vocal and forthright, but there was still a level of shyness at her core that kept her from making a complete spectacle of herself where anyone but her family would see. She wouldn't mind letting her feelings out completely when they were at home, but in public no one would know any more than that she was an avid fan of his music. Suddenly, it seemed like a good idea to have the boys over with Tristan. She'd get more time with him, even if she had to share his attention with three other children. She would get to show off how much more mature she was than a bunch of ten-year-olds.

Was he going to be the reason his daughter got her heart broken for the first time? Should he warn her about not expecting more from Tristan than a star would give a fan? What would happen if Tristan got close to his kids and then things tanked between them? Wouldn't that also break her heart? It was a dilemma for another day. For now, he walked his children back to the shop where Shannon bought one of the miniature mechanical elephants that she could manipulate into different poses.

At home, he decided to wait until he heard from Tristan before broaching the subject of dinner with guests the next day. They ate leftovers before the children went to their rooms, leaving Priest alone in his study, trying not to let his mind wander to the man currently occupying all of his available brain space.

Today's meeting between Tristan and his kids had been serendipitous, making any future time together less likely to be awkward. Still, if the boys couldn't come for dinner, Priest would have to find an innocuous way to explain Tristan's presence, since the invitation had not primarily been meant for him. For entertainment, he imagined it would be easy enough to talk Shannon into playing for Tristan. Maybe he'd play a duet with her to start off, to help her relax enough to do it on her own.

How could he ensure that Mason didn't feel left out? He might have been the more relaxed parent, but he had also always been fiercely protective of both of them as individuals. Shannon was getting to meet her crush, and until Mason could meet *his* favorite band member, he had to ensure that his son didn't feel cheated. He hoped the boys would be able to come. Then everyone would get what they wanted, and if nothing else, he'd at least get to be where Tristan was.

Eventually, after whiling away a couple of hours listening to music, he went up to bed, his thoughts full of the next day's plans. When his phone buzzed five minutes after he'd settled under the covers, he knew without looking who it was.

"Hi." Lord, he'd never been as lost for words as he was around this man.

"Hi." Tristan's low voice echoed in his ear, sending warmth flooding through his body. "Henry and Gen are taking the boys out tomorrow, so they won't be able to join you for dinner."

Priest's heart sped up. "Will *you* still be able to come?" His children could have their dinner date another time. It had been an open-ended invitation.

"Will I be welcome without them?" Tristan's voice held a note of teasing laced with uncertainty.

"They may be momentarily disappointed until I tell them that the boys can come the next time they're available. And you'll be a great consolation prize. After all, which kid who isn't the child of a rockstar has one over for dinner? Even Mason won't have an issue with that!"

Tristan's chuckle chased away Priest's earlier apprehension. "Whew! I guess I'll have to make do with second best if I want to see you, then," he joked.

Something in the words set Priest on edge. Tristan wasn't second best, and if they made this thing between them work, Priest would have to make sure to show him that. Still, he didn't want to get too serious and spoil the moment, so he let it slide.

"It was good to see you today," he said instead. "A really lovely surprise."

"I wasn't sure how you'd feel about me meeting your kids unrehearsed," Tristan admitted. "I know you like to plan…"

Priest interrupted him. "How do you know that?" Was he really *that* transparent?

"It seemed like a safe assumption to make given how long it took you to get back to me."

Priest chuckled. "Touché!"

"It was great to see you too, by the way." Tristan's voice had gone low again.

A weighty pause lingered between them. Part of Priest wanted to hold onto it, to savor the heated tension, while the other part felt it like a bird ready to fly away.

He fisted his hand, then opened it, as if to set the bird free, and said, "I'd better get to bed. I'll have a bit of cleanup to do before you get here tomorrow. You said five, right?"

"Yes. I'll see you then. Goodnight, Priest."

"Goodnight, Tristan."

Over breakfast the next morning, Priest broke the news that only Tristan would be coming for dinner. Mason was disappointed for about a minute, while Shannon was clearly elated. Then Mason said, "Dad, can I ask him to play a video game with me?"

Shannon frowned, and Priest could see her struggling with herself. He could almost hear the arguments she wanted to sling at her brother against the idea and he let her be. He had no idea whether or not Tristan played video games, but that would be something he could do to bond with Mason. The thought was as unsettling as it was compelling.

"You can, son. I don't know if he will or not, but it never hurts to ask."

The doorbell rang promptly at five and Shannon rushed to answer it, knowing that Priest was right behind her since she wasn't allowed to do so without an adult present. Her smile was wide and welcoming as she opened the door and Tristan returned it cheerily. Onesie woofed in welcome, widening Tris's smile.

"Hello, Shannon!" His tone was as open as his smile, and Priest watched his daughter preen when Tristan added, "Lovely to see you again."

"Hi, Mr. DeVere. Thank you. Please come in."

Tristan stepped inside and she closed the door behind him, before he added, "Who's this?" he asked, putting his hand out for the dog. "And where's your brother?"

"This is Onesie," Shannon said. "He's friendly. You can pet him. And Mason's probably still in his room deciding which game he wants to ask..."

Priest interrupted her. "Why don't we let Mason explain himself, Shan, hmm? Don't want to steal his thunder, do we?"

She shrugged, feigning disinterest and failing dismally. "Sure."

Priest hid his grin at her tacit disapproval of his directive, casting Tristan a glance over her shoulder. "That's very kind of you, love. Why don't you go up and get your brother?" Without waiting for her to respond, he turned to Tristan, indicating the shopping bag he carried. "Let's get those things into the fridge, shall we? Come through."

They were barely in through the archway leading into his kitchen before Tristan chuckled. "That was not a pushover move back there, Dad," he teased, but Priest could hear the note of admiration in his voice. "She didn't even *try* to argue." He placed the bag on the kitchen island, sitting on one of the stools and adding, "You were having me on."

Priest smiled. "Some things just go without saying. Besides, it gives me the chance to do this."

Leaning across the counter, he bussed Tristan's lips, briefly accepting his tongue when Tristan offered it. Then he pulled away, not willing to start something neither of them could finish any time soon. His hands shook just a little as he unpacked the ingredients that Tristan had brought with him. Even quick kisses with this man could undo him, it seemed.

Tristan was lavishing Onesie with attention, but both children returned before he could answer Priest, and Mason immediately asked the question that had been burning on his tongue all day.

"Will you play a game with me after dinner, please, Mr. DeVere?" At least he'd asked politely, but Priest couldn't let him get away without a greeting.

"What did you forget, Mase? Before you can ask a guest for favors, you should…"

Mason hung his head for a moment, then looked directly at his father and said, "I should say hello first."

"Good lad. Why don't you do that, and then you can ask again, hmm?"

The boy turned to Tristan, an embarrassed flush on his cheekbones, but he held the star's gaze as he spoke. "Hi, Mr. DeVere. I'm sorry, sir."

Tristan smiled at him. "That's okay, Mason. Tell me about your video games, then."

Shannon's eyes narrowed, and Priest could see a storm brewing if Mason took any more of Tristan's attention than she thought he should have. Time for another intervention.

"Mason, please take Mr. DeVere into the lounge. Shannon and I will bring the refreshments."

"Why does *he* get to go with Mr. DeVere?" Shannon complained as soon as they were in the kitchen. "He doesn't even care about their music!"

Her frustration and ire were almost palpable, though Priest could tell she was doing her best to contain them because she kept her voice low enough so only he could hear her. He sighed. Today wasn't a good day to try his patience, given his own unstable reactions when Tristan was around, but he *was* the adult *and* the parent, so he'd act the part.

"He gets to go for that very reason, Shan. He doesn't have as much in common with our guest as you do. Is it too much to ask you to be kind to your brother and let him find a way to form his own connection with Tristan? Unless there's some other reason you wanted to be the one to entertain him while I got the snacks ready?"

He was putting the finishing touches to the platter he'd been preparing when Tristan arrived. Stacking the last of the crackers and studiously keeping his eyes off his daughter, he waited for her to respond. He knew the answer to his question—he wasn't an idiot, after all—but he needed her to confront her own motivation so he could help her deal with it.

Aside from the fact that she was just too young for Tristan, he already knew that Tristan's interest would never be in her, no matter how old she was. It was his job to protect her, even if it meant hurting her feelings a little bit. Assuming, of course, that she was honest with him. If she couldn't bring herself to admit what the real issue was right now, he'd cut her some slack, since he hadn't told either her or Mason about his bisexuality until two days ago, and only because he'd been forced to do it. Three years was a long time to keep that admission to himself.

The platter was ready, and Shannon still hadn't responded to his question. Priest wouldn't pursue it. Now wasn't the time.

Stealing a grape, he said, "If everything is okay, will you take this in for me? I'll bring everything else."

This time, he watched her expression and saw when she understood what he was doing. Thank heavens for a sharp kid. She smiled, looked up at him, and said, "Yes, Dad. I can do that." She picked up the platter and just before she turned to head into the lounge, she added, "Thanks, Dad." Then she was gone.

"Crisis averted," he murmured aloud as he set drinks, plates, forks, and napkins on a tray and followed her.

Sometimes, it really *was* the little things. He'd take his victories where he found them. Larger issues lay ahead for both of them. A reprieve right now was gold.

Chapter 20

Tris

His mind went back to their sleepover
and heat rode up his spine.

Watching Shannon walk into the lounge bearing a platter of delicious treats made Tris smile. She looked so mature and capable, and behind her he could see her father's face beaming as he also watched her walk ahead of him, managing to avoid the dog who was doing his best to get in the way. She placed the platter on the coffee table that Mason had cleared earlier. The little boy had been excited to learn that Tris played video games with Henry's sons, and they'd spent the few minutes reviewing what games Mason had and how good he was at them.

"Please help yourself, Mr. DeVere," Shannon said when the platter was set in front of him.

Priest placed a tray with drinks and other things, and Shannon handed out the plates and then sat next to her dad and waited while Tristan helped himself. Her gesture reminded him so much of Gen—the perfect hostess—that he wondered if she was remembering how her mother entertained guests and tried to emulate her.

It was sweet and he needed to tell her so without encouraging the crush he was almost sure she was harboring. That was not a situation he was ever comfortable with, and it would be even worse because she was a child, and more specifically the child of the man he had been to bed with.

"Thank you, Shannon," he told her with a smile. "You're such a great hostess."

Her answering blush was reward enough for his effort, and he looked up to find Priest regarding him with a pleased smile. Score! Having her father approve of his response somehow made it even better that he had tried to be careful with her. It could only up his boyfriend cred in Priest's eyes, right?

Whoa! Slow down, Tris! Where had "boyfriend" come from? It wasn't something they'd discussed. His heart kept pushing him to make things more serious than his head was ready for. Were Henry and Gen right? Was he putting obstacles in the way because he was afraid of rejection? But really, who *wasn't*?

"Are you okay, Tristan?"

Priest's question brought him back to the moment and to the fact that he hadn't put anything on his plate. He cleared his throat.

"I'm fine. I just ... remembered something I have to do." It wasn't exactly a lie, even though Priest's raised left brow and amused gaze said he knew it wasn't exactly the truth, either.

He helped himself to a few grapes, some crackers and cheese, and accepted a glass with what looked like lemonade. The silence after he sat back with his food, his drink on the table in front of him, gave him time to pull himself together and prepare for conversations about general topics unrelated to his confused musings.

"So, who plays piano?" he asked, having taken note of the piano by the window.

He knew from his company's website that Priest played, and that Shannon did as well because Priest had told him so. Still, he wanted to engage her in something of interest to her so she didn't feel left out, since he'd already done the same for her brother.

"My dad and I do," she answered, unexpectedly shy.

"I'll bet you're better than he is, right?" he teased.

Shannon blushed and Priest chuckled. "One day soon she probably will be since I haven't played in a while. And in my limited experience, it's not exactly like riding a bicycle. Muscle memory only happens as a result of continual practice, so I can't just sit in front of it and play like a pro without some advance warning."

"Dad is really good," Shannon offered, looking over at her dad with a puzzled expression. "He plays duets with me sometimes."

Tris grinned, assuming she didn't understand why Priest was downplaying his talent. He wanted to hear them play together. Maybe after dinner he'd make a request. For now, he turned his attention to Mason. "And what do *you* play?"

Mason eyed him warily. "I play football," he answered after a long hesitation.

Tris chuckled. "So, you play with your feet, not your hands, huh? That's cool. Do you think you'll want to play rugby like your dad?"

Mason shrugged. "I dunno. We have a footie club in our school. Only the older boys get to play rugby."

Everyone dug into their snacks then, ending all talk for a few minutes. Halfway through, Priest rose, setting his plate down. "I'll be right back," he informed them, excusing himself to the kitchen.

"Mr. DeVere, do you only play the bass guitar?" Shannon asked a second after her father left the room.

"No. I also play the cello, like my younger brother, Tag."

"Tag?" Mason's brow was a furrow of confusion.

Tris could see him trying to decide if he should ask the rest of his question. He chuckled and gave him the answer anyway. "His name is Teagan, but we all call him Tag."

"Does he play the bass guitar too?" the boy wanted to know next.

"No, but he does play the viola, as well."

"Did you always want to be a rockstar?" Shannon asked, casting an irritated glare at her brother.

"Not for a while. I always knew I wanted to play music for a living, though. That's what I studied at uni."

Shannon's eyes widened. Tris wasn't surprised at that. Most fans never thought about who their favorite entertainers were outside of their role as musicians. They were not real to fans, not people with lives and ambitions and goals. They were their instrument, or their looks, or their reputations.

He watched her think for a moment before she continued, "What do you study to become a rockstar?"

He silently applauded her for not asking, as so many others might have done, why he needed to go to uni to play in a band. She had asked a great question, so he'd give her a serious answer.

"I studied music theory and particular genres including classical and jazz music and took performance classes. You can do all sorts of good things with a degree in music," he told her. "You just have to be sure that that's really what you want to do, because being a musician is hard work, like every other profession."

The children asked more questions about his life, his family—he sidestepped those as much as he could—and other things like his hobbies and pets. Priest came back in to hear the rest of the conversation, but he contributed nothing other than an attentive ear, chuckling sometimes at their questions or Tris's answers. Eventually, he called them all to dinner.

The meal was delicious. Tris loved lamb, and shepherd's pie was one of his favorite ways to enjoy it. The fresh garden salad and lightly steamed mixed vegetables made it a perfect meal. He went back for seconds of the pie and rubbed his belly when he polished it off as well. He could feel Priest's eyes on him, but he avoided his gaze, instead looking over at Mason, who had also cleaned his plate.

"That was good, wasn't it, Mason?" he asked with a grin. "Your dad cooks well."

Mason grinned with him, nodding and licking his fork to get the last remnants of the potato and meat mixture off it. Priest chuckled while Shannon rolled her eyes at her brother, and Tris felt a new warmth settle in his chest. Memories of his own childhood, seemingly idyllic until his sexuality brought public notoriety to him and shame to his father, clamored to resurface, but he pushed them away. This was not the time for the emotions they would bring.

"I promised Mason I'd play a game with him, but I'd love it if you and your dad would play for me first, Shannon," he said. "If that's okay with you, Priest?" he added, turning to his host.

"That's fine with me," he began, "if you're not going with the original plan for dessert." He raised a brow in question.

Tris nodded, having forgotten that he'd planned to make dessert with the children. But before he could try to sort out a new plan, Priest continued, "Of course, I'm sure that Shan will love helping me make it so she can show off her skills in the kitchen, yes?"

Tris's admiration for Priest shot up sharply. He was really rather good at the whole parenting thing, because he'd obviously anticipated and had a plan in place to address his daughter's inevitable upset over not having their guest's full attention. Tris looked over and smiled his gratitude, then glanced at Shannon who was a little pink in the cheeks. Mission accomplished, it seemed.

"Right then," he said, turning to Shannon. "I'll help your dad clean up while you go and pick the music you want to share."

"And Mason, you can choose the game and bring it and the controls down so you can play down here."

"Well played, Dad," Tris teased when they were safely away from little ears. "I can't imagine how you managed dating while parenting."

"I haven't brought any of my dates home," Priest admitted slowly. "Until now."

Suddenly unable to suppress the need coursing through him, Tris moved to where Priest stood at the island and reached for him, heedless of how exposed they were. He leaned in and kissed Priest's lips tenderly.

"Thank you."

He smiled into the next kiss and let Priest in when he swiped his tongue across Tris's lips. They made out for a few seconds, stifling moans and keeping their bodies away from each other. Finally, their need for air broke them apart, and Tris reoriented himself to where he was.

"I guess that will have to suffice for now," he said. "And a good thing too. What if one of the children had wandered in just now?"

Priest shrugged, placing the plates in the dishwasher. "They'd have gotten an eyeful, and they'd have learned who the new guy I met was."

"You wouldn't mind that?"

Tris was curious more than anything else. Priest hadn't seemed overly eager to come out to his kids, so why would he be okay with them finding him snogging Tris? And if what he suspected was true, Shannon was deep in a teenage infatuation. How would she react when she discovered that she and her dad liked the same man? He had no experience with preteen girls, aside from his younger sister, but based on those memories, he didn't think things would go well for Priest.

Did he want to be the cause of disharmony in a household where, for the most part, the members loved each other and got along well together? Coming from a fractured family himself, he didn't like to think about such a consequence for the Priestleys because of him. He had no idea how he could fix that, short of removing himself from the picture, but at this point, he knew that was not going to be easy, even if Priest agreed with him. And Tris wasn't at all sure that he would.

"I don't know." Priest's honest reply was oddly refreshing. "Anyway, let's not buy trouble. And thanks for your help. Now let's go be entertained."

Shannon proved to be an excellent pianist, well above her age range in ability. She forgot where she was, once the first wave of shyness passed, and Tris watched as she lost herself in the music she was playing. Her focus was completely on the notes she was reading, her body swaying gently to the music.

"How long has she been playing?" he asked Priest, who was sitting with a large cat on his lap, stroking its fur absently.

"She started sitting with me on the stool when she was three, and by the time she was four we knew we had to get her lessons."

"She's really good."

"Make sure you let her know that, please. It will make her night and maybe the rest of the week."

The melodious sounds ceased and before their applause had ended, Shannon said, "Dad, can you play with me now, please?"

She beckoned him over and Priest went willingly. The cat eyed Tris as if wondering if he should risk his lap, then settled instead in the seat that Priest had vacated. Tris's eyes took in the size and sexiness of the man as he walked over to his daughter. He was breathtaking with or without clothes. His mind went back to their sleepover on his houseboat and heat rode up his spine.

Shaking his head at his randy thoughts, he focused on the pair at the piano, loving how they flowed together as they played a bit of Pachelbel's "Canon in D" first, followed immediately by some of Mozart's "Turkish March." A final fun piece, "If I Only Had A Brain", had Mason singing along and giggling.

Tris was utterly charmed as he watched the little family. Priest may have lost the love of his life, but they had shared the gift of two beautiful children, one of whom was very talented in music. He'd never thought about having children of his own because he'd decided relationships weren't for him, and he would never willingly become a single dad.

But watching and listening to the three people completely engaged with each other, he wondered if he was missing out.

"Brilliant!" he exclaimed, clapping enthusiastically when they stopped and took their bows. "I'm truly blown away by you two. Excellent playing, Shannon," he added, beaming at her and loving the sweet blush that rode up her cheeks as she said shy thanks. "And you're not as rusty as you pretend to be, Dad," he ended, turning to Priest with a raised brow.

"Thank you." Priest's eyes held his for a moment longer than necessary before he turned to the kids and asked, "So, who's ready for dessert?"

"Me!" Mason yelled.

While Priest and Shannon left to make the dessert, Tris played Mario Kart with Mason, loving how competitive the boy was and relishing the tense excitement of the game. They were halfway through when dessert arrived, and Mason happily paused the game to devour his treat. The sundaes went down well, and Mason predictably asked for seconds. Everyone laughed, but he clearly didn't care.

"Just another scoop, son. Shannon, help him, please." When the children walked out of the room, Priest added, "I despair of getting any alone time with you. How are you so cool?"

"I'm enjoying myself. The family closeness is very sweet." He fought to keep envy or hurt out of his voice. He was happy for Priest and his children. He just wanted to share in the warmth and quiet comfort that they had.

"I'm glad. My kids can be a lot sometimes."

"They're fine. I feel like I've known them for more than a few hours."

Priest nodded. "Mason will love you forever," he said with a chuckle. "Anyone who plays his games with him and clearly enjoys being with him is a hero. He's the quieter one, but he feels things deeply, especially since Jane passed." A shadow slid across his face for a second, then disappeared as he ended, "And you already know Shannon thinks you're the moon and the stars."

Tris laughed. "Not even my siblings think that, and they *like* me. But I'm glad she finds something to admire in me."

Priest grinned knowingly. "Yeah, we both know what she finds to admire in you," he teased.

"So, you're saying *you* know, as well?" Tris replied, daring to flirt just a bit. Words were easier and safer than actions when others were in the vicinity.

Before Priest could reply, the children returned, but the look he shot Tris said the conversation, or the flirting—he couldn't be sure which—wasn't over. He acknowledged the challenge with a raised brow, then turned his attention back to the game. He loved how much the boy enjoyed every twist and turn of the game and how he seemed to lose himself in it in the same kind of way that his sister immersed herself in her music.

Needless to say, Mason came out on top, probably because Tris had been distracted by the boy's focus, enjoying it too much to be particularly careful about his own plays. Tris didn't care. He returned the child's enthusiastic and uninhibited hug when he jumped up, thrilled at having won, laughing at his exuberance.

"Bedtime in fifteen minutes, Mase," Priest said at last, interrupting the boy's celebration. "You've both got school tomorrow. Time to say goodnight to Mr. DeVere."

"Can I call you Mr. D?" Mason asked, looking up at Tris hopefully.

"Of course. You both can," he added hastily, catching Shannon's sour expression. He'd forgotten that she was still in the room watching them play.

"Goodnight, Mr. D," Mason continued, completely unaware of his sister's reaction. "I hope you'll come back again."

He walked over to his dad and hugged him. "Can we have him over again please, Dad?" he asked, not even attempting to lower his voice. "He's cool." He didn't seem to care that Tris could hear him.

"I'm sure if Mr. DeVere's got any more free time and you both ask nicely, he'll be happy to return. Maybe he can even bring your new friends with him next time."

While Mason picked up his game paraphernalia and set the area they'd played in back to rights, Shannon came over and extended her hand. "It was nice to meet you, Mr. DeVere," she said politely.

Tris took her hand with a smile. "It was nice to meet you too, Shannon. You play really well, and I enjoyed listening to your performance."

He wouldn't push her to shorten his name if she didn't want to. He'd be the first to admit that he didn't understand much about women, and girls were even more of a mystery to him, so he'd let her choose how to interact with him. He just didn't want her to be too angry at her brother, though he could well understand why she might be. Her handshake was decisive, and she returned his smile, holding his gaze for a moment before retreating to bid her father goodnight.

"I'll come up to check on you both in a bit, Shan." Priest managed to sneak a kiss to the top of her head before she pulled away from their brief hug.

Alone with his host again, Tris watched as Priest approached him, his eyes warm. He remained where he stood and waited for Priest's next move. Without hesitation, Priest stepped into his personal space, planting his body against Tris's, and wrapped his hands around Tris's neck, holding him while he took the kisses they'd denied themselves all evening. Tris mirrored his hold, letting Priest have his tongue, and they ravished each other, stifling their groans when their hardening bodies strained against each other.

"I'm sorry we can't do anything more here," Priest finally said, dragging his mouth away from Tris's. "I can't risk the children finding out..."

"It's fine," Tris said, though his heart fell at those words. "Your kids are great. Anyway, I have to go."

He pulled himself away from the enticing sight of Priest's swollen lips, willing his heart to slow down and his face not to show the creeping hurt that he didn't want to feel. He knew they couldn't lie together in Priest's home before his children knew about their relationship, and Priest had already said they didn't know who the person was that he was seeing. Logic said Priest was right. But Tris's heart had no interest in validating any reasonable response to the situation.

"Thanks for inviting me over," he continued, heading to the front door, doing his best impression of pleased and happy, even if his body was still buzzing from their heavy make-out session moments before in direct contradiction to his emotions. "I had a lovely time, Priest."

Priest had been following him silently and when Tris turned to face him at last, he could see Priest's conflict etching his features in frustration.

"Tristan..." he began.

Tris interrupted him. "It's fine, Priest, honestly. You're right. We need to be careful around them. They won't necessarily understand without an explanation that you'll need to give them first," he said, feeling proud of himself for not sounding more than slightly disappointed.

"Will you come again?" Priest asked, holding Tris still with hands on his shoulders.

Tris understood the question for everything Priest meant. Did he really want to return to a house where Priest's children didn't know who he was to their father? A house where he'd have to be careful not to let any of his growing feelings show? Was it fair of Priest to ask him to do that? He may not still be in the closet with his kids, but he still wasn't being fully open with them about his interest, and Tris didn't think he could handle that. He needed to be acknowledged, especially knowing the full reason for his notoriously disastrous breakup with Devon.

"That depends on you, Priest," he told him honestly. "Have a good week."

Priest let him go without responding, which seemed like an answer to Tris. Still, he waved as he rode away, refusing to let him see how despondent it made him to think he was still being kept a secret from the people who mattered to Priest. The jury was still out on whether or not he'd see Priest again before he told his children about Tris, and even if he wasn't happy with it, Tris was determined to abide by the decision he was almost sure he was going to make.

Chapter 21

Priest

Priest's heart broke, but he shoved the pain away.

The last thing Priest needed was to have to entertain anyone while his head was still full of worry over the way his date with Tristan had ended. It had been pretty obvious to him a week ago that Tristan was upset with him for not being willing to show his kids who Tristan was to him. And Priest could understand that. No one liked to be anyone else's dirty little secret, which was likely how Tristan felt, and with good reason, if Priest were to be honest.

Why couldn't a forty-five-year-old man just be completely honest with his kids? He knew they loved him, and even if Shan would be cross with him for a bit, she'd get over it soon enough. Teenagers were moody like that. But more than his concern for how his daughter might react was a basic fear that he would let someone new in and forget Jane. He never wanted to do that. He never wanted to feel like he was betraying their love by falling for someone new, by bringing that person into his children's lives.

And now, to add fuel to the fire that was raging in his heart, Angelina McGraw was back in town to promote her newest movie and he'd let her persuade him to take her out to dinner, as her friend was stuck at the airport in some African country until a storm blew over.

"I know you hate surprises, B," she'd said as she sat in nonchalant elegance across from his desk at work. "But Gerry left me no choice. He was supposed to be here already. It's a good thing his man knew I was expected, or I'd be stuck in a hotel for God knows how many days." She sighed, then grinned impishly. "I suppose this is what you get for being a world-famous travel photographer and blogger. I can't say I envy him at all, to be honest. Movie stardom is easy in comparison. I don't have to go too far too often to impress people or bring in the big bucks, as they say." Her chuckle was amused.

"I suppose," he'd agreed, all the while wishing she'd just go so he could wallow in peace. Tristan hadn't called or texted, and Priest had been just as silent, not really knowing how to bridge this new chasm that was growing between them, yet fully aware that his silence was only widening the gap more.

Thankfully, she'd left after wringing an invitation to dinner out of him. They'd been an item for a minute back when he was at uni, but their paths were very different, and she'd been the one to say, after they'd hooked up a second time, that they'd be better off as friends.

"I'm not looking for babies, B," she'd said quietly. "I want my life to be unencumbered by people who will make me feel guilty for not prioritizing them. I know, that makes me a selfish bitch, but better that than a selfish mother. There are enough of those in the world, don't you think?"

"Well, Socrates did say 'Know thyself,'" he'd replied, admiring her for her brutal honesty, especially since he knew she spoke from painful personal experience.

She had always been plain spoken and unapologetic in her opinions and tastes, and that was why they were still friends. He knew she would never tell him what he wanted to hear unless she believed it too. She was the female version of Lachlan, and he wasn't really too annoyed that he'd have to squire her out for a meal.

But as he dressed to go out, his mind went back to the man who held his complete attention and when he examined his heart closely, much of that as well. He needed to tell the children about Tristan, but just as before, he'd waited too long and now everything he was beginning to want again, despite his fear, was poised to disappear if he didn't pull himself together and fix what he'd broken.

Downstairs, he found Shannon at the kitchen table finishing her homework.

"Where's Mason?" he asked. "Is he done already?"

"He only had some reading and some maths problems to do, and he'd already done the reading at school. Something about finishing his work before the others."

Shannon didn't raise her head until she finished whatever she was writing in her notebook. Then she looked up and appraised his appearance.

"You should go out more often, Dad," she declared. "You look good. Is Aunt Angie coming to visit soon?"

"I don't know, love," he told her with a smile. Angelina had gotten to know Jane early on and they'd become fast friends, so she'd been adopted into the Priestley family long before Jane died. "We'll have to see how busy she is."

He turned away to check his appearance one more time in the hall mirror by the kitchen door and was just about to head out to the car when Shannon spoke again, this time more shyly.

"Is Mr. DeVere going to come back for another visit?"

A sharp pain, almost like a knife wound, pierced Priest's chest. He had really messed things up, but there was no time just now to try to fix it.

"I don't know, love." He told her the truth, wishing he had a different answer. "He's probably very busy." Which was also true, but if Priest hadn't been a coward, he'd know for certain.

"Will you ask him? Mason and I were talking about how much fun it was to have him over the last time." She sounded so hopeful that it hurt him more.

"I'll ask." Before he could add more, Mrs. Marks came into the kitchen. "Now, you both mind Mrs. Marks," he told his daughter. "I'll call you when I'm leaving the restaurant, Mrs. Marks," he added, turning to speak to the older woman who smiled kindly at him.

"Your children are a delight, Mr. Priestley," she said. "They're no trouble at all."

He was very grateful for that. He bid them goodnight and left. Angelina's friend lived about fifteen minutes away, and soon she was in the car.

"You look happy," he told her as he negotiated his way through traffic to the restaurant. "Anything you care to share?"

"What makes you think it's anything special?" she asked, clearly deflecting.

"You forget, I've known you for half your life, Angie," he retorted. "If it's none of my business, just say the word and I won't ask any more questions."

She hesitated, then said, "I just don't want to jinx things. I've never been in this situation before ... well, only once before, and we both know how that ended. I'm just being cautious..."

"Wait a bit. What position have you been in before that I know about?" He couldn't think of anything ... he cast a quick glance her way and found her eyes on him. Did she mean what he thought she might mean? "Are you ... seeing someone?"

"In a manner of speaking." She didn't exactly sound sure of herself.

"So, why am *I* taking you to dinner if you're with someone?" Priest was truly confused and a bit apprehensive. He didn't want her new beau thinking that anything was going on between them. "Who is this person? Should I be worried that...?"

"It's fine, B. I sent him a message last night to tell him I'd be out with an old friend. He knows your name because I talk about you sometimes. So he won't be surprised, especially as I'm sure some picture from dinner will make it into the tabloids."

Priest glanced into the rearview mirror, though he'd be hard pressed to say if anyone was following them or not. That wasn't his life, and he was grateful for it. He would think about his picture ending up in the paper once he was back at home. It might happen or it might not. He'd cross that bridge when he got to it. Instead, he turned his attention back to his friend, whom he noticed for the first time seemed nervous.

"Who is he? Do I know him?"

"No. We only met a year ago and haven't spent too much time together. It's been mostly text messages and video chats."

That sounded a bit like him and Tristan. Pushing *that* thought away, because he couldn't handle the pain right now and he should be focusing on Angelina, he said, "Congratulations! And, if I'm understanding your comment earlier, the reason *we* ended was that you weren't ready to be any more grown up than you needed to be back then. Too much else was happening in your life, so I don't want you to mope about that. You did the right thing, calling us off." He reached over and patted her clasped hands on her lap. "And in case I've never told you, Jane and I were very happy that you did."

"I'm very good at minding other people's business, as you well know, B," she chuckled. Then she sobered almost immediately and added, "His name is Rafael Fredriksson."

The awe in her voice struck Priest forcibly. Angelina had never been the sort of woman to be bowled over by anyone, so her obvious astonishment was clear to hear. Was she shocked that she'd finally been bitten by the love bug, or was it something else? No doubt he'd know by the end of dinner.

"I look forward to hearing all about him." It would be good to hear about someone else's love life. That was the best way he knew to avoid thinking about his own.

The restaurant was packed, and Priest was glad when they were finally seated, though he could have wished for a quieter corner than the table for two they were seated at. He looked around, hoping to see somewhere less exposed so he could ask to be moved, but the only other empty table that he saw was right by the hallway leading to the loo. He'd make do with where they were and hope none of the people who clearly recognized Angelina would make their meal uncomfortable for either of them.

Once they'd ordered drinks and were studying the menu, he asked, "So, where did you meet Mr. Fredriksson?"

"At the premiere of "The Only Way Out." Remember my co-star Erik Eklund, that dishy Swedish actor? Rafael is his best mate, and Erik had given him a VIP ticket to the event."

The server arrived to take their orders and once they'd settled that, Priest went back to the conversation.

"So, I'm guessing he was invited to the after-party, and you were introduced. Did you seduce him with your winning ways and smooth words?" he teased.

Angelina's laugh was a tinkling sound of delight, causing several pairs of eyes to follow it to where they sat. Priest ignored them, not willing to break their bubble. He was finally beginning to relax, and he didn't want to mess with that.

"Actually, I was uncharacteristically quiet around him. Aside from polite replies when he spoke directly to me, I couldn't seem to find my voice." She played with the napkin-wrapped cutlery, deep in memories by the look on her face. A wry chuckle escaped her as she continued. "It was rather embarrassing because by the time I was ready to leave, I knew I'd messed up as far as first impressions went, and it bothered me that I didn't like feeling that way."

"Why did it matter what impression you made on him? Is he someone in the industry that you needed to impress?"

"Not at all. He's a surgeon. It had nothing to do with who he was and everything to do with who I suddenly needed to be." Another short pause, then she ended, "Anyway, he got my number from Erik and called me a day later to ask if we could meet for a coffee. He even apologized for calling me unannounced, saying he'd bribed Erik into agreeing not to tell me ahead of time." She giggled. "That was an interesting first date."

Priest smiled at her. "You don't normally answer unknown numbers," he reminded her. "So how did he get in?"

"His name popped up. There was no way I was going to refuse his call, even if I spent the entire conversation thanking Santa for giving me an early Christmas gift."

Priest chuckled with her at that and took a sip of his drink. Just as he went to put the glass down, he saw two men being escorted to a table close by but out of his line of sight. At the last second, one of the men turned and Priest froze. His profile looked so much like Tristan's that Priest blinked, but by the time he looked again, the man had turned away to speak to his friend whose back was to him so Priest couldn't see who he was. *Had* it been Tristan, or were his eyes playing tricks on him?

"B, are you okay?"

Angelina's voice pulled him from his haze. He nodded, taking another sip of his drink. "Yes. I just thought I saw someone I know. Trick of the light, I guess."

He really didn't want to talk to anyone about Tristan just yet, though he knew if his friend asked, he would have to tell her something. It was only fair since she'd just told him about the first man to make her pay attention to someone else. He needed to get back to her revelations, but she beat him to the punch.

"So, it's your turn to share. Anyone new?" When Priest hesitated a moment too long, she added, "We both know that Jane would not approve of you still avoiding rela-tionships, B." The entreaty in her voice wormed past his resistance.

"It's complicated," he said, not really knowing how else to begin. "He's a very public figure, and I have the kids..."

"Who don't know you're bi," she interrupted.

"They do now, and they know that I may have found someone, but they still don't know who he is." There ... he'd confessed his error, like a sinner in the confessional.

"Oh dear! B, that doesn't sound like the kind of decision that will keep anyone around, love."

Their food arrived before he could reply, and they dug in. Priest was grateful for the respite so he could gather his thoughts. Angelina had always understood when he needed room to think and she never failed to give it to him, which was another reason that they remained fast friends. Eventually, though, he'd eaten enough. The food was good, but his mind was on other things. Angelina's touch on his fingers where they lay as he placed his napkin on the table brought his eyes to her face.

"I'm sorry you're still having a rough time, B," she began. "But you of all people know that you can't live in the past. You wouldn't have found Jane if I hadn't broken your heart, love."

The whiff of a familiar cologne caught his attention, and he looked up in time to see Tristan walking by, his eyes caught on Angelina's hand covering Priest's own. The gesture was intimate and completely unguarded, and Priest knew at once that his lover had gotten the wrong end of the stick. He opened his mouth to speak but Tristan kept walking, probably on his way to the men's room. Priest's chest heaved with the need for air.

"Benedict, is everything alright?"

Angelina only first-named him when she was angry or frightened. He didn't want to scare her any more than the worry in her voice told him she already was, so he gulped air into his lungs, pulling his hand away. He didn't want Tristan to pass them again with her still holding his hand. He drained the rest of the water in his glass, finished the drink in the other, and raised a hand to a passing waiter.

"Another glass of water, please," he said. He'd much rather have a Scotch or three, but he was driving and didn't need to be impaired. Angelina belonged to someone now, and he had to make sure she was safe while she was with him.

"Tell me what's going on, B. You're obviously upset. What's happened?"

He couldn't tell her about the man he was falling in love with, not here anyway. He hadn't told his children, and now he'd compounded that mistake by being out with a woman after a week of no communication between them. There was no way that Tristan would come to any other conclusion than that he'd made his choice, and Tristan was the loser. *Fuck!*

"I keep messing up with him," he admitted. "It just sort of hit me, that's all."

Angelina sighed. "I'm sorry, love, but you need to get your head out of your arse and fix things. Starting with telling the kids."

Tristan's cologne drifted by as she spoke, and when Priest looked up, his lover's face was expressionless, his eyes directed straight ahead as if he didn't know anyone at the table. Priest's heart broke but he shoved the pain away. He couldn't afford a meltdown here, not in a public place or in front of his friend. She deserved better than that. They'd come out together to reconnect, and he would do everything in his power to keep his issues to himself.

He nodded, unable still to form words, but as soon as he could, he said, "Anyway, I'm happy that you've finally found someone you want to change for. How long have you actually been together?" Angelina eyed him for a long moment, probably debating whether she should follow his lead or not. He crossed his fingers under the table, praying that she would.

"We've been seeing each other for the whole year actually," she finally said, obliging him.

He breathed a sigh of relief. "Seriously?" he asked, genuinely shocked at her reply. "You've never been impulsive or quick to decide. Especially not with men. So how did this guy win you over so fast?"

Focusing on *her* news would at least keep him from thinking about how to fix the disaster in his own relationship that she was unaware had just occurred. It wasn't her fault, and she didn't need to bear any of the guilt.

"Do you remember how it was with Jane the first time you met her?" When he nodded, she continued, "I guess it was something like that that happened to me. Remember I told you I was almost tongue-tied? It turns out that that was what attracted him to me. That's why he called me, because Erik had told him things he didn't see in me, and he wanted to find out who I really was."

The joy that lit up her face, her eyes, her whole being, made a shaft of envy slice through him. That's how he'd felt with Jane, that she could see the real him underneath all his stoic reticence. That feeling of being in tune with someone else was one of the things he had most cherished about his wife, and one that he had hoped he might find with the man he'd now utterly buggered things with.

"Will you promise me that you'll fix what's broken between you and your man, B? Because I can tell you're unhappy and I don't want to talk about my own happiness while you're so clearly miserable."

Priest looked her in the eye then and smiled. "Thanks, Angie." Taking a deep breath to clear his head, he added, "Ready for dessert?" She deserved a sweet ending to their evening.

"Only if you're sure," she said doubtfully.

"I'm sure. I'll have a coffee, but you can have whatever you want."

Lying in bed after he'd dropped Angelina back at her friend's place, Priest wondered how he could fix things between him and Tris. After tonight's unexpected meeting, he didn't think Tris would be too willing to accept a phone call or text message, but short of going back to his boathouse, Priest didn't see any way to rectify his wrongs.

And anyway, he wasn't sure that he was prepared to grovel. He hadn't done anything wrong earlier. Angelina was his friend, not his lover. They'd known each other forever, and he couldn't deny her the request to spend some time with him. She was even coming over to hang out with him and the kids before she disappeared after the premiere. Why should he feel guilty about that?

And yet, he did. His kids knew exactly who Angelina was to him, to their family, but he was hiding Tris's place in their lives from them. He'd never had to do anything like this before. He'd never had kids before, or lost his first love, or had to declare his sexual orientation. None of this was familiar territory to him. He was never one to rush into action, and now, with his children to protect, he wasn't about to start. But if he kept putting things off, he'd lose the one person who was coming to mean a great deal to him.

Was he willing to break two hearts?

Chapter 22

Tris

*Maybe he needed to face the music, to stop
running from his fear of rejection.*

"Have you called yet?"

Tris glanced over at Rory as they left the studio after their final recording session for their newest album. The heat was a pleasant change from the too-frigid temperature inside and he let himself soak in the warm sunshine, trying to find a way to answer his friend's concern.

It had been another week of silence between him and Priest, this one weighed down by what he'd seen, and the picture in the tabloid of Priest and the woman he'd been with as hard evidence that his eyes had not deceived him. They were laughing, eyes focused on each other as only people very familiar with one another could be.

She was an actress on Broadway and on the big screen, and she'd come over for the premiere of her latest film. The photographer couldn't say more about the shot he'd taken, and speculation was rife as to Priest's identity. They'd soon find out who he was to her ... everyone would, he was sure, including him and all the people who knew he was carrying a torch for the man.

What a way to find out he'd been summarily replaced, and all without the courtesy of a phone call or text message.

"Tris, did you *call* him?" Rory's insistent question stopped his runaway thoughts.

"No," he snapped, walking over to his motorcycle. "What's there to say?"

Rory stepped in front of him, clamping a hard hand on his bicep and stopping him in his tracks. "You tell me. You haven't been the same since you had dinner at his home, and you've been even worse since you saw him at the restaurant with that actress. What haven't you told me?"

Tris might have neglected to tell Rory that he'd seen them holding hands at the table as he'd walked by on his way to the men's room. He didn't need anyone's pity. Besides, what would have been the point? It wasn't as though he had held out much hope for himself after their evening at his home when Priest had made it clear he wasn't ready to announce their relationship to his children. For a minute there, he'd been hopeful that it wasn't about him, that it was about Priest needing to prepare the kids—they *were* his first priority, after all—for the appearance of someone else in his life.

But Angelina McGraw had put paid to that hope, killing it instantly on the vine where it had been languishing for the seven days before that night. He couldn't say he blamed Priest ... well, intellectually anyway. Even though he was angrier than he'd ever been with anyone, he could see why someone who looked like she did and who had *her* pedigree would be a catch for a silver fox like Priest. And only a fool would miss how intimate that gesture between them had been.

"Nothing. It was just obvious that they knew each other really well. You'd have to be blind to miss it. How else am I supposed to take his silence than that he's reconnected with someone he prefers to be with?"

Rory huffed, shaking his head. "I dunno, Tris. You could try asking him about her, about who she is to him. You could try refusing to let him go without a fight. You could try trusting that what you saw is not what you think; that there's another perfectly reasonable explanation for whatever you saw that's led you to believe he's done with you. You could try acting your age instead of *reacting* like the kid your father disowned."

Pure rage boiled up in Tris's chest at the last comment. He knew Rory would only ever utter such callous-sounding words to shake him up, to make him face and deal with the deep anger and hurt that he'd buried inside him for almost two decades. That pain had only deepened after the showdown with Devon, when his ex had humiliated him by announcing his engagement to the woman he'd been cheating on Tris with for almost the whole of their relationship. And on the same night that he'd dumped Tris too. He could still hear the hateful words that the man he'd thought he loved spoke loud enough for the journalist close to them to hear.

"It was a fun ride, baby, but it's time to get serious. You and I were never going to be a thing. You must see that."

Tris's shock had been complete. He'd run out of the room like his arse was on fire, completely ignoring the other guests whom Devon had invited to what he hadn't known until that moment was an engagement party. The following day, as he was moving the rest of his things out of their shared apartment—because he'd taken a couple suitcases of things with him to a motel so he wouldn't be where he could hear the newly engaged couple cop- ulating—he'd plucked up the courage to ask the questions raging in his mind.

"What did I do to make you disrespect me, Dev? If you'd wanted me to leave, surely you could have found a better way, a better time to tell me? Did you have to humiliate me in front of the person you replaced me with and all your friends? Did I mean so little to you?"

Devon's reply had been the ultimate betrayal. "Oh, grow up, Tristan! We were headed nowhere fast, and you know it."

Grow up, Tristan! He realized now, thinking back on it, that the response had been typical of Devon. He never admitted to any wrongdoing, never addressed an issue head on, always deflected. The big difference in their ages should have given Tris pause, but he'd been so flattered and over- whelmed by the attention of the most gorgeous man he'd ever met that he dismissed it. Age didn't matter, only love did.

How very wrong he'd been! He hadn't been loved. He'd been toyed with, used, and discarded. And just at the moment, it felt like history was repeating itself. He couldn't do that again. He couldn't let one more man shove his unworthiness in his face. He wanted to matter to anyone he gave his heart to, and since he wasn't yet all the way in love with Priest, he'd just take it back before it could get completely shattered. And the only way to do that was to break all contact immediately.

A clean break, cold turkey, anything to cauterize the wound that opened wider every day without the sound of Priest's voice or his words in a text message. He could put his heart back together if there weren't too many pieces missing. He'd say he had definitely grown up since that awful night.

"It's because I'm not that stupid kid anymore why I'm not going to call, Ror. I'm an adult, a human being with feelings. He saw me. He must know what I would have thought. Why hasn't *he* called *me*? Why should *I* be the one to make the first move? Here's the perfect opportunity for Priest to show me where I truly stand with him. The longer it takes for him to call, the more certain I am that I'm right and you're wrong."

Rory sighed. "Did you make any promises to each other?" he asked, releasing Tris's bicep reluctantly.

"Not really. Not aside from agreeing to see each other."

"So what I'm hearing is that neither of you is obliged to call first."

Tris straddled his motorbike and switched on the engine. "I'm not calling him, Rory. It's over unless he calls me."

He rode away, gunning the engines in a futile display of heated determination. He wouldn't change his mind. This was too important. Maybe he'd needed this to happen, to shake him out of his complacency. Now that he knew he wasn't broken, maybe he could try again with someone closer to his age, someone with no other priorities than him and what could grow between them. Someone who might not tick all his boxes—apparently only Priest could do that— but would tick enough that he could live the way he wanted to, with a partner, a family, some pets, and a boat on which they could while away the weekends.

Too late, as he headed onto the motorway, he realized he'd just described what he'd thought he was beginning to find with Priest. Willing himself not to speed as pain shafted through him—because who benefitted if he killed himself riding while angry?—he made his way back home, slammed his way onto the boat, shut off his phone, and drank enough beer to sink a ship.

When he woke up, it was almost three in the morning, and his head was one large, thudding ache that his tired neck and shoulders could barely support. His mouth was as dry as the desert and tasted like he'd been drinking sewer water not beer. And to add insult to injury, he was ravenous. Knowing he wouldn't make it back to bed before dawn, he showered and went to find food, leaving his phone on the bed where he'd dropped it.

Half an hour later, the throbbing in his shoulders was mostly gone, though his head felt like the pain that had filled it earlier had been replaced by cotton wool. His belly was full, and he felt almost human. At times like these, he wished he had a pet. He could do with stroking a cat or petting a dog to help relieve the stress he was still carrying in his spine and across his shoulder blades.

Maybe when it got light out, he could go and see the progress on his house. He'd been avoiding the place since his last time with Priest, needing to avoid any further accidental meetings. But he wanted to see how far the workers had gotten since they'd started a few days ago. Maybe they'd let him help them break down a wall or something. He needed to use up all the pent-up energy building in his bloodstream. Until then, he'd listen to some blues and hard rock.

Dozing off sitting up on the couch in his living room had not been the smartest idea, as Tris discovered when he woke with a start. The morning was gray, and a light rain misted down as he tried to work the kinks out of his neck and back. It was past ten and though he had nothing planned for the day, he still felt like a bit of a waster lying about sleeping instead of being productive. The band had a few days off ... maybe he'd go visit his sister until work started again. The break would do him good.

Fetching his phone, he turned it on to make the call and found far too many missed calls and messages from his bandmates. He ignored those, zooming in instead on three from Priest ... a missed call, a voice message, and a text message. He was torn. Was he ready to be booted to the curb before he'd even managed to step fully into Priest's life? Was he ready to be told his reading of the situation at the restaurant was incorrect?

He stared at the notifications, wondering why he was fighting so hard to hold onto the hurt, why he was considering ignoring the messages from Priest. He had no real reason, no excuse other than fear that the outcome of holding onto hope would be heartbreak a third time. His father's rejection, a betrayal of the trust he had thought existed between them as father and son, had left him a wound so severe that he still didn't know, after all these years, how to heal.

Forgiveness was impossible unless the hurt was erased, and how was he to do that when he hadn't spoken a word to his father in more than a decade, when he would gladly ignore his mother's pleas to reconnect with her, at least, rather than face the possibility that he might run into his sire and be left speechless again? And Devon's betrayal, cutting in a different way from his father's, only added to the rage he had never truly addressed.

Any bad news from Priest would be the last straw and he wasn't feeling up to that just yet. He opened the messages from the other guys in the band and abandoned his decision to call his sister immediately in favor of calling Rory, who had threatened to come over unannounced bringing Henry with him, because Tris wasn't answering his calls or messages.

"Nobody needs to come anywhere," he said as soon as Rory answered his phone, bypassing the usual niceties of polite phone conversation. "I was asleep, and I'd shut the phone off. Nothing more. I'm fine."

"Have you called him?"

Tris rolled his eyes. He wasn't even remotely surprised that Rory was singing his tune of the month. His friend was tenacious and wouldn't let it go until Tris did something other than dither about.

"*He* called *me*. Left a voice and a text message."

"And?" Rory's tone said Tris would be in trouble if he gave an unsatisfactory answer.

"And nothing. I just opened my phone. I'm calling you lot first."

His friend wasn't to know that he'd only given him half the story. Half-truths were better than lies every day. Maybe Rory would let it go? Tris could dream.

"Why are you calling me when you should be on the line with your man?" Rory's impatience was barely held in check. "Have you even read or listened to them?" Tris's silence seemed to rile him up even more. "Bloody hell, Tristan! Get off the phone and *call him!*"

Before Tris could respond, the hum of a disconnected call sounded in his ear, an admonishment and an opportunity. *Grow up, Tristan!* Devon's mocking words rang in his ears again as clearly as if they had just been flung at him from a sneering face. Maybe his ex was right, after all. Maybe he needed to face the music, so to speak, to stop running from his fear of rejection, to grow a spine and really be the man he'd spent all these years pretending to be. How hard could it be to hear what Priest had to say? They had only just begun to forge something between them, so a break wouldn't tear him apart this time. He might even have grown a strong enough armor to protect him from the worst that could happen.

Priest's text message was simple:

[Priest: Please listen to the voice message.]

His voice message was longer and harder to hear. "I know what you must be thinking after the other night, Tristan, and I'm sorry it took me this long to reach out. I've been thinking about the best way to say everything I need to say to you, and I'd rather do it in person. When and where can we meet to talk? Please let me know and I'll be there. Thanks."

No explanations, no excuses, just an apology and a request. Tris could hear the strain in Priest's voice, despite his effort to sound cool. Whatever he had to say, he was also clearly affected by this unexpected breach between them. Tris knew they didn't know each other well enough to be certain of anything, but he couldn't imagine Priest as the kind of man who would be deliberately unkind to anyone.

Still, he needed time to get out of his own head, so he'd be ready to really listen to anything Priest had to say. He owed them both that, at least. So he sent a text message—he also wasn't quite ready for Priest to answer his phone—in reply.

[Tris: I've listened to your message. Thanks for reaching out. I'll be away for a few days. If you're free on Sunday afternoon, we can meet in Hyde Park. I should be back by early afternoon, so you can choose where in the park to meet, and I'll see you there.]

He hit Send before he changed his mind and then rang his sister. He really would go away for a few days, just so he wouldn't make a liar of himself and also because now that he'd decided to hear Priest out, he needed to get rid of all the negative thoughts and emotions clogging his system. Some time with his family would definitely help. Tara's phone went immediately to voice messaging, and Tris bit back a disappointed sigh before speaking.

"Tee, I'd like to come up for a few days. Are you free?"

They both loved Mr. Humphries from the '70s Britcom *Are You Being Served?*, one of whose most famous lines, spoken in a singsong voice, was "Are you free?" They had adopted it as their own when Tara was a teenager. Tris hoped she was free for a visitor, or he'd have to find another way to spend the next few days to keep his mind off Priest and whatever he was going to say.

Deciding that a long ride was just what he needed while he waited for his sister to call, he dressed quickly and set off, choosing to ride where the road took him rather than planning a route. Hours later, after a leisurely lunch at an Indian restaurant and some lazy meandering by a lake in a park, he felt more at ease than he had when he'd woken up as he walked down the slope from the house where he'd made his final stop to see what progress had been made. Maybe he'd spend the time helping where he could if Tara wasn't available.

His phone buzzed as he stepped onto the houseboat, and he answered without checking it.

"Where the bloody hell have you been, Tristan?" Henry's voice telegraphed ire, worry, and frustration. "I've been ringing since this morning. You've not answered your phone or responded to the texts that Gen made me send. What's going on?"

Tris sighed. "Sorry, Henry. I went for a ride to clear my head. I got pissed last night and woke up with a hangover."

He knew his explanation would only raise more questions, but he could handle them better now than a few hours ago. Since Tara still hadn't answered him, he had some time to spare.

"I know things haven't been good recently and though you haven't told me exactly what's wrong, I assume it has to do with Priest. Have you talked to him?"

Tris knew that Rory wouldn't break his confidence, so Henry didn't know about the latest issue between him and Priest. He knew he didn't owe anyone any explanations for his behavior as long as it didn't interfere with his work, and since he'd been using work to hide from the problem, no one had any reason to complain. But Henry was his friend, his older brother almost, the band's father figure, to all intents and purposes, and Tris knew he worried about the others. He wouldn't let his friend add any unnecessary burdens to his shoulders.

"Something else has come up, but I haven't talked to him, exactly. I need to prep myself for whatever he might say."

Henry's sharp intake of breath was all the notice Tris got before his friend was lambasting him. "That's always been your way, hasn't it, Tris? When are you going to stop running away from confronting an issue head on? Nothing gets fixed your way, and you know it." He paused, unaware of Tris's pounding heart and red face. "Look, I don't know how deeply involved you are with him, and it's really none of my business, is it? But what happens with you *is* my business, Tristan."

Using his full first name meant Henry expected Tris to take heed to his words. "You're family. Gen and the boys and I care a great deal about you." Henry's words made Tris's heart swell. He knew that. He really did. "Please tell me you're going to speak to him. Whatever is going on, you need to fix it, not just for yourself but for all the rest of us who can't stand to see you hurting and not be able to help. It's a selfish demand but live with it." Tris smiled at Henry's attempt to lighten the mood before he ended, "And give me your word you'll handle this now, not whenever it becomes inevitable, after things have gone to the dogs."

"I give you my word."

"Now, what are you doing with your time off? The children want to go to Brighton. If you've nothing planned, want to come with us?"

That was just like Henry. He was always looking out for others, to include them so they'd never feel alone.

"I'm waiting to hear from Tara. Depending on what she says, I may or may not be able to join you. I'll let you know as soon as I know."

"Good enough."

Thank God for friends like Henry. Tris knew he'd never have done as well as he had without them.

Chapter 23

Priest

Never deny how you're feeling.

The last time Priest had seen Tristan almost two weeks ago, he'd been certain that the feelings growing between them would become stunted, would wither and die on the vine. However, no matter how good he'd thought he'd been at hiding his distress, the people closest to him at home and at work had noticed. He'd made up a story about being tired to soothe his kids' anxiety, but Lachlan didn't believe it, as Priest knew he wouldn't. The man knew him too well.

They were having lunch in Lachlan's office when his friend said, between bites of his sandwich, "Since I know it's not about the kids, what's bothering you, Priest? You've been little better than a bear with a sore paw. Why are you so unusually bad-tempered these days, mate?"

Had he really been that bad? Priest didn't normally suffer fools gladly, but he was usually able to keep his impatience to himself. Apparently, though, he'd lost that control sometime between seeing Tristan in the restaurant and this moment.

Swallowing the bite he'd just taken of his own sandwich, he answered, "Sorry about that. I thought I was handling it." Which wasn't an answer, as Lachlan let him know at once.

"That doesn't explain why, Priest. So since you want me to guess, let's see." He tapped a finger against his pursed lips, humming softly as he thought. Then he snapped his fingers as if he'd had a Eureka moment and continued, "I've got it. You've had a falling out with the rocker over Angelina." He resumed eating, an eyebrow cocked at Priest as if to say, "Well, am I right or am I right?"

"I hate you," Priest grumbled before stuffing his mouth with a huge bite of his sandwich.

Anything to avoid giving an immediate answer, but Lachlan waited patiently, eating and drinking as though they had all the time in the world instead of the twenty minutes left in their lunch break. A reluctant grin creased his cheeks when Lachlan chuckled at his grousing.

"With haters like you, I'll live a long and healthy life. So, what's going on with the rockstar?"

"Nothing." A bald, painful truth, but Priest didn't have the energy to prevaricate with his friend. "He was at the restaurant the night I took her out for dinner. He saw us…"

His pause made Lachlan's eyebrows lift in alarm. "And? What exactly did he see, Priest?"

"Angelina's hand was covering mine on the table when he walked by to go to the men's room. He saw it, and you can guess the rest."

Lachlan eyed him assessingly for a long moment as if Priest were a puzzle he was trying to solve. When he finally responded, Priest shook his head, not surprised by his insight.

"I'm going to assume that you didn't go find him and bring him back to introduce him to Angelina, and worse, that you haven't called or texted him, or that if you have done either of those, it wasn't immediately. How am I doing so far?"

Priest hated the smug look on his friend's face. He threw down the rest of his sandwich. He'd lost his appetite anyway and couldn't tell what he was eating if you asked him. Lachlan didn't wait for him to answer, but ploughed on, uncaring of his discomfort.

"What did I tell you the last time we talked about you fooling with this man?"

That stung. "I'm not *fooling* with anyone," Priest snapped back, more angry with himself than with his sharp-eyed friend.

"And you think ignoring him after what happened is proof of that, do you?"

Lachlan's "I told you so" stare was on full blast, and Priest hated how he had to fight not to squirm beneath its weight. He was not the man he'd always thought he was since he had allowed this misunderstanding to go on for so long without reaching out. Maybe marriage had made him complacent, but now, without Jane to hide behind, he was forced to concede that he was probably nowhere near as sensible about relationships and nowhere near as brave as he'd thought he was.

"Look, I know the problem is mine, not his. And I know I should have called sooner."

"Oh," his friend's eyebrows rose. "So you *have* actually called him?" If the slow clap he executed had a tone, it would be beyond sarcastic.

"Shut it! Of course I did!"

"Eventually," Lachlan added. "How long did it take you? A few days? A week, two?" He shook his head and gestured at Priest. "Never mind. It doesn't matter. What matters is what you said." He stopped speaking again and waited expectantly.

Priest sighed. "I asked him to name a time and place where we can talk face to face."

This time, the tone of his friend's applause was exuberant. "Well, congratulations on making the first smart move since this relationship began." He leaned forward, his elbows on his knees, and regarded Priest with a serious gaze. "Do you know what you're going to say to him? How you're going to fix this mess?"

"Not really. All I know is that if I don't let the children know everything before I talk to him, it won't be worth the time and he'll definitely cut me off for good."

"I don't get it, mate. Why is it so hard to tell the children you're interested in someone? Do you think they'll object because it's a man? I mean, I understand that there's a difference between knowing your dad's bisexual and actually meeting the evidence of that in the flesh. Do you think they won't accept him? Is that the reason you've been putting it off all this time? Or is it that you're ashamed of it, now that you've finally had to face it head on?"

Priest's chuckle was humorless. "You know I'm not ashamed of who I am. I've just never had to be more than one part of that personality for so long that it feels ... strange, now. And I guess I haven't told you that Shan has a bit of a crush on him. Has since before we met. Now that they've both met him in person and the children actually like him, how do I break my baby's heart by telling her he's interested in me and will never be in her? I mean, she *knows* he's too old for her. She's said as much. But won't it seem like a betrayal to her when I tell them what we want to be to each other?"

Lachlan's eyes filled with warm understanding. "Don't forget the part you haven't said. You're afraid that if you speak it into existence, you will feel like *you're* betraying Jane, no?"

Priest slumped against the back of the chair he was in and crossed his arms over his chest. "We're meeting on Sunday at four at Hyde Park Corner. We'll just wander about, I guess."

"I'm sure you can understand why he wouldn't want to be cooped up inside with you," Lachlan murmured. "Will you be alright?" He reached out to lay a sympathetic hand on Priest's knee.

Priest huffed. "I'll have to be, won't I? If he doesn't choose to forgive me, what can I do?"

"Well, that rather depends on how you feel about him, doesn't it, mate? You didn't let Jane put you off even for a second, no matter what she tried. And we both know you're not the sort of bloke to throw in the towel without a fight. As my dad would say, courage, my boy! Into the fray!"

Priest laughed in true amusement at his friend's too accurate imitation of his father's tone and volume. "You're completely bonkers, but I love you, anyway," he said.

"Well, when you've got me for a friend, you really have no choice, do you?"

Lachlan's self-satisfied smirk as he blew on his fingers and buffed the nails against his shirt made Priest laugh harder, and somehow, he felt lighter. His friend had always been able to make him laugh, to ease the weight that his problems sometimes laid on his shoulders. The intercom buzzed and Lachlan's PA spoke.

"Please pardon the interruption, Mr. Elliott, but your one o'clock has arrived. Shall I bring her round?"

He muted the speaker before saying, "Bollocks! I'd forgotten all about the old windbag," Lachlan groused. "Now I'll have to waste thirty precious minutes listening to her whine about the latest change that she ordered but now doesn't like and showing her why it's better for her to adjust her attitude."

Another chuckle escaped Priest. "Sorry, but that's what you get for being a softie at heart. You know what to do if you need me to bail you out."

Lachlan echoed his wry amusement. "Thanks, mate." He told his PA to send the client around and as Priest was leaving, after throwing out their lunch trash, he added. "And by the way, the feeling is mutual. That's why we're friends. Never forget that."

Saturday morning found Priest at the breakfast table watching his children eat their porridge—which they still wanted most Saturday mornings, as if to remind themselves of their mum—and rehearsing how he would break the news that he was thinking of dating Tristan. He'd have to word it that way, because at the moment he didn't know what Tristan was thinking anymore. He could only hope that the spark was still there, that he hadn't completely ruined his chances because of his cowardice.

"Dad, don't you like the porridge?"

Mason eyed him curiously, and Priest realized he hadn't taken even a spoonful of his food. Hurriedly shoveling a few mouthfuls in, he wiped his lips on the napkin and smiled at his son.

"Sorry, son, I was just woolgathering." He turned to Shannon and added, "And thanks for helping me with breakfast, Princess. It's good."

Shannon grinned at him. "I like it when we make it the way your friend showed you. It's so good with toast and jam."

Priest smiled at the memory that her words conjured. Adding cream and berries jazzed up the flavor. They finished their porridge and were spreading jam liberally on the toast when he spoke again. Time to rip off the plaster.

"I have something to tell you," he began, sipping the tea he'd just poured for himself. English courage ... the thought almost made him chuckle. "Remember when we talked about me never having had a boyfriend?"

That conversation, which he'd been dreading, held nothing like the intensity that this one had the potential to hold. Pulling his thoughts together, he sucked in a deep breath and began.

"I've met someone, and we like each other well enough that we might like to become boyfriends someday." He cringed at the word "boyfriend," watching their faces as he spoke and seeing innocence and curiosity in Mason's gaze. Opening his mouth to continue, he stopped when Shannon interrupted with a question.

"Is it someone we know?"

When Priest turned his attention to her, he found her eyes alight with something like suspicion, and her question was sharp with some emotion he couldn't identify. She sat back in her chair, her back straight, shoulders tight as they'd been in the hospital when he'd had to tell them that their mum had died.

"You do. It's Mr. DeVere."

What now? Neither child spoke for a moment and when one finally broke the silence, it was the one he'd expected would do it. Mason eyed him curiously.

"Is that why he came to visit?"

Easy question, thankfully. "No, Mase, we were just getting to know each other a bit more, and he wanted to meet you both."

Still nothing from Shannon. Priest gave her time to think and, after a minute of silence while he sipped his tea, was just about to ask her what she was thinking when she said, "May I please be excused?" She avoided his eyes, staring down at her plate.

Priest sighed. "Clear your place first, and then you may go."

She scraped the chair back from the table and took her breakfast things to the sink before rushing from the kitchen like she was in fear for her life. Priest knew he'd have to go up and talk to her, but he'd give her time to calm down first. He needed time himself to plan the best way to comfort his daughter who was growing up much too fast for his liking. In the meantime, he still had to find out what Mason's reaction would be.

Turning his eyes back to his son, who was polishing off the last of his toast, Priest said, "So, what do you think, Mase?"

"Does that mean we'll get to see him more?"

"It does."

Mason smiled. "Cool!"

And that was that. Mason helped him wash and dry the dishes, and then he too went off to his room, no doubt to play one of his video games. Time to face the music with Shannon. He knocked when he got upstairs to her door and waited. No response. He knocked again, heard nothing and tried the door. Thankfully, it was unlocked. Shannon was sitting cross-legged on her bed, writing in a notebook.

"May I come in, Shan?" he asked, waiting by the open door before he stepped inside.

She nodded but didn't look up from her writing. Priest walked over and sat on the edge of her bed and watched her for a few seconds, noting her stiff posture on the buttercup-yellow bedspread.

"Are you ready to talk now, Shan?" he began. "I'm always here when you need me."

Glancing up at him, she nodded again, then went back to writing. It seemed that he would have to do the talking for them both. That was okay with him.

"Are you upset that I'm seeing someone? Or are you upset that it's Tristan?"

Her pen paused, fingers still wrapped tightly around it. Then she finally looked at him and spoke.

"I know it's stupid to be mad about it, but…" She shook her head. "It's fine. It doesn't matter, Dad."

"But what, Shan?" Priest insisted. "Tell me. I promise I won't be angry with you."

"Why couldn't he like girls?" she grumbled.

He dared to move closer, catching a glimpse of what she was doing in the notebook. There were doodles everywhere, curlicues, hearts, arrows, lightbulbs, some faint, some bold, some half and half. That must be how she was feeling, he supposed, like worlds of different emotions that she had never felt before trying to fight their way to the surface.

"Why can't *you* like girls?" he asked her. When she didn't reply, starting on another doodle instead, he continued. "We are attracted to people for a lot of reasons, and there's nothing wrong with any of that. But you can't make yourself like someone you don't. And anyway, didn't you tell me a few weeks ago that you know Tristan's too old for you? So what's the real problem, love?"

He wanted her to admit that she wasn't comfortable with the idea that he was moving on and that it was with a man. He also wanted her to acknowledge that perhaps she was a bit jealous, because he wanted to be able to reassure her that it was okay to feel how she felt. He never wanted her to hide her feelings because she was afraid he'd be angry with her.

"I..." she hesitated, and Priest waited patiently. This was too important for him to rush her. "I know he's a grownup and I'm just a kid, Dad. I just..." She stopped again, sighing heavily. "I just wish I was a grownup too." Priest heard the catch in her voice, but she rallied, holding back the tears no doubt brimming in her lowered eyes. "And I feel bad that I'm mad at you because I know it's not right."

"Are you just angry with me, or with me and Tristan?" Better to start with the easier question first.

She sniffled and pressed her thumb and forefinger over her closed eyes. "I don't know. Both of you?" She huffed in frustration.

Priest chose to bail her out. She was only twelve, after all, trying to act like a grownup when she needed to be the child she still was. If Jane were here, she'd have known what to say to their daughter, but she wasn't, so it was up to him to do the best he could.

"It's okay to feel what you feel, Shan, even if you can't explain it. It's okay to be disappointed and angry when your wishes can't come true. Never deny how you're feeling. But at the same time, don't wallow in it, especially when you know it won't change what's upsetting you."

He paused to let that sink in. It would take some time, perhaps years, for her to fully grasp what it all meant, but it was a lesson adults needed to embrace as well, so he didn't worry that she'd never understand. Now came the part where he'd help her to accept what she couldn't change so she could move on.

"Can you think of any way that Tristan and I being together might be a good thing?"

She brought the pen to her lips, pressing it against her bottom lip the way she did when she was trying to figure out a maths problem or solve a riddle. She glanced up at him, looked away, looked back, and then shrugged.

"I guess it's good that you like each other because then we'll get to see him more. And maybe he will really like me and not just because I play the piano."

Sometimes his children surprised him, and Priest had learned never to underestimate their insightfulness and ability to think critically. He smiled and opened his arms, cradling Shan close when she uncoiled her legs to accept his embrace. He kissed the top of her head and pulled back to look into her eyes.

"I'm sure he'll love you both because you're good, kind, thoughtful, loving children." Planting another kiss on her cheeks, he asked, "Better now?"

She nodded against his chest. He inhaled deeply and let her hold him as long as she needed to. One hurdle down. A bigger one loomed and Priest could only hope that *that* conversation would go as well or better than this one had done. Only time would tell.

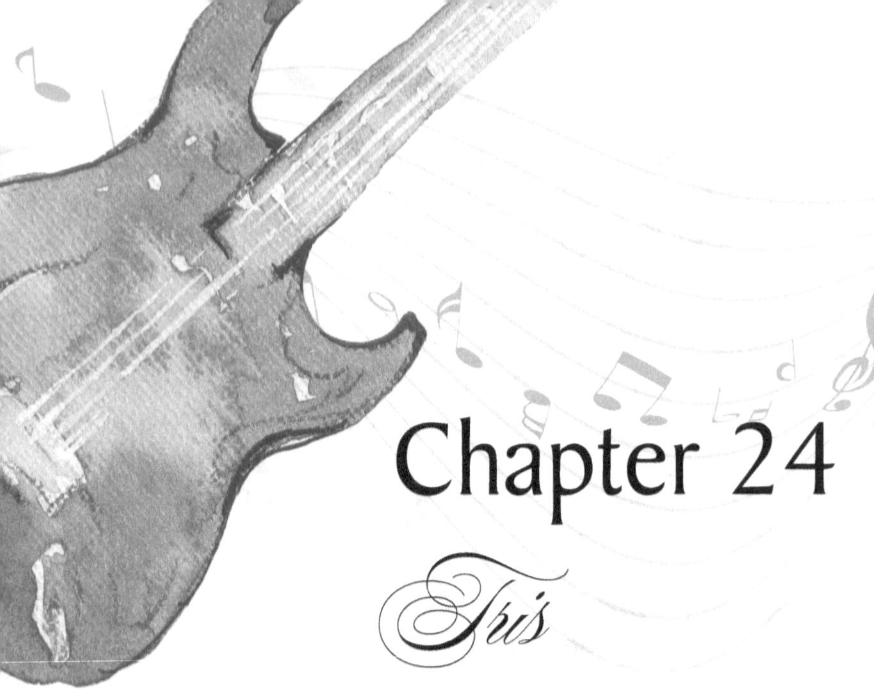

Chapter 24

Tris

He had to learn to trust that Priest
would be his soft place to land.

"**G**ood luck with your guy," Tara said in Tris's ear as she hugged him goodbye.

Tris chuckled. "You're a hopeless romantic. You know that, right?" He kissed her cheek and turned to hug his niece and nephew as she continued speaking.

"There's nothing wrong with wishing the best for my big brother. It's high time you find yourself someone real. Everyone needs joy."

Stooping to squeeze the children one last time, he stood again and said, hoping the conflicting feelings rolling through him didn't sound in his voice, "From your mouth to God's ears, Sis."

The drive back to London was thankfully uneventful, unlike the drive up which had been delayed by a big accident on the motorway. He had time to think about all he needed to say to Priest, once he'd established that he needed to say anything at all. If Priest still refused to acknowledge who they were to each other to his children, there'd be no need to bare his soul and open his painful past to yet another person's eyes. Not that he thought Priest would judge him, but it was important to Tris for him to understand that what had happened the last time with the actress in the restaurant had triggered memories of the pain, mistrust, and fear that had pushed him to build high walls around his heart to begin with, and he was never going to live that way again.

Happy to come upon a car moving out as he drove around looking for parking, Tris maneuvered his Evoque into the spot, checked his pockets for his wallet and cell phone, and locked the car before walking away. The walk to Hyde Park Corner took about five minutes and as he waited at the light to cross, he scanned the area, searching for Priest. He was halfway across the road before he saw him emerge from the gateway next to the Diana Princess of Wales Memorial Walk. He did his best not to move any faster. He had no wish to appear more eager than Priest, whom he could tell had seen him and was waiting to greet him with a carefully neutral expression on his face.

"You came." No smile, no other word of greeting, just pure relief shining in his eyes.

Still not sure how to trust Priest's words, Tris cleared his throat and said, "Yes. Shall we?" Stepping ahead, he led the way into the gardens, stopping to watch as a guard on horseback rode by, stately on the beauty of a horse that was completely black except for the two white socks—or whatever they were called—on his hind legs.

"You like horses a lot, don't you?" Priest asked.

Tris withheld his startled reaction, because why was Priest being close enough that he could smell his cologne a surprise? He knew they'd been walking together, more or less, but he'd been so busy trying to distract himself by watching the horse and rider that he'd blocked Priest from his mind.

"Yes. It's one of the things I love most about visiting Sam's estate."

They walked on, passing the map showing the spots of interest in Hyde Park where some tourists were gathered, trying to get their bearings. Tris knew that he and Priest weren't there to sightsee, but he didn't know how to start the conversation that they *were* there to have. He breathed a sigh of relief when Priest spoke first.

"Angelina is one of my dearest friends, whom I've known for a long time. If you read the papers, you know that she was in town for the premiere of her newest movie. We were just catching up as we haven't seen each other since before Jane died. Originally, she was supposed to go out to dinner with someone else, but he was delayed in another country, and she asked me to go with her."

Tris swallowed. "So she knew Jane?"

"Yes. They became great friends. The children call her Aunt Angie."

He felt foolish for asking the next question, but he didn't feel like keeping any more of his uncertainties where Priest was concerned locked away inside him. "Were you ever...?" He paused, licking his lips before speaking again. "Involved with her?"

"We had a fling briefly back in college when we first met, but one time together was enough to show us that we were better suited as friends. Angelina broke things off because she wasn't ready for the commitment that she knew I wanted eventually. And she was right, because when I met Jane, we both knew she was who I was meant to be with."

A weight that Tris hadn't realized that he'd been carrying since that night at the restaurant lifted, and he felt almost giddy with relief. Priest was not Devon. He knew that, had always known it on some level, but hearing it confirmed was what he'd needed. Now it was his turn to bare his soul, to tell the part of his past that he'd kept buried out of sight and out of mind. But how was he to begin?

"Why didn't you say something when you walked by us in the restaurant? I know what you saw, and I knew at once what you thought it meant when you walked back to your table without even acknowledging me."

The puzzlement in Priest's question was the spur that moved him into speech. "Seeing you with a woman brought back memories I've done my best to bury for well over a decade." Tris heard the husky note in his voice and cleared his throat, not wanting Priest's pity. "I was in a relationship with an older man in my early twenties," he continued. "I thought we felt the same thing for each other. I never knew he was just playing with me until he announced his engagement on the same night that he called it quits with me, to the woman he'd apparently been cheating on me with."

"Bloody hell!"

Priest's exclamation was somehow the most reassuring thing that Tris had heard in a very long time. The tone was equal parts shock and anger. Tris hurried on, not wanting Priest to say anything for fear those words would undo what he was feeling.

"That night at the restaurant, I saw how she was holding your hand, and you didn't seem to mind. It just felt like déjà vu. And given how our last evening together before that had ended, it didn't seem too far-fetched to think it meant you'd decided to move on without me."

Priest winced as though Tris had punched him. "I guess I haven't given you any reason to trust that I wouldn't hurt you like your ex did." His voice bled regret. "I'm sorry, Tristan. I *am* a better man than he was."

Tris felt the intention-filled silence stretch between them and didn't break it, knowing instinctively that Priest wasn't finished speaking, merely gathering his thoughts. They had another big issue to address that was Priest's burden to bear. Tris could let him have the space to think now that his own dark secret had been shoved into the light.

They'd been walking aimlessly for some time, and Tris looked around, trying to get his bearings. They were standing just below the Wellington Monument, the statue of Achilles imposing and virile. Tris thought the location was ideal for the conversation they were having. It had left them both vulnerable to the deep wounds only anger and fear could inflict, but it had also helped to establish that they were strong men, able to face their demons unwaveringly.

"There's something else you need to know," Priest said into the lengthening silence filling the warm afternoon air. "I've told the children about us."

Tris's heart skipped a beat, a second and third time. He hadn't known what to expect, hadn't wished to open his heart to hope, but this was clearly the best news. Priest wanted to be with him, to own what was happening between them. Unbridled relief wrapped his spirit in warmth, and he turned a smile at Priest.

"Thank you." He was too full to say more for a moment, letting himself bask in the glow of acceptance. Their relationship was still new, but he understood that going forward, they had to be open with everything. No more hiding from each other and the people they loved. "How did they take it?" he finally asked, needing to be prepared in case the children had been less than receptive.

A wry grin pulled the dimples into Priest's cheeks. "Mason is cool with it. He just wanted to know if that meant he'll get to see you more often."

"And Shannon?" He knew very little about teenage crushes, but he hoped Priest had been able to let her down lightly, so *he* wouldn't have to. He'd freely admit that he was a coward when it came to handling women and their inexplicable emotions.

"Shan is hurting a little. And she says she's angry with both of us. But she's also angry she's not a grownup, even though she doesn't seem to get that you still wouldn't be interested in her because you're gay.

Tris sighed. "It's hard when your feelings for someone aren't reciprocated. And it's harder when you're a teenager. What can I do?"

Priest stopped their aimless ambling to face him again. "Just be you. She'll probably be distant for a bit, but she'll come round. It's the way of all crushes, isn't it? Also, I think a more than twenty-year age gap will eventually..." he paused, clearly searching for the right word, then continued. "Gross her out, as the kids say these days."

"I *am* old enough to be her dad," Tris supplied, glad of the lightened mood.

Priest's gaze sharpened. "Which is a good thing, if we can get our act together." His tone held equal parts question and answer.

Tris understood. Anything he did with Priest's children could become more than friendly. If they chose to deepen their relationship to the place where they became partners, maybe even husbands—though he dared not think about that now—he would undoubtedly find himself taking on the role of parent. It wasn't something he had considered before, but he still chose to answer the question Priest hadn't asked.

"I agree. We'll have to trust each other completely. Not leave anything out, not dismiss any question, not hide any emotions. Which means there's one more thing I need to tell you."

This would be the hardest part. He never spoke about his relationship with his parents, particularly his father, these days. After the fiasco with Devon, which had made the news given that his ex was a well-known restaurateur, Tris had fallen afoul of his father, who hadn't appreciated having the family name "dragged through the mud" as he put it. After his ultimatum—"Reconsider your predilections or be disinherited!"—Tris had moved out of his family home and never returned.

"My father and I are on the outs. I haven't spoken to him in well over a decade, and I rarely speak to my mother." *Damn, that had been hard to speak into existence!*

They'd meandered their way to the Diana Princess of Wales Memorial Fountain and sat on the edge. Tris watched Priest trail his fingers in the water and memories of those fingers in his hair took him by surprise. A sudden need to touch the man unaware of his scrutiny overwhelmed him and for once he went with his desire for the comfort of a touch. He reached out, resting his hand atop Priest's, letting the cool water wash over them, a balm to his wounds.

Priest's eyes were alight with heat when he met Tris's gaze, and when he turned his palm over so he could link his fingers with Tris's, they held on for a long moment before he released Tris with a smile. The patience in his waiting, combined with the promise of more comfort whenever he needed it, bloomed in Tris's chest, a flower opening to the sun.

"Thank you for telling me," Priest said. "I can only imagine how difficult it must have been to be set adrift from everything you've ever thought you had, from everyone you thought would support you. I'm glad you still have your siblings."

"So am I." Tris was certain that the pain he usually kept in check bled through those words, but he didn't care. He had to learn to trust that Priest would be his soft place to land when the complicated mix of emotions surrounding thoughts of his family whipped around inside him with gale force strength.

"Thank you for meeting me here. I know you didn't have to..." Priest began.

Tris interrupted him. "I didn't. And for a moment, I didn't want to."

He caught the touch of hurt in Priest's gaze before he blinked, and it was gone. He couldn't manage anyone's hurt but his own right now, and he was sure Priest would get over it. At least he'd told the truth. He would never lie to this man in any way again.

"But I wanted to believe you were different from my ex," he continued. "Better than him, *more* than he could ever be. So I came, and I'm glad I did."

They were headed back the way they'd come, walking in a silence that was laden with all the things still to be said that could wait now that the apologies and truths had been spoken. When Priest reached for his hand, hope glided into the quivering places that Tris had hidden with expert attention from the world and calmed their fearful tremors. He had not even shared those most secret wounds with his siblings whom he loved and trusted, or with the men who were his found family. He held onto Priest's hand, appreciating not only the gesture but the comfort of his touch. It was as though Priest knew what he needed and willingly gave it, ignoring whatever *he* might be feeling about the simple PDA.

"So, where were you for the past few days?" Hesitant curiosity laced Priest's voice.

"I went to visit my sister. It'd been a while, and I was feeling the need for ... some sibling comfort."

Priest squeezed *his* hand this time, acknowledging that he understood why Tris had needed to run away. "Are you closer to her than to your brother?" he asked.

"Not really, though she *is* older than Tag. We share the burden of being older than him, but she's the only girl, and the expectations of her were different from those for me, as you can imagine. But she's married with children, and I knew she would give me a different perspective on things."

"My only sibling is a younger sister as well, also married with children, living in the Caribbean with her physician husband. My parents live in Spain, so our family is pretty scattered. The closest we've been to each other in the last five years was after Jane died. They all came to spend time at the house, mostly for the children, but also for me I guess."

Tris had lost his only living grandmother when he was a small boy, and sometimes, when the weight of his anger with his father settled over him, he wondered how such a warm and sweet old lady had given birth to such an arsehole like his dad had turned out to be. He had never known his grandfathers, and only aunts and uncles who had been as distant as older relatives tended to be with young children. Or at least, that was *his* experience.

"I'm sure you were glad they were there, even if you wanted like hell to be alone to wallow in your grief." He could understand that complexity of emotions, especially after Devon. "I know what happened with my ex is nothing compared to your loss, but my therapist at the time warned me never to compare my situation to anyone else's." That had been a loss of such a magnitude that his barely adult heart had been completely crushed. "But if you felt like I did," he continued "like my heart didn't know how to beat, like I was drowning and couldn't get air, then I know how you felt."

"It *was* hard. Thank goodness it isn't like it was anymore."

They'd found their way back to where they'd started, and as they walked past the column at the entrance where a man still sat manning a white booth whose sides boasted the word "Legalize" and a painting of a green marijuana plant, Priest said, "I took the tube, so I'm headed that way." He pointed over his shoulder in the direction of the train station.

"If you don't mind, I can give you a ride home. I won't come in," Tris hurried to add, "because it'll probably be too soon for Shannon."

Relief shone in Priest's eyes. "Thanks for understanding. I wouldn't want you to think I'm still hiding by not asking you to come in."

Tris smiled. When he was pleased to, he could be all grown up. The thought made him chuckle, but Priest didn't ask why, so he just led the way back to his car. They didn't talk much on the way back, but Tris didn't mind the silence. It was the comfortable kind that meant there would be time for talking later, and he was all for it. When they were stopped at the foot of Priest's driveway, he turned to Tris with a smile.

"Thanks for the lift. And for the talk and the forgiveness and the trust. I won't let you down again."

That ... that right there was his complete undoing. That Priest would acknowledge that *he'd* been the one to mess up was huge for Tris. When had he ever known a man he cared about and trusted to do that without being pushed into it? His father would never admit to being wrong, to being a disappointment, to being less than he thought he was. And his ex? Devon always saw the faults in others as the reasons for his actions. And here was Priest, proving that Tris's mistrust of emotion and refusal to allow himself to feel anything permanent for anyone had run its course.

It really was time to move on. He nodded. "You're welcome."

The sweet kiss, a simple press of lips as Priest said goodbye, was everything that Tris could wish for, a silent promise of better things to come.

Chapter 25

Priest

A man who is secure in his sexuality is invincible.

"That's brilliant!"

Priest's eyes lit up as he followed the contractor through the renovations already begun on Tristan's house via video call. The space had opened up nicely, and despite the early issues with mold in some of the baseboards and the need to rip out the fireplace, which was unstable and required a new plan that he'd had to run by Tristan while he was away on business, things were moving along swimmingly.

"I'm pleased with how things are going, yes. Bit of bad weather right now, so we'll do some of the work in the basement. The soundproofing will make it the perfect man cave, once we've finished raising the floor."

Priest laughed. "I guess it will." He didn't bother to correct the contractor's assumption.

They chatted briefly before he rang off, eager to get his day done. He and Tristan hadn't been able to spend any time together in person after their talk more than a week earlier, because he'd been away for business, and Tristan and the band had been deep in rehearsals for a benefit concert to raise funds for Elder Care Initiatives, an organization established to support the work of old age homes.

Tonight, though, they had another date. Priest had agreed to leave the planning to Tristan, who'd refused to give him even a single clue to where they were going or what they'd be doing. He'd only made one request ... he wanted to say hi to the children before they went. It had been a week, and since Priest had told the kids that he and Tristan were going on a date, he saw where that was a smart move on his lover's part. Best to get the first-time awkwardness over with, especially since Shannon was slowly thawing.

Tidying his desk and setting the rest of his office to rights didn't take long, and as he was slipping on his suit jacket, Lachlan walked in the door, clearly ready to leave as well.

"On your way out?" he asked.

"Yeah. I need a shower and a shave before Tristan shows up." The smile on Priest's face was as inevitable as sunshine in summer.

Lachlan's answering smile was part amusement and part affection. "I'm glad you've finally pulled your head out of your arse. How's my baby girl doing?" Lachlan loved his children like Priest was sure he'd love his own, if he had any.

"She's speaking to me in more than monosyllables now."

Lachlan chuckled. "Well, consider yourself lucky, mate. She could have kept you at arm's length until she found her next crush, and Lord only knows when *that's* going to be. I mean, what boy can ever measure up to your man?"

Your man. The words resonated inside Priest, comforting and rewarding, a validation and a blessing. "Guess we'll just have to wait and see." He walked over to where Lachlan stood waiting and they exited together, Priest closing the door behind him. "I'm just a bit nervous about the pre-date meet-up. Tristan wants to say hi to the kids, and I'm not sure how Shan will react."

Lachlan sighed. "Preteens. Better you than me, my friend." He clapped a sympathetic hand on Priest's shoulder as they waited for the lift.

"Soon-to-be-teenager. Which reminds me, are we still doing the party at yours?"

"We are indeed. And you'd better bring the rocker with you. I've given you enough time and grace." Lachlan wagged a finger at him as he spoke, doing his best to stifle his amusement and utterly failing.

The laughter he shared with his best friend lifted Priest's spirits even more as he drove home and let himself into the kitchen. Returning Onesie's doggie kisses with some belly scritches further settled his jitters, and despite the unusual quiet, he felt hopeful that everything would be okay. Mrs. Marks would be there in less than an hour, so he'd need to get a move on.

"Shan? Mase? I'm home," he called out. No answer meant they were in their respective rooms. Would he have to coax Shannon out of hers when Tristan came? Time enough to worry about that after he was dressed and ready to go. Deciding that black slacks and a white shirt were classic and tasteful and would be appropriate anywhere they went, he made quick work of showering and dressing before going in search of his children. It would be better all around if he didn't keep the news a secret.

Mason stood outside his door when he opened it, fist upraised to knock. "Dad, I was just coming to find you. Mrs. Marks is here."

Priest resisted the urge to ruffle his hair, remembering at the last moment that his son had suddenly become less tolerant of the affectionate gesture. They were both growing up too bloody fast if you asked him.

"Thank you, son. Please let her know I'll be right down."

Knocking on Shannon's door, he waited until it opened to reveal her already in her pajamas. Immediately, concern replaced the nerves.

"Are you feeling alright, love? Do you need anything? Mrs. Marks is here. I can have her bring you up whatever you like."

"I'm fine, Dad." She eyed him warily. "Is tonight your date?"

"Yes, and I need you to change, please. Tristan would like to see you both before we go."

Her eyes clouded. "Why?"

"He wants to say hello." Keeping it simple seemed to be the best option. "He'll be here in a few. Go ahead and change and meet us downstairs in the lounge. And don't dilly-dally." He reached out to cup her cheek. "It'll be alright, Shan, you'll see." Then he leaned in and kissed her on the forehead.

When Tristan arrived five minutes later looking dapper and delicious in matching slim-fitting black trousers, a crisp white shirt and a black leather jacket, Priest leaned in to buss his lips after he closed the door behind him.

"Great minds, eh?" he asked, gesturing between them. "You look the part of the rockstar, love."

The tension beginning to pulse between them was sweet and hot, but Priest knew they'd need to temper it for the time being. The children were waiting. "Come on. Let's go to the lounge."

Shannon was sitting in the loveseat closest to the door on her phone, ear buds in her ears listening to music, he assumed. Mason was playing a game on his phone, but he looked up as soon as they walked in, and he beamed a smile at them.

"Mr. D!" he exclaimed, rising to walk over to Tristan.

"Hello, Mason. It's good to see you again. How's the gaming going?" Tristan returned Mason's grin.

"I beat another level on the new game Auntie Angie bought me. Maybe we can play it some time?"

"I'd like that. Maybe when you come to visit me on my boat we can play out on the deck."

Mason's eyes widened. "You have a boat? Is it a yacht? How big is it?"

Tristan laughed. "It's a houseboat. I live on it, and it's big enough. If your dad agrees, we can all have a sleepover on it when you come to visit. There's enough room for all of us."

Priest had only been listening with half an ear, admiring how Tristan was winning over his son effortlessly, and observing Shannon quietly paying attention while still pretending to be listening to her phone. She had pulled one earbud out when he walked in, and Priest had chosen to give her time to gather her courage to say hello. Now, though, he decided it was time for her sulking to end and was just about to call her attention to the elephant in the room when she stood up and came to stand next to him.

"Good evening, Mr. DeVere," she said quietly, barely glancing at him before looking down at her hands.

"Good evening, Shannon. It's nice to see you again," Tristan repeated. "I hope you're well."

She looked at him again, holding his gaze a moment longer as though she understood his unspoken question before she replied, "I'm fine, thank you. I hope you and Dad have a good time tonight."

"Thank you. I'm sure we will. We're going to see an art exhibit. Do you like art?"

"Some of it," she answered, warming up a bit more. "Some of it is weird, though."

Tristan chuckled while Priest watched him charm his daughter out of her funk. "I agree. If your dad likes this show, maybe he can take you to see it before it closes."

This time her eyes were sharp when she held his gaze. "You're not going to be there too?"

Tristan's expression softened. "If I'm invited, I will be, of course." Shannon finally smiled. It was small but real. Message received and accepted.

Priest wished he could kiss Tristan in that moment, he was so relieved. Clearly his man was better at calming ruffled feathers than either of them had given him credit for if he could get a sulking teenager to smile at him despite being angry that he was dating her father instead of noticing her.

"Anyway, we've got to be off. It was good spending a little time with you both. I'll see you again soon."

Priest wondered if the faint uncertainty he'd detected in Tristan's tone was just in his imagination, until his lover spoke as they were driving away.

"D'you think I've been removed from the *persona non grata* list now?"

"With promises of a sleepover on your houseboat and a visit to an art gallery together, I'm sure you have," Priest replied with a chuckle. "I admit to being jealous, though."

"Jealous?" Tristan turned an inquiring glance his way. "Why?"

"I only got to find out where we're going for our date before we get there because you were intent on seducing my daughter into liking you again. That feels like a punishable offense to me," Priest teased.

Tristan's chuckle seduced him with its warm amusement. "Punishment, huh? Kinky fucker!"

"Any more talk like that and we won't be seeing any artwork tonight."

The tension swelling around them held comfort and the promise of satisfaction. Priest relaxed against the seat and listened to the music echoing softly around them in the car, relishing the contentment that had finally settled inside him. Whatever happened next, he was ready for it. He recognized the art gallery as one of the few he enjoyed revisiting when Tristan found a spot to park. He and Jane had been there once to see her friend's work and they'd been pleasantly surprised by some of the other brilliant work on display.

"Who are we seeing this evening?"

"I thought you'd enjoy spending some more time with Averille Shand's work," Tristan replied as they walked together into the gallery. "Tonight's the opening night of this show, and they've done it up with cocktails and finger foods and a live band."

Tristan stopped at the table set up to welcome guests and handed over two tickets before they entered the lobby where a low hum of conversation swelled as the number of guests grew. Servers moved among them offering drinks and food. Priest helped himself to a glass of bubbly and some delicious shrimp bites. He saw the artist, a tall, elegant woman, standing near the door to the gallery itself and pointed her out to Tristan.

"There's Averille. She hasn't aged a day."

Seeing her reminded him of the friendship she and Jane had shared, one in which he'd been included. They hadn't seen each other after Jane's funeral, though she had called him a number of times to check up on him. What would she think of his new relationship? They'd never discussed such things when the three of them had been together, and he didn't know much more about her than most people did.

As though she knew he was thinking about her, Averille looked up, saw him, and smiled widely. She said something to the man she was standing next to and headed over to where he stood with Tristan.

"Get ready to be introduced," he murmured as she approached. His body hummed when Tristan seemed to move closer to him, as if he needed protecting.

"Benedict, how lovely to see you, my friend!" Averille pulled him into a tight hug, holding on longer than necessary before releasing him to plant a soft kiss on his cheek.

"Good to see you too, Av! This is my friend Tristan DeVere."

"A pleasure, Mr. DeVere," she purred, turning her light brown eyes on him. "Third Generation bass guitarist, am I right?"

Tristan's eyes widened, as surprised as Priest was that she knew anything about him or the band. "That's me," he answered. "It's nice to meet you too, Ms. Shand."

"I understand that you won the bid for 'Hope's Promise'," she continued. "I'm so glad you appreciate my work."

"It's a marvelous piece and beautifully executed. And I couldn't resist the treble clef, after all."

She grinned. "Indeed. I'm surprised Benedict didn't beat you to the punch on that one. He knew when I started it and wanted first dibs on it."

Priest felt Tristan's eyes on him then and saw the calculating tilt of his head and his narrowed eyes as he figured things out about the bids on the fundraiser night. Thankfully, before he could say anything, Averille turned to Priest and continued speaking.

"How in the world are you, my friend? I'm sorry I've been such a stranger lately, but you know how it is." Remorse shadowed her eyes, but Priest would have none of it.

"No need for apologies, Av. I understand. The kids and I are fine. How about you?"

"All good here. Making my annual pilgrimage into the outside world before I head back to my hermitage." She laughed quietly, and Priest joined her.

"It's always good to see you, Av. Maybe someday, when you're ready, I'll come by with the children. You know they love it when you let them play with your watercolors."

"Ladies and gentlemen," a male voice broke into their conversation. "Welcome to the opening night of our 'Stars Aligning' exhibition. We're thrilled to be showing the work of two of Britain's greatest artistic talents, Averille Shand and Omari Achebe. Ms. Shand's paintings are a magical and spiritual delight, and Mr. Achebe's sculptures are power and sensuality in 3D. Both artists are here with us this evening and are happy to talk about their work with you. And now without further ado, I'm happy to declare the exhibition open."

The doors to the gallery swung open as the man added, "Please leave all food and drink in the lobby. Refreshments will remain available for all guests throughout the evening."

The guests filed through the doors into a high-ceilinged room where the art works were displayed with spotlights in various soft hues. Each piece had a descriptive note below it, and there were two boards displaying pictures and a bio of each artist to either side of the entrance. Soft music surrounded them as they moved through the space, and without his conscious volition, Priest found his hand at the small of Tristan's back guiding him through the room, pausing when Tristan did, moving when he moved.

"This is sexy as sin," Tristan declared as they stood in front of a glazed, mid-sized sculpture in flaming colors titled "Drive". The man leaning nonchalantly against a fragment of wall was burly and heavily muscled with a sharply chiseled face and full lips. His eyes were almost glowing, the slight frown marring his forehead giving him a formidable air. He was buck naked, his cock and balls partially hidden by the position of one leg depending on where you were standing.

"Can't argue with the truth," Priest replied, holding Tristan's gaze for a long moment before looking back at the sculpture. "I wonder what he's frowning at? What's got him thinking so hard?"

Tristan wandered around to the back of the piece, which showed a strong back and tight arse cheeks. For some totally unknown reason, Priest's cock shifted in his slacks, his mind going unerringly to Tristan's body after their last time together. The way the sculpted man's feet were planted on the ground, and how he held his shoulders ... everything spoke of the sexual power intended by the title. A flush warmed his flesh, but Priest couldn't look away.

Tristan smiled at him, his eyes gleaming with knowledge. It wouldn't be a stretch to imagine that the younger man knew exactly where Priest's thoughts had gone, most likely because his own were there too. And that idea made his cock jerk harder. Only the fact that they were in a fairly crowded space stopped him from adjusting himself, though he did beg the gods of randy men not to let anyone notice his predicament. Because who got aroused by a sculpture?

"Are you alright there, Priest?"

Tristan's question brought him up sharp. "I'm fine, thanks. Shall we move on?"

Tristan nodded, and Priest followed him to the next few pieces, thankfully cooling his overheating body before Averille joined them again.

"So, how are you finding the exhibition?" She looked at Tristan as she spoke.

"You've always been one of my favorite painters," he began with a charming smile at her. "And now it seems I'm developing a liking for sculpture, as well."

Her eyes twinkled as she chuckled at his comment. "I think Omari's 'Drive' has made a convert of many art lovers. And it's no wonder, either. That's his best piece by far in this show. It's one of a series. You should ask him about it."

"I will," Tristan promised. "I'd love to hear more about it. I also noticed that you've got a few other paintings in the same style of 'Hope's Promise'. Are any of them for sale?"

"Not at the moment, no. But I'll be making an announcement about that in a few weeks."

She turned to Priest to add, "My annual garden party will be in a few more weeks, and I expect you to be there. No more hiding away." She wagged a finger at him. "Bring the children and any other guests you'd like to bring." She grinned impishly, winking at him before adding, "Just let me know how many will be in your party so I can make the appropriate arrangements."

Priest didn't have a chance to respond before she was whisked away by a rather official-looking gentleman who whispered something in her ear that had her following him immediately. He turned his attention back to Tristan, whom he knew had heard every word and probably realized that somehow, his friend knew that they were together.

"She's either very intuitive or we're not doing too good a job of disguising our connection," Tristan murmured as they moved on to another piece.

"Definitely the former," Priest replied. "I don't know how she does it, but she's skilled at reading people."

"Must make it difficult to lie to her," Tristan commented.

"I've never had reason to," Priest said, understanding Tristan's unspoken question. And because Averille had figured out that they were together, answering her inevitable questions just got a whole lot easier.

Omari Achebe was standing with a small circle of interested people around him at the sculpture they'd been riveted on, and by mutual consent, they walked over in time to hear him speaking in strongly-accented English.

"A man's base of power partly resides in his awareness of himself as a sexual being. It is innate to who he is, to how he views the world, to how he achieves intellectual, spiritual, and moral authority. A man who is secure in his sexuality is invincible."

Provocative words, for sure, but Priest was barely listening as Mr. Achebe's audience took him to task, questioning his meaning. He was too busy thinking about himself, about how hiding who he was had been curiously emasculating, and he hadn't been aware of it until he'd had to make the decision to come out to his children. He'd gained personal power once he spoke his identity into existence. The piece was at once a psychological and emotional, as well as an erotic, triumph for the artist.

They'd been snacking on the plentiful hors d'oeuvres as they gone through the exhibition but by the time they were ready to leave, Priest was ready for real food, as was Tristan.

"Time for dinner. We've got a date on the Thames."

"A dinner cruise? Sweet." Priest loved Tristan's romantic impulse, but he did have one concern. "What about the publicity?" he asked. "Will that be an issue?"

Tristan glanced at him as they drove to the pier. "I thought that it was only fair," he began, navigating around an illegally parked car. "That if you've made some public moves to secure what we are building, so should I."

"Are you absolutely sure about this, Tristan? I don't want you to feel obliged..."

"But I *am* obliged, Priest. We're in this together. And after all these years, it's time to be completely open. Enough of the wild speculation. If we're seen together and anyone has questions, I'll answer them this time." He paused, then added, more uncertainly, "Unless you don't want to? I know it can be a lot, and I don't know how it will affect the children..."

Priest stopped him. "It's okay, Tristan. We'll cross that bridge when we get to it, yes? I know that you'll work with me to do everything we can to protect the kids. I'm a grown man. Don't worry about me."

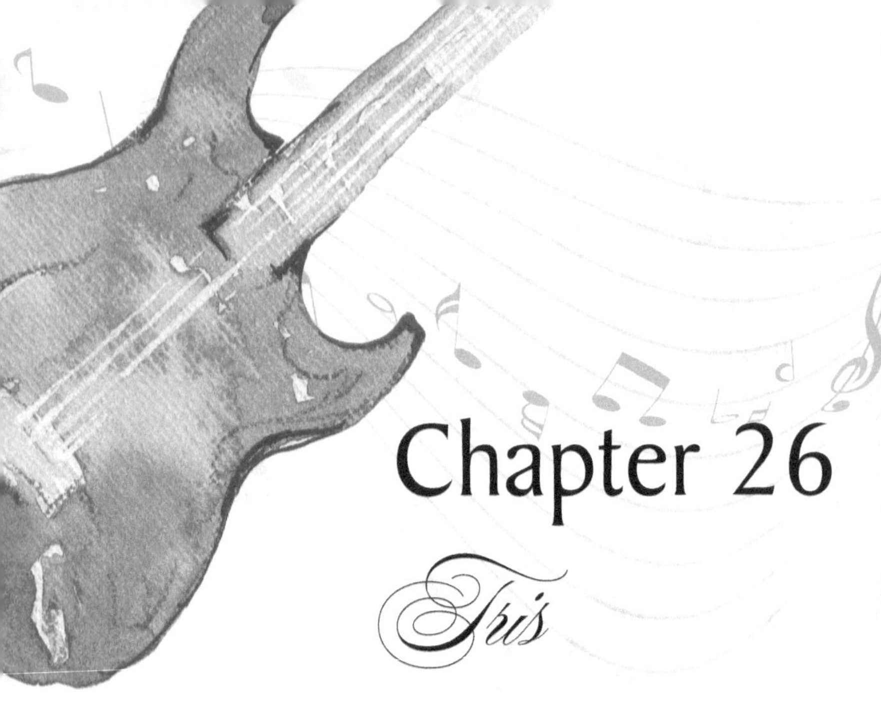

Chapter 26

Tris

I'm sure we'll play well together.
I already know you're very talented.

They were quiet the rest of the way, not speaking again until they'd been seated at a table for two by a window on the big boat. No one seemed to notice them, which was a good thing, although Tris wouldn't care if anyone did. He was fine being open with the man he wanted to be with more than he wanted to remain hidden from the world, and he was grateful that Priest was right there with him.

"I've never been on one of these cruises," Priest said. He clinked his complimentary glass of bubbly against Tris's and took a deep swallow. "This is grand. Here's to moving on."

Tris smiled. "Cheers!"

It was jazz night on the boat, and as they ate their three-course meal that included some kind of delicious ham and chicken terrine, confit of duck with veggies, and a mouthwatering coconut and vanilla crème brûlée, they were treated to delightful music played by expert musicians. Tris could feel Priest's eyes on him, and he knew his face was beaming as he enjoyed the music. Would music be a theme of all their dates? He wouldn't say no to any of it.

Surprisingly, their table by the window somewhat cocooned them away from the other guests, which made Tris almost feel like he was dining in a bubble. He wished that Priest would reach over and hold his hand, but despite his words earlier, he wasn't sure that Priest was quite ready for that level of PDA. But when he felt a foot tapping his own under the table, his heart swelled. It seemed they'd been battling the same wish. Thank God for long tablecloths!

"Footsy, Priest?" Tris teased, raising an amused brow.

"Would you prefer handsy? I'm game if you are." Priest held his gaze, his own smile predatory with how wide it stretched his cheeks.

Tristan chuckled. "Maybe later, on the way home? That might be more ... rewarding."

Warmth stole into his cheeks, no doubt giving Priest a fair idea of where his mind had gone. Priest nodded, and Tris suddenly wished they were off the damn boat. He'd had enough of shipboard romance for the night. Time for more. He was beyond ready for more, even if he didn't know where or when that would happen. But holding hands in the car would be a start. He'd take it. As the cruise wound down, they let their gazes catch on some of the sights visible on the river ... The Tower of London and Tower Bridge, London Bridge, The Houses of Parliament, and Big Ben.

Driving home next to an aroused man was an exercise in patience for both of them. Tris made lazy trails up and down Priest's thigh, while *he* did his best to keep Tris on edge, teasing his growing cock with glancing touches as he also stroked Tris. Only when he needed both hands to make turns did Tris remove his own, but after a while, he reached down and held Priest's hand, stopping him from further teasing.

"If you want to get back to your children in one piece, you're going to have to stop," he managed to rumble out, squeezing Priest's hand in his fist. "You're much too good at this kind of handsies, and I'd much rather enjoy it when I'm not in danger of wrecking the car."

Priest grinned, pulling on his hand, but Tris resisted. "May I have my hand back then?" he asked, chuckling.

"I never said I didn't want to hold your hand. I just need you to stop edging me with it."

Priest turned his palm up then and linked their fingers, and they drove the rest of the way home like that. On his driveway, he turned to Tris again, still holding his hand.

"Do you want to come in?"

Tris shook his head. "I'd love to, but I don't think I'd be able to stop myself from taking things too far. I'd rather not be interrupted when we have make-up sex, you know?" He winked at Priest, trying to ease the sexual tension between them and pulling a laugh from him.

"Are you driving home tonight?" Priest asked without responding to his comment. "It's a bit of a drive after the evening we've had." They hadn't indulged aside from a second glass of champagne, but it had been a long evening, with a long afternoon before it.

"I'm staying with Henry overnight, then going home in the morning."

"Come for breakfast before you go. Bring your nephews. Shan and Mase will love to hang out with them again." Desire leaked through Priest's invitation.

"I'd like that." Tris leaned over the console and Priest met him in the middle, sealing their lips together.

The flame that had been on low all evening flashed higher as they invaded each other's mouths, groaning into fierce, hungry kisses, slowing to nip and tease, then powering back up to ravage each other. Tris's cock, which had been on edge all evening, surged to life again, pulsing with its own heartbeat in his trousers.

"Fuck!" Priest groaned when Tris's hand dropped to his lap. "We can't, love."

Tris inhaled sharply, squeezing the hard flesh beneath his palm before releasing it and pulling away. "I know. I just wish..."

"I know," Priest echoed him. "Me too. I'll see you in the morning."

He leaned in to kiss Tris's cheek and then got out of the car. Tris hated to leave him standing there, but he knew they'd made the right decision. It was one thing for his children to know that Priest was dating Tris, but it would be a different thing for them to find out that they were sleeping together. Shannon wasn't a fool, and she'd be bound to wonder about how fast they were going and whether that meant her dad had been lying to her. Not to mention making love with children around wasn't something Tris had ever done, and he wasn't sure he was quite ready for that. Still, he'd be lying if he said he didn't want to fall into Priest's bed for some wild sexy times.

Henry's house was quiet when he got back, and he did his best not to wake anyone as he made his way toward the staircase after downing a glass of water. He should have known that he wouldn't escape Henry's grilling, though. His friend was sitting in the lounge, a single lamp on, nursing a drink.

"Ah, sneaking in after curfew, are you?" he asked, chuckling.

"No, Dad," Tris answered sarcastically. "My curfew is after midnight, remember?"

Henry's lunatic cackle was pitched low enough that only Tris would hear him. "So, how did it go?" he asked once his amusement had abated.

Tris sighed and sat down opposite his friend. "It was brilliant! Thanks for suggesting the dinner cruise, by the way. It was the perfect end to a great evening."

Henry sipped his drink. "Good. How did it go with the children?"

"Surprisingly well. Certainly better than I'd expected. Which reminds me, Priest has invited the boys over for a play date with his two. I'm to take them to breakfast with me."

"Breakfast, eh? Maybe I'll come get them and bring his with ours to the zoo. That's where we're going tomorrow afternoon."

"I wouldn't want to mess with your family time..." Tris began, but Henry shushed him.

"Do you or do you not want some time alone with your man now that you've both fixed things?"

"Of course I do, but we'll just have to be patient."

"Or you can take the gift I'm offering you and enjoy the time with him while they're out. We'll even keep them for dinner if he'll be okay with that and bring them home after."

Tris wanted that more than he could say. "I'll ask him when we get there and text you as soon as I know."

It took far longer than he wished for Tris to fall asleep. Images of Priest's face as they eyed each other over dinner, hunger and affection pouring out of him, and memories of their goodnight kisses, kept his body on a low hum. Jerking off wouldn't help with the deep-seated need to be in Priest's orbit, even if that was all he could have. He loved the feeling of having someone he could feel that way about yet hated that it might make him seem too needy.

He wanted to quench his thirst with the man who was causing it, but he didn't want to be the only one feeling this desperate ache. Should he call for a last goodnight? His cell phone said it was long past midnight. Priest was likely asleep. He should really do the same. He put the phone away and forced his body to relax.

By the time he got downstairs next morning, the boys were up, dressed, and raring to go. Tris laughed at their antics as he poured himself a cup of coffee.

"Settle down, you two. We'll leave in ten minutes."

He turned as Henry walked in, heading over to his wife to plant a quick kiss on her lips.

"Morning," he grumbled and poured himself his own hot drink. "What time's breakfast?" he asked Tris.

"Nine. We'll leave soon."

"We'll be there to get you at noon, boys," Gen said, coming over with a container that she placed in front of Nick. "You be sure to thank Mr. Priestley for inviting you over for breakfast and hand these to him."

"What's in the bowl?" Tris asked.

"Cranberry scones. I made a couple of batches yesterday, and since you're taking these two off our hands for the morning, I thought it'd be nice to give your man something to help feed the hungry masses."

Tris laughed. "They *are* growing boys, you know," he said, ignoring the "your man" comment.

"Can we go now, Uncle Tris?" Luke interrupted. "I'm hungry." And as if to verify his statement, his stomach rumbled loudly enough to be heard.

"Good Lord!" Tris drained the last of his coffee and took the mug to the sink. "Let's get going. I don't want to be the cause of your demise from starvation."

Henry and Gen laughed as Gen took the mug from him. "Have a good time," she said for his ears only and smiled, all cheeks and teeth. Tris chuckled, then laughed outright when Henry winked and added, "Make the most of the time, mate."

Thankfully, the boys didn't notice his heated cheeks. They were too excited about having breakfast with their new mates and going to the zoo, as well. Their chatter was full of speculation about what kinds of games Mason played, about which part of the zoo they liked the most—"I love the butterfly house," Nick declared—about what other bands they liked to listen to. Clearly, there wouldn't be any lapses in conversation or in entertainment. Each boy also had his favorite race car and had brought along an extra so that if they were allowed, they'd race them with Mason.

Shannon opened the door when they arrived, offering them a shy smile and inviting them in. Priest stood behind her, his eyes devouring Tris who returned the favor before following the boys into the house. Animated good mornings flowed around him as the children greeted each other but his whole attention was focused on the man now standing next to him. The heat from Priest's body felt a hundred times higher than it was, and the urge to pull him in for a kiss was almost overpowering. He joined in the greetings instead, declining Mason's invitation to join the boys in playing car races after breakfast.

"Breakfast first, then playtime."

Priest didn't sound nearly as flustered as Tris felt. That must be one of the perks of parenthood ... iron control.

"Mum said to give you this, Mr. Priestley," Nick said, remembering his task and offering the bowl of scones to Priest.

"Thank you. Come through, everyone. Breakfast is ready. Shan, show the boys where to wash their hands, please."

Tris waited until they stood in the kitchen together alone before turning to meet Priest's gaze. The desire that greeted him made the quick kiss they stole sweeter and more precious than any they'd shared so far. Tris breathed softly against his lips, prolonging the moment, before pulling away, both mindful of the children nearby.

"Henry has invited your kids to go to the zoo with their family this afternoon. If you agree, they'll be here to pick them up around noon."

Priest's eyes glittered. "All of them?"

Tris chuckled. "All of them. And if you don't mind, they'll even feed them dinner before they bring yours back."

A deep breath later, Priest replied, "You'll need to tell me your friends' taste in wine so I can get them a case of it."

"I'm sure a single bottle will do," Tris teased as the sounds of children returning reached his ears. "I'll just send them a message now."

"A special thank you for today seems in order," Priest insisted, then turned to say to Mason, who appeared first, "Right then, son, you get going on the juice. Shan, toast, please."

"Can I help?" Tris asked, finished with his text message to Henry.

"Well, if you like, you can tell me what the boys will like best."

Eventually, everyone settled at the table and before long, the happy chatter of the children made any conversation he might choose to have with Priest impossible. He listened idly as the boys asked Shannon if she'd like a turn racing cars, and when she declined, Luke asked, "So what are you gonna do then?" Tris loved that the boy was always trying to make sure everyone was involved in fun times.

"I guess I can be the referee, or whatever you call the one who declares the winner and gives out penalties and such."

"That's football, Shan," Mason said condescendingly. "We don't need a referee for racing."

Before the discussion could devolve into an argument, Priest interrupted. "You won't have too much time to play, anyway. Once we've cleared up from breakfast, it'll be time to get ready for your outing."

"Outing?" Mason tilted his head excitedly, a piece of sausage on his fork halfway to his mouth. "Where are we going, Dad?"

"You've both been invited to go along with the boys and their parents to the zoo. They'll be here to get you all at noon. And if you're good, you'll even get to stay for dinner."

The switch from deciding what Shannon would do while they raced cars to what animal was the coolest in the zoo was the subject of heated debate for the rest of the meal. Shannon was well pleased with Tris when he agreed with her that tigers were by far and away the best of the bunch. He did love tigers, so it was an easy win for him.

"See? Even Mr. D agrees with me, and since he's our guest, he wins. Which means I win," she declared.

Tris registered the "Mr. D" in her sketchy argument at the same time as Mason's protests. "Luke and Nick are our guests too. Why can't they win?" he demanded.

"Because they don't have the same vote, silly!" She couldn't have sounded any more satisfied. He could almost see her dusting her hands off in triumph. He chuckled when she added, "Most votes win." Then she finished her orange juice and closed the knife and fork on her plate before announcing, "I'm going up to my room after we clean up. I'm going to find something cool to wear."

Priest grinned at his daughter but said nothing. The children, including Nick and Luke, all cleared away the dishes, and while Shannon packed the dishwasher, the boys went to play with Onesie, who had been lying next to Nick's chair the whole time snoozing. Tris wandered into the lounge and sat at the piano, idly passing his hands over the keys while he waited for Priest to reappear.

"You play piano too?" Priest asked from right behind him.

"I dabble," he replied, struggling not to shiver. "When I'm writing a song, I use it to flesh out the melody and figure out chords and such."

"Maybe we can play together when the children leave." Smoky tones roughened Priest's words, inducing a hard shudder that Tris couldn't control.

Keeping his eyes on the keyboard for fear he would lose control if he looked into Priest's face, Tris said, "I'm sure we'll play well together. I already know you're very talented."

Priest's dirty chuckle sizzled up Tris's spine, and he'd never been more grateful for a little boy's intervention than when Mason rushed into the room.

"Dad, Shan and I are going to wear our new band t-shirts." He was already dressed, even though they still had more than an hour to wait. His excitement filled the kitchen with energy that snapped and sizzled around them.

"Try to stay clean, son," Priest begged him. "We don't want the Thackerys to think I'm raising a hooligan."

"We're only going to play race cars, Dad. We're not going to wrestle *this* time."

Turning without waiting for his father to respond, Mason rushed away to suit action to his words while Tris and Priest chuckled in amusement. The heated moment of verbal foreplay was broken, but the buzz remained in Tris's veins, keeping him attuned to Priest's every move.

"Would you like a tour of the house? The last time you were here you only got to see a little of this level."

Tris would do anything for alone time with Priest. Visions of schoolboy antics in each room … a stolen kiss here, a grope there … flooded his mind and he managed to disguise his groan in a cough. The ground floor had the kitchen, a lounge and a formal sitting room and dining room as well as a guest washroom. The kitchen door led to the garage, which had a door leading to the back garden.

"Next time, we can have supper out there. It's lovely in the summertime," Priest informed him as he led the way upstairs. "The children love to play out there until late when it's warm."

Upstairs there were three bedrooms, the master suite including a beautifully appointed and clearly newly-renovated bathroom with a clawfoot tub with a shower attachment. Tris thought he could let all his troubles float away in the room with its navy-blue walls, pale blue tiles, and white window treatments. He noted the open shelving filled with towels and washrags, and the robe hanging on a hook behind the door. Toiletries, a hairbrush, a shaving kit, and electric toothbrush were set neatly on the counter between double sinks.

The bedroom housed an enormous mahogany wardrobe in lieu of a built-in closet, a single tallboy, with a bedside table and a standing lamp on opposite sides of the bed. *That* was a king-sized affair, dressed in midnight blue with bright yellow and orange pillows for an exciting pop of color. Would they enjoy some playtime in it? The idea sent a harder buzz zapping through Tris's veins.

"You must live like a king in this room," he observed, needing something to fill the silence.

"A king without a consort," Priest rumbled, shutting the bedroom door they stood next to with his foot.

He pulled Tris close and raided his mouth as they stood just behind the door. Tris gave himself over to the passion spilling from Priest into their kiss, holding onto his waist to anchor himself in the embrace, in the moment of desire. Priest's groan as they pulled apart echoed his own feelings on the matter before they walked out, leaving the tempting bed behind them.

The rest of the tour was a blur. They barely glanced into the children's rooms, their bathroom, a door leading to the attic—"I'll take you up there after they leave," Priest promised him—before they made their way back down to supervise the excited children. The boys were racing their cars in the hallway, and Tris assumed Shannon was still getting ready. He held back an impatient huff when he checked his watch and saw they still had half an hour to wait.

Priest's chuckle brought his eyes up. "What?"

"Whenever I was feeling extra randy, Jane would remind me that patience is a virtue." His grin was wide, even though his voice was soft with memory.

"Where's the virtue in being cockblocked by a bunch of preteens?" Tris groused, though a smile ticked his lips upwards.

"Anticipation makes it sweeter," Priest said.

"Promise?" Tris sounded like a teenager himself, but he didn't care. He was enjoying this charged banter too much.

"Promise."

A firm touch at the small of his back held the heat Tris knew meant he'd get his fill of this man and then some once the children left. When Henry and Gen arrived, he and

Priest walked out with the children so Priest could say hello and thank them. Once they'd waved goodbye and watched the big car drive off, Priest turned to him, his eyes blazing with desire.

"Ready?"

Tris nodded. His voice had deserted him, but that was okay. No words were necessary. His actions would speak for him.

Epilogue

Priest

*As happily ever afters went, this was
the best way to start theirs.*

"He's good for you, my friend."

Priest turned to find his best friend watching Tristan, who was kicking around a ball with Mason and the Thackery twins. Their shouts of joy rent the air each time they managed to wrangle the ball away from him.

"Yes, I have to agree with you there."

He let his gaze rest on the man he was in love with, and a fist tightened around his heart. They hadn't been together long, in the grand scheme of things, but Priest knew that someday soon, he was going to take the next step in his journey back from grieving and ask Tristan to marry him.

When the rest of the band arrived with their women a few minutes later, pandemonium broke out in Lachlan's backyard. Shrieks and shouts of greeting met them before they were completely surrounded by children. Priest watched the men as they high-fived and fist-bumped them all.

"Where's the birthday girl?" Henry asked above the din.

Shannon raised a hand, and Gen stepped forward with a bag full of gifts. She smiled and said something too low for him to hear before offering his daughter a hug. Priest's heart swelled with gratitude for these people who had accepted him into their circle and made his family their own. Inevitably, his thoughts went to Tristan, whom he could no longer see. Where had he disappeared to?

"I'm glad they're here now, because I'm starving." Lachlan laughed as Priest swung around to find Tristan approaching. "And I'll bet I'm not the only one."

Priest leaned in to buss his lover's lips. It had been six weeks since they'd renewed their relationship, six weeks of learning and loving, and tonight, for the first time since then, Tristan would be staying the night at Priest's after the party. In fact, he'd be staying the rest of the weekend. They'd talked about it that day, after they'd mauled each other while the children were with the Thackerys. Memories of that day, of those things they'd said and done to each other rushed in again, and his cock woke with a start. Maybe Tristan had the right idea. Feeding everyone would redirect his randy thoughts to safer paths.

"Why don't I help settle your friends while you and Tristan bring the food out?" Lachlan suggested, a smirk on his face. He'd been more than happy to hear that Tristan and Priest had patched things up, and he'd taken every opportunity to get them together "like any good matchmaker would do," he'd declared.

Priest shook his head but happily walked back into the house, aware of Tristan close behind him, almost crowding him. Inside, the door shut behind them, he turned to find his lover nose to nose with him.

"Need something?" he asked, reaching up to cup Tristan's cheek.

"A kiss would be great for starters," Tristan rumbled against his lips before taking what he wanted.

Priest let him have his tongue for a long, breathless moment before pulling away. "We're supposed to be getting the food out. Do you want everyone to know what we're doing in here?"

Tristan's exaggerated pout sent him into a fit of childish giggles that he fought hard to control as he placed platters on the food cart. Tristan slapped his arse as he walked by with another cart laden with sweet treats.

"I'll make you pay for finding my desire amusing, mate."

"I can't wait," Priest answered with what felt like the cheesiest grin he'd ever worn plastered on his face as they took the food out to the tables already set up for them.

When everything was ready and everyone gathered to fill their plates, letting the birthday girl go first, the feast began. Priest didn't pay too much attention to what he ate. In fact, he couldn't say with any certainty exactly what he put in his mouth. Whatever it was, it had all tasted really good. He wasn't hungry anymore ... at least, not for food.

"Aren't you glad I'm keeping the munchkins until you surface in time to come get them for Sunday dinner?" Lachlan chuckled at Priest's missed punch. "They're so thrilled to be spending extra time with Uncle Lanny that you should be thanking me, not punching me."

"Just wait until it's your turn, mate. Remember what they say about payback."

Thirteen looked good on Shannon, Priest had to admit as he turned to see where she was. Dressed in a short skirt and high boots, with a form-fitting top that just managed not to emphasize her budding breasts, she was aglow with happiness and contentment and looked more like her mum than he'd ever seen before. When she sidled over to him after they'd cut the cake and everyone was enjoying it, he hugged her to his side, dropping a kiss on her head.

"Happy thirteenth, Shan! You're growing up so fast on me," he murmured against her hair.

"Thanks for the party and the sleepover, Dad." She squeezed his waist and looked up at him. "Will Tristan still be there when we get home on Sunday?"

Priest smiled, unsure where she was headed with the question. "Do you want him to be?"

"Yes, please. Mase and I have a surprise for him."

Priest held back his sigh of relief and nodded. "Then he will be, pet."

He suspected the tie-dyed t-shirts they'd been working on were the surprise. It had taken her a long time to thaw completely around Tristan, but this sounded more than promising. The family visit to the art gallery had been a success, but they hadn't managed the sleepover on the houseboat yet. She hadn't mentioned it, and Tristan had said he'd wait until she asked. Maybe now she would.

Later, once the fire of their hunger had eased—rough, impatient sex up against a door was highly underrated, even if his thighs disagreed—Priest and Tristan showered and lay in Priest's big bed, arms wrapped around each other. Desire still burned bright in his chest, warming his body as he held Tristan to him. Contentment settled. He could do this forever, and if Tristan agreed, he would for the rest of their lives.

There was a lot they still needed to learn about each other, but Priest knew that one day he'd have this man as his life partner, his second chance for forever with the love of his heart. Falling in love was so unpredictable, so unexpected, like sunshine in a thunderstorm or dancing at a wake. But Priest wouldn't change a thing about what he was feeling now, except for the fumbles he'd made that might have lost him the precious gift snuggled against his chest, breathing warmth into his skin and into his heart.

"What are you thinking so hard about?" Tristan's voice was heavy, whether with drowsiness or lust, Priest couldn't tell.

"I'm just marveling at how happy I am, how contented with you here in my arms."

Tristan shifted until he was looking into Priest's eyes. "And?"

Priest chuckled, shaking his head. "What makes you think there's anything else?"

He wasn't surprised that Tristan knew he hadn't said everything on his mind. The man had apparently learned to read him like a book in the three months that they'd known each other. He couldn't deny that he loved being known so intimately. It was as good as Tristan learning what made *his* motor run, what sent him over the edges of pleasure, and Tristan was definitely learning how to make him lose his mind with need and lust.

Tristan pinched a nipple hard, making Priest hiss. "Are you saying that was all you were thinking about?"

Priest reached down to silence him with a kiss, the sharp pain in his nipple spreading heat across his chest and shooting pleasure down to his once-again interested cock. Tristan rolled his hips so their dicks slid together, and they both hissed this time. Priest moaned when Tristan sucked on his tongue, owning the kiss and pulling them deeper into each other.

"I was thinking that you'd make a great king's consort, that you fit in so well in this big bed with me, that I'd like it if this could become a permanent arrangement. Someday, you know..."

Why was he fumbling for words? He knew what he wanted, but he had definitely not meant to utter any of his wishes so soon. How did this man have the power to make him say things he meant to keep quiet? That wasn't even how he would have proposed, for heaven's sake, but it sure sounded like he'd just told Tristan that he was going to ask him to marry him.

This time, Tristan initiated the tongue action, dragging Priest's head down and pulling him in to devour him. Their tongues played, hot breath washing each other's lips as they paused for air. Then Tristan rolled, pulling Priest with him until they were lying chest to chest, Priest's heavier body draped over him. Their cocks were hard and leaking against each other, when Tristan suddenly pulled his lips away to say, "When that day comes, I'll be happy to fill the position."

And if that wasn't a yes, Priest didn't know what was. He growling against the mouth once more seeking his and took the kiss beyond teasing to foreplay, letting himself go and wallowing in the need overwhelming him. Tristan's hand was on his dick, leading him to where they both wanted him to be, drove lust right through him, a power punch to the gut that made him gasp as Tristan rolled and settled over him to ride them to ecstasy.

Priest growled and set his hands on Tristan's hips, raising his own to meet his lover's downward thrusts. As happily ever afters went, this was the best way to start theirs, and as they drove each other over the edge, he thanked his lucky stars he'd faced the music and earned a second chance at love.

Holding Tristan tightly to him as they came down together, he whispered, "Welcome home, love!"

The End
♪ ♪

Keep reading for a sneak peek from *Playing It By Ear*, Book 3 in the *No Strings Attached* series.

Brandon

Zane looked coolly at Brandon when he opened the door. "Hey, your roomie in yet?"

"He's passed out in bed. Why?"

This close, Brandon could feel the heat radiating off the bodyguard's tall, powerful frame. He knew that Zane could feel the electricity that sparked between them every time they were in the same room, and this close, within touching—kissing—distance, the pull was dangerous. He gripped the door hard to stop himself from reaching out to touch.

"Just doing the rounds before turning in," Zane said. "The others are secure. You know how to reach me if you need me."

"What if...?"

Brandon hesitated. Did he dare speak his desires to the man who had steadfastly been refusing to surrender to the attraction between them? Was he just being a brat, trying to force something more than Zane wanted? He had never been the one to push for more than a partner was willing to give. But Zane was not his partner. He was his bodyguard, and he had made it clear that they needed to remain professional.

"What if what?" Zane's question brought his attention back to the moment. "Do you need something, Brand?"

Brandon raised his eyes to Zane's, letting the ripple that started in his chest run through him at the sound of his nickname on Zane's lips. He searched his gaze for a moment before replying, "You can't help me with what I need." He moved to close the door. "Goodnight, Zane."

He wasn't prepared for how fast Zane moved to stop the door from closing. "How do you know what I can or can't do for you?" He pressed his index finger hard against Brandon's chest. "I didn't hear a question. How can I respond to a request you haven't made?" His eyes had gone black, his expression unreadable.

"That's how you want to play this, Zane?" Brandon demanded, suddenly angry. "Fine! What if what I need from you isn't in the rule books? What if it crosses those professional lines you're always so careful to keep drawn between us? Can you help me with that? Huh?"

When Zane didn't immediately respond, Brandon huffed and stepped back. "I thought so. I'll just turn in now so you can go off duty." His logical mind told him he was being unreasonable, but the desire addling his brain didn't much care.

Zane's hand on his bicep zapped a few more of his barely-functioning brain cells. "Help you with what exactly, Brand?"

His question was dangerously low, a heady seduction that Brandon could no longer resist. He let go of the door and pulled the big man against his chest.

"This! Help me with this!"

The memory of the kiss that had kept him up all night still made him shudder now as Brandon listened to the MC opening the show. Zane's lips had been delicious, a warm, succulent treat. His mouth had been a feast for Brandon's starving libido, and when Zane had pulled him in with a hand at his nape, Brandon forgot where he was. Eighteen hours later, he was still riding the edge of that fiery exploration and reveling in the high from that small victory.

"Ladies and gentlemen, please welcome Blackbeat!"

Brandon inhaled deeply, closing his eyes to center himself, to shake off the last of the inevitable jitters—why *that* still happened almost six years after his musical career took off, he couldn't say—and stepped into his role as he walked onstage with his friends. He refused to think about the man watching from beyond his line of sight, making sure that he and his friends remained safe. Zane was doing his job. Brandon would do his. There would be time to think about that scorching hot kiss in his room after the show.

Book Discussion Questions

1. Which of the following tropes in this novel appeal to you the most: second chance, single dad, widower, rock-star, later in life love, bisexual coming out, hurt/comfort?

2. In what way(s) is Tristan like/unlike your idea of a rock-star? Does it increase or lessen your appreciation of his character? Why?

3. What do you like most about Priest the man (not the father)? What do you like least? Why?

4. How do you rate Priest as a father? Why?

5. Do the descriptions of the different settings in the story help you to feel like you are there with the characters? If not, what would have made them better?

6. Of the important adult secondary characters—Henry, Gen, Rory, Lachlan—whom do you most appreciate? Why?

7. What do you like best about this love story? What do you like least? Why?

8. Which secondary adult character's story would you want to read in a separate novel?

9. Did you find the story realistic? Why/Why not?

10. Did Priest's struggles with coming out to his kids and admitting to a relationship with Tristan seem reasonable or far-fetched? Explain.

11. Does the epilogue satisfy your need for an HEA? If not, what else would you have included?

12. If this novel were to be made into a movie, who would you cast in the role of your favorite character?

13. How does the book's title help you understand/appreciate important issues in the story?

About
The Author

A. J. Buchanan has been ghostwriting M/M love stories since 2017. With over twenty of those ranging from short stories to full length novels—including a five-novel series—under her belt, she's more than ready to tell stories in her own name. *Facing the Music* is the second book in AJ's series, *No Strings Attached*.

When she's not creating worlds with men who grow to love each other, A. J. consumes novels in every genre but horror and plays amateur photographer with her trusty iPhone. She loves Britcoms, hangs out with her grown children, and plays Redecor, Word Crossy, Bingo Story, and Solitaire on her phone.

Social Media

https://www.facebook.com/authorajbuchanan
https://mybookdates.wordpress.com
https://linktr.ee/awjb

More books from 4 Horsemen Publications

LGBT Romance

AJ Buchannan
Orchestrated Love

Eskay Kabba
Hidden Love
Not So Hidden
Signs of Affection
Deeply Devoted to Him
Honest Love
A Plane and Simple Connection

Lucas LaMont
Roman's Reckoning: Type 6
Mikaél's Moment: Type 6
Stephan's Resurgence: Type 5
Anastasia's Arrival: Type 6

Stormie Skyes
Check Yes, No, or Maybe

V.C. Willis
The Prince's Priest
The Priest's Assassin
The Assassin's Saint
The Champion's Lord

Discover more at
4HorsemenPublications.com